THEY WERE ...
AND T...

Katherine Ransome Cole: She had it all—fame, passion and power—and had to risk it all, in a televised interview that exposed her deepest secrets and jeopardized her empire, to save the future of the children she adored. . . .

Richard Sears: A rich kid who lost everything in the Depression, he climbed to the top of the Hollywood heap. He was a superstar who sold his body to the studio boss's daughter, but couldn't divide his heart in love. . . .

Leo Cole: Hollywood—and Katherine—made the penniless Hungarian gambler into the man he always wanted to be. But only Richard knew the unholy bargain that transformed Katherine into Leo's wife. . . .

Maria Lashman Sears: The gorgeous Hollywood princess owned Richard Sears and would never let him go. Her father's studio made him famous. But her own scandalous sexuality and the threat of ruin would hold him fast. . . .

Rosalind Cole: Tormented by her mother's past indiscretions that turned her own life into a lie, Roz escaped into the deceitful arms of love—only to return to Katherine when there was no place left to go. . . .

HOLLYWOOD HILLS

Gabrielle Kraft

POCKET STAR BOOKS

New York   London   Toronto   Sydney   Tokyo   Singapore

An *Original* Publication of POCKET BOOKS

 A Pocket Star Book published by
POCKET BOOKS, a division of Simon & Schuster Inc.
1230 Avenue of the Americas, New York, NY 10020

ISBN: 0-671-73646-9

First Pocket Books printing August 1993

10 9 8 7 6 5 4 3 2 1

POCKET STAR BOOKS and colophon are registered trademarks of Simon & Schuster Inc.

Cover art by Punz Wolff

Printed in the U.S.A.

Chapter

1

A young hawk hovered high over the Hollywood Hills, its brown wings trembling on the light wind sweeping down from the wide expanse of the Mojave Desert to the east. The bronzed bird made a long, slow circle, sailing blissfully on a silent thermal, and trained its dark eyes on the underbrush, scouring the hillside for game. But the hawk saw nothing running over the ground below and, too fat or too uninterested to continue its desultory search, it dipped past a woman standing on the edge of a long redwood deck jutting out over the lip of the canyon.

Their eyes met, and for a millisecond the woman and the hawk regarded each other with mutual interest, two dissimilar creatures briefly sharing a suspended slice of time in the dry California foothills. The moment of recognition passed, and the hawk wheeled joyously in the sky, its wings cutting through the still air as it headed over the next range of hills toward the Pacific Ocean shimmering in the distance.

Katherine stood on her deck and kept her eyes on the hawk as it flew out toward the sea until it became an etched V in the flat horizon beyond, wishing she could skim along with it. The power of freedom and flight momentarily filled her thoughts with blinding intensity until she forced her attention back to the view spread out below her.

For years Katherine had used the constantly shifting view of the city like a rope of worry beads. The view fascinated and soothed her, and whenever she had a problem to solve or a decision to make she went out on the redwood deck and let the glinting city calm her nerves.

Now a tiny breeze edged nervously along the gentle sloping hills into the hollows of the canyon below and scurried down to the city as the early evening lights broke through the iridescent twilight and the first sharp dazzle of night spread across the seamless distance. Katherine smiled as she watched L.A. slip into its evening clothes and get ready to rock and roll.

Below her the huge metropolis lay spread out like a genie's magic carpet, the colored lights glittering into action like an intricate pattern of knotted thread in the twilight. How the city had changed! Twenty-five years ago the Hollywood Hills were sleepy and quiet; thirty-five years ago there was no smog. Today a mass of glass boxes covered the landscape like a legion of gigantic warriors, reflecting the burnt orange light of the dying sun in their tremendous windows. The city had changed, as time had changed, as she had changed. . . .

But despite the transformations, she adored it, still saw it as her city, her prize, her reward for a life spent in its hectic embrace. Her lifetime in the City of the Angels had taught her that the essence of the city's power lay in its metamorphic talent; L.A.'s genius was its ability to shift shapes and recreate itself like a phantom in the night.

She loved L.A.'s changeable, quicksand nature, so well suited to the movie industry it harbored. She loved its pastel colors, its foolish architecture, its warm Santa Ana winds, the throbbing, pulsing lifeblood pushing through the car-choked veins of the city. She loved it now just as she'd loved it when she first came to the city searching for . . . For what? she wondered. For love, for fame, for a career, for wealth? I've had it all, Katherine thought, as panic plunged through her like a falling elevator. I've had fame and passion and power. Will I lose it all tonight?

She shook her fear away and stared into the lights below, hoping the glitter would hypnotize her anxiety away. As always, the kaleidoscopic view filled her with energy and infused her spirit with strength and purpose. Suddenly Katherine felt young and alive again, and she knew she'd need every drop of her vitality to survive the ordeal to come, the few moments ahead that would inevitably change the shape of her life and reinvent her past, her present, and her future.

A hundred million years ago she'd been safe, protected by the Hollywood Hills, cradled in the arms of the wealth provided by a great city. But no longer. Tonight she was vulnerable to destruction. Like the city she loved, Katherine was poised on the precipice of change; a vast abyss stretched below her, filled with unknown dangers.

She tried to remember how long she'd lived in Los Angeles and it shocked her, as it always did, to realize she had first come to the city in 1936. Now it was 1987 and that meant . . . Katherine knew what it meant, and fifty-one years rang inside her head. "The bell tolls for you, baby," she murmured absently. But I'm no different now than I was at eighteen, she thought urgently, her mind twisting and turning like a small silvery fish caught in a net. I'm no different. "Who am I trying to kid?" she said ruefully as she leaned forward on the cold wrought-iron railing and looked down at her slim hand.

The hand was a jolt. A delicate tracery of protruding blue veins against a backdrop of pale white skin. Thin skin, no longer resilient. In the back of her mind Katherine always expected to see a young girl's hand. The contrast between the memory of the young girl who'd come to Los Angeles so many years ago and the reality of her hand, of her body, was a shock. The young girl had vanished long ago, and in her place stood the formidable founder of the Cole Agency.

"I feel the same," Katherine said aloud. "I'm the same person inside." But as she straightened up, a tiny stab of pain in her lower back told her she'd lied; age had exacted its price. She wasn't the same at all; she was only a version of herself. Like the city she loved, Katherine had changed. Time had rewritten the woman she'd been, and now she was a doctored script.

Katherine looked back across the garden at her beautiful house looming up in the oncoming night like a great white cloud and a huge sense of accomplishment swept over her. She thought, as she did every time she saw the structure from her favorite vantage point on the deck, what a wonderful house it was.

It lay nestled in the dense jungle greenery of the garden as if it had been born there, surrounded by an explosion of cascading bougainvillea, lush water-hungry palms, and banana trees that actually bore hefty yellow fruit. Its thick white stucco walls, red tile roof, and picture windows were perfect, complete, and there was even a sound track hovering behind it all—the gentle gurgle of the tiny waterfall feeding over the rocks and into the koi pond below.

It was past six-thirty in the evening now and all of the outside lights were on, casting a network of jagged shadows across the garden, the pool, the pool house that lay on the other side, and the tennis court beyond. Katherine watched the growing shadows quiver in the breeze. My children are grown, a voice sang in her head. Rosalind and Olivia and Charles are all grown up now, adults with adult lives. I am no longer the young girl I was when I came to Los Angeles; I am no longer the young mother who lives in my memories. I am an old woman with grandchildren.

The kitchen door banged, and the characteristic sound punched through Katherine's uneasy thoughts like the sharp crack of a pistol as reality returned her to the present. I'd know that sound anywhere; I could pick the bang of that kitchen door out of a police lineup of a hundred kitchen doors, a thousand kitchen doors. . . .

"Mother? Are you out here?" Rosalind called uncertainly, peering into the garden. "The limo is here. It's time to go.

Mother?" Roz was dressed and ready, her deep red silk suit emphasizing the burnished highlights of her long auburn hair caught in a thick knot at the nape of her neck.

Katherine watched her older daughter proudly, filled with a maternal sense of accomplishment. Roz looked like a hot red ruby as she stood framed and backlit by the glowing golden square of light in the kitchen doorway.

"Mother?" Roz called again, tapping her nails on the door impatiently. Roz was always darting from one thing to another, always quick and fast and impatient. "I can't see you. You're there, aren't you? It's time to go."

Katherine stepped out of the shadows and waved. "Here I am, darling," she said softly. As she watched her daughter, Katherine was flooded by a wonderful sense of relief. How sure of herself she looks, how strong and competent. After everything she's been through, Roz is sure of herself at last.

Roz walked briskly across the deck, her needle heels clicking out a light staccato on the weathered redwood. "We have to go," she said as she stopped a few feet away from Katherine and scrutinized her mother's face. "The show tapes at eight, and Olivia wants us there early. You don't want to rush right before you go on camera, do you? Are you ready?"

"Of course I am," Katherine said, the strength in her voice covering the harsh charge of dread coiling around her heart like a snake. Her life was dangling on a raveled thread. . . .

Suddenly she was frightened and she couldn't let go of the rail. She had the horrible sensation that she was plummeting, careening into a bottomless vortex. If she let go of the chipped wrought-iron rail she'd tumble end over end across the canyon, a lost astronaut whirling away into black, endless space. Katherine shook the brief feeling of panic away and smiled at her daughter, her fear hidden beneath a calm mask.

"Mother," Rosalind said, carefully watching Katherine for a reaction. "Are you sure you want to go through with this? We can pull out; it's not too late. Are you sure?" Rosalind's anxiety was clear. A tremulous frown creased her pale forehead, and her face twittered with nerves buried just below the surface.

"I'm sure," Katherine said, her voice stronger. The falling sensation evaporated. She let go of the rail and ran her hand across Rosalind's cheek. "It's your future at stake, yours, the children's. Are *you* sure? It's only my past we're going to rake over the coals," she said lightly. "And my past was over years ago. Are *you* sure?"

"Nope," Roz said promptly. "But I won't let that stop me."

"Good." Katherine laughed. "Ten points for honesty, darling. And ten points for knowing there's no such animal as a sure thing."

"Daddy always said that." Roz's crisp voice softened as she turned away from her mother and looked down the canyon at the shimmering city, her face hidden. "Daddy always said there was no horse in the world named Sure Thing." Her voice was suddenly soft and small, the voice of a little girl. A little girl lost . . .

It was the voice she used when she talked about Leo. The voice she *always* used.

"And he was right." Katherine knew Roz was vulnerable and kept an image of Leo locked in her mind as an icon and a guardian. Leo was still with them, protecting his makeshift family in his own makeshift way. Leo would always be with them. . . .

Katherine sighed and looked away, the hills darkening now into a deep, rich chocolate brown. Tears hit her eyelids, and a thick knot balled up in her throat like wool, but she shook it away. She didn't like to think about the tough past behind her, but tonight that past leapt out from behind every shadow.

"Mother," Roz said, "whatever happened between us before, I've let go of it. Can you forgive me for being such an idiot? I love you, and from now on we have no differences,"

Rosalind added emphatically, slicing the night air with one hand.

Katherine took her daughter in her arms, folded her up like the child she'd been years ago, the little girl she'd loved then and loved now. . . . "Long live the future," Katherine announced, her voice thick with hidden tears.

"Exactly," Roz said as she pulled back from her mother and touched her shoulder. "No more differences," she repeated firmly. "Now . . . ready, steady, go?"

Katherine felt that cold hand constrict around her heart again as she looked across the twilight hills for one last glimpse of the tiara of lights below. "Almost," she said slowly, the fear sweeping over her again as the same urgent thoughts battered her mind: I've had it all, love and marriage, money, fame, and power. Will I lose it all tonight?

Katherine stepped into the black Cadillac limo waiting in the driveway and settled herself in the corner of the huge car. Leo had kept a car and driver in the old days when he first made it big, but now it was easier to call for one than to maintain it. That was so long ago, another world, another life. . . .

As it was during all desert nights, the air had turned cool, and Katherine pulled her sable coat around her shoulders to keep out the chill. I probably shouldn't have worn it, she thought as the car rolled silently down the street, past the great houses of the lower Hollywood Hills. A fur coat was once a symbol of success, but fur wasn't politically correct in the New Hollywood. Still, some symbols remain the same, she thought as she looked out the window at the huge white-elephant mansions whose time had come and gone and come around again. The smaller houses on the upper end of the street were being torn down to make way for larger, more palatial homes as the last of the best priceless land in Los Angeles prepared for the century ahead.

Katherine was quiet as the black car rolled past the curlicue wrought-iron Hollywood Hills gate, past the low white building that housed the Hollywood Hills Patrol, then turned into the jeweled flow of traffic on Sunset Boulevard.

She dozed quietly until they reached the Sunset Strip, and as she opened her eyes she had a flashing photorealist memory of the Strip as it used to be, lined with fabulous cars and fabulous people; Mocambo, the Trocadero, the Player's, Ciro's, and all the other glamorous restaurants and night-clubs catering to the free-spending movie crowd. When she first came to Los Angeles, the Strip was the only place in L.A. to combine passion and fun, to live life as a movie star's rhinestone fantasy. But now the landscape was com-monplace and the once-brilliant Strip was just another dingy street dominated by rock clubs. Tonight the street was limp and wrung out, jammed with lonely, feral children with blank cartoon eyes, shuffling their feet underneath the gigantic gaze of billboard celebrities. Like the rest of the city, the Strip had changed, the glamour was long gone, and the once great street was tawdry and sad.

Katherine closed her eyes again as the car climbed up Laurel Canyon toward the Valley. Change is the lifeblood of Hollywood, she thought as her mind drifted quietly, and here she was, still changing, unafraid to keep pace with the city she loved. Here in Los Angeles change is everything. Her thoughts blurred as sleep struggled to take hold. . . .

Each scrap of my life combines with others to create a crazy quilt just as each light in the city combines with others to create a blinding carpet of brilliance. . . .

Faces of the people she loved shimmered like a mirage in a waterless desert, shifting from one to the other, a quick series of intercut images. The montage again, a calendar flipping its pages to indicate the passage of time, the pages tossed away into a Hollywood whirlwind. That endless loop of memories dancing just out of reach. . . .

People. The people she'd loved and cherished and fought to protect were all around her. But in a few minutes she'd go on television and expose every mistake she'd ever made, every cut corner, every wrong move, every little glitch and error she'd kept hidden away in the back closet for years and years. . . .Was she going to heal old wounds, or was she about to destroy the one thing she'd fought all her life to protect? The one thing that gave meaning to her life, to fifty years in Hollywood?

Was she about to destroy her family?

Chapter

In August of 1936 the summer sun beating down on the west end of the San Fernando Valley was hot enough to fry a lizard flat on a rock, and the company of *The Arizona Kid* didn't like it one bit. *The Arizona Kid* was the fourth feature film made by Lashman Films, Edgar Lashman's fledgling production company, and Lashman's skinflint vision of "taste without waste" meant the actors and the crew were lucky to get a stale baloney sandwich and a glass of tepid water for lunch, if they were lucky enough to get lunch at all. They weren't happy about that either.

The west end of the Valley was mostly open land. A few citrus ranches hugged the ground, surrounded by fragrant orange groves that flowered and bore fruit courtesy of William Mulholland, who drained the Owens Valley dry so the growing city of Los Angeles would never go thirsty. But though much of the Valley was now rich and green with irrigated land, the particular corner occupied by the company of *The Arizona Kid* was hot, hard, and dry, exactly right for Edgar Lashman, who wanted a desert mise-en-scène for his current epic. Just dirt and dust and gophers and the occasional sleepy rattlesnake sunning itself under the same blue skies shining on the bustling town of Beverly Hills, a few miles across the Santa Monica Mountains as the crow flies.

Most of the cast and crew knew the picture wasn't much good. It was just a programmer, another no-good oater for the bottom half of the weekly bill at the neighborhood movie theater. To the writer, an ex-reporter from Chicago who'd never met a nag that finished in the money, *The Arizona Kid* was merely another inconsequential horse opera he wrote on weekends to pay his bar tab at the Brown Derby. To the director, a Hungarian refugee who'd escaped the growing storm in Europe but didn't quite understand he wasn't in Budapest anymore, it was a job that paid the rent. But to three people on the set that day, *The Arizona Kid* was an entrance into a new life, a chance meeting marking the source of their intertwined futures. To Katherine Ransome, to Richard Sears, to Leo Kartay, it was the beginning.

Katherine Ransome was a slender redhead from the wetlands of the Northwest who thought *The Arizona Kid* was the most wonderful, the most thrilling event of her life—all eighteen years of it. The picture was the first big break of her young career, a success, something to write home to Seattle about. In Katherine's shining eyes her new life as an actress was ensured, even though her tiny part as the Kid's token love interest bordered on the invisible.

Katherine Ransome was ambitious. The picture business was the escape hatch she'd seen in the rain-driven wind sweeping across Puget Sound, a bright lucky moment up ahead that had kept her sane as the gray water of the Pacific storms streamed down all around her, month after wintery month. As she huddled by the fire in her mother's apartment overlooking the Sound and waited for the sun to come out, she promised herself that someday, somehow, she would shed the cold and the gray and the endless mildewed wet-sock smell of the air. She would live in the sun and eventually bake the dampness out of her bones before she got dry rot and died. And then, at sixteen, as the bitter, snarling Depression ravaged the face of the country, Katherine Ransome won a marathon dance contest at the Tulip Ballroom and parlayed the prize money and her mother's meager savings into a ticket to Hollywood, California, where the skies were clear and blue and it never rained and the sun shone every damn day.

Since then she'd worked at a variety of day jobs, waitressing and, most recently, selling dresses at Chapman's Department Store. She'd managed to land a few parts as a bathing beauty or a chorus girl. Once she'd played a hatcheck girl with three lines of dialogue in a William Powell detective picture, but *The Arizona Kid* was her first big part and she'd quit her job at Chapman's to take it, though she didn't have much to do in the way of acting. Mostly she watched the Kid do rope tricks or looked at him with tear-filled eyes or astonished eyes or smiling eyes and read lines like "But I didn't know *you* were the Arizona Kid!" or "Arizona, you've got to help Dad save the ranch. You've just got to!"

The star of the picture was Richard Sears, a handsome young actor with an overflowing fountain of energy fused to a wild ambition fueled by poverty. Unlike many of his new friends in the movie business who were refugees from the destitute shores of Europe, Richard Sears had grown up as a spoiled rich kid, a product of East Coast schools, debutante balls, and lazy summers at the family home in Newport. So when the Depression hit and his father went belly up in the grim aftermath of the debacle, Richard Sears was painfully aware of exactly what he'd lost.

As the Sears family money spiraled down the rusty drain of the Depression, Richard wandered west in search of whatever luck he could manufacture, and the stark aura of determination hovering over him set him apart from other young men his age. Richard Sears was determined to be rich again, no matter what price he had to pay.

Leo Kartay, the third member of the burgeoning triumvirate, was older than Katherine and Richard, and his experience had made him wiser. As Hitler's shadow darkened the face of Europe, he had made his way to America where there was a future, perhaps, for a poor Hungarian Jew with little prospect of surviving the next few years in the capitals of Europe. Leo Kartay had seen his future burned in the sun of California and had persuaded his friend Eddie Gibbon, a fellow Hungarian who was directing *The Arizona Kid,* to let him spend the day on the set. Leo Kartay watched and waited.

"No, no, no!" Eddie Gibbon shrieked. "Sears, an idiot you are! Keep that up and the horse will be killed!" Gibbon, who'd changed his name from Emeric Gambo the moment his feet touched the soil of Hollywood, slashed the air savagely with his fist and slapped his forehead dramatically. He was a small, florid man much given to large gestures.

"The horse? Who's the star of the picture, me or the horse?" Richard Sears demanded exultantly as he wheeled the roan stallion to a stop directly in front of the camera and sent a cloud of dust and grit whooshing into Gibbon's knotted face.

"The horse! The horse!" the crew chorused as Gibbon spat the dirt from his mouth in disgust.

Sears grinned and shook his fist at them. "Quiet, peons!" he demanded.

Gibbon buried his head in his hands and groaned. They'd been shooting for six hours straight, the temperature was well over a hundred degrees, and Sears was acting the movie star.

"Please, Mr. Cowboy Sears, Mr. Matinee Idol, do it right this time. On my knees I'm begging you," Gibbon moaned.

Sears laughed, doffed his white ten-gallon hat, and held it over his heart in a classic cowboy pose. "The position was made for you, Eddie," he said as the crew wolf-whistled and razzed Gibbon.

"Sears, just grab, uh, what's-her-name from behind and ride off with her, yes?" Gibbon croaked. "Look at the clouds. We're losing the light," he moaned. Blue afternoon shadows had begun to stretch out along the ridges of the low purple mountains.

Richard Sears hooked one leg over the horn of the saddle and stared down at the little director, whose face was a mask of anguish and concern.

"Eddie," Richard said, his voice calm and unhurried, "you want it to look real, I do it my way, okay? Otherwise, I'm telling you the God's own truth, it's gonna stink like the high school play."

"How do you know, Mr. Cowboy Sears?" Gibbon demanded. "You're only an actor. Nothing you know."

"I know horses, is how I know." Richard's smile was unperturbed.

Gibbon sighed in resignation and glared at Katherine. "And you, uh . . ."

"Katherine Ransome."

"Right. Katherine. Dear, look frightened, yes?" Gibbon simulated fear, his plump red face a grotesque round-eyed mask. "You think he's a cattle rustler, yes? You don't know the Arizona Kid he is. You're terrified!" Gibbon rolled his eyes and only succeeded in looking demented.

Katherine nodded in agreement, but she didn't know what Eddie Gibbon was talking about. She thought she *had* looked frightened. She certainly *felt* frightened. They'd shot the scene twice, once too often for a quickie Lashman film, and each time Richard Sears had scooped her up into his arms and galloped off on the pounding roan stallion, she'd felt a rush of bottomless terror pumping blood through her veins and turning her heart to stone.

He was strong, this cocksure young man masquerading as a cowboy, but what if he dropped her? What if she fell off and the horse crushed her under its sharp hooves? What if . . . ? There were a thousand what-if's, but Katherine pushed them resolutely away. *The Arizona Kid* was her chance, the break every would-be actress in Hollywood dreamed of while she slaved away at her day job, and Katherine Ransome couldn't afford to fail. "Yes, Mr. Gibbon," she said, hoping her tone was suitably docile.

Betty, the combination makeup girl and wardrobe mistress, rushed forward and powdered her down again.

"Honey," Betty warned, "try not to sweat. We've got to get the dress back to Logan Costume, and if you sweat, they charge extra."

"Crazy director," Richard Sears mumbled angrily as he reined in the horse and trotted off out of camera range.

Katherine hit her mark at the edge of the corral, her gingham sunbonnet swinging from her fingers, and smoothed her apron over her blue and white schoolmarm's dress. Then she noticed him again, a tall, thin man in a dusty suit standing behind Eddie Gibbon with one foot up on the dented bumper of the little director's secondhand Pierce-Arrow. His face was angular, with high cheekbones, his mouth was turned into a knowing half smile, and his black hair was combed straight back to reveal a high forehead. But his dark, glittering eyes constantly roamed over the milling crowd, and the intriguing intensity lurking behind those curious eyes reminded her of a hawk searching for prey.

He'd been there all day, studying the confused scene with keen interest, watching the crew milling around the camera, the actors, the wranglers watering the horses the Arizona Kid would need when he led the victorious posse in a wild ride across the desert. Whoever he was, he was reserved, almost studious, and his serious air and dark suit were completely out of place in the dry heat and rough-and-tumble atmosphere of the San Fernando Valley location.

Katherine tried to watch the man without gawking. A long, slim cigar hung delicately between two fingers and sent a tail of smoke curving up into the blue sky and turning to tiny shreds until it disappeared. Once or twice she'd seen him speak to Eddie Gibbon, nodding and gesticulating, but despite the passion of their conversation, there was no real friendliness between them, only polite reserve.

Katherine thought the stranger was oddly serious amid the freewheeling location atmosphere, yet he was watchful and alert and there was a sharp, intelligent light in his eyes. Clearly he was drinking in the scene with every meditative inhalation of his long cigar, and his dark eyes flicked from one member of the company to another like those of a curious, hungry bird.

The stranger was still leaning lightly on the bumper of the Pierce-Arrow when suddenly he turned and saw Katherine watching him. He smiled—rather sweetly, she thought—and dropped his head in a small but formal bow.

She bobbed her head in return, momentarily embarrassed that he'd caught her studying him, and turned her attention back to Eddie Gibbon while she waited impatiently for her cue. She was playing Gail, a courageous western girl whose beloved brother had been killed by a band of cattle rustlers, and Richard Sears was the Arizona Kid, a lawman working under cover as a member of the gang.

To tell the truth, Katherine was in awe of Richard Sears; she sensed that he was different, only pretending to be one of the boys. He was tough and handsome, and his self-confidence made her shiver. He laughed and joked with the crew and was scrupulously polite to her, but like the watchful stranger in the ragged suit, Richard Sears was reserved, cautious.

She'd seen Richard Sears staring at her once or twice and though he'd looked away very quickly, those few seconds when his blue eyes were unveiled had told her there was another man bottled up inside him like a ferocious genie struggling and straining to get out. A steel core was visible in those cobalt eyes, a rod of determination and anger spilling out over his oddly battered face. Katherine had heard the gossip about his wealthy upbringing and she thought that for a fellow who'd been born to the purple, he looked as if he'd been in a fight. Maybe more than one.

"Action!" Eddie Gibbon screamed through his cardboard megaphone.

Katherine stood at the edge of the corral and anxiously scanned the desert for the brother who would never return as Richard Sears thundered up behind her on his stallion, scooped her up, and carried her off across the dry floor of the San Fernando Valley.

"Yah! Yah! Keep going!" Eddie Gibbon's reedy voice

trailed off in the distance as Sears rode on across the sandy ground. His white hat flew off, and Katherine desperately clamped her arms around him. Terrified, she felt herself slipping off the horse, but Sears pulled her closer to him and she felt the hardness of his body. She struggled futilely in his arms, pretending to fight off the Arizona Kid.

"Cut! *Cut!*" Gibbon shouted.

Richard Sears urged the horse onward.

"Sears! You fool!" Eddie Gibbon shrieked, his voice wispy as it faded into the distance. "The scene! It is finished! Come back!"

Sears laughed wildly as the horse kicked up a fine spray of rocks and sand behind them, and Katherine felt his arms tighten around her, pressing her even closer.

"Hold on, Red," he shouted as they thundered across the Valley.

She was in front of him on the saddle, her arms twined around him, her face buried in his neck. Her lips were half open and she could taste the salt on his sunburned flesh and feel the heat of his skin.

Behind them she barely saw Eddie Gibbon dancing up and down in rage like an infuriated jack-in-the-box. "Cut! Cut!" he screamed again. His tiny figure disappeared into the distance as Richard Sears laughed and spurred the horse on into the dark blue hollows of the low California foothills, as dark and blue as Richard Sears's eyes.

They galloped toward the hills of Calabasas, the brown and gold and green underbrush whirled by in a wild blur of color, and the clouds threw a dizzy pattern of light and dark shadows on the ground underneath the horse. Hot wind tore at her skin as Richard Sears pulled her tighter against him on the saddle, one arm around her waist, one hand on the reins.

"What are you doing?" she cried, but her mouth was buried in his neck and her words were whipped away in the wind.

He urged the horse on, his chest heaved against her and she was hit by a series of bone-crunching thuds as the animal pounded across the dry valley floor. Sears laughed again, a strange, exultant sound, and once again a shiver of expectancy ran through her, a warning bell, a signpost pointing to an intricately textured future.

"Christ," he yelled in her ear. "I hope Gibbon's got the camera rolling. The horse won't last much longer."

"The horse!" Katherine cried. "What about me?"

Sears laughed, and his breath was hot on her cheek. Katherine felt a vibration thudding up from the ground, through the horse, into the saddle, and into her own heart as she clung to Richard Sears. The wild ride was making her dizzy, but it was more than just the ride. She'd never been this close to a man before, and she was frightened but terrifically excited by this wonderful new experience. Suddenly she felt exhilaration coursing through her like a molten river, and the strange combination of the galloping horse and Richard Sears's straining body penetrated her like a knife.

As the feeling flooded over her she gave herself up to it, melting into a pool of ecstatic new sensations. Whatever this was, she wanted more of it, and she wanted it for the rest of her life, every minute, every hour, every day, forever. She laughed triumphantly. Richard Sears felt it and pulled her even closer. The ground below was as brown as the rough shell of a Brazil nut and faint green flashes whipped over her eyes as mesquite and tall grass moved by in an endless blur.

Abruptly Sears reined in the horse and it pulled up sharply; it stamped its feet, panting and blowing happily in the warm air. Sears laughed as he held Katherine away from him and looked at her possessively. "You liked it, didn't you?" he said, surprised. "Tell the truth, Gail."

"Katherine," she told him, annoyed that he didn't remember her name. She felt deflated, and the ephemeral pleasure she experienced during the wild ride evaporated into the blue sky. She had a momentary vision of the stranger's cigar smoke shredding into the air in tiny jagged puffs as she wiggled and tried to slide out of Sears's arms. "Gail's the character; I'm Katherine Ransome."

He shrugged, quickly leaned forward, and gave her a brief, teasing kiss that barely grazed her mouth. "You liked that too, Katherine Ransome," he said as he pulled away from her. "How about I do it again?"

The horse snuffled nervously under them, shifting heavily from leg to leg.

She wanted him to kiss her again, but she didn't want to admit it. She didn't like the way he was so sure of himself and simply assumed she'd let him kiss her. She wondered if that was what money did to you, if it made you sure of yourself. Impulsively she leaned forward, wrapped her arms around him, and kissed him possessively. He hadn't expected it, and as he buried one hand in her hair he groaned in surprise, his mouth slipping softly over hers.

Katherine felt him react, and she pulled away quickly, unwilling to give him more than the prelude he'd given her a moment ago. "Two can play at that, Mr. Cowboy Sears," she said shakily.

"Well, well, Miss Ransome," he said admiringly. "I dare you to do it again." His hands were stroking her sides the same way he would stroke a horse if it got wild one night and tried to kick down the stall. Suddenly Sears looked into her eyes, then let her slip to the ground.

Flustered, Katherine stared up at him angrily. "Why did you ride off like that?" she demanded.

"You don't want to play with me, Red. Too dangerous," he said meditatively as he lit a cigarette.

"You think a lot of yourself, don't you?" she said, still looking up at him, framed by the sun. Yet behind her bravery she knew he was right: he was dangerous. He was handsome, but there was an ancient soul lurking in his eyes, a timeless knowledge scrutinizing the world. He laughed, but his eyes weren't joking, not those smooth cobalt stones. He smiled, he joked and played cards with the crew, and now he'd kissed her, but behind it all was a look that made Katherine wonder what went on inside Richard Sears. Once, when he was talking to Eddie Gibbon, she'd watched a cold self-interest sweep over Sears's face, and she realized that same icy draft would sweep across anyone who stood in his path. Suddenly she was afraid to be alone with him in the dry wooded hills, afraid her game had gone too far.

"Mr. Gibbon's going to be furious with me," she said uncertainly, backing away from the stamping horse.

Sears shook his head cavalierly. "Don't worry about it, Red. I'll take care of it."

Katherine wasn't so sure. "But you weren't supposed to gallop off with me."

"Hell, I had to do *something*. The scene was getting dull, y'know?" Sears looked guilty, like Tom Sawyer in trouble with Aunt Polly. "I was over at the Warner lot the other day, having lunch with Jimmy Cagney, and I tell him this horse picture I'm on is no good and I'm afraid I'm in trouble. Cagney laughs—you know how he does—and he says, 'Fella, it sounds like a cuff opera to me.'"

"Cuff opera?" Katherine asked.

"Sure, sure," Sears said impatiently. "He meant I ought to do it off the cuff—make it up as I go along. He does that with Pat O'Brien all the time, and it's done him a world of good at Warner's. The Warner boys are tough, too. Shoot top pictures in sixteen, seventeen days. You've got to be good to stand up to that schedule."

"And that's why you rode off with me? Because of something Jimmy Cagney said at lunch?"

Sears shrugged awkwardly and grinned. "Had to do something," he said again. "Kids watch these serials, they want excitement, a little git-up-and-go on a Saturday afternoon. Eddie's a nice guy, but he's Hungarian. What does he know about the wild wild West?" He smiled knowingly at Katherine, still half a kid himself. "You're a good sport, Red."

Her uneasiness disappeared. "Take me back, will you?" she asked, holding her hands up so he could hoist her into the saddle.

Surprisingly he pranced the horse just out of her reach. "If I do, will you kiss me again?"

Anger flashed through her, red as her hair. Kisses were

one thing, her career quite another. "Look, you don't need this job—"

"Don't you believe it, Red." His voice turned grim. "I need this job bad as anybody else."

"Well, so do I! I worked hard to get it, I need it, and I can't afford to lose it. If something goes wrong, they won't blame it on you. You're the star."

"The star? In a Lashman picture? Don't be a fool," he said shortly.

"Please, take me back," she demanded, holding her arms up to him again.

"You win," he shrugged as he offered her a hand up into the saddle. The game was over. "What makes you think I don't need this job?" he asked as she settled behind him. He turned the horse back toward the location, clucking at the animal and roughing up its mane with his free hand.

"Thanks," she said gratefully as she put her arms lightly around his waist. She pulled back slightly, away from the heat of his body. She didn't want him to feel her pressing against him. "Oh, I don't know. You look . . . well, rich."

He snorted. "Rich? I'm just another struggling actor. I need this job just like you."

"But you're not afraid to lose it and I am," she said frankly.

"True enough, Red," he told her, exhaustion in his voice. The horse trotted slowly over the hard ground toward the movie crew, outlined in the distance like a set of lead soldiers lined up for a toy battle. "I've lost so much in my life already, I guess I'm not afraid of losing any more."

She thought it was curious he'd make such a revealing comment. "Not afraid of losing any more? What have you lost in the past?"

"Everything, Red. Everything there is." Richard Sears fell silent for a second too long, then grinned, trying to make a joke out of his honesty. "Maybe I'm afraid of falling off this no-good nag and splitting my head open on a rock, and maybe I'm afraid of losing at poker, but you're right: I'm not afraid of losing this part. Gibbon can't get anybody better'n me, or you either. Besides, he's shot too much film to back out now. Lashman would have his Hungarian head on a plate. You'll be great, Red—don't worry so much. I'll take care of you."

Surprised, Katherine leaned forward and tried to get a look at his face, but that was impossible. The horse trotted on unaware.

They cantered back to the dusty set, and Katherine saw that Eddie Gibbon and the camera crew were busy shooting a few desultory reaction shots of the other members of the cast. The elderly gentleman playing her father, an alcoholic stage actor who'd fallen on hard times, was gazing blearily across the barren desert as his bloodshot eyes parodied concern for his lost son.

Gibbon glanced angrily over his shoulder as Richard and Katherine trotted up to his side. "Where haf you been?" he blurted out in a rush. "I said *cut,* yah? *Cut* means *cut,* yah? Why don't you do what I tell you once?"

"Don't kick, Eddie." Sears laughed as he reined in the horse and let Katherine slide to the ground. He swung his leg over the horn of the saddle and jumped down in one smooth acrobatic movement, then stroked the animal's velvet nose and kissed it. Briskly he stripped off the saddle and blanket and turned the panting horse over to a wrangler.

"You think I like yelling at air?" Gibbon said as he danced furiously around Richard Sears like an aggravated Rumpelstiltskin. "Where haf you been?" In his anger, the tiny director had lapsed into a heavier than normal Hungarian accent so it came out "Vere haf you bean?"

"Vere vee bean?" Sears mocked. "Eddie darling, I love you." Playfully he swiped the director's brown fedora and dangled it above Gibbon's head.

Gibbon was not amused. He snatched vainly at the hat, trying to grab it back, but Sears was at least a foot taller and wouldn't let go. He reached out and rumpled Gibbon's hair, spinning the hat on his finger like an old vaudevillian with a plate on the end of a stick. His voice turned serious.

"Looked real this time, hey, Eddie?" He let Gibbon grab the hat.

Gibbon scowled as he jammed the brown fedora down around his ears. "Yah, yah, right," he said grudgingly. "You look good this time too, Miss, uh . . ."

"Katherine Ransome," Sears said pointedly.

"Yah, right. Katherine. You look scared this time, dear."

"I was sca—" Katherine began, but Sears waved at her to keep quiet.

"This little lady's one talented actress," Sears said expansively, one hand on Gibbon's shoulder. "We're lucky to have her on this show. Matter of fact, Eddie, let's expand her scene in the hideout. It'll help the picture. Give her some more dialogue in the scene where the rustlers have us tied up."

Katherine felt a rush of gratitude toward Richard Sears. She'd been in Hollywood long enough to know that many people made promises but nobody kept them. You had to help yourself, reach out and grab what you wanted before somebody else got there first. But Sears had actually put in a good word for her with Eddie Gibbon. Maybe he'd meant it earlier when he said he'd take care of her.

Irritated, Gibbon shrugged off Sears's friendly arm. "Vat, now you're a writer? Please, don't help the picture any more, Mr. Cowboy Sears."

Behind them, Katherine heard the dull rumble of a car engine. Richard Sears's smile never wavered, but his eyes hardened as he looked over Gibbon's shoulder at a long gray limousine winding its way toward them up the rutted dirt road. He frowned, and she sensed the downward shift in his mood as all the fun fell away from his face and it became an enigmatic mask.

Katherine didn't know anything about cars—she'd recently bought a third-hand Model T and thought it was the most wonderful car ever made—but she knew the limousine was terribly expensive. The car was huge, driven by a liveried chauffeur sitting behind a glass windshield, a gray cap on his head and goggles over his eyes to protect him from the clouds of dust spewing up as the car continued to grind slowly toward the movie company.

Katherine watched Richard Sears in confusion. Suddenly he was a different man. Not only had he lost his exuberant sense of humor, but the calculating veneer that dulled his eyes like cataracts was frightening. A second before, he'd been laughing and joking with Eddie Gibbon like a kid playing stickball on a city street, but the moment he saw the big gray car his cobalt eyes had turned as dark and hard as a flat river rock.

Eddie Gibbon saw the change too, and his mouth twisted into a cynical smirk as he followed Sears's gaze to the oncoming car. The little director didn't miss a beat.

"That's all for today, Mr. Cowboy Sears. Now maybe you have other fish to fly," he said, leering as he shifted his attention to Katherine. "Dear, I want to do now a little close-up, yes? You stand by the gate, you look out, you're sad for the brother who is dead. Tears well up. Can you well up on cue?" he asked anxiously, afraid he wouldn't get the tears he needed to make the scene work. "I hope yes?"

"I . . . think so," Katherine said, fascinated by the gray car and confused by the change in Richard Sears.

"Betty I haf to send for this, Sears," Eddie Gibbon said, handing him the white ten-gallon hat that had blown off in the wild ride across the desert. Sears took it without a word and abruptly stalked away. Little clouds of dust rose from his bootheels and mirrored the dust from the oncoming limousine.

"Whose car is that, Mr. Gibbon?" Katherine asked. She tried to sound as if she didn't care one way or the other.

Gibbon looked at her sharply, knowingly, then frowned. "It's a gray car, it's a Lashman car. Always they have with the gray cars," he said shortly. "Like a—what do you call?—a trademark. It would be Miss Maria Lashman in the gray car. Now we shoot, yes?"

As the cameraman reloaded, Katherine obediently went back to her mark by the corral gate. Everyone in town knew Maria Lashman, the daughter of Edgar Lashman. The daughter of Lashman Films. Katherine watched as the limousine glided to a stop about a hundred feet away, next to Gibbon's Pierce-Arrow.

Wearily the chauffeur got out from behind the wheel and vainly tried to dust himself off as he walked around to the passenger side of the car. He glanced up at the clouded sun and wiped his sweating forehead with a gray silk handkerchief that matched his elegant gray livery.

Eddie Gibbon yelled frantically at the crew to get the shot set up before "vee lose zee light," and Katherine watched in fascination as the chauffeur opened the car door. She'd heard of Maria Lashman, Edgar Lashman's elegantly spoiled only child, but they'd never met. In Hollywood, a thick social curtain hung between hopeful actresses who waited on tables to make ends meet and Hollywood princesses. Maria Lashman was famous for her extravagant clothes, her wild parties, and her excessive spending, and her name was often featured in the columns. Her photo appeared in movie magazines as if she were a star, and Katherine had seen her beautiful, spoiled face many times.

A small dark young woman looked out of the car, shielding her eyes from the sun's glare with one red-nailed hand. Cautiously she put a peach-slippered foot on the powdery soil and stepped out of the car, but her foot instantly sank into the sandy ground. She looked around and grimaced prettily as her foot sank deeper into the sand, which covered her thin shoe up to the heel. She stood there helpless, half in and half out of the car, one hand on the chauffeur's arm, one braced on the car door. Clearly she didn't want to put the other foot down lest it, too, sink into the dirt.

Katherine watched, fascinated. Maria Lashman was a doll, a dark, exquisitely clothed doll, and she was the most beautiful creature Katherine had ever seen, on or off the screen. Certainly Maria Lashman was as beautiful as any movie star, as Claudette Colbert or Loretta Young. She was perfect, a scissored silhouette of femininity cast in sharp relief as she stood carved against the unlikely backdrop of scrub oak and dried weeds; the thin peach silk dress whipping around her legs gave her a fragile, helpless air.

Yet there was something wrong with that beautiful face, something disconcerting, out of place. True, her face was beautiful, but her eyes were shrewd, and she reminded Katherine of a darling little ferret, a clever animal with bright eyes and sharp, sharp teeth. A mass of dark, close-cropped black hair hugged her head like a crown of curls. Her face was expressive, and she didn't have the thin, penciled eyebrows that were the current style, but dark, arched brows that accentuated her slanting eyes.

Maria Lashman watched as Richard Sears slowly walked over to her side, and Katherine saw pride of ownership gleaming in her eyes as she smiled up at him. Suddenly Katherine was painfully aware of her own dowdy gingham costume, and she knew that even if she were dressed in her best, she'd never measure up to this fabulous Hollywood heiress.

Richard Sears slapped the dust from his white cowboy hat, the complete movie hero, the perfect match for a Hollywood princess. He bent down, and as the tiny dark doll prettily put up her face to be kissed, Katherine felt a wave of shame push through her, shame liberally mixed with anger. Her cheeks turned red, and as she balled up her fist, wishing with all her might she had something to hit, she realized the tall, ragged stranger in the dark suit was watching her reaction intently.

As Richard Sears kissed Maria Lashman's smooth peach-flower cheek, Katherine Ransome knew she'd been played for a fool. Sears was trying to spice up the picture when he rode off with her; he'd told her so. But the worst part was that the ragged stranger had been watching the entire time, and he'd caught her staring at Maria Lashman like a bumpkin ogling a queen.

"Country mouse," Katherine mumbled angrily at herself.

Sears was toying with her as if she were a cheap chorine, and Katherine Ransome didn't like it one solitary bit. She felt a gnawing embarrassment as she remembered her excitement when the horse pounded across the flat Valley floor into the foothills. Richard Sears, the cowboy hero, had held her in his arms, and she'd kissed him and tasted the salt on his flesh, but she wanted more. Another wave of anger and embarrassment flooded her body, and Katherine knew she was as red as the side of a barn.

"Okay, okay," Eddie Gibbon said. "Now the reaction shot we do. Time now to cry, yah?" he asked hopefully. "Just a little tears, darling. It'll look zo nize when we come in on the close-up."

Katherine sighed and turned her face to the camera's cold, glassy eye. If there was anything she hated, it was being played for a fool and getting caught at it. "All right," she said, raising her chin and straightening her spine. "A little tears . . ."

Chapter

3

Katherine shot her close-ups, and her tears welled up on cue without any trouble, though Eddie Gibbon didn't know they were tears of anger, not the bright professional tears of an accomplished actress. As she was finishing the scene Katherine saw Richard Sears, wearing a light gray suit that blended perfectly with the long gray Lashman limousine, climb into the car beside Maria Lashman and drive away down the winding dirt road, the omnipresent dust rolling up behind them like swollen clouds as they disappeared toward town.

Katherine was tired, heartsick. She felt as if she'd been shot from a great height and fallen down to earth, a bird skewered by an arrow. Her momentary triumph had turned gritty, like the dust spewing up from Maria Lashman's long gray car. Maria Lashman was so elegant, so effortless, so . . . so everything Katherine was not. . . .

Finally Eddie Gibbon released the company, and the brutal day in the hot sun was over. Katherine changed into street clothes and trudged blindly toward the grimy station wagon waiting to take her back to the studio, her feet burning on the still-warm ground.

Ten hours on location, an hour in the studio car, another hour in her own car driving back to the tiny West Hollywood apartment she shared with Madeline Gerard, and a five o'clock call in the morning. Katherine wondered if she would survive.

She didn't bother to wipe off her makeup, and she fell asleep as soon as she climbed into the backseat of the big Ford station wagon. When she woke up fifteen minutes later, she was slumped on the bony shoulder of the tall stranger in the ragged suit, the man who'd been watching her on the set. She struggled away from him, still half asleep, half caught in a net of disturbing dreams.

"How do you do?" he said gravely as she opened her eyes, dropping his head in the same polite nod that passed for a bow.

Katherine was embarrassed to find herself wedged up against him in the car, and she had the certain feeling that he'd been watching her sleep. She was annoyed he'd caught her in a private moment—now more than one. They were alone in the car except for the driver in the front seat, and he couldn't hear much over the rattle of the road and didn't care anyway.

"My name is Leo Kartay," the stranger said, his voice soft and courteous. He had the same accent as Eddie Gibbon, but while Gibbon's speech was overblown and bordered on the comic, Leo Kartay's intonation was curiously perfect, and his accent was more in the inflection than in any mispronunciation of his words. "Yours, I already know, is Miss Katherine Ransome."

"Yes," she said, still confused by sleep. Once she realized that Leo Kartay was a foreigner, a friend of Eddie Gibbon's, her old-fashioned manners surged to the fore. She put out her hand, twisting awkwardly in the backseat of the car.

Leo Kartay took her slim hand in his, turning it slightly so his lips met the meaty part just above her thumb. He smiled as he kissed her hand, lifting his black eyes to meet hers, and the penetrating glance was sensitive and intimate. His eyes were large and dark, and the crooked bridge of his nose gave his face a predatory cast like that of a bird of prey.

A funny thrill tickled across her arms and down her body. She'd never had her hand kissed before, and it was a new and erotic experience. Where Richard Sears's kiss on horseback had been exciting, all sunshine and healthy warmth, Leo Kartay's polite kiss on the hand was refined, secretive, and the momentary flutter of his lips promised her that a deeper knowledge lay ahead.

"I watched you today," he said formally as he released her hand. "I want to learn about the movies."

"Are you an actor?"

"I will be." He nodded with complete certainty.

"I saw you talking to Mr. Gibbon. Is he a friend of yours?" Katherine was still tangled in sleep, flustered.

"We are both Hungarians." He shrugged. "Two Hungarians in a strange land are more than friends, less than brothers. And you? How long have you been in California, Miss Ransome?"

"How do you know I'm not *from* California?" Katherine countered.

A sudden smile flashed across Leo Kartay's face like summer lightning, and she saw that while his beak nose and intense eyes weren't handsome, his smile was compelling, a revelation of the intelligence of the man within.

"I have been in California for six weeks now," he informed her carefully, "and I have learned one important thing: no one in the city of Los Angeles is *from* Los Angeles; everyone here is from somewhere else. You know, Miss Ransome," he said, his eyes flicking past her to the dusty orange groves outside the car window, "when I learned this, I knew I had found the home I have been looking for ever since I left Hungary. Your Los Angeles is an immigrant's dream."

Katherine laughed in agreement. "You're right, it is. I feel like an immigrant myself sometimes. I'm from the northwestern part of America, and it's very different up there."

"Yes? I have never been there. How is it different, please?" he asked, interested.

"Well, it's very beautiful," she said, the memory of rich brown earth and endless green rain forest covering every inch of the land flooding her mind as she saw the dry roadbed ahead. "It's wet and as green as . . . Oh, I don't know. As green as Ireland's supposed to be. Yet the northwestern landscape is closed. I love it, but it's too gray for me, too dark. It isn't open and free and hopeful like California. I like the light, I always have. My mother said when I was a baby I used to play on the carpet in the patch of sun coming in the window. But on days like today I wonder if I made the right choice. This heat . . ." Katherine sighed as she pushed her straggling hair back from her forehead and wondered why she was talking so much. "Sometimes I wonder if L.A.'s too hot for a northwesterner who's used to cool green days."

"I hope I'm not impertinent, but you look like a strong person, Miss Ransome," Kartay said as he fished in his pocket and pulled out a worn leather cigar case. He flipped it open, frowned, and snapped it shut again. There were only two cigars left.

It was a small gesture, but telling, and it wasn't lost on Katherine. Her eyes traveled down to his cuffs, neat and clean yet ragged at the edges. His shoes were dusty from the day, but clean and polished, though the black leather was old, cracked, and worn thin. Even his shoelaces were knotted in two places. Katherine deliberately turned her attention out the window so he wouldn't realize she'd noticed his poverty. He was nice, this Hungarian stranger with his eagle's stare, and she didn't want him to be ashamed or embarrassed.

He'd noticed nothing. "Ah, well," he said as he replaced the cigar case in his jacket pocket. "This city has its flaws like any other, but it's wonderful. Not green, you are right. But beautiful like the Arabian Nights stories my mother read to me when I was a little boy. And here you can be whoever you want to be. You agree?"

Katherine was puzzled. "I think I do."

He smiled that brilliant smile again. "My English is not good enough yet. But I will improve."

"Your English is perfect. Better than mine."

"Thank you. Most kind. What I mean is"—Kartay groped momentarily for words—"you can make yourself up in Los Angeles, like Scheherazade made up the Arabian Nights tales. That is what I will do, and it is why I will become an actor. So I can create myself, yes? Los Angeles will make me the man I always wanted to be."

How strange, Katherine thought as she felt her eyes closing against her will and a thick grainy sleep tugging at her mind. The twelve-hour day hit her like a landslide, and though she knew it would be horribly rude to fall asleep, she couldn't stay awake. "I'm sorry," she told him, "but I'm so tired. . . ."

She slept uncomfortably, a heavy, weighted sleep that brought strange dreams. She dreamed a lion carried her off into the lush green jungle and she rode on its tan back like a princess. The lion fell into a bottomless pit and just as it turned to devour her and she was whirling into its terrible red mouth, she woke with a start, terrified of the abyss in front of her.

Leo Kartay was shaking her, a little roughly. "You cried out," he said as she opened her eyes.

Her body jerked back at his touch, and she pulled away from him, automatically straightening her matted hair. "I'm sorry. It's been a long day."

"No need to be sorry," he said, his gentle voice a sharp contrast to his momentary roughness. "In Hungary we say that a beautiful woman never needs to apologize. Look," he said, pointing out the window. "We are at the studio."

As the dirty station wagon pulled into the circular driveway in front of Lashman Films, Katherine saw the small, ferocious figure of Edgar Lashman stalking out of his office toward the sound stages, his trademark bamboo cane in one hand, a rolled-up script in the other. Lashman was a restless man filled with boundless energy, and he had the ambition to match. He wore a military mustache, and he was trim and taut from the tennis weekends he hosted at his Spanish palace at the top of Beachwood Canyon.

Lashman Films was a small studio very near Uncle Carl Laemmle's much larger Universal Studios in the east end of the San Fernando Valley. Though Edgar Lashman's operation was nowhere near as grand, he was a tough, hard-driving businessman and he had an unshakable belief that he could promote his small company into the ranks of the majors. Like the rest of Hollywood, Edgar Lashman had big plans.

Lashman Films was a conglomeration of beige Spanish-type stucco offices clustered around the sound stages, surrounded by carefully tended flagstone walkways edged with moss. In the flower beds on either side there were thickets of bamboo some foolish gardener had allowed to run wild when the small studio was built in 1923 for Knocky O'Malley, a onetime silent comedy star who killed himself after the coming of sound made his life and career obsolete in one painful pratfall.

By 1935 the stand of bamboo had taken over most of the grassy areas of the studio, and the maintenance crew struggled constantly to keep it under control. When Lashman bought the run-down studio from Knocky's estate, the symbolism of the ferocious, uninhibited bamboo that constantly threatened to overrun the little studio wasn't lost on him. He took to carrying a gold-handled bamboo cane for effect and bought bamboo furniture for his personal office, giving the room a poolside quality that put the unwary at ease.

Edgar Lashman turned his lot into a little town, complete with a one-man police force and a mayor—Lashman himself—and he often strolled through the darkened lot at night, checking up on his empire.

"Will you be on the set tomorrow, Mr. Kartay?" Katherine asked as she got out of the station wagon. The sleep had done her good; her mind was clear, and she felt alive and cheerful again, rejuvenated despite her momentary gloom over the beautiful Maria Lashman. Somehow the sight of Edgar Lashman patrolling his domain put her life back in perspective.

Katherine Ransome had a streak of practicality running through her as deep as a vein of gold buried in a mountainside, and she knew there was no point in running haywire over Richard Sears and his teasing kiss, no sense in losing control. Maria Lashman had been willing to drive all the way out to the end of the Valley in her limousine for Richard Sears, and Katherine knew that kiss or no kiss, a country mouse from Seattle could never compete with the beauty and sophistication of a Hollywood princess—or with her money. Nor would an ambitious actor like Richard Sears throw away a chance with Maria Lashman for a flirtation with a penniless hopeful like Katherine Ransome. Better to forget him.

"Most certainly," Kartay nodded, interrupting her train of thought. "I have the opportunity to learn by watching, yes? I will take advantage of it."

"See you tomorrow, then," she said as she waved and headed for the cramped dressing rooms at the back of the studio. But despite her good intentions, her mind was still on Richard Sears. He was handsome and it *had* been exciting, that freewheeling moment as they galloped through the barren desert on his roan stallion, more romantic than any movie. . . . She shook the memory away. Despite her embarrassment and the emotional slap in the pride she'd felt when Richard Sears kissed Maria Lashman, Katherine knew the most important event of the day was her scenes. She'd done well, she could feel it. Her tearful close-ups were right on the money, and the day was a professional success. That's what counts, she thought as she walked briskly back to the dressing rooms to cream off her smeared makeup. That's what counts because Hollywood is my future.

Suddenly she realized Leo Kartay had said the same thing about himself, and the realization momentarily confused her. She hadn't thought of herself and the stranger in the dark suit as kindred spirits, but maybe they were. Certainly one thing he'd said was true: in Hollywood you created yourself.

Forty minutes later Katherine was chugging up Cahuenga Pass in her rickety Model T when she saw a familiar figure trudging stoically along the side of the two-lane highway toward Hollywood. She pulled up ahead of him in a veil of dust, reached over, and opened the door. "Get in, Mr. Kartay," she said in her Gail-the-schoolmarm voice.

"Miss Ransome, how nice to see you again," Leo Kartay said politely as he dusted himself off and got in beside her.

"Why didn't you tell me you didn't have a car?" Katherine asked as she pulled out onto the road again.

Leo Kartay shrugged philosophically, mopping his face with a white handkerchief. "A man shouldn't advertise his poverty," he smiled sheepishly. "It's not correct."

Katherine laughed at his aristocratic notions. "Don't let it bother you. We're both in the same boat. I gave up a job as a salesgirl for this part. I've got a tank of gas in the car, but I won't have a dime till payday. Most of the kids in this town are just getting by, job to job, hand to mouth. Being broke is part of an actor's life, so don't be embarrassed," she said gently as they passed the Hollywood Bowl. She was trying to make it easy for him and let the lonely man from another country know he wasn't completely alone.

"You have no money? How will you eat?" Leo frowned curiously.

"I'm thrifty, Mr. Kartay." She laughed. "When I get paid, the first thing I do is buy a kitchen full of groceries, get a tank of gas, and put something away for the rent. I don't have any cash between paydays, but you can bet I always eat. Look, I live in West Hollywood, not far from here. Let me make you a sandwich when we get there, okay? My roommate, Madeline, has a date tonight, but she'll be back early.

Maybe you'd like to meet her," Katherine added hastily, so he wouldn't misunderstand her motives. A sandwich was the only thing she had in mind for Leo Kartay.

"A sandwich?" he asked, a touch of longing in his voice. "It would be most nice, but—"

"Fiddlesticks," she said gently. "I know you're hungry, and it's just a sandwich, after all. I told you, most of us don't have much money, so we have to look out for one another."

Leo regarded her closely, his black eyes dark and shrewd. "You're very good at looking after people, aren't you? But who looks after you?"

Katherine laughed self-consciously. "I look after me. Always have." The conversation was verging on the personal, and she changed the subject. "Do you miss your home?" She'd forgotten where he was from. Someplace in Europe.

Leo Kartay stared out of the open car window before he answered, and when he did, his voice was sharper and carried a new, bitter edge. "In these times, Hungary is a good place to be from, not a good place to be."

"I don't understand," she said uncertainly.

"You don't follow politics, Miss Ransome?"

"I'm afraid not very much. I know things are bad over there, but usually I just read the movie columns."

"Americans . . ." Kartay said lightly, shaking his head. He gave her a sidelong glance, and his tone softened. "I am a mixture of things," he said gravely. "A mixture of races, a mixture of religions. Mostly Catholic and Jewish, but I have Gypsy blood as well." He grinned, and the dark eyes flashed happily. "Or so I like to think. But these days there are people in Europe who do not like mixtures of blood."

"Mutts, we call them," she said. "My father died when I was little, but he used to say a mutt dog had a stronger heart and loved you more than a purebred dog."

"Yes? I like your father. So I miss the thought of Hungary but not the reality. There is no future in Europe for a . . . mutt like me." Leo shifted his thoughtful gaze to the tall palm trees lining the side streets, their dry fronds cutting the air like oars through the sea. "Europe is dead. But the future is alive in Hollywood."

"I was just thinking the same thing," she said as she turned onto Santa Monica Boulevard. "I was just thinking that my future is here, in Hollywood. You're very sure of yourself, Mr. Kartay," she ventured. Leo Kartay had the ability to turn her thoughts inward, and that was a new experience for her.

He smiled and the hawkish face looked happy and free. "If I am not sure of myself, how will I make others sure of me?" he asked lightly. "If you will permit me, when we know each other better, I will give you a wonderful dinner at the Magyar Café, a place I know. But tonight, as I am embarrassed for funds"—he lifted his hands in the air and shrugged meaningfully—"I will be happy to join you for a sandwich."

"Good." She smiled. "I'm glad."

A few minutes later she pulled up in front of the white Spanish-style building on Hayworth Avenue where she shared a two bedroom apartment with Madeline Gerard, another hopeful actress. Several banana trees with heavy green fingers of fruit were clustered in the center of the courtyard, and a thick patch of untended red geraniums flowered wildly against the far wall.

Leo and Katherine got out of the Model T, and as Katherine led the way up the stairs to her apartment at the back of the building she heard Bing Crosby's voice drifting out of the open windows and across the courtyard into the lazy evening air. She had a sudden sinking feeling. Madeline was playing the radio too loud again, and that invariably spelled trouble. "Oh, dear," she said nervously, glancing at Leo. She slid the key into the lock, but as she pushed open the door it jammed on the security chain inside.

Leo hovered behind her, hands thrust deep in his pockets. "Something is wrong?" he asked politely.

"I don't know. Madeline?" she called. "It's me. Let me in!"

The music stopped abruptly and a moment later a pair of startling blue eyes framed by tousled blond hair peeked around the doorjamb. "Hi, sugar, you're back early. Who's this?" the blond asked, her blue eyes traveling slowly over Leo Kartay.

"Mr. Kartay's a friend of mine," Katherine said impatiently. "C'mon, Mad, let us in. I promised him a sandwich, and we're starved."

Madeline Gerard stepped forward so her body was visible through the crack of the doorjamb. She smiled at Leo over Katherine's head and let her aquamarine kimono slip open slightly, watching him for a reaction.

He studied her coolly, but didn't react.

"Friend, huh? If you say so, hon. Look, kids," Madeline whispered conspiratorially, glancing back into the apartment over one white shoulder. "You gotta give me a few minutes, okay?" The kimono slipped open wider, revealing Madeline's large bosom and pale, flawless skin. "I'm engaged," she rolled her eyes and arched her thin eyebrows in a meaningful parody.

"Madeline," Katherine said with a sigh, "come on! I've had a long day."

"Please sugar, forty-five minutes," Madeline begged.

"Madeline baby," a man's voice called from inside the apartment. "Let's go!"

"Coming, sugar," she called over her shoulder. "Please? This guy's an agent!" she said as she closed the door.

Katherine balled up her fist and furiously whacked the thick oak door until her hand hurt. "That Madeline," she said, rubbing her fist.

Leo Kartay stepped forward and took her hand in his own. "Miss Ransome, do not worry yourself," he said gently. "Come with me, please."

"Where?" Katherine snapped, fighting back tears of frustration. "Neither one of us has a dime, and I'll be damned if I'm going to sit in my car for an hour while she . . . Madeline!" she yelled as she kicked the door. "Mad! I mean it!" The apartment was quiet; then the radio flicked on and

Fred Astaire's thin voice echoed "Cheek to Cheek" across the courtyard.

"That Madeline," Katherine mumbled furiously. "I'd like to strangle her! An agent, my foot! Probably books dog acts at county fairs!"

Leo grinned down at her, and there was a rakish, almost piratical look in his dark eyes she hadn't noticed before. "Miss Ransome. Katherine. Please not to worry yourself. I'll take care of you."

Who lived behind those dark eyes? Who was Leo Kartay? "Well, Leo," she said frankly. "If you do, you'll be the very first man I've known who could."

The Magyar Café was a small restaurant tucked away in a quiet side street just off Fairfax Avenue near the Farmers' Market. The outside of the building was a nondescript storefront that looked blank and empty, but inside, the café was bustling with life. The tables were crowded with men and women eating, drinking wine, and laughing, and Katherine felt instantly comfortable and at home in the warm, cozy atmosphere. Lace curtains covered the windows, and an assortment of mismatched kitchen tables and chairs gave the room a friendly air, like a house where a happy family lived. The café was gaily decorated with odds and ends, brightly colored embroidered wall hangings were everywhere, and gleaming brass utensils crowded walnut shelves at the far end of the room. The colors of the hangings were mainly red, white, and green—the colors of the Hungarian flag, Leo explained as they sat down at a spotless table in a corner. "Mihály!" he called out to the waiter. "My old friend."

The waiter frowned unhappily when he saw Leo. He was a thin, sallow man with a drooping mustache and the pushed-in face of a pug dog. "Leo," he whispered, glancing uneasily at Katherine. "Positively no credit. Especially positively no credit for two."

Leo held up a placating hand. "Who's in back?" he asked calmly.

Mihály frowned again. "Gambo . . ."

"That is Eddie Gibbon," Leo explained. "Gambo is his Hungarian name. Who else?"

"Leo, last time you lost enough to feed all three of us for two weeks, yes?" Mihály complained.

"That was last time." Leo laughed as he looked happily across the table at Katherine. "Tonight I think the lady will bring me luck. Who else?" he prompted.

Mihály gave a dramatic sigh and pulled nervously at his long mustache. "Gibbon, Nagy, Kertesz . . ."

"Michael Curtiz, the director," Leo told Katherine. "Good, Curtiz has money."

"Curtiz works; Curtiz has money. You do not work; you gamble," Mihály said.

Leo shook his head. "Tonight I win," he said decisively. "Mihály, bring us some wine, triple goulash for the lady, and for me . . . smothered chicken smitane, yes?"

"Smothered chicken smitane, no. Not without money." Mihály's voice was sorrowful but adamant. "I am a Hungarian, not an idiot."

Leo stood up and put a friendly hand on Mihály's shoulder. "My friend, have I ever failed you?" he asked kindly.

"Many times." The waiter's voice was mournful. "But I won't shame you by speaking of it in front of the lady."

Leo shrugged, then turned back his lapel to reveal its underside, removed a gold stickpin capped with a small cabochon ruby, and held it out to the waiter. "I need twenty for a stake. You get ten percent of my winnings and this for security," he said, wiggling the slim gold pin enticingly.

"Again the stickpin?" Mihály said wearily, shaking his head. "Keep it. By now the stickpin and I are practically brothers. I'll bring the food on one condition. You win, you pay your entire bill here first, yes? The entire bill," he stressed. "Not just a piece. Before you go elsewhere and buy champagne for the lady. No offense to you, miss," he said quickly as he turned back the lapel of his white mess jacket and unpinned a rumpled twenty dollar bill.

Leo's hawkish face broke into another brilliant smile of triumph as he pocketed the twenty and shook hands with Mihály. Leo sat down at the table and grinned broadly. "Also some Liptauer cheese would be nice," he called as the waiter retreated to the kitchen.

It was the oddest negotiation Katherine had ever seen. The two men danced backwards and forwards in a mild tango of insults until they reached a decision that was obviously predetermined from the moment they'd seen each other. She was confused, yet intrigued. "Your friends have changed their names," she observed. "Are you going to change yours?"

"Of course," Leo said firmly. "If I am to be an American actor, I need an American actor's name, yes? Short. Simple. One that people will remember, but it must also fit the . . ." He made a square with his hands. "What do you call it? Over the theater?"

"Marquee," Katherine told him. "Leo Kartay. Leo Kartan. Leo . . ."

"No *K*," he said, his voice decisive. "Too foreign. I need a name that is sophisticated but simple to remember."

"How about Leo Cole?" she said with a happy burst of inspiration. "Like Cole Porter, the songwriter. There's a sophisticated name for you."

"Cole." He nodded, smiling as his long fingers toyed with his worn cigar case. "Leo Cole. I like it. Yes. I think I will be Leo Cole from now on. Good, you have decided for me, and you now bear responsibility for the newborn lamb. You'll be my godmother, then?"

Laughing, Katherine dipped her fingers into her water glass and flicked the droplets across the table at Leo. "I dub thee Leo Cole," she said imperiously. "Go forth, Sir Knight, and conquer!"

"Now I am a new man," he said, his eagle's face bright with happiness. "First we eat. Then we go in the back room, and you watch Leo Cole win money. In Hungary we always say that a beautiful woman brings luck."

"I thought that in Hungary we always say that a beautiful

woman never needs to apologize. I'm beginning to catch on to you, Leo," Katherine laughed, wagging her finger at him.

Leo shrugged easily and toasted her with his water glass. "In Hungary we always say that a beautiful woman can say anything she wants."

Two hours later Leo Cole was sitting at a battered wooden table in a hot back room at the Magyar Café playing poker with Michael Curtiz, Eddie Gibbon, and Nagy, a composer at Fox who only used one name and refused to change it. Leo was down a hundred dollars that he didn't have, but fifteen minutes later a trio of benevolent queens brought him luck and he was up two hundred. "Here," he said, as he handed Katherine a hundred dollars and exhaled a cloud of smoke from a freshly purchased Monte Cristo. "Give forty to Mihály for my tab and tell him to keep ten for himself. You hold the rest for me, yes?"

"Yes," Katherine said, marveling at the man as she took the money and went out to the front of the restaurant. Leo Kartay—now Leo Cole—was the most amazing character she'd ever met. His quicksilver nature exuded confidence, yet he was both mercurial and tough. How did he have the nerve to walk into a restaurant without a dime and order dinner? How could he play poker with only a twenty dollar stake? Somewhere inside, did he know he was a winner? "Whoever you are, Leo Cole, there's nobody like you in Seattle," she told herself as she waved at Mihály across the crowded restaurant.

The waiter bustled over to her side, a large tray of steaming bakonyi pork and caraway dumplings balanced carefully on one shoulder.

"How long have you known Leo?" she asked as she held out the bills.

The waiter looked at her sharply. As he rested the tray on the back of a chair it tipped slightly and bumped against a customer sitting at the table.

"Hey, bud, watch it!" the man growled in irritation. Then he looked Katherine up and down, grinning.

Katherine stepped back involuntarily. In contrast to the rest of the diners, the man was plainly American, in a cheap suit and a cloth cap he hadn't bothered to remove.

"Apologies, apologies," Mihály said quickly as he pocketed the money and guided Katherine away from the irritated diner. "Why do you ask, miss?"

"Call me Katherine," she said as she slipped the rest of Leo's money into her purse. "I just met him this afternoon. He's an unusual man. Very resourceful," she said, groping for the right word.

"Hungarians are—"

"Now, don't you start that Hungarian routine with me," she said, laughing. "I've heard it from Leo since the moment I met him."

Mihály shrugged dramatically. "Hungarians, they are not like other people."

"Fiddlesticks," she said briskly. "My father used to say that about northwesterners, and I told him it was fiddlesticks too."

"No, no 'fiddlesticks,' Miss Katherine, you don't understand. These days, if you're a good Hungarian, you're a good survivor," Mihály said slowly, his eyes veiled. "Otherwise you're a dead Hungarian. Leo is a good Hungarian, a good survivor."

The night air outside the Magyar Café was refreshingly cool and vaguely damp as Leo and Katherine slowly walked toward her car. Pools of light from the concrete and iron streetlamps illuminated the sidewalk, and a calico cat skittered across their path as they turned the corner. "Do you do this all the time?" Katherine asked curiously. The entire day had a bizarre, unreal quality, and the full extent of it surprised her—kisses on horseback, Madeline and her dog-act boyfriend, a gambling Hungarian who claimed to be part Gypsy—not what she'd expected when she walked onto the *Arizona Kid* location at six that morning.

"Do what?" Leo asked, his cigar clamped between his

teeth. "Eat? Gamble? Of course I do." He grinned mischievously as he knocked a glowing ash into the gutter where it hissed briefly and went out.

"You know what I mean," she said seriously. "Go into restaurants and bargain for meals you haven't eaten with money you don't have."

"All the time." He laughed. "Only because I have no choice. But now I am Leo Cole, and I think my life will change for the better. You remember I said I wanted to create myself?" he asked seriously. "It was a true thing I told you. A dream I have had since I left my country. . . ."

Suddenly Leo stopped dead and put his finger to his lips. There was a small shuffling sound in the darkness, and he cocked his head to one side like an alert watchdog, smoothly put one hand under Katherine's arm, and guided her behind him just as a big muscular man stepped out in front of them, grinning.

Katherine felt a wave of fear clutching at her back. It was the rough-looking man from the restaurant, the man Mihály had bumped with his tray when she handed over Leo's poker winnings. He must have seen her put the rest of Leo's money into her purse, Leo's hard-won treasure, the treasure marking the first victory of the newly named Leo Cole.

"Got a match, bud?" the man asked, gesturing helplessly at the unlit cigarette hanging between his lips. He was big, broad in the chest, and he easily outweighed Leo by fifty pounds.

Katherine sucked in her breath nervously. She knew they were in danger. It was obvious the man meant to rob them, but the street was silent and deserted, and there was nobody to help, no one to rescue them. Surreptitiously, she pushed her purse under her arm, though it was a futile gesture. The man knew she was carrying at least a hundred dollars. A fortune. These days, with the Depression stalking the land like a hungry giant, many people were poor and hungry. Leo's poker winnings were a windfall for a man like this, a big man, a brutal man. . . .

"A light?" Leo didn't hesitate, and his voice was pleasant

as he patted his pockets absently. "No matches, I'm afraid. But here, use my cigar." He stepped forward, holding out the glowing tip of his Monte Cristo.

Katherine was shocked and suddenly afraid. Leo was a gambler, a survivor. How could he be so naive? Why didn't he do something? Didn't he know what was going to happen? Katherine was frightened and suddenly very sorry for poor Leo Cole. The man was tough and strong, and Leo would probably take a beating, but that wasn't the worst part. The embarrassment of a robbery would destroy Leo's victorious evening and cut into his pride far deeper than the mere loss of his winnings.

The man smiled crookedly and bent forward, holding his cigarette outstretched toward Leo as if for a light. Suddenly, in one graceful motion, Leo lashed out and kicked the big man savagely in the kneecap. The sick crunch of breaking bone echoed hollowly across the empty street, and the man howled in surprise, then whined in pain like a wolf in a trap as he collapsed heavily on the ground, clutching his ruined leg.

Leo shook his head as the man writhed on the ground. "My friend, you're not a very good robber. I saw you leave the café just before we did, I heard you breathing, waiting for us. I'm afraid you must find another line of work. Do you understand me?"

"You bastard," the man snarled, his voice thick with pain. "I'll kill you for this."

"Me?" Leo sighed as he blew all traces of ash from the tip of his cigar. "I think not." Quickly he bent down and held the hot tip of the cigar to the man's cheek, searing the skin.

The man screamed in pain, struggling backwards across the pavement and away from Leo as the stench of burning flesh wafted through the cool night air. Katherine felt a grim wave of nausea sweep over her, and it was all she could do to keep from being sick to her stomach. She gasped as the man's animal wail of agony cut into the sleeping streets around them. "My God," she whispered, surprised and horrified. It was the most deliberately cruel thing she'd ever seen one human being do to another, vicious and hard and awful. It repulsed her, and yet at the same time she was fascinated by Leo's ruthlessness, by the raw brutality of the moment. As she stood on the quiet side street watching the man writhe on the pavement in front of her like a fish starving for air, she realized that she'd miscalculated and misjudged Leo Cole. He was far more complex than she'd imagined and far, far tougher.

Leo straightened up and tossed his snowy handkerchief on the ground beside the wounded robber. "My friend, listen to me," he said, his voice soft and quiet. "You have a broken kneecap, and you will have that scar on your cheek forever. The knee I gave you because you are a bad robber and you chose the wrong man to rob. The scar I gave you because you threatened me. Never threaten me again. Never let me see you again. If I see you, if you think of following me or the lady, *I* will kill *you*. You are lucky to be alive, my friend. Do you understand me?"

The man moaned but said nothing. Leo poked him gently with his toe. "Do you?" he asked again, his voice tougher. The man nodded his head. "Good," Leo said. "Then we are finished with each other." He reached into his pocket, took out ten dollars, and tossed it on the ground beside the would-be robber. "If you'd asked me for money, I would have given this to you because this has been a happy night for me. Come," he said firmly to Katherine. "Now we go."

Gratefully Katherine let Leo half drag, half propel her back to her car. They got in, and she drove away without saying a word as a strange whirl of thoughts battered her mind like a tornado.

Leo sat next to her, quietly looking out the window and smoking the remains of his cigar. "You think I was cruel, yes?" he asked softly, his craggy face hidden in the shifting light. "Not so. He would have killed me and done worse to you, if I had let him. I told you I would take care of you, but you must understand that sometimes taking care is not easy. Not pretty. You see"—Leo's tone was gentle, a father patiently instructing a wayward child—"here in America you don't know how hard it is to survive. You haven't learned yet that life can be very ugly. Very unrelenting. If you want to win at life, you have to be very tough in order to stand up to it."

To think she'd believed, even for a minute, that he was naive! Leo Cole was the most complicated man she'd ever met and the least naive. And he was all the more hazardous because of the sharp, dangerous edge hidden behind his sunny, seemingly open smile. She was confused, exhausted, and she wanted to go home, sleep, and put this strange night away from her. The long, tiring day swept over her again, and Katherine knew she was drained of emotion and couldn't take much more. "Is that another thing we say in Hungary?" she asked, her voice trembling.

"In Hungary? Oh, no," Leo Cole said, his eyes on the lights shining above them in the Hollywood Hills, his hoarse voice far away and sad. "I think that is something we say in Hollywood."

Chapter

"**W**ho's the boyfriend?" Madeline asked as Katherine let herself into the apartment.

"I'm not talking to you, Mad," Katherine said. She threw her bag—minus Leo's winnings—on the mahogany side table by the front door. "And he's not the boyfriend. He's not my type."

"Oh, yeah?" Madeline hooted. "You better get busy, sugar, if you're ever gonna find your type. You want to die an old maid?" Madeline, still wearing her favorite aquamarine kimono, was lounging on the flowered print sofa with a cup of tea and a copy of *Photoplay*.

Katherine glared at her. It was easy to get angry at Madeline, but hard to stay that way. Madeline pretended to be a hard-bitten bachelor girl, a smart blond cookie who knew every trick in the book, but she wasn't as sassy as she appeared. She'd been badly scarred by a hard-luck childhood, and underneath her brittle exterior lay a wistful tenderness and fragility she hid from her endless procession of boyfriends. "I said I wasn't talking to you and I mean it!

You're such a rat! That poor man was starving to death, and so was I."

Madeline sighed. "I'm sorry, I'm sorry. But this new guy is a doll, *and* he's an agent. Can you believe it?"

"No," Katherine said shortly. "Not a word."

"C'mon, sugar," Madeline nagged, laughing. "Who is he, anyway? I bet you had a good time."

"Oh, Mad, I did!" Katherine confessed as she kicked off her shoes and peeled off her stockings. "Darn it, I've poked my toe through . . ." she moaned as she collapsed on the sofa. "You wouldn't believe the day I had. The most amazing things happened!" Katherine stopped abruptly. Should she tell Madeline about the robbery first? Richard Sears's kiss? Leo Cole's new name? The wild horseback ride across the desert? "All kinds of things," she trailed off. For one more moment she wanted to hold her secrets close.

Madeline didn't notice. "He's kinda cute," she said, ignoring Katherine. "He foreign? Looks kinda foreign. So you gonna poke the guy?" Madeline rubbed her fingers together suggestively.

"You are so awful! It's a good thing my mother can't hear you talk like that. She thinks you're a nice girl."

"I *am* a nice girl. But I like to . . ." Madeline gave a bad-girl grin and rubbed her fingers together again. "So who is this guy? How'd you meet him?"

"He was on the set. He's a friend of the director's."

"Eddie Gibbon doesn't have any friends." Madeline snorted, sipping her tea. "Too poor. Can't afford 'em."

"Well, Leo's poor—"

"Ooooooh, you're calling him Leo already!" Madeline bounced up and down on the sofa like a happy child, slopping tea on her kimono. "It must be love."

"It is not! But I'll tell you who *is* handsome—Richard Sears."

A frown flicked over Madeline's face like a thin whip. "You watch out for him, sugar. Richard Sears is too rich for your small-town blood."

"You think I'm not good enough for him?" Katherine snapped. "Well, he kissed me today!" she said, showing off just a little. Madeline was worldly-wise, went out with men, and went to bed with them, too, an adventure Katherine hadn't yet experienced.

"He kissed you?" Madeline was astounded, and her red lips made a big round *O*. "Tell all, sugar! Don't leave out a heartbeat! You gonna . . . ?" Slyly, she rubbed her fingers together again.

"You are so awful! No, I certainly am not. We had a scene on horseback, and then he rode off with me into the desert and kissed me." Katherine sighed dramatically, hiding the rush of anger and humiliation she'd felt earlier. "But then Miss Maria Lashman came to pick him up in her car, and off he went."

Madeline put her teacup on the table and pulled her kimono tight around her, frowning. "Sugar, let Aunt Mad tell you the hard facts of life in this town, okay? Sears and Maria Lashman are gonna get married. Period. Word's all over town Daddy bought him for her Christmas present. Get it? That's the punch line."

So, he was going to marry the Hollywood princess. Katherine felt a disconcerting hollow sensation, a sudden wrench like ripping cloth. Probably heartburn, she told herself. Too much rich Hungarian food. "I know *that*," she lied. "I just thought you'd want to know he kissed me."

Madeline sighed and rearranged herself on the sofa. "Okay, here's the lowdown on Richard Sears. Fade in. Comes from some fancy back east family that went belly up in the crash." Madeline shrugged. "Came out here, worked as a lifeguard until—whaddaya know, folks?—he meets Billie Law, and all of a sudden they're the cutest pair of lovebirds you ever saw, living in the Hollywood Hills in Valentino's old house. You remember Billie Law?"

"Sure, she was a big star. Didn't she kill herself?"

Madeline nodded slowly. "Tried to. Now, Billie, she's the gal who used to have the USC football team in for palm readings every Saturday night, so she knows the score. But she gives it all up for Dickie bird. Rumor has it she's in l-o-v-e with him and she's got her tootsies on the straight and narrow. Wants to keep him sewed up forever in that Chinese opium den she calls her bedroom. Okay, cut to Billie, cooking dinner and wearing a print housedress, slippers waiting by the fire."

Madeline lit a cigarette and put her head back on the couch, her long white throat shining like a dove in the half-light. "But Dickie bird doesn't want to be tied down. Dickie's an adventuresome bird. Turns out he wants to be a star, rolling in money. Billie's given him a few lines in all her pictures, so he ain't a lifeguard anymore. Now he's an actor! He's the third lead in some *Beau Geste*-type remake at Columbia, and somebody tells Billie they saw him playing patty-cake with Patricia Montaigne in her dressing room, and Billie hits the roof. Takes a potshot at Dickie over on Gower Gulch, then goes home and slashes her wrists in the Chinese love nest. Like it so far?"

"How do you know all this, Mad?" Katherine said slowly.

"Pishposh, sugar, everybody knows. Doesn't get in the papers 'cause the studios don't let it. Except how Billie tried to kill herself. That got in the papers because the studio boys were tired of her. She was late and overweight; she was expensive, and her pictures were losing money. So . . . no more movies for Billie Law 'cause now she's a whoring slut. But Dickie bird? The boys like him; he's one of their own, went to Yale or some such, and he's a big man with the ladies. So they give him a chance, see how he does. Now he's doing his first lead for Lashman, and he's gonna marry Lashman's daughter, and Edgar Lashman's gonna run this town one of these days. Fade out and the audience goes home."

Katherine felt a sudden emptiness in the pit of her stomach. "Madeline, why did you tell me this?" she asked slowly as she digested this disturbing information. Why do I care? she wondered. Why am I frightened?

"So you watch where you step, sugar. Sears eats up women and spits 'em out. Ever since he came to this town he's been climbing up the ladder of love, and now he's got a little chunk of Hollywood royalty right in the palm of his hand. Get it? He's won Miss Maria Lashman, the biggest Kewpie of them all. Billie Law's broke and busted. You think he gives a damn? She handed him a career, opened all the right doors, and he threw her away when she was used up," Madeline said. "Honey, Hollywood's one big easy lay, and don't you forget it."

"It was just a kiss," Katherine said. "Nothing else happened."

"Are you sure?" Madeline sighed. "Did you like it?"

Katherine nodded. Outside, the Santa Ana winds swept in from the northeast, carrying the dry heat of the desert with them.

Madeline twisted the belt of her kimono around her finger. "Two men in one day, huh? That's a lot, for you. Katherine, it hurts me to say this because you know how I feel about money, but stick to the poor guy. Richard Sears is way out of your league, *and* he's dangerous. Wants to hit the big time. I saw him with Jimmy Cagney over at the Warner's commissary last week."

"He told me they had lunch."

"Forget about Sears," Madeline insisted. "Listen to me, 'cause men are the one thing I know something about. So, tell me about the poor guy. You really not interested in him? 'Cause I think he's kinda cute. Think he'd like to take me out for a late date sometime?"

"Madeline, you are so . . . forward!"

Madeline threw back her head and laughed. "I can hear your mother saying that to you the day you left home. 'Now, Katherine,'" she mimicked expertly. "'Don't you be forward. Don't you go and throw away your girlish treasure on some ne'er-do-well. Save it for your wedding night!' And the screen goes soft focus."

"This dialogue is making me queasy," Katherine said. "I'm going to bed."

Madeline hooted with laughter as Katherine headed for

her small bedroom at the back of the apartment, still thinking about Richard Sears. Was he really the calculating user of women Madeline described? She shook the thoughts away as she washed up in the tiny pink and blue tiled bathroom. She didn't mind sharing the bathroom, even though Madeline's makeup littered the sink and her washed-out stockings hung over every towel rack, but Katherine's own bedroom gave her privacy to dream at night.

Katherine knew Madeline's faults; most of them were painfully obvious. She was shallow, but charmingly so. She was vain and selfish, and yet she'd do anything for you, if you were on her side. So when Madeline teased her about her virginity and her caution with men, Katherine generally took it well. Tonight it got to her, though. Katherine *was* saving herself, but she didn't know why. For what? For whom? she wondered sleepily as she went into her own room. For Richard Sears on horseback? For Leo Cole, savagely burning a man's face?

Her eyes closed heavily as she vainly tried to brush her thick red hair the required hundred strokes. Waves of exhaustion swept over her, and the white sheets of her narrow bed shone invitingly in the darkened bedroom. You have a five o'clock call, a voice told her. Better go to bed and let this day end. The right man hadn't come along yet, and there were times late at night when she wondered if he ever would. Perhaps Madeline was right and there was nothing to love but fun. Nothing to it but parties and kisses behind closed doors and rumpled sheets . . . Katherine looked at her creased bed and wondered, objectively, how it felt to be handled, the way the agent handled Madeline while Leo Cole played cards in the back room of the Magyar Café. Was it all the same? Fatigue pulled her down as she stripped off her dress and got into bed naked. The warm night air came in through the windows, and the Wellington palms on Hayworth Avenue rustled in the night. As she lay alone in her bed Katherine wondered if Richard Sears was handling the beautiful Maria Lashman, marking her with kisses, stripping off her thin peach silk dress. . . .

The disturbing images faded and sleep came. . . .

In the morning Katherine felt relieved, wonderful. She didn't know why. She'd hardly slept, and she felt she ought to be tired, but as she drove back over Cahuenga Pass to the Lashman lot she was exhilarated and optimistic. She climbed into the studio station wagon, and as the car made its way across the Valley she focused on the brilliant white clouds moving in across the wide expanse of the blue domed sky like travelers heading for home after a long journey. She fell asleep almost instantly, and by the time she arrived at the location she was completely renewed.

Eddie Gibbon was sitting on the running board of his car, munching a doughnut.

"Good morning, Mr. Gibbon," Katherine called.

The little director gave her the fish eye. "Seventy dollars I lose to that crook and you say 'Good morning, Mr. Gibbon'? Bad morning, I say. Mr. Cole, he calls himself now. Where is he?"

"Leo?" she asked, uncertain. "He's certainly not with me!" Katherine was far too prim to let Eddie Gibbon think Leo had spent the night in her bed.

Gibbon grinned widely, and a chip of glazed sugar fell from his mouth to the dry valley floor. "He's not, huh? Good. I feel much better he shouldn't win at everything, Miss . . . uh . . ."

"Katherine Ransome." She sighed, determined not to blush.

"Yes. Good crying yesterday. I like an actress who knows how to cry," he said, returning to his doughnut. "We shoot the hideout soon now. You get more lines."

"I do?" she said, excited. "Thank you."

"Oh, not me, my dear," Gibbon said. "Thank Mr. Cowboy Sears." He pointed at Richard Sears, sitting on an upended milk crate playing cards with the cameraman, a wrangler, and a driver.

Just as Sears dealt the cards, Leo Cole appeared from behind a nearby truck. He was wearing the same threadbare black suit, but today he had on a new white shirt and a purple silk tie. He sauntered over to the game and casually took a kibitzing position behind the cameraman, cigar in hand. Sears said something, there was raucous laughter among the men, and Leo sat down to play, a flashing smile on his mobile face.

Katherine couldn't take her eyes off Richard Sears.

"You want advice?" Gibbon asked in a surprisingly gentle tone as he watched her. "Probably not." He sighed. "So I'll keep my mouth shut for once." Abruptly he got up and walked away.

"Mr. Gibbon?" Katherine called hesitantly. "Why don't you give Leo a job? He's your friend. Your countryman . . ."

Gibbon turned, pointing at Katherine with the remains of his doughnut. "Red-haired women are trouble," he said. "Old Hungarian saying."

Wisely Katherine said nothing about Hungarian sayings. "Please? He wants to be an actor. There must be something he can do in this picture."

Gibbon snorted and waved toward Leo, his black suit and distinctly foreign features out of place in the harsh valley sun. "What, please to tell me? The Ellis Island Kid looks like a cowboy to you?"

Katherine had a flash of inspiration. "No, a peddler!" she said excitedly. "He could be a peddler in town!"

Gibbon sighed. "Why did I ever get into this business? You know, my father had one of the largest furniture stores in Budapest. *This* I chose? Sears wants me to give extra lines to you. You want me to give a job to Leo."

"Mr. Gibbon?" Katherine said, an insistent, wheedling edge creeping into her voice. "Look at him. He *could* be a peddler."

Gibbon screwed up his face like a pug dog with indigestion. "A peddler? So now you're an agent? I thought you were an actress, Miss Random."

"Ransome," Katherine said firmly.

Eddie Gibbon looked at Leo Cole for a long, uninterrupted moment. "Okay, why not a peddler?" he said grudgingly. "If Lashman don't fire me after yesterday, he'll never fire me. Leo! Come here once!" he called. "I have a favor for you."

Leo Cole looked across the makeshift set at Katherine and Eddie Gibbon, and a sunlit smile of understanding spanned his face. "Of course, Eddie," he said eagerly. "What can I do for you?"

The funny thing was, he was good. But the amazing thing was, he was a natural. Betty, the wardrobe mistress, togged him out in an odd pleated smock she dug out of her emergency trunk, and Leo made himself a belt looped with keys, tin cups, spoons, and dangling pocket knives and crowned the outfit with a pair of Ben Franklin glasses and a dented top hat. In a matter of minutes, Leo Cole transformed himself from a hungry immigrant into a Wild West peddler with snake oil, love potions, and lucky charms in his tattered pack. Though it was only a bit part, the way he turned his head and twisted his mouth into a wickedly knowing grin when Richard Sears rode by gave the boring snippet of film a flash of excitement. Clearly, Leo Cole stole the scene.

Eddie Gibbon groaned as he grudgingly let the camera linger on Leo. "The camera likes you, Leo," he called. "I hate to admit it, but it is so."

Richard Sears wheeled his horse around and rode back to the camera in a whirling cloud of dust. Briefly, Katherine was afraid he was angry, jealous. Maybe he'd persuade Eddie Gibbon to cut out Leo's bit or do it himself by forcing the horse to kick dust in Leo's face or by pulling some other savvy actor's trick.

Sears reined in the stallion and jumped down out of the saddle, silver spurs clinking as he hit the ground. "Try it this way," he told Leo. Sears demonstrated, ducking his head even lower and cocking an eyebrow as he imitated Leo's grin. "Eddie's right. The camera likes you. See, the camera's a curious girl. Once she's got her eye on you, she'll want to know all about you, who you are, what you're up to. Don't forget that, Leo," he said seriously. "It's important. Remember, the camera is a human being, a woman. I always think the camera's the best-looking dame in the room and she's only got eyes for me, get it?"

Leo peered out over his wire-rimmed glasses and nodded seriously as he took in Sears's impromptu acting lesson. "Of course I do. Richard, I'm sorry you lost so much money to me this morning," he said gravely. "This afternoon I'll let you win it back."

Sears laughed as he swung back into the saddle, his eyes on Katherine. "Forget about it, pal. I'm gonna get every dime you've got, but I'm gonna do it the hard way. Acting's only a game, but cards and love are serious business. Besides, the Arizona Kid never gives an inch!" he yelled happily as he rode off out of camera range, waving his white hat.

The crew razzed him good-naturedly, and Leo doffed his dusty top hat and bowed in gratitude.

As the cameras rolled once again, Katherine stood next to Eddie Gibbon and watched Leo, delighted with the progress of her protégé. But her attention was constantly drawn to Richard Sears as he slouched in the saddle, his horse neighing and pawing the ground in excitement against the backdrop of the brown California foothills. Was he really the womanizer Madeline had described? Was he really just another selfish actor? He'd persuaded Eddie Gibbon to give her more lines, and he'd helped Leo without a second thought. Generosity of any kind was a rarity in Hollywood, but it was astounding to find it in an actor. So many actors were egomaniacs who believed they'd lose their immortal souls if they weren't on camera, couldn't bear to be out of frame for an instant, couldn't bear to watch the camera turn its loving eye on someone else. But despite his reputation, Richard Sears had a wide streak of generosity running through him, and he constantly worked to improve the picture as a whole, instinctively knowing that good supporting actors made him look even better.

For the first time, Katherine realized the ancient superstition was wrong: the camera didn't steal your soul, it created a new one every time it opened its lens. Once again, her eyes were drawn to Richard Sears. He was watching her, but now he was smiling.

By lunchtime, she hadn't spoken a word to him, but every time she looked up, Richard Sears was watching her with his cobalt eyes. Katherine wished Madeline wasn't so foolish about men; she wished her mother wasn't straitlaced and far away. Who can I talk to? Who can I ask? He's there, watching me, waiting for me to tell him yes without speaking. I know he's wrong for me, and I know he's trouble. There's another woman waiting for him. I know if I turn toward him and tell him yes, it will cut a new channel in my life like a river flooding an unplowed field. I know he's wrong for me. I know he's a terrible, lasting mistake. I know I don't want to, but I know I will. . . .

Katherine tried not to look at him. She looked at the camera, at Eddie Gibbon, at Betty fussing with the costumes, but her eyes continually slid toward Richard Sears. He's not forcing me; he's not persuading me. I'm persuading myself. . . . How will I escape the inevitability of the future?

"You are very kind to me, Katherine. I will not forget it." It was Leo in his makeshift peddler's costume, dark eyes glittering above the glasses.

"It—it was easy," Katherine stammered. "I saw my chance and moved."

"Now I owe you my name and my first job," Leo said. "A big debt. Will you have your sandwich with me?"

"I promised one of the girls," she said, pointing at the extras clustered around the back of the station wagon.

He bowed slightly. "Another time."

Katherine took her dry sandwich, fled to a corner, and ate with the extras. She wanted to be alone.

Sears, Leo, Eddie Gibbon, and some of the other men hauled out the milk crates and dealt the cards, laughing and smoking cigars through the brief lunch break. True to his word, Leo lost to Richard Sears, and from her vantage point near the group of gamblers, Katherine wondered if the loss was deliberate.

The shooting day was long and hard, but Katherine knew she'd done well, especially with her added dialogue in the hideout scene. Then, at the end of the dusty day, Richard Sears came up to her as she climbed into the studio car. Leo was nowhere to be seen. "Meet me tonight at the corner of Laurel Canyon and Sunset Boulevard," Sears said in a low voice. "Ten o'clock. I'll take you for a ride."

"No," she told him.

"Don't be coy, Red." He laughed and pulled gently on her hair. "I've got you pegged for the adventurous type who just hasn't found her adventure yet. Am I right?"

She shrugged, wondering what she meant by it. Is this how my life starts? she wondered. On the set of a second-rate Lashman film? Is this where the chain of events begins? She looked up at Richard Sears, his white cowboy hat circling his face like a Hollywood halo.

"So c'mon and meet me." He grinned. "We'll go for a ride. What've you got to lose?"

"Nope," she said as she walked away. But she could hear him laughing behind her. He knew she would be there and so did she.

She was deliberately late, and as she drove the Model T up to Sunset, she wondered if he'd still be there. She hoped he would; she hoped he wouldn't. But if he wasn't there, she would know he was with Maria Lashman. . . .

He was waiting for her, sitting in his black coupé a little way up Laurel, head thrown back on the seat, one arm dangling out the window with a cigarette trailing a thin stream of smoke into the warm, starred night. She pulled up next to him, and there was a tiny span of time when he didn't see her, one more moment when there was still time to escape Richard Sears. Katherine thought she was balancing on a precipice.

Then he saw her, and she knew she wasn't going anyplace, except with him. "You're late," he said gently, flicking the cigarette away into the street. "But not too late. C'mon, Red, hop in."

She parked her car and got in beside him. "I don't know why I came—"

Sears cut her off. "Sure you do," he said, his voice soft. "And so do I. I'll make you a deal, Red, and I swear I'll stick by it. I won't lie to you, and I won't use you. This is a tough town. It's full of liars and fools and tough guys and a few right guys, and I'm all of them at once. I'm not dependable, but I'll always tell you the truth and I won't try to con you, okay? Why do you think I rode off with you the other day?" he asked shortly, swinging the car up into the Hollywood Hills.

"People say you're ambitious and you thought it would make the scene better," she said promptly.

"People say?" he teased. "You've been asking about me? You're right; I'm ambitious. My career is the most important thing in my life, but I wanted to be alone with you and sink my hands into that red hair of yours. That's why I spurred the horse after Eddie said 'cut.' See? An honest answer."

"Why did you want me to meet you tonight?" she asked, her voice shaky. What a strange man. He was so sure of himself, so certain life would go his way. Had anybody, any woman, ever unsettled him?

"To see if you wanted to go to bed with me. You ever been to bed with anybody?" Sears asked. He kept his eyes on the road.

"None of your business."

"Thought not," he said. He grinned, then reached over and roughed up her hair the same way he'd roughed up the horse's mane. "Scared? Don't be. I'm not going to seduce you, and I'm sure not gonna rape you, so don't get skittish. You know I'm gonna marry Maria Lashman, don't you?"

"Yes," she said quietly.

"Good. I'm glad you know. I'm not in love with her, and she's not in love with me, though she's playing at it right now. Maria's smart, but she thinks Daddy's money can buy her any damn thing she wants. She hasn't figured out that Daddy's money only rents."

"If you don't love her, why are you—"

"Money and power, Red," he said, his voice harsh. "See, I'm a rich kid—or I was before my father lost it all and decided to take the easy way out."

"What happened?" she asked. "You don't have to tell me. . . ."

"Same old song." Sears shrugged. "My father was a Wall Street booster, one of those hail fellows who *knew* the big boom would never end and the market would go up and up and up like a Fourth of July rocket. He'd come home in the evening, we'd drink champagne cocktails, and he'd tell me the facts of life on Wall Street. 'Son, there's no ceiling,' he used to say. 'No ceiling.'" Sears laughed bitterly.

"You see," he went on, "the boom lasted so long that he forgot the old rule. There are only two emotions on Wall Street, fear and greed, and fear always wins. So, when the market started to fall, there was no stopping it. No ceiling, hell, there was no floor! The market dropped like a lead weight. Some of the guys at J. P. Morgan tried to hold it, but it didn't work. Dad was convinced the market would turn around, so he threw a million of his own money into it. A million dollars . . . One evening when he realized he was broke he quietly came home, quietly went upstairs, quietly put his revolver in his mouth, and quietly blew his brains all over the bedroom. Yeah. Some ceiling," Sears said bitterly.

So the stories about his past were true. Katherine was taken aback by the depth of Sears's sudden highly personal revelation, but most of all she was frightened by the caustic anger boiling inside him, the rage and fear burning as the soft rug of money slid out from under his feet.

"I'm so sorry," she fumbled helplessly.

He hadn't heard her. He wasn't listening. Sears plunged on, the words tumbling out in a rush. "He left me in college and my two sisters and my mother without a dime. Now me, I can take care of myself, but my sisters and my mother, Christ, they're like lost puppies. Without money they'll shrivel up and die. No coming-out party?" he mocked. "No hats and dresses and furs and . . ." He cast a sidelong look at Katherine as the heavy car whipped around the curves of Laurel Canyon. "You don't understand that kind of woman, do you, Red?"

"No," she said, shaking her head. "Work didn't kill me, and it won't kill your sisters."

Sears snorted a harsh laugh. "That's where you're wrong."

"It won't hurt them to learn to work. It might make them stronger. Waiting on tables isn't so bad."

Sears pulled the car to a stop in a deserted stretch of road lined with eucalyptus trees and flicked off the headlights. "You're strong, Red. You're tough 'cause you were raised tough. But Claire and Lila are like . . . Oh, hell, what's light and fragile and delicate and useless? Some kind of ugly hothouse flower? An orchid, maybe. God, I hate orchids. Anyway, I have to take care of them, so I'm marrying Maria. See, I'm going to be a big star, and she's going to help me," he said, turning toward Katherine in the seat as he lit a cigarette and stared down the empty canyon at Los Angeles below. He reached out with one hand and lightly caressed her breasts, the eucalyptus leaves hissing in the background. "Don't be frightened, Red. We're not going to make love here."

His honesty flustered her. She was excited by the casual way he ran his hands over her body, and she didn't want him to stop. "I—I didn't think we were," she stammered.

"Oh, yes, you did." He smiled, exhaling a trail of smoke as he slowly took his hand away. "And I have to admit, I had hopes. But not tonight, not here," he said. "See, something happened between us yesterday. You know it and so do I. I told you about Maria so you'd know how my life was going right off. I'm going to marry her in a few months, but I want to see you. Understand?"

"Yes," she said quietly. "I understand."

"Think about it. Picture'll be over in a week. If you decide you don't want to see me, you won't have to ever again— unless we work together on another picture, in which case I'll try again. See?" Suddenly he was unaccountably cheerful. "Honesty. Here I am, telling you what I want. No lies, no pretense. I want you," he said. "You're beautiful, you're strong, you're . . . Christ, I think you're just like me, but you're a woman. I hate those damn hothouse orchid types."

"Like your sisters?" she needled.

"Damn straight. Men have enough burdens without some helpless female hanging around their necks." Sears pitched his cigarette out the window and stared at it moodily as it flickered on the pavement and went out.

"Helplessness works, doesn't it?" Katherine laughed. "You're going to marry a woman you don't love so you can take care of your sisters whom you don't like. Orchids always get their way," she said ruefully. "It's just my hard luck I'm not one of them. I guess I must be a weed. Something that grows in rocky soil."

"Can I kiss you?" he asked. "I want to more than anything. Actually, I want to make love to you right here in the car, but I'm restraining myself."

"You're the strangest man!" she said. "Can you kiss me? Yes. But not the rest," she said as he reached out for her. "Just a kiss."

He was around her like a blanket, warm, enveloping, kissing her passionately, rubbing her body up and down with his hands. She tried to pull away from those searching hands, from the magnitude of his feelings and the hard pressure of his body, but it was no use. Richard Sears raked up emotions she'd never known and sensations she didn't recognize. Who was she if a kiss could arouse her so deeply? "Just a kiss to see what it's like," she whispered as he started to kiss her again. "Just to see . . ."

* * *

An hour later as Katherine walked slowly up the stairs to her apartment the musky odor of cigar smoke came drifting down the steps to meet her. Inside, she found Leo and Madeline sitting at the red enamel–topped kitchen table drinking tea and playing gin for toothpicks.

Madeline's eyes flicked over Katherine very quickly, and she raised her thin eyebrows imperceptibly as she took in her breathless, faintly disheveled air. "So," she continued without missing a beat. "I let Lashman chase me around his big bamboo desk; then I ran out on him. He's not a bad guy, but his crying act gives me the willies."

"Crying act?" Leo asked, folding his cards as Katherine joined them. Courteously he started to stand up, but Katherine waved him down. "I don't understand," he told Madeline.

"You *are* new in town," Madeline said. "Lashman's famous for weeping. If he doesn't get his way, he starts to cry. Gets down on his knees, begging and moaning. Big—whadda-you-call-'em?—crocodile tears rolling down his cheeks. Tells you Daddy'll take care of you if you'll just climb up on his lap and sign on the dotted line. Want some tea, sugar?" she asked Katherine. "Pot's almost empty, but I think there's a smidge left."

"I'll put the kettle on," Katherine said as she lit the gas jet on the white enamel Clark Jewel stove. "Who's ahead?" A mean thought clawed at her mind, and she tried to shake it off. Had Madeline taken Leo to bed? After what she'd seen last night, she doubted Leo Cole would allow himself to be taken anywhere by anyone. By any woman . . .

"Leo, of course. He came around looking for you, but since you were out, we decided to play a few hands," Madeline said, clinking her spoon against the heavy mug.

Leo's dark eyes were unperturbed. "I brought something for you," he said to Katherine. He reached into his pocket and pulled out a small black velvet jeweler's box. "A token. Since you have given me my name and my first job, you must have a memento of the great occasion. Not much, I admit, but later on, when I am rich, I promise you diamonds." Politely he held out the little box.

Her mother had warned her not to take gifts from men, but Katherine knew if she refused, Leo would be deeply wounded. "Thank you, Leo," she said as she opened the box and took out a small silver and marcasite pin in the shape of a jaunty bow. "It's lovely." She was oddly moved by the little gift. Leo was very different from Richard Sears, she realized as she pinned the gleaming bow on her dress. He was poor and he probably hadn't had much schooling, but Leo Cole had the manners and attitude of a gentleman.

What a contrast to Richard Sears, who came from a world of wealth Katherine had never seen except in the society pages. Sears was rough, ambitious, and hard. He freely admitted he was marrying Maria Lashman for her money and connections. Did he think he was royalty? Did he think he was creating an alliance of power by uniting two great families? The memory of Richard Sears's hands caressing her body played across her mind as she smoothed down the rumpled fabric.

Leo smiled, turning his cup around and around in his long fingers, his black eyes on Katherine, his predatory face hungry.

Madeline was unusually silent as she watched Leo and Katherine. "I'm working at Metro tomorrow," she said finally, anxiety playing over her voice. "Some musical. I've got a two-line bit with the second lead, and if the numbskull doesn't upstage me all the way to Alaska, I'll get a good piece of film out of it."

"I'm glad you like it," Leo told Katherine. "A token, as I said. But there *will* be diamonds."

An uncomfortable silence filled the room, and for an isolated moment the three of them were frozen in the still kitchen, caught in time like butterflies. Horns honked in the distance and somewhere a trolley bell sounded. Suddenly the kettle began to shriek, and the awkward moment was shattered. Katherine took the kettle off the stove and poured hot water into the fat brown teapot to revitalize the tea leaves.

"You must be tired," Leo said, dark eyes darting between Katherine and Madeline.

Madeline coughed.

"Yes, I am," Katherine admitted. "I have an early day tomorrow."

"Then I will say good night to you both," Leo said. He rose quickly and grazed Madeline's hand with his lips. She was too astonished to say anything and simply let her hand drop, holding it slightly away from her body as if he'd kissed a star onto her soft flesh. He turned to Katherine, took her hand, and gravely kissed it as well. "No need to see me to the door."

The two women listened as Leo left the apartment and closed the door behind him. His light feet skittered down the tiled stairs and he was gone.

"That's a first! I've been kissed in a lot of places but never on the hand," Madeline laughed, waving her hand in the air. "So what happened with Richard Sears?" she asked curiously. "Dish the dirt."

"Oh, God, I don't know. He told me he was going to marry Maria Lashman and then we kissed for a while."

"I knew *that* the minute you walked in," Madeline said. "So did Leo, by the way."

"You think he did?"

"I *know* he did. Still waters run deep as the Grand Canyon. You watch out for Leo, Katherine, I'm telling you. He's not a run-of-the-mill guy. If he falls in love with you, you've got him for life. There's something special about Leo Cole. I see it even if you don't."

"I *do* see it and I like him. He's dark and . . . a little frightening, but I don't want him to . . ." Katherine broke off lamely. "Mad," she said helplessly, "Richard makes me feel something inside, and I don't know what it is! I've never felt it before, and it's scaring me to death. I feel as if I jumped off a cliff into a lake sometime yesterday afternoon and I haven't hit the water yet. I'm not like you; I'm not used to men. . . ." Embarrassed, she let her voice trail off. "I don't know what to do. I know what men want, but I don't know what *I* want!"

Madeline stared at her for a long minute, then broke into soft laughter. "You are a child, aren't you? You better be careful, sugar. These are grown men you're fooling with, not high school boys hanging around hoping you'll let 'em carry your books to the malt shop. You think a man like Richard Sears is going to play kiss-kiss with you forever? He's had every dame in town, and he's working his way up the ladder toward the Hollywood princess. See, he's the kind of guy wants to fuck one kind of girl and marry another."

"Don't say that word, Mad. It's so ugly."

"Grow up, sugar pie. He uses women, Sears does. Which is okay if you're after a quick roll in the hay. I'd take him on anytime, anywhere, but you're a high-minded gal. Anyhow, you're missing a bet. This guy, Leo Cole? Boy, he's divine. I'd like to rub up against him on a slow boat to Hoboken for a week or so. I bet he knows some foreign tricks that Mr. Tall-in-the-Saddle Sears hasn't read about in the Sunday supplements."

Katherine stood in the kitchen doorway and stared out through the French doors in the living room, over the flat tar garage roofs toward Fairfax Avenue as Madeline's words rolled over her unheard. It was a warm night, and the breeze blew the palms against the windowpanes with the dry, comforting sound that signified California. Was this love? This confusion? Was this how your life took shape? She sipped tepid tea and went to the sink to rinse out her cup. "You don't love the men you . . . ?" she asked Madeline without looking at her.

"Not usually," Madeline said. "Big waste of time. The guys I go with don't want to settle down, and neither do I. I don't know if I ever want to be tied to one man, a house, kids. Christ! My mother had a dozen of us, I ever tell you that? Twelve times she got swollen up and ugly, and twelve times she almost died, and you know what? As soon as she finally *did* die, my father took off and left us all. The truth is, we kids killed her. Or maybe he killed her. I dunno, maybe there's no difference. But I was old enough to know she thought settling down meant one thing, and he thought it meant another. Katherine, be careful. Listen to me. This is good advice I'm giving you, and it's free."

"I know it is, Mad." Katherine sighed. "But I don't know what to do about it."

Leo wasn't on the set in the morning, and Richard Sears had a black eye and an ugly slash over his eye that looked as if it would leave a scar. Eddie Gibbon was furious, once again dancing up and down in anger. "What now, Sears? What did you do this time? Leo I have to match in this shot, and he's gone! And you look like you been ten rounds in the ring!"

Sears looked guilty and drew Eddie Gibbon off to one side.

Katherine heard them muttering, two angry men, toe to toe, one towering over the other. Gibbon finally threw up his pudgy hands and scuttled off, yelling at the cameraman.

A few minutes later Katherine went over to Richard Sears, who was halfheartedly twirling a rope. "What happened?" she asked anxiously. "Where's Leo?"

"In jail," Sears answered shortly. He looped the rope over his arm and affected an Edward G. Robinson delivery. "Don't worry, see. A pal of mine's busting him out, see. We're gonna get some gats and—"

"Richard!" Katherine said, furious. "Stop it! What's happened to him? What have you done?"

Sears looked like a kid again. "How come everybody thinks it's me? Besides, I can't tell you."

"Why not?" Katherine pressed.

"I can't tell you," Sears said again, embarrassed. "You're not the kind of girl I can tell this story to."

Katherine looked at him in disbelief. "Richard," she said

slowly, "will you please tell me what happened? Why is Leo in jail?"

"How did I get myself into this?" Sears groaned. "Well, I promised you honesty, Red. Let's see how you like it. After you left me in the car last night, I went up to Clara's place."

"Clara's?"

"The house with the blue door? Clara's?"

"Who is she?"

Sears sighed. "Clara runs a very special cathouse, cookie. Very fancy. All the girls look like famous movie stars. They'll look like anyone you want 'em to look like. You want Jean Harlow, there's a girl who looks just like her. You want a redhead . . ." He reached out and took a strand of Katherine's red hair in his hand, watching her closely for a reaction. "Get it?" he asked, pulling gently on her hair.

Katherine thought she was going to die. Maybe, if she was lucky, the ground would open up and she'd sink into the desert. "Oh, you didn't."

Sears laughed. "Nice color of red, Red. You turn that way all over?"

"You didn't," she said again, helplessly.

"I did and I felt a lot better afterward. Just think of it as a medicinal tonic. Like a doctor's prescription?" He grinned.

"And Leo was there too?"

"Yes, but not upstairs. He was playing cards. Winning, too." Sears laughed. "We had a few drinks, and I guess a fight broke out 'cause the police showed up. Leo got me out the back way, but he was too slow and he got caught. Don't worry," he said as he saw the concern on Katherine's face. "I'm bailing him out. He's a right guy, Leo."

"You ought to be ashamed of yourself!" That sounded terribly prissy, but it was the only thing she could think of.

"Why do I think you sound just like your mother?" Sears laughed again. "I *am* ashamed of myself, but mostly I'm ashamed I let Leo get caught. Guy pushes you out a window when you're half baked, you have a duty to get him out too."

"He pushed you out a window?"

"Fell on my head, too. No damage." Sears grinned. "Do me a favor, Red. When Leo shows up, don't let on I told you, okay? He's kind of straitlaced. He wouldn't want a lady to know he got caught in a whorehouse raid."

"I am never going to speak to you again," Katherine said firmly as she walked away.

Behind her, Richard Sears was laughing.

70

Chapter
5

~~~~

"Leo *Cole*, Leo *Cole*, Leo *Cole*," he chanted as he walked up the dark and silent street above the Sunset Strip toward the house with the blue door. His new self-created identity reverberated in his head like the bronze bells of a cathedral tolling over a Sunday morning city. He felt invincible, as if he were sheathed in metal.

Leo Cole. Leo Cole, the actor. At last his luck had changed! He had felt it the moment he saw Katherine Ransome on the dusty set of *The Arizona Kid,* perfectly etched against the blue California sky. And as she stood beside him at the Magyar Café, he had never doubted the cards would fall his way; he'd actually felt victory flying across the table into his arms. His luck had changed. Good fortune shone out of her face; it was reflected in her hair. *She was his luck.*

Leo Cole was a man who lived by luck, and like all true gamblers he believed luck came in runs and streaks. A run was a river of fortune; you dipped your cupped hand into it and drank freely, because there was always more luck cascading down from upstream, filling you up with its brilliance. But a streak was quick, hard, and fast. If you didn't seize it, it was merely a moment seen out of the corner of the eye, a flash in the pan, a spark of lightning momentarily bottled up in a jar until the jar exploded under the pressure. The important thing was to recognize it, seize it, and play it for all it was worth.

He'd had a long run of luck. It had carried him to New York. It hadn't been easy slipping out of Hungary without money, without capital, without cash for tips and bribes and drinks, the important things that oiled a man's way through a dangerous life, for a man could survive only so long on his charm. By the time he arrived in New York—foreign, broke, and desperate—Leo's luck had run dry and his soul was as hard as a flake of rock. He felt nothing. There was a desert inside him, a flat, barren stretch of arid salt, and until it quickened again there would be nothing.

Oh, he'd tried to renew it. He'd tested his luck at cards and dice and horses, secretly hoping it had changed. But no. The cards were always sour, the dice were always cold, and the desperate anger of the unlucky gambler gnawed at him every night as other men raked in piles of coins. Luck had slipped away as surely as the winning cards slipped across the calm green surface of the table into the hands of other players.

The life he'd dreamed of as he lay in his narrow bed in the back of his father's tailor shop, the life he'd craved when he fled Hungary after his mother's death and turned his hopes toward the unknown shores of America, that life danced out of reach. Poor, unable to speak English, he had languished in the ghetto on New York's Lower East Side as he tried to understand this strange new country, this strange America where everything was possible.

But even a man with no luck had to eat, so Leo had found work as a tailor, his father's one legacy, a trade he despised as he had despised his father, a small, wretched, pinched-faced man who spent his life knotted up in a corner. Always the old man's image hovered over him like an evil angel as Leo wetted thread between his lips and stitched lapels for gentlemen, an endless stream of pinpricks marking a high-way of blood on his long, thin fingers. While other men starved and begged in the ravaged streets of New York, Leo Kartay's dreams turned to ashes in his mouth as he mended and pressed the clothing of his betters.

But at night Leo Kartay had no betters, and as he wandered through the streets of New York, he was entranced by the sky, fleetingly glimpsed above the concrete canyons, hidden like a fabulous necklace in a black velvet jeweler's box. Perhaps he'd hit a run of bad luck, but at least he was in America, where a man could rise above his birth and his class, where a man with the ability to transform himself could become anyone he wished. Leo had roamed the city, thinking and learning, hunting for his lost luck in the rain-slick streets, the dark saloons and cafés, in alleyway crapshoots and poker games in dingy back rooms.

He watched the rich climbing in and out of their glistening black limousines on Park Avenue, the long fur coats of the ladies trailing unnoticed across the dirty sidewalk as they entered the great hotels where they ate and danced under the sharp glitter of multifaceted crystal chandeliers. Outside, the world was savaged by the Depression, but in the brightly lit hotels and the great New York houses the rich danced on as if the gathering storm knocking on their door was only a light spring breeze. As the rest of the world shuddered in chaos, as a dank wind of hate blew across Europe, the American rich danced on unaware. The rich dined, and the poor scuttled beneath their tables and hunted for crumbs.

All this was no surprise to Leo Kartay. He'd seen the great European capitals, he'd heard the older men telling stories of their youth, and he knew this was as it had always been. But unlike the timid sons and the failed old men, Leo Kartay believed he had the ability to change his life and become greater than the sum of his parents, for as Europe faded before his eyes, change was a living possibility in America. Not for him was the life of the tailor, the life of the peasant, the life of a servant in a rich man's house.

Then Leo Kartay discovered the movies.

The movies were his college course in America, and the tuition was only fifteen cents. Like many an immigrant, Leo used the flat white expanse of the movie screen as a magnifying glass in his attempt to decipher the riddle of his huge, complex new country. He spent endless hours seated in cramped theaters, thrilling to the tales of adventure and romance being spun across the screen like a panoramic web, for up on that flickering screen all men were equal, rich or poor. Gradually Leo Kartay began to transform himself from the man he was to the man he was inside, no longer the son of a shabby Hungarian tailor, but an American. And so, every Friday and Saturday night, he went to the movies, the wide open doorway to the new life he craved.

If he had a bit of extra cash, he went to the great movie palaces in and around New York. Loew's Paradise on the Grand Concourse, which featured moving clouds dappling the blue sky set in the ceiling above, the magnetic Radio City Music Hall, or the height of glamour, Loew's 175th Street. As the clouds drifted by overhead he dreamed he was a prince and the movie palace was *his* palace, his home, the glittering foyer of his kingdom.

Slowly he realized he would find his future up on that flat white screen, among the movie princes in California. There he would become the man he longed to be. There he would find his—a shudder of anticipation ran through him and pounded at his heart—his destiny?

Yes, destiny. And his skill with cards and with horses, his mobile face, and his adaptive tongue would make it all possible.

Leo had always had an ear for languages, for the nuances of dialect, and he learned English quickly, mimicking the vocal timbre of Ronald Colman, the pitch and control of Fredric March. Very soon he could speak without a trace of his characteristic Hungarian accent, and by the time he was ready to leave for California and the movie industry on the other side of the vast, playful American continent, Leo

Kartay had only the barest inflection, a faint but aristocratic foreign accent, which he could turn off and on at will.

Soon he would be a totally created man, created and recreated at will, and in California he would start afresh and shake off the past. For Leo knew he was born for more than a tailor's life, as surely as he knew the tailor with the blood-spotted fingers was not his father.

Leo knew this, believed it, because of a memory lingering in his mind he refused to release. Once, as a small boy, he was walking with his mother along the banks of the Danube when they passed a Gypsy camp. One of the men, tall and dark, with a proud hawklike face, came out and talked to his mother for a long time, looking all the while at Leo. The Gypsy never spoke to him but stared intently at the little boy as Leo waited patiently for his mother under a linden tree and watched the water.

Then, as his mother turned to leave, the Gypsy called out. "Boy," he said. "Keep this for luck." He took a gold coin out of his pocket, kissed it, and tossed it into the air.

Leo watched as the coin tumbled end over end in the air, catching the light in the green river valley as it flew toward him. He reached out his small hand and caught the golden coin, feeling a tiny bite as it hit his palm. "Thank you, sir," he said, a little afraid of the Gypsy.

The Gypsy snorted derisively. "He calls me 'sir,'" he said to Leo's mother, laughing, then stood and watched as Leo and his mother continued down the road. As they reached the crest of the small hill leading to the village, Leo turned back and saw the Gypsy wave at him. "Good-bye, boy," he called out. "Keep the coin. Good luck!"

Leo stared at the kissed coin in his damp palm and put it carefully in his pocket. I am the son of a Gypsy prince, the little boy said in his hidden heart. I am made for more than this barren life.

From that day forward, Leo believed the Gypsy was his father and the tailor was not. He kept the coin, and at night he lay in his bed and dreamed of being a Gypsy, dreamed of gold coins, dreamed of a new and shining life. Leo had always known he was different from those around him, and now he knew why. The other children had dirty faces, and they were lazy, stupid hoodlums who couldn't read and were deliberately cruel and vicious. But his face was never dirty, and his mother had taught him to read and write and do his sums. His beautiful mother had died too soon, simply from the poverty and ugliness around her . . . and when she died the light had disappeared, the light shining like a gold coin in the dark night as Leo Kartay lay in his narrow bed.

But now his luck was back. Katherine. She was responsible for his luck, his new luck. From the moment he'd seen her on the set of *The Arizona Kid* his luck had changed. He felt good fortune running in his blood as surely as if it had been written in the clouds moving across the wide San Fernando Valley. No more dried-up luck hanging out of reach like a bunch of desiccated herbs in his mother's smoky kitchen, his luck was full and round again.

She was his luck, the redheaded girl. He'd felt it as they'd stepped into the Magyar Café together; he'd felt it as she stood behind him during the game. With Katherine beside him, he would win. He'd known he would win, he'd known it! She was his luck; he could not lose. "Katherine, Katherine," he said, rolling her name around in his mouth like honey. In one glance she had transformed him from the man he never was to the man he knew he could be.

Leo Cole. Now, *that* was a name for an American actor. Leo, like Leo the Lion, roaring over MGM, the greatest American studio of them all. Cole, for Cole Porter, the most sophisticated American songwriter. Leo *Cole,* Leo *Cole,* Leo *Cole* . . .

Leo Cole touched the gold coin in his pocket and knocked on the blue door. A butler who looked exactly like the character actor Arthur Treacher opened the door, and music and laughter and the happy sound of ice on crystal rushed out to envelop him.

The house with the blue door was run by a lady named

Louise Bindel who had come to California from Ohio in 1927. Like every other girl in the world with curly hair and straight teeth, she had come to Hollywood to get into the movies, but circumstances beyond her control killed her budding career every time she set foot in a casting director's office. They all said the same thing: "Gee, kid, I'd love to help you, but the problem is, you look just like Clara Bow."

Louise had heard the same line in Ohio in 1925 when Clara Bow first made it big in movies, but she'd never seen it as a problem. Matter of fact, she idolized Clara's unbridled hoydenish sexuality and regarded the resemblance as an asset, especially because, when she came to Hollywood in 1927, Clara Bow's star-power vehicle *It* was burning up screens all over the United States. But no one wanted a second-rate Clara Bow. Louise Bindel's chances for stardom were quashed, and she was reduced to waitressing at a Hollywood eatery.

One night, lonely and bewildered, Louise succumbed to the blandishments of a shirt salesman named Harold Adler, who said he loved her. But when he cried out, "Clara, Clara, my darling!" at the crucial moment, Louise realized it was time to convert her liability into an asset.

She scoured Hollywood for girls who looked like the reigning movie queens of the day, and it wasn't hard to find them. Girls who worked as waitresses or extras, girls who never took money but often accepted presents, girls who were Hollywood's castaways. With a little persuasion, careful makeup, and an expert dye job Louise turned them into exact copies of important movie beauties. Then she rented the house with the blue door high above the Sunset Strip.

And very soon hundreds of lonely men discovered that they could be star makers, for a price. Here, lounging by the pool on a warm summer evening or listening to the soft music of the piano, a butter-and-egg man from Wichita could meet a woman who looked like a famous movie star and fulfill his wildest dreams. He could dance with the woman of his imaginings, kiss her hand, ask her—politely

—if she would care to go upstairs with him. Gloria Swanson, Jean Harlow, Bette Davis, even Mae West—all of them said yes.

Only Louise, her red hair and bee-stung lips perpetually recalling the Roaring Twenties, rarely entered into the fun and games that went on in the house with the blue door. Scandal finally killed off Clara Bow's career as a film goddess but the "It Girl" lived on in the heart of Louise Bindel from Ohio.

"Leo," she said, holding out her hand to be kissed. "I'm glad to see you. Cards or . . . ?"

"A game of cards would be nice, Clara," he told her gravely, declining her unspoken offer of female company with one of the false stars. Leo never availed himself of the pleasures waiting upstairs at the house with the blue door, for another secret hidden in his heart was that Leo saw himself as a lover. The act of sex was twined with love. He would no more think of it as sport than he would part with his Gypsy coin.

The living room was a long, low room filled with comfortable couches, lamps casting soft pools of light that never revealed too much. A walnut bar at one end was manned by an Eric Blore look-alike in a red mess jacket with gleaming brass buttons. Rows of bottles and glasses cast a hundred chips of light multiplied a thousand times in the reflection of the mirrored backbar. Near the bar stood a black baby grand piano topped with a tall crystal vase of graceful white lilies. A piano player in black tie sat on a low stool tinkling out "We're in the Money." At the far end of the room a row of French doors led to a large, quiet terrace overlooking a blue tiled pool. It was a weeknight, and only a few men were sitting in the living room, listening to the piano, talking to young women who, in the soft and flattering light, resembled the women of their dreams.

As Leo made his way toward the card room on the low mezzanine he saw a familiar figure following a redheaded girl upstairs, his hand resting casually on her hip. Richard Sears.

Leo smiled, shaking his head. He liked Richard Sears. He was open and tough and free and his Wild West temperament fit the immigrant's dream of a true American. But Leo saw something else in Richard Sears's easy nature; he saw a reverse image of himself. Richard Sears was an American prince who saw himself as a man of the people while Leo Kartay, the immigrant commoner, dreamed of being an American gentleman.

Leo shrugged, amused. He went into the card room and played a few hands with some of the blue door's regulars: Curtiz, Nagy, and one of the few women who frequented the place, the icy blonde, Constance Bennett. Bennett was a demon gambler, and her snappy chatter and golden beauty were an asset to any game. She won often, but not tonight. Tonight belonged to Leo Cole. The cards fell his way just as they had at the Magyar Café, just as he'd known they would. He had his luck.

The game was loud and raucous, Bennett and Curtiz told dirty stories, and Leo, the big winner, bought several bottles of champagne. The game broke up about midnight, and Curtiz drove Connie Bennett home because she had an early call in the morning. Leo wandered out to the bar for a nightcap, wondering if he should get a hotel room or ask Clara for the loan of her couch. Richard Sears was standing there alone, staring at the reflected room in the mirror and playing an imaginary piano on the walnut bar.

"Leo," he called, closing the imaginary piano case. "Having fun?"

Leo smiled. "A few hands of poker, nothing more."

"Nothing?" Sears said, gesturing to Clara's rhinestone stars lounging on the broad sofas. "Amid all these riches?"

"These riches are not to my taste," Leo said.

"No?" Sears grinned. "Money solves all problems, my friend.

"It would certainly solve all of mine," Leo said lightly. "Scotch," he told the bartender.

"On my tab," Sears said. "You like your part in the picture? You have a beautiful agent."

Leo smiled, controlling the anguish he felt. If Katherine melted away into the arms of Richard Sears, would his luck go with her? Earlier, when Katherine had walked into the small apartment as he sipped his tea with Madeline, her flushed face and shining but uncertain eyes had told him she'd been with a man. With Richard Sears. How deep had the river cut its path? "But what good is beauty without luck?" he said lightly. "Old Hungarian saying."

Sears laughed, and the two men raised their glasses in a silent toast.

Leo patted his pockets for his cigar case, Sears rattled the ice in his glass, and the silence was broken as a stunning version of Mary Astor ran outside to quiet a pair of angry writers fighting in the front yard. Both men sensed the undercurrent, both men felt something for Katherine Ransome, something unusual. But in the way of men, neither was able to express his feelings openly but could only allude to them obliquely.

"You're Hungarian?" Sears asked. "I read it's getting rough in that neck of the woods."

"Politics interest you?"

"I read the papers; I'm interested in things other than the movies. I read about this guy Hitler, and I don't think I like him or his Brownshirts either. Sounds like a goddamn bunch of foolishness to me."

"Oh, do not underestimate Hitler," Leo said. "Never underestimate a madman."

"That's a mistake I never make. We got our own madmen in this town," Sears said. "Power mad. A guy who likes gambling ought to do well here. After all, Hollywood is the last big crapshoot in America. It's a no-limit game with high stakes. That's why guys go nuts and turn into midget Hitlers. The high stakes in the movie racket drive 'em crazy," Sears said cheerfully.

"Some men are corrupted by high stakes. I am not," Leo said.

Sears laughed, then cocked his head as they heard a thud outside the blue door. "I bet you're not. You've got the lean and hungry look of a man starving for action. Say, what the hell's that?" he asked as heavy fists slammed at the door and the sound of men yelling filled the room. "The cops? If those two writers can't keep it in their pants . . ." He groaned. "Damn it all to hell, I can't afford to get caught here. If Maria doesn't kill me, her father will. The old skunk won't like it if his Arizona boy gets nailed in a whorehouse raid."

Leo knocked back his drink, listening. "Yes, I think it's the cops." He grinned, then balled up his hand and laughed, his eyes shining. "The sound of a policeman's fist pounding on a door sounds the same in any language. Not to worry, my friend. Follow me."

Quickly he led Richard Sears into the card room on the mezzanine, empty except for the remains of the game scattered on the green baize table, and bolted the door behind them. There was a window at the far end of the room, and Leo went straight for it, Sears right behind him. Leo pulled open the window. "Jump," he told Sears.

Sears stuck his head outside and took a fast look around the backyard. "Jump? Down there? The hell I will. We're on the goddamn second floor," he said in surprise. "That's a fifteen-foot drop!"

"You want the cops or you want to jump? Out. Grab the sill, hold on, then drop down. You're a lucky man, Sears. Besides, if you land on your head you won't break anything." Leo laughed.

Sears grinned and draped a lanky leg over the windowsill. "You're right, I'm lucky and hardheaded to boot."

"Open up! It's the law!"

"Even bad luck is useful," Leo said, glancing back apprehensively as the door squealed loudly under heavy fists. "Go!"

"Open up. It's the police!" A shoulder struck the groaning door.

"Over the top, boys!" Sears yelled as he dropped to the ground. He scrambled to his feet and ran full tilt for the end of the yard, passed the swimming pool, and vaulted the low fence leading to the house next door.

The door squealed, and then the planks shattered as the police broke it down and burst into the room, guns drawn.

Leo held up his hands and smiled, carefully blocking the window to give Richard Sears a little more time to run for it. "Gentlemen, I am yours," he said.

The next morning, after Richard Sears's attorney bailed Leo out of the L.A. County Jail, he took the bus over to the Lashman lot and hung around the commissary until he caught a ride out to the *Kid* location an hour later.

Katherine waved tentatively, but her eyes constantly slid away from him and over to Richard Sears, who was laughing with the crew in between setups. Slowly, Leo took out a cigar and lit it as he paced back and forth by the clutch of cars pulled up in a rough circle behind the location. He looked at the knot of people gathered around the striped canvas umbrella shielding Eddie Gibbon from the sun.

Does she love Richard Sears? Leo wondered. If she loves him and if he wants her, Katherine will choose Richard Sears over Leo Kartay and even over Leo Cole, for Sears is a worthy adversary. He is handsome, and he is going to be a movie star, but he has a fatal flaw. He is both trapped and overwhelmed by his desire for wealth because somewhere, hidden away inside, he does not believe in himself. He believes he will be rich only if he marries Maria Lashman, and she is a force to consider. And there is also Edgar Lashman, the wild card. Leo blew a thin stream of smoke into the air and watched it dissolve in the breathless sky.

Leo shook his head. He didn't like the thought of Katherine—his luck—in bed with Richard Sears. But I must wait, he told himself emphatically. Sooner or later, if I can restrain myself, she will turn to me, because when Sears deserts her the comforting ear of her friend Madeline will not be enough. She will need a man. She will need me.

Eddie Gibbon shrieked for silence: *"Kvhy-yut!"*

Leo tapped a thick rope of gray ash onto the ground, then broke it up with the worn toe of his shoe until the ash blended with the brown earth. If I can wait for her, she will be mine. And I am a man of infinite patience.

A few minutes later Katherine ran up to him. She had on her gingham schoolmarm costume, and her thick hair was caught in a heavy knot at the base of her neck. There was an appealing earnestness about her, Leo thought as he smiled down at her. A face like a flower, an honest flower, like a daisy that sprouts and grows optimistically in the sun.

"Leo," she said breathlessly, "what happened? Richard told me I wasn't supposed to ask, but I can't help it."

"I spent the night in jail," he said calmly. "Believe me, I've slept in worse places and on worse mattresses. At least I had a place to sleep," he said, making light of the unpleasant accommodations at the county jail. He hoped he hadn't picked up fleas or lice.

Katherine frowned. "If I ask you a question, will you give me an honest answer?" she asked. "Please? Don't be embarrassed, Leo. Look, I told you we're all broke here. Where are you living?"

Leo shrugged uncomfortably.

"Nowhere, right?"

"Address unknown. My few things are in a locker at the bus station. Meanwhile, a room here, a room there," he admitted.

"Come home with me and sleep on the couch," Katherine said, putting a gentle but unmistakable emphasis on the word *couch*. "Madeline and I each have our own rooms, but we have a couch and you're welcome to it."

"I know; I saw it. It's a lovely couch."

"It's as lumpy as gravy! But it's inside, and you won't have to wander around all night. What were you going to do, sleep at the . . . uh, place where you met up with Richard?" she stammered.

She had turned quite a pretty flushed pink. Rose pink, he thought, the delicate interior of a rose in full flower. He smiled, touched by her ingenuousness.

"Leo?" she asked. "Say yes? You're going to get paid for

this job next week. You can kick some money in the kitty for groceries, okay? I can't let you sleep on the street."

"If you let me stay with you, I can afford to take classes with Madame Lermontov," he said slowly. "She teaches acting, and I must pay her something."

"That's a good idea. If you want to be an actor, you need to study."

What a wonderful person she is, he thought happily. "You must understand that I was at Clara's house to play cards," he told her carefully. "You understand? Cards only." He wanted Katherine to know he'd gone to the house with the blue door for cards alone, even if Richard Sears had other things in mind. Someday, when Richard Sears deserted her, Katherine would remember that Leo Cole wasn't a man who went with whores.

So Leo moved into the Hayworth Avenue apartment, coming and going very early and very late, always carrying groceries or flowers when he came back, washing the dishes, sweeping the floor while he was there.

Madeline, who wasn't keen on the idea of Leo as roommate at first, instantly discovered he was the ideal companion. "He's the first guy I've ever met who doesn't treat me like a dumb blond," she told Katherine one morning a few days later as they lingered over a cup of coffee. "Plus, he cleans up after himself. I could fall for him in a big way, but he's crazy about you, sugar."

"He's not crazy about me; he's crazy about movies," Katherine said.

"True enough, but he's really crazy about you. You don't see how he watches you? Like a spaniel."

"Don't be silly." Katherine shrugged, uncomfortable at the idea of Leo in love with her while she dreamed of Richard Sears.

Madeline had a screen test coming up, and she was nervous about it. "I've got to make it," she told Leo that night. "If I can't be a movie star, what else can I do? Go to work at Clara's house?"

"Madeline!" he snapped, his voice harsher than Katherine had ever heard it before. "Never say that, never! You are beautiful and you have talent, but you don't work hard enough," he said shrewdly. "You are lazy, and you like parties." His voice had changed, no longer angry, but soft as he cajoled Madeline. He wagged a gentle finger at her. "Don't you know that being an actor is hard work and that being a star is a lifetime of dedication? You go out at night when you should be sleeping; you don't take classes. Come with me to Madame Lermontov. Your work will improve."

"That hag? She never works except when she plays the old maid villager in Lashman's vampire epics. What the hell does she know about acting?"

"We all have to eat," he said philosophically. "Madame was a famous actress on the stage in Moscow. She studied with Stanislavski; she's worked with Michael Chekhov. Soon she is leaving for New York to set up an acting school but now she's here in Hollywood. Study with her, Madeline. Study and learn to use what you have inside you. Let it show on the screen."

"Easy for you to say, Leo," she snapped. "You have talent, damn it. All I have"—Madeline did a quick bump and grind—"is me."

Nevertheless, she went to the next class with Leo and came home more thoughtful than Katherine had ever seen her before. "Leo was right," Madeline admitted. "I can learn; I can be better. You know, Katherine, nobody laughed at me in Madame's class. None of the other kids thought I was just a dumb blond."

"Don't be frightened of yourself, Mad. You're not dumb. Leo's right: you ought to study."

"Leo's right a lot," Madeline said, a new respect in her voice.

"It's funny . . . Leo didn't tell me to go to class," Katherine said thoughtfully.

"You're better than I am just standing still," Madeline suggested.

"No, I'm not," she said slowly. "That's not true. Your

future is up on the screen, and I don't know what my future is. Not yet." Suddenly she felt afraid.

For the next few days Katherine stayed away from Richard Sears on the set, and then the shooting on *The Arizona Kid* ended as abruptly as it had begun. The people who'd come together and been a family for a few weeks were about to split apart, drift away, and perhaps meet on another picture. Katherine wanted something more personal than the warm ginger ale provided by Lashman Studios, so she asked the cast and crew to her apartment for a small, homey wrap party. It wasn't much—some homemade beer a neighbor had brewed in a still he'd set up on his back porch during Prohibition and had never taken down, hot dogs grilled in a pit in the backyard, and potato salad—but it was a wonderful party, full of friends and laughter, jokes and storytelling. Eddie Gibbon got drunk and did a Hungarian folk dance with a napkin tied round his head like a scarf, Leo did sleight of hand, and Richard Sears did rope tricks.

It was close to midnight when the party broke up and Sears found Katherine in the kitchen washing the silverware. "Meet me tomorrow night," he said. "Ten o'clock. Laurel and Sunset. Same place as before." A horn honked outside and he frowned. "That's Maria," he said. "Come to pick me up."

"No," Katherine told him firmly, her hands deep in hot, soapy water. "No, no, no, Richard, I won't." The horn honked again, twice, and Katherine inclined her head toward the impatient sound cutting through the night. "She's waiting for you, Richard. You're going to get married."

"Yes, but not now," he said, pressing the length of his body hard against hers as she stood by the sink. "I don't want to hear about Maria, and don't waste time telling me you're not coming," he said, pressing harder, kissing the back of her neck. "Meet me."

"No, Richard. I won't."

Sears cupped her breasts in his hands. "Yes, yes, yes. Yes, you will."

He pulled her away from the sink and began to kiss her passionately, roughly, as her hands trailed water down her dress and onto the floor. "Yes," he told her and he left the room as the horn blasted a long rude call into the night.

Quickly Katherine dried her hands on a dish towel, walked out to the balcony overlooking the street, and stood in the doorway. Maria Lashman, wearing a red satin evening gown, was sitting on the hood of her gray car with a glass of champagne in her hand. Her dark eyes swept the stairs as Richard walked slowly down the outside staircase, through the courtyard, and toward the car. She looked up and saw Katherine standing in the balcony doorway looking down at the street below.

Maria threw back her head and laughed in an exaggerated gesture, then lifted her champagne glass to Katherine in a mocking salute. Roughly, Richard pulled her down from the hood of the car, and she threw the champagne full in his face. He slapped her and she melted toward him as the sharp sound of the slap followed by Maria's laughter resounded across the quiet street.

Quickly Katherine stepped back from the doorway, shocked and embarrassed by the scene. Was Maria drunk? She didn't think so. The little show had been for her benefit. She felt Richard's hands on her body, smelled his scent on her neck, her skin, her hair. Oh, God, she thought, I want him. I know I do . . . and the next night she drove slowly up to Sunset to meet him.

"I knew you'd come," he said as he leaned over and opened the door.

"I didn't want to. I wasn't going to until I saw you with Maria Lashman. Doesn't she trust you? She keeps you on a tight leash, picking you up on the set, at parties. Why didn't she come in? Too fancy for the working class?" Katherine heard her voice fraying at the edges with anger she was not sure she actually felt. Was this jealousy? Was this how it tasted? A bitter, bilish aftertaste of cold metal lingered in her mouth.

"Maria? She's like my sisters," he said shortly. "Rich, spoiled, willful, likes to put on shows. A beautiful narcissist. She looks in my eyes and all she sees is her own glistening reflection. She doesn't like me to sleep because she can't see herself when my eyes are closed." He laughed unpleasantly, then gunned the engine, and the car jumped away from the curb.

So he's been to bed with her. Did I think Maria Lashman was as prudish as I am? Katherine thought bitterly. The mouse-brown country cousin. She looked at Richard's profile, etched against the dark sky in the dark car, his face speckled by the oncoming headlights. Why she was resisting him? She didn't want to resist; she wanted to give in, and only the ragged remnants of her mother's protective upbringing kept her from acquiescing. She had a vague vision of herself, back arched, mouth open, in the darkness of an unknown room, and she flushed.

He turned the car up into the Hills and she thought he was taking her to the same place overlooking the Valley, and then he would take her in his arms, kiss her, run his hands . . .

But he didn't. He drove quickly through the narrow streets, up Beachwood Canyon to Lost Lane and pulled into the steep driveway of a two-story white Spanish-style house with wrought-iron bars over the windows and a huge front door spanned by iron bands and dotted with iron studs. A massive bougainvillea hugged the stucco walls.

"My place," he said dismissively as he killed the engine. "Want to go inside?" He watched her face in the darkened car and as the sound of the engine faded, the silence over the sparsely populated, chaparral-strewn hillside was very deep.

She knew what he was asking, knew if she went inside her life would be changed forever. She felt her foot poised above a stairway rising into the rest of her life.

Richard sat quietly, still looking at her. "What I said the other night still goes. People think I take advantage of women." He laughed shortly. "But most of the time it's the other way around," he said, a trace of bitterness in his voice. "That's why I won't try to talk you into anything. See, I want you to want me, Red. Love's a serious game, and it takes two to play it right. Otherwise the hell with it."

Katherine opened the car door and got out.

Chapter
6

Katherine was surprised at the beauty of Richard's little house, which he called "the cabin." But it was hardly a cabin. The atmosphere was an artful parody of a man's hideaway, a western enclave with the edges deliberately left rough, like a refined bachelor's jewel in a rugged setting. Richard Sears wasn't afraid of beauty, and his eye as a decorator was discerning.

The living room was huge, with a long green pool table filling one end. Behind the pool table a graceful wrought-iron spiral staircase led to an open sleeping loft. The walls were plain whitewashed plaster with rough-hewn timber surrounding the diamond-paned leaded-glass windows, and in the center of one wall there was a massive flagstone fireplace surrounded by brightly colored Spanish tiles echoing the blues and greens in the stenciled beams running the length of the ceiling.

Western art lined the walls—Remingtons, Boreins, and Russells, Navajo blankets, a shelf filled with intricately worked baskets. An elaborate silver saddle on a stand filled one corner, and the leather furniture was huge and looked comfortable enough for a long winter's nap.

"Richard," she said, astonished. "It's wonderful! I never guessed . . ."

He laughed self-consciously. "What, that a guy like me had taste? I collect western art and Indian artifacts because I love beautiful things," he said. "Nobody out here appreciates baskets or rugs." He gestured at the collection of brilliantly colored Navajo eye dazzlers illuminating the white plaster walls. "People throw 'em out."

As Katherine examined the details of the room, she realized the eccentric beauty of Richard's cabin only accentuated the differences between them, differences of class, of breeding, of upbringing and education, and she felt intimidated by the extent of his possessions. "Did you know how it would look when you started? Nobody told you what to buy?"

"We don't *buy* our things, Katherine. We *have* them." He laughed self-consciously. "That's what my mother says. She likes furniture with the patina of England, so it looks as if it came over on the bloody *Mayflower*. Maybe that's why I like this stuff. She thinks it's junk, but to me, handmade things are the most beautiful of all."

Katherine nodded. Richard was so concerned with his surroundings, with the placement and choice of objects. Was that a characteristic of the rich? As she looked at the exquisite, careful beauty of Richard Sears's home she realized he was even farther away from her than before, almost unattainable. His house, his taste, his sense of breeding, and his own history created a gulf between them, a vast, unswimmable ocean of class.

For a moment Katherine felt shy and awkward, unable to compete with Sears's casual display of wealth and personal style. Her family was warm and loving, but nothing in her background had prepared her for his voracious love of beauty. Her Presbyterian mother had only two things on the walls: a framed print of *The Blue Boy* in the living room and a calendar over the kitchen stove with a picture of the Washington Monument on it. Katherine felt as if she were standing on the edge of a cliff, looking at Richard Sears across the breadth of a wide river below. Was she out of her league? Out of her class?

She thought back to the wrap party for *The Arizona Kid* and her brief glimpse of Maria Lashman in her red dress, coiled provocatively on the hood of her car, posing like a stylish icon demanding admiration. Wealth hung over her like a fog. Was money the only prize in the Hollywood game?

"What's the matter? Don't you like the house?" he asked easily as he went behind the bar and poured himself a scotch. "Drink?"

"No, thank you. Yes, I like your house but I didn't expect it to be so grand. You caught me off guard."

He laughed, but a bitter rasp made the sound harsh and unforgiving. "What did you expect? Dirty boots on the floor? This is what I'm working for, Katherine." Richard took his drink and sat down on the sofa. "This house is only the beginning of what I want."

Katherine perched tentatively on the edge of a leather chair. "Certainly not dirty boots, but not this." She felt shy; now that they were alone the mood shifted gears.

"I told you I had big plans," he said impatiently, waving at the room. "I *want,* Red. See, I grew up in a sheltered, controlled world, all soft lighting and flat green lawns. But at night I read Rider Haggard and dreamed I was Allan Quatermain, a gentleman adventurer. I imagined going up the Orinoco in a dugout canoe, to the South Pole with Shackleton," he said, a faraway look in his eyes. "I had my life planned like a chess match, but after my father shot himself . . ."

Katherine shuddered.

He saw it and grimaced. "It's the truth." He made a gun with his hand and aimed it at his temple. *"Ka-pow,"* he said, automatically jerking his head back in a grim pantomime. *"Ka-pow* went my world." He got up abruptly and made another drink. "So I changed my plans. Instead of being a gentleman adventurer, I *pretend* to be one. It's a slim difference but a telling one."

Katherine shook her head. "I don't belong in the world of gentleman adventurers. You're rich, you're a movie star . . ."

"Not yet, but soon," he said without a trace of affectation. "At least that way, I can have a piece of what I want. When I was a kid I thought I'd have everything. Now I'm willing to settle for fifty percent."

"We're very different," she said thoughtfully. "The way you live, this house. Richard, you want the moon above and the stars below. It's overwhelming."

"Oh, no, we're not different." He laughed, swirling the ice in his glass. "You're as tough as I am, Katherine, but you're a virgin in more ways than one. You haven't learned how uncompromising Hollywood is, and you haven't caught on to the rewards. Not yet, anyway."

"I wonder." Katherine leaned her head back in the chair, her eyes following the delicate scrollwork on the beams above. A maze. She was lost in a maze, and her lack of experience felt like a noose around her heart.

"What a throat you have, like cream rising. I know just how Bela Lugosi feels. God, this is insane," he mumbled as he came over to her side. Gently he pulled her head back, and as his eyes searched hers, he began to run his hands through her thick red hair.

Then he started to kiss her exposed neck, pressing his mouth down her body as he knelt on the floor next to her. Softly his hands caressed the insides of her thighs, moving upward beneath her dress and gently spreading her legs apart. Suddenly he pulled back, his hands still on her legs. "We're trouble, you and me."

She looked down at him, kneeling in front of her. She was trembling, and she didn't want him to stop. "Trouble? I guess we are." Her body was hot and hard, and she pushed forward against him reflexively. "Then I want trouble. If I want you, I want trouble, and I want you, Richard." She laughed. "I've been safe all my life, wrapped up in a cocoon as strong as a prison. Maybe I left home to break out of it, I don't know. . . ." Katherine looked into his eyes, then took his hand and placed it gently between her legs, pushing forward so the shape of her body fitted into his cupped hand. He was closer to her now than ever before. They were closer to the moment. . . .

Slowly his mouth moved back up her body and he began to kiss her face, her eyes, her cheeks, her forehead. His tongue made a circle around her lips, mimicking the slow, tender circle his fingers made between her legs.

She closed her eyes, smiling, opening herself to him. *Now.* Her future was beginning now.

They met whenever they could; they met at his place, at her apartment if Madeline and Leo were gone, in hotel rooms because they were convenient on all too brief lunch hours. Often it was tricky for Richard to break away from rehearsal on his new project, a more serious western at Paramount. *The Gunman* was a character study of Billy the Kid, a dramatic piece focusing on a brief incident in Billy's life. On the trail of his father's killer, Billy has a chance encounter with a young girl who doesn't know his true identity. Of course, the story was a complete fabrication, but the script was taut and lean with an exciting climax. The project had the smell of success, but no one in the Paramount hierarchy knew the part struck home for Richard Sears.

It was Richard's first starring role for a major studio, and once filming began, lovemaking with Katherine was interspersed with work on the script. They sat naked in bed and drank champagne from the bottle while Katherine cued him on his lines for the next day's shooting.

"I've learned something about acting," Richard told her as they lay in bed at his place late one night, the script momentarily abandoned.

"Yes? Tell me," she said, stroking his thigh. She was amazed she'd learned to love so quickly. When she was alone she thought only of him, of the sight of his body covering hers, or of his face as he lay beneath her and she moved rhythmically above him. He had a perfect body, she thought idly. He was smooth and muscled, and there was a springy tension running beneath the surface of his skin that made him seem forever on the verge of striking out.

"Leo says an actor has to search out a place in his heart where you and the character are one," he said, hands behind his head as the fan slapped a slow pulse of cool air across the ceiling.

Katherine shifted uncomfortably, pulling the wrinkled sheets around her like a sarong. Leo's name in their bed disturbed her.

Richard noticed nothing. "Take this part, Billy. It's a natural for me. Paramount doesn't know why and I ain't gonna tell 'em, because why doesn't matter. On the surface it's because Billy is tracking down his father's killer, but there's a piece of Billy that's just like me. Billy was a ruthless son of a bitch. There's a killer in him and maybe there's a killer in me. . . . Drink?"

The ceiling fan blew cold air across Katherine's naked skin, and she pulled the sheet even closer. "No," she said slowly. "But I'm hungry." It wasn't true; the emptiness inside her had nothing to do with hunger. Was he as ruthless as he pretended to be? Was he only pretending to love her? If there was one chance, she would take it. . . . Maria Lashman's face danced in front of her like a spoiled sugarplum, and out in the hills a coyote barked. Suddenly Richard's house didn't feel so private and cozy and secure.

But during the day, she couldn't stop thinking about him and often found herself staring at nothing, standing with a dish towel in her hand, like a child playing a game of statues, her mind wrapped around Richard in a kaleidoscope of shifting color and changing shape as the colored stones reformulated in the sharp triangle of mirrors. Did love always feel like this? How did people stand it?

Katherine didn't have any work lined up after *The Arizona Kid* wrapped, so she made the rounds, dropped off some eight-by-ten glossies, talked to secretaries, and tried to talk to casting directors. She wondered why her agent, a worried man with a tendency to plead, didn't do more to drive her career forward after her slim lead in *The Arizona Kid*. After her brief flash of success at getting Eddie Gibbon to give Leo a part in the picture, it had occurred to her that she'd make a good agent; it was easier to get work for other people than for herself because she could press and cajole without embarrassment. But she'd saved most of her salary from *The Arizona Kid,* and it would keep her for a month if she was careful. For now she was content to drift.

Meanwhile Leo got a job as a sniveling hood on a Warner Brothers picture, *Dead End,* starring Humphrey Bogart. So, with a little cash in hand, Leo moved out of their apartment and into two furnished rooms over a garage on De Longpre Avenue for twenty dollars a month. He never mentioned Richard, though Katherine knew Richard had gotten him a character part in *The Gunman*—a role that was threaded through the entire picture. And of course she knew Leo and Richard played cards together and gambled and drank frequently. Very quickly Leo became part of Richard's rowdy crowd of men friends—actors, writers, and directors —who went sailing, played tennis, and drank on the weekends. Leo often took Katherine out to dinner, and though he said nothing, she saw danger and worry in his dark eyes.

Madeline, too, was unusually quiet. "Be careful, Katherine. Sears is dangerous," she warned. "I told you, he's tough and he's ruthless. You're not. This is the first time you've been in love. He's your first guy. I don't want you to get hurt."

Katherine didn't know what Madeline was talking about. "Hurt me? How? Richard wouldn't hurt me," she said. She knew he loved her, though he never told her so. His love surrounded her every time they lay in his bed with a slick film of sweat between them. He loved her, she knew it, she was sure of it. So she drifted through the days and waited for night to come. She slept late and lounged around the house in her bathrobe drinking coffee with Madeline. Two weeks seeped into three, three into five, into six. . . . Richard was deep into *The Gunman*, and Katherine got a week's work at RKO on the new Astaire-Rogers picture, but they still met every night.

Richard never mentioned Maria Lashman, but Katherine thought about her a good deal. A pastel picture of her with Irene Mayer Selznick and Edie Mayer was in the latest issue of *Screenland* with an article titled "Moguls' Mites," about the beautiful daughters of the rulers of Hollywood. Maria Lashman stared seductively into the camera, lips wet and parted, neck encircled by a three-strand pearl choker, shoulders bare, dark curls glistening. The caption read, "The Fairest of Them All." Katherine stared into Maria's blank eyes, and dread pierced her heart.

When she lay in bed with Richard, her hair trailing across his chest like an encompassing vine, she knew he would never give up these passionate moments, never remove the scent of his body, which was imprinted inside her body as a signet ring melts into red sealing wax. He would never marry Maria Lashman.

But afterward, when she went home to the dark apartment on Hayworth Avenue in the cool, damp air of early morning, passing the Adohr milkman on the way up the stairs, in those quiet moments when she was unbearably, unalterably alone with her thoughts, she was besieged by doubts and assailed by fear. He was too hard; it would never last. It was impossible. She remembered strange moments when he talked business on the phone and his voice was harsh and his eyes turned as black and hard as a stone. The Richard she knew and loved disappeared, and there was only a movie star inhabiting his body. The movie star was emerging as she watched. . . .

Richard Sears was on the cusp of success in Hollywood. Everyone in town knew it. Everyone in town read success as though it were burned into his forehead, Katherine thought idly. Even Louella Parsons loved him, and she used her powerful gossip column to promote his burgeoning career. She'd been on the *Gunman* set and had raved about the picture in the effusive prose she usually reserved for her darling, Marion Davies. Madeline, always a conduit for gossip, said Paramount was ready to push Richard Sears in a big way, send him on tour of the sticks and to New York for interviews. The publicity blast for *The Gunman* was going to focus on Richard.

Katherine felt desperation closing off her breath like a fallen trapdoor when she heard Paramount was poised to give him the star treatment. A movie star doesn't marry a bit player, her mind nagged. A movie star wears white flannels and plays croquet. A movie star tangos the night away at the Trocadero or the Coconut Grove. A movie star marries the Fairest of Them All.

Was she playing the fool? Early on, he'd told her he intended to marry Maria Lashman, and though he'd never mentioned it again, he'd never told her otherwise. Never looked into her eyes and lied, never whispered a half-truth in her ear. He'd promised her honesty, and honesty lay between them like a knife. For even as he buried himself in her, shuddering with joy, he never said he loved her. Richard Sears never lied to her. He'd been utterly honest. But was she lying to herself?

Then, at the end of a particularly long, slow day Katherine was sitting on the balcony of the apartment, watching the sun on Hayworth Avenue shift into twilight. The street was quiet; the Spanish-style buildings silent except for the sound of children playing in the front yards. Lately she sat here often, her mind lazy, her thoughts focused on the night to come. She was waiting for Richard, doing nothing, letting time twist by like an unraveling spool of thread.

She heard the car before she saw it. The deep growl of the engine reverberated through the street. Then a long gray limousine pulled to a stop in front of the building and the chauffeur in his gray livery opened the door for Maria Lashman.

She got out of the car, and her eyes found Katherine sitting on the balcony looking down at her. Without hesitation, Maria gave a jaunty wave, spoke to the chauffeur, and walked briskly through the courtyard and up the stairs toward Katherine.

The visit was so sudden Katherine was flustered and didn't know how to react. Maria's heels clicked like the keys of a typewriter as she ran briskly up the tiled staircase, one hand shielding her eyes from the final rays of the ocher sun slanting across the sleepy street below. She was wearing an elegant white shantung suit and pearls. Her head was bare, and her cap of black curls glistened and bounced as she stopped at the top of the stairs.

"I thought we should talk," she said quietly as she held out her small white hand. "I'm Maria Lashman."

Katherine's heart was pounding, but she refused to give in to fear. "Katherine Ransome," she said. She took Maria's outstretched hand with the formality of a society matron at afternoon tea. "Don't sit down; you'll dirty your suit. We'll go inside."

"Lovely," Maria said, arching her slanted brows.

The two women sat down in the living room. The French doors were open, and the noise of the traffic on Fairfax Avenue drifted across the alley behind the building and in through the open windows.

Maria Lashman's dark eyes lazed over the room, her glance falling on the shabby couch, the spindly potted plants with their dusty leaves, Madeline's aquamarine kimono tossed carelessly over the back of the overstuffed chair, the bookcase piled with magazines and secondhand books, the scarred beehive radio.

A smile flickered over Maria's red mouth as she crossed her legs and smoothed her white skirt. For the second time Katherine realized Maria was like a small but dangerous animal. Silk stroked silk as she pointed her foot and rotated her ankle.

"I know all about you and Richard, so don't bother to pretend," Maria began suddenly in her breathless voice. "I won't scream and yell, so don't worry about *that*. I hate scenes; they're so pointless. Let's just have this little heart-to-heart and then I'll leave, all right?"

"What do you want, Maria?" Katherine said, her voice as level as she could make it. I'm damned if I'll let her see I'm afraid, she thought.

"Is he the first man you've . . ." Maria let her voice trail off delicately. "The first one you've been interested in? Seriously interested in, I mean?"

"That's none of your business, is it?" Katherine said flatly.

Maria ignored her. "He's not a wise choice, but the first man rarely is," she said. "The first man I fucked was a gardener. I was fourteen. I trapped him in the shed behind our house and told him if he didn't fuck me whenever I wanted it, I'd get him fired. So the first man doesn't really count." She raised her eyebrows. "I adore Richard, but I see his faults clearly, and believe me, they're legion. He's vain and ruthless and ambitious, and that's exactly why we make a good couple—we're so alike. In many ways Richard reminds me of my father, and that's another reason we get along. Richard uses up women and throws them away, but *I* do not intend to be thrown away. Richard belongs to me, and I intend to keep him, but I have no illusions that I'm the only woman in his life or ever will be, and that suits me down to the ground. These days, a modern marriage demands tolerance on both sides, don't you think? We all have our little quirks, and I don't intend to give up mine any more than I expect Richard to give up his," Maria smiled meaningfully and recrossed her legs. *Slick-slick,* went the silk as it rubbed together.

"You don't *care* that Richard and I have been seeing each other?" Katherine asked slowly. There was a strange undercurrent in the room, and she didn't understand it.

Maria laughed, cold silver bells clinking on a metallic Christmas tree. "Well, I won't say I don't *care*. But it doesn't worry me unduly. As I said, we all have our little quirks." She leaned forward on the couch and looked deep into Katherine's eyes, then put her small, red-nailed hand on Katherine's.

Maria's touch was confusing, unhealthy. Katherine squirmed inside, desperately wanting to pull away, but she refused to show fear to Maria Lashman. Katherine smiled coldly and didn't budge.

After a long moment Maria sighed and pulled her own hand away, leaning back on the couch. "Richard's fucked lots of girls, lots. Let him fuck you if he wants to," she said carelessly.

Katherine was startled by Maria's coarse language, and she was stung by her blasé taunt. Obviously, Maria Lashman didn't care what anyone thought of her.

Maria continued, oblivious to Katherine's discomfort. "Some men *need* to fuck a lot of girls; they don't think they're men otherwise. And as I said, Richard reminds me of my father. My father's laid every ingenue in Hollywood. He keeps a diary! Isn't that funny?" Maria laughed humorlessly. "I got into his desk a few years ago and read it. Don't ever fuck my father, 'cause he'll describe every mole on your pretty ass in loving detail, and one of these days it'll get into the papers," she said with relish. "Think of that as a warning from a friend."

Maria gave a wise smile, and suddenly Katherine wondered if she was telling the truth. Maria had beauty and intelligence, but there was a soft core of ugliness lurking behind her beautiful face. Was Maria talking about her father or was she talking about herself?

Maria stood up and straightened her white skirt over her slim hips. "Glad we could have this little talk," she said primly. "I hope you understand me?"

"Oh, you're easy to understand," Katherine said, furious at Maria's arrogant attitude. "You've had life handed to you on a plate, Maria. I haven't. I work for what I want. I expect to go on working, and that doesn't bother me. But you bother me, Maria. You're rich and spoiled, and you think all you have to do is open your hand and Richard will fall into your palm."

"Just like a piece of overripe fruit," Maria mocked.

"How wonderful to be so sure of yourself," Katherine said.

"Oh, I'm not sure of myself." Maria laughed as she got up. "I'm sure of Richard."

After Maria left, Katherine sat down on the flowered couch and shakily watched the shadows cross the darkening room. Maria's unpleasant visit had loosed an acrid current in Katherine's heart and she felt uneasy.

Later Katherine told Madeline about Maria Lashman's unpleasant visit. "I told you Richard Sears was dangerous," Madeline said, her blue eyes cloudy and confused. "And so is Maria Lashman."

A few nights later Katherine came in late and found Madeline and Leo sitting at the kitchen table drinking tea. Madeline shot Leo a quick glance and disappeared into the bathroom to wash her hair.

Leo looked at Katherine with the sad eyes of a parent filled with concern for a foolish child. "Listen to me, Katherine. Come to me when you have need. Yes? I am your friend, I will take care of you as I did on the night we met. Remember? Remember how I told you taking care is not always easy? Come to me when you have need."

"That's very kind, Leo," she murmured, aware of an unfamiliar urgency between them. But she didn't understand why he was offering help, and she didn't understand why he offered it now.

Later as she lay in her narrow bed listening to the leaves rustle in the courtyard, Madeline's warnings ricocheted uneasily through her thoughts, but she shoved them aside. Richard would never leave her, never. Other men deserted girls, but he'd never change; he would always be the same gentle lover. Despite the little worms of mistrust twisting into her brain when she thought of him as a movie star prince or saw Maria Lashman's photo, Katherine knew Richard would never marry Maria Lashman.

So, a few weeks later when Katherine realized she was pregnant, she didn't worry. Briefly, she kept it to herself, treasuring her new knowledge and feeling the silent weight of their love locked within her body for a last solitary instant.

She decided to tell Richard on Friday night.

"Katherine, I won't marry you." Richard's voice was as flat and hard as rock. He spat out the words as if he felt nothing.

A fist drove through her heart. "What?" she said stupidly. "You won't what?"

"I told you a long time ago I'm going to marry Maria Lashman. Nothing can change that." He turned away; he wouldn't look at her.

"Damn Maria!" Katherine screamed. "We're going to have a baby! Don't you care?"

"Of course I care! But I'm marrying Maria."

She felt sick. "But I thought you loved me," she said.

"Stop it!" he snarled. He whipped around and smashed his fist on the back of a chair. Light from a streetlamp slatted across his face through the venetian blinds in the corner window, and for a moment he looked like a prisoner. "Don't make this situation worse than it is. Look, I'll help you. You have to get an abortion."

"Never," she said flatly. "I can't do that. Our child?"

Richard shook his head angrily. "Don't be stupid, Katherine. You're not the first woman to face this problem. Get rid of the baby and go on with your life. But it's your choice. If you don't want an abortion, I'll give you all the money you need. You can go away, have the baby, and give it up for adoption."

"Give it up?" she said blankly. "Just give it away like an unwanted Christmas present? Richard, what's happened to you? You don't give away a human being because it's inconvenient! When did you become so callous, so shallow? Or were you shallow all along? People told me you were ruthless, and I didn't believe them," she said, all emotion drained out of her. "If you won't marry me, I'll have the baby and I'll keep the baby. I wanted you. I got you, and now I'll have to live with the consequences. My God"—she laughed bitterly—"my mother was right! If you get what you want, you have to live with what comes with it."

"You can't keep the damn baby," he insisted.

"Really?" Her voice was ice. "Why not? Other women do. I'll just be another on a long list of fools."

"Damn you for being so stubborn," he said impatiently.

"Stubborn! Richard, you're a bastard. You love *me,* but you're going to marry Maria Lashman because you have some ridiculous ideas about money and power and fame. You're a gold digger, Richard. Or maybe just a whore." Just saying the word made her feel dirty and used.

He looked at her, anger and disbelief flooding his face.

"Well?" she mocked. "Tell me I'm wrong. You're marrying Maria for her money, aren't you?"

He turned away, refusing to look at her.

"You're a whore, Richard. My God, is everybody in this town mad for money? You're in love with money, and your greed has made you weak. You think Maria will bring you the security you had as a child. I know she won't. She'll be a prison, because you don't love her and she's incapable of loving at all. She loves money, she loves possessions, and most of all she loves herself. There's nothing left for you and there never will be. She'll destroy you, Richard. She's rich and vicious, and she likes to break things. Shatter things and throw them away when she's used them up and spit on them so no one else can have them."

It was no use; she was talking to his back. "Richard darling, we love each other . . ." She was pleading, and she stopped because she couldn't bear the ragged sound of her own voice.

He turned around, his handsome face warped with anger. "You know nothing about me," he snarled. "Nothing! I mopped my father's *brains* up off the floor after he shot himself because he didn't have money, do you know that? His *brains!* He shot his head all over the goddamn room, and I got down on my hands and knees and cleaned up the mess before my mother saw it. Then I threw up until there was nothing left inside me. It's not just Hollywood, Katherine, it's everywhere. Money rules the world. I swore, as I was wiping up blood and flabby little slivers of my father's flesh, as the bile choked me, I swore I'd protect myself. From now on, nothing comes between me and what I want. Nothing, do you understand? You're right, I don't love Maria. Not the way I love you. But she knows what I want."

"Does she? How nice for her." Katherine's voice was acid.

"Stop it! I told you when we started, I have a family to protect."

"Richard darling," she begged. "Don't you see, I need your protection, *I'm* your family. I'm going to have your baby."

Richard's face was expressionless as he looked up at her. "So is Maria."

There was nothing left. Nothing. The room was filled with a tremendous, palpable calm, an unbroken silence as cold as a northwestern beach after a winter storm. Gray, seamless, nothing. Katherine leaned her head back on the couch, emotionless, drained, empty. She had nothing left but the child in her stomach.

Every ounce of pride was erased, and Katherine knew she'd been lessened. Madeline had told her, Leo had warned her. She'd heard, but she hadn't listened. Maybe no woman listens when she thinks she's in love, she thought dully. At least I'm not alone.

The palms rustled outside, and for the first time she hated their ugly jagged leaves and their endless scraping against the windows every time the Santa Anas blew.

Rock-a-bye-baby on the tree top . . . My first lesson in the language of Hollywood. I'm not the same anymore. I'm changed, grown up, and there's something hard inside me that will never dissolve, a shard of glass lodged inside me like a bitter arrow. A picture of Saint Sebastian flashed in front of her. She laughed, and the new, bitter sound didn't surprise her.

A piece of me will be standing outside looking in for the rest of my life. "I feel as if I've lost my faith," she whispered. Her words soaked into the big room, and silence covered her. "Richard . . . I didn't know I had faith to lose. . . ." But she was talking to herself.

Chapter 7

Leo Cole was dining alone in the main room at Musso and Frank's on Hollywood Boulevard. He'd managed to slip in a day's work on Metro's latest Gable picture between two down days on *The Gunman,* and the Gable picture wasn't easy. Now it was late and he was dog tired, but the steak in front of him was pumping him back to life. As he reached for one of Musso's huge french fries he saw Richard Sears take a stool at the long bar running along one side of the room, toss back a scotch, and signal the bartender for a refill. Leo left his steak on the table, crossed the big room, and tapped Sears on the shoulder.

Sears spun around so quickly he almost knocked Leo over, and his empty glass clattered awkwardly across the bar. For a tense moment Leo thought Sears was going to punch him. Then Sears's handsome face sagged with relief.

"Leo! Have a drink?" he asked, his voice taut.

"I was going to invite you to join me," Leo said, pointing to his table. There was a lonely note in Sears's voice he'd never heard before, and it sent an alarm running through his head.

"Same again," Sears told the bartender. He took his glass and followed Leo to his table.

Leo sat down and resumed eating his steak. "Have some sourdough, Sears," he said, pointing at the bread basket with his knife. "Best in town. You look like hell."

"Feel like hell, pal," Sears said, ripping off a thick piece of crust and slathering it with butter. "Worse'n hell."

"A problem with *The Gunman?*" Leo probed.

"A problem with a woman."

Leo felt his stomach knotting and unknotting like a slippery rope, but his face betrayed nothing. His intuition was right. "Women can be a serious problem," he said casually.

Sears was thoughtful as he chewed on the sourdough. "You've had quite a bit of experience in that line, haven't you?"

Leo shrugged meaningfully. "I like women; a few have liked me."

Sears downed his scotch. "I've got two pregnant women on my hands," he said flatly. "I'm in big trouble."

Leo sat quite still, his heart choking him. A burst of energy rushed through his body, the exhaustion of the long day disappeared, and he was completely revived. In a moment of brilliant clarity he could see the future. He knew exactly what he would say, exactly how Richard Sears would respond. He saw every line of dialogue written in ten-foot letters of fire.

Behind them the clash of dishes and the snarling of Musso's bad-tempered waiters faded into the background as if an invisible sound man had turned down the volume on the big, noisy room and left only two men staring at each other over a white table.

"One pregnant woman is trouble," Leo said carefully. "Two is a disaster."

"You know the ladies involved?" Sears asked.

"Hollywood is a small town with no secrets. I presume you're going to marry Miss Lashman and not Katherine?"

"It's always been that way, damn it! She knew about Maria from the beginning. I'm not a . . . rat," Sears said defensively, his voice rising. "Or maybe I am," he said, helpless.

The couple at the next table glanced at them uncomfortably, and Leo held up a warning finger. "Get hold of yourself, my friend. You're not on your way to the guillotine."

"Not yet. Maria's a smart cookie. She doesn't care about Katherine."

"Keep your voice down," Leo warned. "Be discreet."

Sears lowered his voice. "But her father's another story. He finds out, I'm dead. Maybe not literally, but certainly professionally."

"A problem," Leo agreed. "But not an insoluble one. Do you love Katherine?" He said it casually, trying to give the impression that Sears's answer was of no concern to him.

"Love?" Sears looked helpless, as if Leo were speaking a foreign language. "Love her? Sure. Yes, but—"

"No 'yes but,' my friend. Either you love or you don't."

"Don't patronize me, Leo," Sears snapped. "I'm in up to my goddamn neck as it is."

"No offense intended," Leo said gently. "But love is straightforward."

"For you, not for me," Sears said, irritated. "I marry Maria, I'm on the right track. I don't, I'm a has-been who never was. Leo, I have responsibilities; people depend on me. I can't just do what I want."

Leo raised an unbelieving eyebrow. "Richard, you are a nice fellow and not a bad poker player, but spare me your attempts at collegiate altruism. Maria is rich and beautiful; her father is powerful. Katherine is lovely, but"—Leo raised his hands eloquently—"as we say in Hungary, money lies down with money. That's the way of the world. You've offered Katherine the usual choices?" he asked, steering the conversation back on course.

"Of course," Sears said impatiently. "And she refused."

"Didn't you know she would?" Leo asked curiously.

"Who the hell knows what I thought?" Sears snapped angrily. "I didn't think. Maybe I thought with the wrong goddamn part of my anatomy."

"But now you are thinking Katherine will have the baby and sooner or later Maria will find out."

"I told you, I can handle Maria. It's her damn father I'm worried about. And if it gets into the columns . . ."

"Your patron, Louella, is growing more powerful every day. You would be ruined," Leo agreed thoughtfully.

"I'll be the Fatty Arbuckle of my time," Sears said with grim humor, draining the last drops of scotch. "And once I was destroyed, then Maria would leave me. She's tough, she can live with anything I dish out and sling it right back at me. Matter of fact, I guess that's what I like about her—she's as tough as I am. But she won't live with failure. I'm in the soup, pal."

Leo ordered brandy, waiting until the waiter set the glasses down before he spoke. "Suppose Katherine got married?" he said bluntly, turning the snifter in his long, thin fingers. As the big wheel began to spin beneath his feet he knew this was the moment to stack every chip on one number. To win all you must risk all . . .

Sears looked at him in surprise as the full impact of Leo's question struck home. "Married? To you?"

"Yes. To me." When you play in luck you can't lose; when luck is on your side and in your pocket, every time the ball skids around the red and black wheel the only number that can come up is your number, and Leo Cole knew the wheel would spin faster and faster until the tiny ball clicked into place on his number. "I will ask her to marry me and she will accept."

"You're insane," Sears snorted.

Leo shrugged. "Perhaps. But very serious."

Sears stared at him across the table, a deep gleam of self-interest shining in his eyes. "Just for the sake of argument, what makes you think she'll marry you?"

"It's a sensible plan, and basically Katherine is a sensible woman despite the fact that she has acted foolishly with you." An emotion he couldn't control passed over Leo Cole's transparent face.

Sears saw it and tilted his chair back on two legs, his self-interest replaced by compassion as he stared at Leo for a wordless moment. "You're in love with her!" he said, his voice low. "Christ, I didn't know! I'm sorry, Leo. Believe me, I wouldn't have brought it up if I'd known. I may be a bastard, but I wouldn't . . . Does she know?"

Leo nodded and sipped his brandy. "I've said nothing, but I imagine she half knows."

Sears knocked back his scotch and looked around the crowded room. "What a screwed-up little world it is, my friend. All right," he agreed suddenly. "You marry Katherine, and I'll give you twenty-five thousand when I marry Maria. I won't have it till then," he added with a grim laugh.

Leo considered the offer, rolling the brandy around in his snifter. "The baby will have my name, and you will swear not to see Katherine again. Swear on your honor?"

"My honor? You're not serious. After this conversation you think I have any honor left?" Sears mocked himself bitterly.

"Oh, yes, in abundance. The past doesn't concern me, Richard, as long as what happened between you and Katherine is finished once she is my wife. I will never mention your name to her in anger, the baby will be mine, and Katherine will be mine. Do you agree?"

Sears looked at Leo admiringly. "God damn, you're a cool son of a bitch! Too bad you're a foreigner, you'd make a helluva President."

"You agree?"

"If she'll have you, of course I agree. But, Leo, why didn't you balk about the money?"

"Balk?"

"Protest. Tell me you're a gentleman and a gentleman doesn't take money for marrying a woman he loves."

Leo's dark eyes were cold and hard. "I thought you knew me better, Richard. I can't afford the manners of the rich, so I leave them to the rich. Why shouldn't I take your money?

Or rather, Edgar Lashman's money. I need it. Money is green paper; it has no morals and no feelings. You're a gentleman, not me, and you're ready to discard Katherine without a backward glance."

"That's not true," Sears said sharply.

"No?" Leo said, his voice soft and insistent. "Then tell me what *is* true."

"I love Katherine, but I need Maria. If I marry Maria, I get what I want. Guy like you should understand that, Leo, getting what you want. You see, it's very simple. I'm not giving Katherine away; I'm giving her up. Big damn difference, pal."

"Perhaps so. Perhaps an uneducated foreigner like me can't see the—what is the word?—the nuances?"

Sears grinned and leaned back in his chair. "Don't grope for words, and don't hand me that pitiful-immigrant routine. Maybe you didn't go to Harvard, but three months ago you were a guy with one suit, and today you're ridin' the escalator to the sky. Damn," he said ruefully. "Leo, I don't know what the hell you are. You're the strangest duck I've ever met. You're an actor and a gambler and a hard customer, and maybe you're a lying bastard and you're gonna take money for marrying a woman you love, but you've got ethics all the same. You play the Hungarian, you play the gambler, you play . . ." Sears stopped, and a shrewd, knowing look filled his cobalt eyes. "Christ, you're always acting, aren't you? You're on all the time. Maybe that's why you're a natural on screen. Me, I work like a damn dog to be natural, to make it look smooth and easy. But you just walk out there and—"

"Find my key light and say my lines," Leo said simply. "Yes, my life has an unreal quality, even to me." He paused and extracted a cigarette from Sears's gold case lying between them on the table. "Only a few years ago I was sleeping on a pile of rags in a wet cellar."

"Only a few years ago I was playing polo."

"And while I was stitching lapels in Brooklyn . . ."

"I was a lifeguard in Santa Monica."

"And here we are together, two gentlemen dining at the same table. Life twists you and turns you until she has you in her grip. We both love the same woman." Leo paused as he blew a series of smoke rings and watched them drift toward the ceiling. "We're both actors, yes?"

"We're both scoundrels, and you know it." Sears shoved his chair back from the table. "I'll have my lawyer draw up the papers, and I'll transfer the twenty-five thou within a week after I marry Maria. My word on it."

"As a gentleman?" Leo said archly.

"Hell, no." Sears laughed. "As an actor. At least that way you know what to expect. I'm going over to Clara's. Care to join me?"

Leo shook his head. "No, thank you. No cards tonight. I have other business."

The light knock on the door woke her up, and Katherine stirred hopefully, momentarily thinking it was Richard, knowing it was not. "Go away," she whispered. "Go away and let me sleep." He's back, a voice called in her ear. He's not marrying Maria, she isn't pregnant, he loves me after all. Thoughts washed back and forth in her mind, the detritus of a low tide.

Get up, get up, the voice said. You can't lie here in the dark.

It was Leo.

"May I come in?"

Her brief hope sputtered out, and she turned away, ashamed to let him see her face. "Leo, I'm so tired . . ." She stood slumped at the thick oak door, hands trembling on the wood.

Leo's eyes searched her face and the darkened apartment beyond. Gently he nudged the door open. "Please? Only a few minutes, Katherine. Let me make you a cup of tea."

"Tea, yes. I suppose." It didn't matter. Nothing mattered.

They went into the kitchen, and Leo turned on the lights. Katherine sat at the enamel table, watching him put the kettle on the stove, warming the cobalt blue Hall teapot with hot water. His thin fingers knew every object in the kitchen. When the tea was brewed, he slid her cup in front of her and stroked her hair like a patient father. "Drink," he told her.

She obeyed, grateful for some order in her new, empty life.

"Katherine," he said as he sat down opposite her. "I know you are pregnant."

Shame and exhaustion combined to produce . . . nothing. She was still empty, completely barren despite the child in her belly. "How do you know?" she asked, barely able to force out the words. "Even Madeline doesn't know."

Leo sidestepped the question. "She knows. And I know, because I have eyes to see with. I know because I know you." Was his answer too enigmatic? Would she question him further?

She did not. "What else do you know, Leo?"

"He will not marry you," Leo said calmly.

"Nope." She laughed, her voice bitter. "Nope. He won't. I thought he would, you see." She raised her eyes to him, empty, washed-out eyes reflecting only loss. "I read too many romantic books when I was a girl, and I thought love conquered all. I thought when I told him I was pregnant he would fall on his knees in front of me and beg my forgiveness. Kiss my . . . my stomach," she said, touching herself gently.

"But he did not do this," Leo said, his voice still patient.

"No, he did not, so my pathetic dream of love has evaporated into a special-effects fog. He offered me an abortion, which I refused. He offered to send me away and have the baby adopted. I refused." She sighed, running a clawed hand through her damp hair. "Then he told me Maria was pregnant and left." Katherine laughed sardonically, and the harsh new sound surprised her. It didn't sound like her voice; it sounded like the voice of a girl who worked at the house with the blue door. "Leo, I have not only made a goddamn fool of myself, I have also ruined my life."

"Katherine, will you marry me?"

She was surprised and touched by his unexpected offer. "Don't pity me, Leo. I'll survive. I don't know how, but I'll survive."

"I don't pity you; I love you. Haven't you known it all along? True, you've made a foolish mistake, but you're not the first woman to love a man who . . ." He paused delicately. "How to say it? A man who did not live up to her expectations. So I do not pity you. I love you. Will you marry me?"

Katherine drank her tea, warming her cold fingers on the porcelain. "But, Leo, I don't love you. How can I marry you?"

"Marry me because I love you. The baby will be mine, and it will have my name—Cole, the name you gave me. I ask one thing of you—one thing only. Promise me you'll never see Richard Sears again. Never see him alone," he said, his tone easy and gentle. "It does not concern me that you have loved him or that you will have his child. Once we are married, he will be in the past, and the child will be mine." The smile on Leo's hawk's face was knowing. "Some men are foolish about women. They don't want a woman who has loved before. I am different."

"You are *very* different," she agreed. She felt tears knotting her throat at his kindness, his sweetness. Why couldn't I have loved *him?* Why Richard? "But, Leo, dearest Leo, you haven't answered my question. How can I marry you when I don't love you? I'm so fond of you, I *do* love you, but not the way . . ." she foundered, drifting toward jagged rocks. "Not the way you love me," she finished lamely.

"There are a hundred kinds of love," he said simply. "A thousand. You will understand when you are older. I believe you will come to love me. For me, for now, it is enough that I love you. Katherine dear, you cannot have a child without a father in Hollywood. You couldn't work as an actress, and once the news got out, the columnists would tear you apart. Eventually people would discover that Richard was the child's father, and the publicity would ruin him as well."

"Good," she said emphatically. "Let him suffer. Maybe Maria will kill him."

Leo shook his head impatiently. "Unlikely. She is too clever to do that, especially if she is having a child herself. The embarrassment of publicity will only hurt you and the child. So be wise. Accept my offer. I will be your husband, the child will be mine, and you will be safe," he said.

Katherine looked at him, profoundly curious to know what motivated her improbable savior. "Why do you want to do this, Leo, after I've told you I don't love you? God, I don't want to hurt you, but I care for you too much to lie."

He got up, took their teacups to the sink, carefully rinsed them out, and set them on the drainboard. "I told you I love you, and it is true. But you are more to me than love alone. Do you remember when we first met I told you I had Gypsy blood?"

"Yes."

"It may be true. It may not be true. I don't really know. But it is an idea I carry around with me like a talisman." Leo looked over her head, out the kitchen window at the palm fronds scraping on the glass with a dry, sore sound. "You are my luck, Katherine. I felt it the moment my hand touched yours that first night at the Magyar Café. Do you remember?"

"Of course. You had no money, but you won at cards."

"I'd been losing for months. I won that night because you are more than love to me; you are my luck, my fortune." Leo reached out and wound a burnished strand of her hair around his forefinger. "You created Leo Cole, the man I am now, and if you marry me, you will create the man I will be. You have created Leo Cole, and he will take care of you. I said that too. Do you remember?"

"Yes," she told him slowly. "Yes, I remember." She had the strangest feeling she was stepping onto a path that had no turning.

"I am taking care of you now. Will you accept my proposal?"

She got up from the table, stood next to him at the sink,

watching the dry, windy California sky. The palm fronds still scraped their dry fronds in the Santa Ana winds, the crickets still hummed in the grass, but her life had cut a new path.

Once again Katherine felt a void beneath her heart, and for a millisecond she panicked. What does it mean to be a man's luck? Richard, Richard . . . A final memory crashed over her like a wave, and then it was gone. He was gone. She had nothing, and she needed nothing. Nothing but the child curled inside her like a peaceful snail in its shell. Without looking at Leo she took his hand and put it on her stomach. "I accept," she said softly. "The child will be yours, and I will never see Richard Sears alone again. Never. And, Leo? I promise——"

Leo laid his long, cool finger on her lips. "No need to promise more, Katherine," he whispered. "Not tonight."

Brilliant sunshine flooded across Highway 101, turning it into a long ribbon of butter stretching into the brown California foothills. They were driving up the coast to Santa Barbara. Katherine Cole watched as the cloudless sky above and the green sea below scrolled over the windshield as if it were projected on a movie screen, but she was unmoved by the beauty in the frame. She still felt nothing. No pain, no happiness, no anger, no emotion at all, not even relief. Bitterly she'd discovered she had an immense talent to deceive. Was she an actress at last? If so, this was her best role.

She was about to create a new woman out of the cold ashes abandoned by Richard Sears. She would be Katherine Cole for the rest of her life, and the woman she used to be, the old Katherine Ransome, would live silently inside her skin. But as the acid residue washed in and out, she knew the part she was playing wasn't on film; it was permanent.

People had spoken to her, congratulated her on her marriage, and she had stretched the appropriate mask over her face, smiled, and mouthed the correct words. No one seemed to notice she was deadened, though Madeline had been unusually somber during the past week, and her pretty face was worried. Ironically, Katherine felt worse when she knew her ruse was successful. Marriage to Leo stretched out in front of her like a long, twisting road. . . .

But she had to marry him, for the child. It was the child who counted. It was the child spurring her on, pushing her into her new life as Katherine Cole. Richard's child. She was empty but for the child. Flat. Filled with lead. Her new gold wedding band felt unfamiliar on her hand, and she twisted it anxiously, covering one hand with the other so Leo wouldn't see what she was doing. She kept the little half smile pasted on her mouth, carefully keeping her lips upturned. She would manage; she was determined to play her part in order to protect the child. Leo would never know how empty she was. She'd spare him that. In her own way, she would protect him, too.

He'd said little in the last week, and Katherine was grateful he'd taken all the decisions out of her hands. He arranged the brief ceremony at the home of a justice of the peace in Santa Monica, bought her the plain gold wedding band, arranged for a week's honeymoon on the beach at the Santa Barbara Biltmore before he began work on a new movie, a featured part in *Mask of a Gangster.*

Katherine behaved correctly. She smiled, nodded, agreed —and felt nothing. This morning, as she put on the new blue suit she'd bought at Bullock's Wilshire for the wedding ceremony, she decided she'd sleep with Leo when he wanted it. He'd indicated he would make no demands on her, but that couldn't last. He was a man, after all, and Katherine knew—now—what men were like. Besides, it was little enough, and what would it matter to a woman who was dead inside?

Katherine was determined to carry off her farcical marriage with good grace if she could muster it, and with scrupulous politeness if she couldn't. Stoicism was the only answer, she thought as she watched the foaming whitecaps dappling the water. The whitecaps reminded her of the icing on her wedding cake, the wedding cake she'd cut only a few hours ago. . . . She would pretend—now that she knew that her life ahead was only an acting job—and Leo would never know. She'd be a good wife. Absently she wondered if Leo would be a good lover. Would he be gentle or would the ravenous nature she sensed inside him break out and . . . But it didn't matter, she thought as she looked over at him. His sharp, thoughtful profile reassured her. He would be kind to her because he loved her. At least she had that. But what did Leo have?

He gave her a sidelong glance, frowned, and turned his eyes back to the road as he maneuvered the secondhand Lincoln Phaeton he'd just bought over the rutted two-lane highway toward the Biltmore. He'd learned to drive in an afternoon; he was a quick study. "The hotel is quite close now," he said.

She was grateful; he was giving her time to compose herself.

"Arranged marriages are very common in the rest of the world," he said.

"But not in Hollywood." She kept her tone neutral, as if they were strangers discussing strangers.

"People can grow into love. Become friends, learn to trust, then love. Love is the . . ." He groped briefly for words. "Love can be the end result of marriage even if it is not the beginning."

"We're friends now, Leo." She felt a rush of tenderness for him, then realized it was the first emotion she'd felt in weeks. "Thank God," she whispered, glad to feel anything, anything at all. "Maybe I'm not dead." Hot tears came to her eyes, and then, without warning, the dam broke. Katherine heard someone sobbing far away, the pitiful howl of a damaged child, and as a sharp noise like ripping cloth tore out of her body she realized *she* was the child, *she* was making those dreadful sounds.

Quickly Leo pulled the heavy Lincoln over to the side of the highway and stopped. He leaned back against the door, fished his handkerchief out of his pocket, and gave it to her.

"Damn, damn, damn," she mumbled helplessly as tears

and pain overwhelmed her. "I'm sorry, Leo." She clutched the handkerchief and blotted her face. A smear of jaunty red lipstick stained the white cloth, and the bright, color made her unhappiness worse. She couldn't stop crying. Richard, Richard, Richard . . .

Leo rolled a cigar back and forth in his fingers, watching, saying nothing.

She cried for ten or fifteen minutes until there were no more tears left, until she was as blank as slate, as empty as death. Finally she leaned her head back on the leather seat as the tears, the sobbing, and the pain gave way to a frightful peace, the peace that comes after a particularly destructive hurricane has scoured the beach clean and there's nothing left to be destroyed because everything has been smashed. Shards of her life lay scattered on the shore like broken shells.

But at least I feel *something,* she thought fiercely. At least I'm not dead. A new spirit infused her as pain gave way to anger. I'm damned if I'll let this kill me. I won't be dead, I *won't.* I want to live, I have to live, and I won't give up. Baby or no baby, Richard or no Richard, I won't roll over and die. Leo's a good man and he loves me. Maybe I can't have what I want, but I can have something. Even if I can't love, I can *be* loved. But will that be enough? Stop it! she told herself savagely. You've made your choice, now live with it.

Abruptly Katherine struggled out of the car and walked a little way up the road to a small lookout point on the other side. The car door slammed, and she looked back to see Leo leaning against the side of the Lincoln, lighting a cigar. He touched his forefinger to his forehead in a characteristic salute, guarding her with his presence. He looked up at the sky where brown hawks hunted across sunburned hills.

Katherine stood on the cliff looking into the seamless blue distance. The cliffs were gold and green, the perennial colors of the California landscape. The sky was a brilliant blue flecked with clouds. What a day to be married. What a day to be unhappily married. . . . I wonder if he thinks I'll jump. I won't. I wonder what he sees in me. I wonder why he loves me. The sea sparkled, the waves rolled in like unwary soldiers, and she laughed in spite of her blotchy face and red eyes. Did I think the world would stop for me? Maybe Leo sees a strength in me I can't see in myself.

Leo walked over to her side. "Feel better?" he inquired.

"I'm surprised, but I do. Much."

"Crying is good for you. Cleans out the heart," he said sympathetically, tapping his chest.

"Tears aren't a very good way to start a marriage," she said, apologetic. "Leo, I'm sorry you've married such a dope. But I'm so grateful . . ."

He clamped his cigar between his teeth. Smoke whipped away in the breeze, and behind his predatory eyes she saw the ravenous hawk inside him struggling to break out. "Don't ever be grateful to me. I don't want gratitude. I want you."

She pulled back from her husband, and the wet ocean breeze whipped her blue skirt around her knees as clouds billowed across the horizon. She felt as if she were in a Vorkapich montage; skies moved and changed to indicate the passage of time, all light and shadow and disturbed perspective. "Leo, give me time," she said frankly.

He reached out, took her hand, and kissed it, then gently rubbed her new wedding ring with the tip of his finger. "For luck," he said. "Katherine, you and I have all the time we need. But we can never have too much luck."

She looked at him, and happiness flooded his face as he saw her flickering smile. She didn't love him; yet suddenly she felt an emotion greater than love springing up in her as she realized that she trusted him unconditionally. He was as steady as a rock, as unbending as iron, and she could rely on him absolutely. But was trust greater than love? Or was trust a different kind of love, an endless current running back and forth between two people like electricity?

"Come. It's been a long drive, and we're tired. Put on your dark glasses so people don't think I beat my new wife." Leo grinned. "We'll be at the Biltmore in a few minutes."

The bellboy brought their luggage to the room, then

disappeared after Leo pressed some folded bills into his hand. The room was beautiful, simply furnished in white and gold, with a view of the lush gardens surrounding the sprawling hotel and the groomed golf course lying beyond. There was a large wicker basket of fruit on the side table and a pair of champagne bottles cooled in sweating silver buckets. Glasses sat waiting, turned upside down on a square pink napkin. Dazzling late afternoon sunlight streamed in through tall windows.

Leo thrust his hands in his pockets uncomfortably as he looked around the room. "I'm going to the bar for a drink," he said.

"You can have a drink here," Katherine said, pointing to the champagne.

"I'll open it for you." Leo popped the cork on one of the bottles and poured a glass for each of them. "Happiness and long life," he said as he raised his glass and drained it. He poured himself a second glass and drank it off, then kissed her on the cheek. "But I'll still have a drink at the bar."

He disappeared before Katherine could answer, and once again she was grateful for his consideration. She needed time to sort herself out, wash the tears away from under her sunglasses, fix her face. She sank down in an armchair and slowly drank her champagne. To my new life, my new self, she toasted as she poured another glass. She was tired, and though she still felt the effects of her breakdown in the car she was calm now, almost clinical as she unpacked Leo's things. My first duty as a wife, she thought as she slid a neatly folded pile of shirts into a drawer, laying socks and boxer shorts next to them.

She drank another glass of champagne and opened her own suitcase. The blue silk nightgown from Bullock's Wilshire lay on top. She picked it up and felt the softness of the silk drift over her skin like feathers, the champagne warming everything as if with a soft-focus lens. The same day she bought her wedding suit she'd seen the gown lying in a glass display case in the lingerie department, and she had bought it on an impulse, a whim. She'd never bought anything like it before, nothing so beautiful, extravagant, and overtly sexual.

She ran her fingers over the silk and the thin, almost transparent lace along the yoke. She knew what the nightgown meant. It meant she would sleep with Leo. It meant she *wanted* to sleep with Leo and superimpose his flesh on Richard's, and she realized the thought excited her. Leo's new touch would cancel out the old.

She bathed and put on the nightgown and its matching peignoir. As she smoothed it over her imperceptibly fuller figure she looked at herself in the full-length mirror. Her belly was still flat, but her breasts were lush in a new way, and the gown's sweetheart neckline accentuated her body. Exhaustion and champagne overcame her, and she opened the windows to let in the sea breeze.

She stretched out on the bed, the thin silk of the gown molding itself to her body. She closed her eyes and let the cool wind sweep over her, chilly with the salty moisture of the ocean, but still clean and good. Despite her bath, her face was hot from crying, but the evening air calmed her prickly nerves.

She fell into a half sleep, champagne ironing out the rough edges of her nerves. Outside, the patio garden rang with the faint and happy laughter of the rich at play. Running water splashed in a nearby fountain, the tinkling of ice in tall glasses rang like wind chimes, and behind it all, the waves beat down on the sand in an insistent rumba.

Katherine dreamed of that day on the set when Richard carried her off on his horse and the scrub oak and golden brush of the San Fernando Valley whipped by in scattered flashes of color. She felt her body pressed to his, her arms tight around him, the smell of his flesh. Once again she slipped to the ground, felt him kiss her, saw herself in his big white bed in the Hollywood Hills. . . .

The door opened and Leo stood silhouetted in the triangle of light from the hall.

Without a word he closed the door, opened the second bottle cooling in the dripping silver ice bucket, and poured some champagne. He sipped thoughtfully, and Katherine knew he was watching her, waiting for her to give him a sign.

She held out her arms to him. He came over to the bed and sank down beside her. Slowly he lowered the thin straps of her blue nightgown and ran his hands possessively over her breasts and down her body.

For a brief moment she pretended he was Richard, Richard's lips were on her, Richard's hands were caressing her, but when she opened her eyes it was not Richard at all. It was Leo, dear Leo, smelling pleasantly of scotch and cigars. He dipped his finger in the glass of champagne and ran the liquid down her throat and between her breasts.

He began to kiss his way down the line of warm liquid beading her body, and despite her dreams of Richard she was thrilled by his touch. She felt a new erotic tremor as his stranger's hands played over her, rousing her to excitement as light and sound from the garden outside coalesced and dappled her skin like drops of rain. She closed her eyes again and saw Richard, Leo, Richard, Leo, and Richard melded into one man.

Leo kissed her throat, licking the champagne from her shoulders, the hollow of her neck, and though his mouth touched her only briefly, his hands were strong and confident.

She felt dreamy, caught on the cusp of an experience she couldn't fathom. A sudden picture of Richard astride Maria Lashman flashed across her mind—Maria, with her ruby nails curled passionately on his back, her head thrown back, her mouth open—and Katherine had an urge to bolt. Then Richard was gone and only Leo remained.

Katherine opened her eyes as Leo's dark head moved down her body in the half-light. I will not stop him, she thought. I told him yes, I told him yes. And slowly, as Leo continued his languorous journey down her body, she knew it was too late to stop. Besides, she thought dreamily as passion flooded over her, I don't want him to stop. . . .

Chapter
8

A week later Leo turned the dusty Lincoln up into the Hollywood Hills and followed the crooked road to a street dead-ending in hillside and chaparral. Together Katherine and Leo left the car in the sandy driveway and walked up a brick pathway paved in a herringbone pattern, through an ivy-covered white lath trellis toward a two-story Spanish-style house lying at the end of the walkway. Thick white stucco walls, deep arched windows shading the rooms within from the sun, and a red tiled roof framed by huge eucalyptus trees gave the house a peaceful, classic southern California feeling.

There were no signs of life—no red wagons scattered on the long expanse of green lawn winding around toward the backyard, no clothes flapping on the line, no shouts of laughter floating from the kitchen. A young orange cat skittered past Katherine's feet, batting a dry eucalyptus leaf with a furious paw. It flopped down directly in their way, and Katherine stooped to stroke its warm fur. "Who lives here? Do you?" she asked the cat as it curled its paws playfully around her outstretched finger in the warm afternoon sunlight.

"We live here," Leo answered. "I own this house, so I hope you like it."

"You bought it?" she said incredulously. "Just like that? Leo, where did you get the money to buy a house?" When Leo had told her they had a stop to make, she'd assumed they were visiting friends or perhaps collecting a gambling debt.

"I didn't say I bought it; I said I owned it." He smiled. "I was cutting cards with Nagy, and the fool bet me double or nothing. Queen high and Nagy begins to whine he has no money. I explain to him that when you lose, you must pay, and he says he has this house. So now the house is mine. Ours." He stopped abruptly by the hand-hewn oak planks of the front door, hoping his lie had gone undetected. He'd used Richard Sears's money to buy the house and had put it in Katherine's name. A good investment, a house in the Hollywood Hills . . . "Over the threshold, yes?"

Katherine laughed as he hoisted her into his arms, puffing and blowing, pretending she was too heavy for him to carry. There was an endearing sweetness hiding behind Leo's hawklike face; it wasn't a quality she usually thought of in connection with men. Men had strength or intelligence or character or power, but rarely sweetness.

Leo pushed open the door, and as he carried her into the house and into the living room, she saw the unfamiliar wedding band shining on her finger. He put her down, and Katherine rubbed the ring for luck as she looked at her new home for the first time. "We can be happy here," she whispered to herself. *"I* can be happy here."

And as the weeks stretched into months, Katherine gradually realized she *was* happy. She busied herself with furnishing the house, and she found the new experience both difficult and interesting. Where to get furniture? Where to put it? How to arrange the rooms? Fabric, curtains, dishes, silver—all of the jigsaw bits and pieces of daily life were new to her, and she immersed herself in the trivial details of her first home.

Leo worked every day at the studio, first on *Mask of a Gangster,* then, without a break, on a Warner's melodrama with Bette Davis. But at home he watched and waited. He gambled less often but with greater intensity. Money flowed through his hands and piled up in his pockets, and when he came home at the end of a long evening he'd toss a wad of bills on the kitchen counter for the housekeeping. A few hundred, a few thousand, the amount meant nothing. Money meant nothing unless you didn't have it.

Leo couldn't lose, because when he played, the thought of Katherine echoed in his mind like a church bell. She was his luck, and when the cards flew across the table it was as if he sat before an exploding star. Money, cash, coins, and bills of all nations exploded outward with it, fiery comets of money hurtling through the universe. Katherine was his luck and his fortune.

Often he took her out for dinner and dancing. Often he led her into the shops to buy expensive dresses, silk scarves, and underwear, foolish toys for the unborn baby lying peacefully between them. She was still small and had barely begun to show, and her soft, rounded belly fired his desire for her to new peaks. "Here," he said, piling his winnings in her hands as if the money were water. "Be beautiful. Dress like a star—not a movie star but a star in the heavens."

Leo watched her grow happier, more confident, and just as before, he waited. Like all people who had experienced fear, he was an expert at waiting. He knew how to tremble, still and soundless, in a burrow until the fox had passed. He'd waited all his life—waited to escape Hungary, waited to escape New York and begin his new, reinvented life in California—and he was willing to wait for his wife to love him. Katherine was his wife and his luck, and although he was inexorably linked to her he knew part of her was still trapped in her own past, trapped in the memory of the few brief months of her affair with Richard Sears.

One Sunday afternoon he saw her open the *Herald*

Examiner and quickly put it aside. Later, when she was in the bath, he skimmed curiously through the paper, hoping to find out what had startled her. A photograph of Maria Lashman stared out of the society page, flanked by a handsome Richard Sears in riding clothes. The caption read, "The beautiful Mrs. Richard Sears, the brightest star in Hollywood."

Leo threw the paper aside, but that evening when she responded to him with unbridled passion, he knew she'd been fired by the photograph of Richard and Maria in the paper. If only Richard and Katherine had had more time together! Time to grow tired of each other, time to see all the warts and wrinkles and inevitable bursts of temperament that either spelled disaster for a love affair or turned it into a marriage. But Richard and Katherine hadn't had time; they'd parted while they were still perfectly in love, and the memory of that passion formed a bond between them as strong as the unborn child they had created.

A few warm evenings later, with ten thousand dollars stuffed in his pocket after a high-stakes poker game, Leo wandered into a jeweler's shop in Beverly Hills and walked away with a diamond necklace a princess would have envied. The faceted stones reminded him of glittering snowbanks reflected in an icy pond, and, slightly drunk, he wondered if the gold links of the necklace coiling around her neck would link her to him.

At home, he draped it over Katherine's toothbrush and silently slipped into bed. Her breathing remained steady. She was used to his late hours now and rarely stirred when he tucked the long smooth warmth of her body to his. Her beauty roused him. She looked like a princess in a fairy tale. "Rapunzel, Rapunzel," he whispered, "let down your hair. . . ."

She turned to him. Her eyes fluttered open, and a sleepy smile curved her lips. "Leo dear, what time is it?"

"Do you love me now?" he said urgently, one hand raking her red hair. "Katherine, beautiful Katherine, tell me you love me. I've waited so long. . . ."

For the first time she felt desperate urgency in the hard thrust of his body as it pressed against her. "You're the most wonderful man in the world, Leo."

"But do you love me? Can you? I can wait, but I must know that someday . . ."

For a long moment she held him, and as his body vibrated like an earthquake, she realized she did love him. Not the way she had once loved Richard, but was that important? Richard was unattainable, a fantasy lover receding into a dim past, but Leo was her husband, the man she would live with forever. Did one love have to cancel out the other? "I *do* love you, Leo," she told him. "I love you, and I always will."

He collapsed on her body like a starving man, his dark head buried in her neck, his mouth pressed against her skin.

"My God, Katherine, never leave me, never leave me, never, never," he whispered fiercely. Outside, the dry wind rattled the dry leaves as it always did. . . .

Madeline took a silver-backed mirror out of her handbag and carefully inspected her lips, straightening an imaginary smudge with her nail. She blew herself a kiss, put the mirror back in her bag, and arched a curious eyebrow. "What's wrong, sugar?" she asked anxiously.

Katherine didn't answer as she slowly looked Madeline up and down. "You look different. What have you done to yourself?"

Madeline kicked up a tiny heel and held the pose, the seams on her silk stockings perfectly straight. "Your Leo told me how to change my look, take the act uptown. This is the all-new Madeline Gerard. You like?"

Katherine stared at her appraisingly. Madeline *did* look more elegant. She was wearing a beige suit and a silk blouse that exactly matched the new color of her hair. She'd tamed the peroxide and brass and given her hair a deeper golden glow. Her eyebrows, once elaborately thin and arched, were a little fuller now and her lips a little less luscious. The old good-time gal with the voluptuous figure was gone, and in her size fives stood a new vision of controlled sexuality.

"Yes, I do," Katherine said as she studied her friend. "You're less an ingenue, more the leading lady."

"Star, dear. Say 'star.' The word has such a lovely ring to it, don'tcha think?" Madeline put a hand over her heart and batted her eyelashes.

"Leo put you up to this?"

Madeline nodded happily. "And Madame Lermontov. I mean, hell, Norma Shearer I ain't, but maybe I can give Joan Crawford a run for her money. That bitch," she added. "I don't understand acting too well—all this turning into somebody else like Leo does—but maybe I can learn to pretend better. It's awful strange, though. We were doing an exercise in Madame's class the other day where you had to imagine what you wanted most in the world and then act out what you'd feel if you knew—really *knew*—you'd never get it."

Katherine looked out the window and through the eucalyptus trees shading the front yard. "Yes?"

"Leo, he sits there for a minute, all alone in front of the class in a wooden chair. He closes his eyes and . . . Christ—" Madeline broke off. "Maybe I shouldn't tell you this."

"Leo and I don't have secrets, Mad. Go on," Katherine said impatiently.

"He closes his eyes, his face goes as gray as a dirty rag, and then he gives out with this terrible yell. It was the most frightening thing I ever heard, honest. I got honest-to-God goose bumps, and so did everybody else. Didn't he tell you?"

Katherine shook her head as she realized Leo never discussed his work with her. "We don't talk about things like that. It's not a secret," she explained lamely. "It just isn't something we talk about."

"Really? Huh." Madeline looked puzzled. "What *do* you talk about? I always wondered what married people found to talk about, since they see each other so much. Maybe nothing's new if you're married."

Katherine realized she was uncomfortable with the idea of Leo baring his soul in front of a roomful of strangers. That was a side of his character she'd never seen. Maybe his actor friends weren't the strangers. Maybe *she* was the stranger, standing on the outside of his life, looking in. The baby felt heavy in her stomach, and she touched it involuntarily. Perhaps the baby will be an entrance, a doorway into a life I thought was closed to me, she thought. After I have the baby I'll sink into a daily routine, and my life will be ordered forever. I'll wear an apron, roll out piecrust. The baby will sit in a wooden high chair wearing a bib with ducks on it.

"Katherine? Hey, you there?"

"Just dreaming," Katherine said slowly.

The pregnancy was easy. Day by day Katherine grew quieter, heavier, retreating into a secretive, comfortable world she shared only with the child within her body.

Leo was working on *Fight Game,* a Fox flick with a boxing background. He was playing Collie Malone, the hero's crooked manager, and he was enjoying the part.

"Playing the heavy is so easy," he told Katherine one evening as he sat at the kitchen table and watched her straightening up after dinner. His fingers tapped restlessly on his cigar case. "So easy to remember past cruelty and become it, just for a minute, then let it go at last and forever. It's a catharsis," he said proudly. "Nice word, yes? I was over at Metro yesterday, and David Selznick was at the next table. I heard him use it. But it's so. You play the villain, you're washed clean of all the indignities of the past."

"Sometimes I forget that your past and mine aren't the same," she said, twisting the red checked dish towel in her hands. "When we're here like this, alone at night in our house, I feel very close to you, as if we're brother and sister and we've shared everything."

"That's a good sign, my love," he said, looking up from the table with bright dark eyes.

"But don't you think it's strange?" she pressed. "That we should feel so close when we hardly know each other?" She fumbled, not wanting to tear the fragile spiderweb of love hanging between them.

"Not at all. We met a year ago, do you know that? *The Arizona Kid* was a year ago. A lifetime. And besides, it's fate, yes?"

"You and your Gypsy blood!" she teased. "Cross my palm with silver?"

"Not with silver. Gold and diamonds for you, my love," Leo said. He took her hand and kissed the palm, damp with water and fresh with Lux soap flakes.

"Oh, my God," Katherine gasped as a sword of pain thrust through her. She bent over double, clutching her stomach and involuntarily pulling away from Leo as spasm after spasm swept over her.

"What? My God, it's too soon." Fear choked Leo's throat with iron hands. "Darling girl, is it—"

"I don't know," she groaned as she slumped down on a straight-backed kitchen chair. "Oh, God, Leo, call the doctor!"

Katherine lay in Good Samaritan Hospital for three days, her mind a blur of pain, drugs, and weariness. Leo stayed by her bedside constantly and slept upright in a chair.

Madeline, who'd recently become interested in Christian Science, instructed Leo to keep Katherine's healthy image in the center of his thoughts and gave him a copy of *Science and Health*. Leo thanked her soberly but ignored the book.

On the morning of the third day, when the doctor assured them there would be no immediate change, Madeline insisted Leo come home with her for a few hours. "You have to eat; you have to sleep," she told him. Dazed and hungry, Leo agreed.

Madeline piled him into her car and drove to the little apartment on Hayworth Avenue she now had all to herself.

As she went to the kitchen to put the kettle on, Leo wandered uncomfortably around the living room, touching familiar objects—a vase, a pillow. "If she dies . . ." he said, his breath harsh and grating.

"She won't die," Madeline said confidently, startling him. "I'm telling you, sugar, it ain't gonna happen. You have to project positive thoughts."

"From your lips to God's ear," he said, sinking down on the flowered couch he'd used as a bed in those few weeks he'd stayed with Katherine and Madeline.

Madeline sat down next to him. "C'mere, hon," she said as she put her arm around him and pulled him close.

Leo recoiled as he felt the heat of her soft body touch his. "Madeline, for God's sake—"

"Oh, can it, Leo!" she said, exasperated. "You oughta know me better by now. This is just between friends, okay? Nothing personal. I may not be the smartest dame in the world and I'm not a slut, but I do have a heart of gold, and you need a little comforting." Madeline smiled sympathetically and put a hand on her bosom. "I'm asking you to sleep on me, not with me."

Leo groaned and sank onto her, exhausted. As the heat of her body saturated his, he instantly fell into a thick, dreamless sleep that felt as if he were floating peacefully on a calm, warm, and endless sea.

Madeline waited, watching him sleep. The one man I love, and he won't love me, she thought grimly as Leo's breath rose and fell in deep, even strokes. The one man I even *like*. Well, kiddo, that's how it goes. . . .

When he woke up, Madeline slipped on an apron, filled him full of bacon and eggs, coffee, and toast, and pushed him out the door and back to the hospital.

Katherine was very weak when she brought little Rosalind home from the hospital, and Leo promptly hired Mrs. Gebhardt, a short, stout woman with a rough voice, work-hardened hands, and a surprisingly gentle manner despite her crusty exterior. She was recently widowed and had lived most of her life in Santa Monica with her husband, a construction worker hard hit by the Depression. Mrs. Gebhardt was glad to have the work, and she put herself out to do extra for both Katherine and the baby. Almost instantly she became a fixture in the Cole household. She cleaned and cooked and cared for the baby, and as Katherine recovered from the difficult delivery she was reassured by the large, placid sight of Mrs. Gebhardt seated at the kitchen table poring over the childlike color pictures in her oversize Bible.

In a few weeks Katherine was on her feet again, weak and drained, but whole. It came as a surprise that her life was completely changed by the baby, by Rosalind, for that was the name Leo chose. "A girl should have a beautiful name," he said. "And a name from Shakespeare's *As You Like It* is appropriate for an actor's daughter."

Sometimes Katherine would slip into the baby's room and watch her sleep. "The baby." She still thought of Rosalind as "the baby." It was hard to believe this tiny creature lying in her lace and ribboned bassinet was going to be Rosalind, a living human being who would grow and change like a plant.

The little hand outstretched, fingers curling and uncurling in a fitful dream. The infinitesimal eyelids with their fragile blue veins fluttering. Katherine stood and stared at the angle of the leg, drawn up protectively, the smooth sheen of the pink skin, the soft, rounded arm.

As she watched the baby sleep, Katherine knew she would kill to protect this tiny thing she had produced, this unexpected, unwanted treasure that suddenly meant more to her than her own life. Rosalind's little body lying helpless in the bassinet pulled Katherine into a pool of emotion deeper than any she had known before, a bottomless well of feeling fiercer than love and stronger than hate. The child's breath whooshed in and out and as flickers of thought passed over the small face, Katherine knew she would never love anyone or anything as much as she loved this child.

* * *

Over the course of the next year Richard Sears's career was in phenomenal ascent, a shooting star climbing higher and higher into the sky, a star that never fell to earth. Richard signed a seven-year contract with Edgar Lashman, and Lashman handled his son-in-law brilliantly. Sears had one splendid success after another, and as one forceful starring role led inevitably to the next, Lashman began loaning him out at a hefty profit. First to Metro-Goldwyn-Mayer for *Carolina* with Clark Gable and Joan Crawford, where there were hushed rumors that Joan got Richard into her bed on the rebound from her on-again, off-again affair with Gable. But the rumors died as soon as the picture wrapped. Then Lashman sent him to Warner Brothers for *Smokescreen* with Bette Davis, the acknowledged queen of the Warner's lot. This time the rumors were quashed before they had a chance to begin, and the elegant Maria Lashman Sears was always present on the set.

Both pictures were financially successful, and finally, Lashman felt justified in risking big money on his new star. His smart, fast-talking backstage comedy *Heartthrob* with Carole Lombard brought Richard critical plaudits and, he joked to the press, gave him a chance to wear a dinner jacket for the first time on-screen. There were rumors he'd taken the bawdy Lombard to bed, but this time Lashman didn't seem to mind the idle talk as long as it brought publicity. No doubt about it, Edgar Lashman had a red-hot property on his hands.

But despite the rumors of sexual escapades, Richard Sears's marriage to Maria Lashman remained secure. Like other wealthy wives, Maria Lashman Sears took up charity work to pass the hours while her husband single-mindedly pursued his career. She founded the Swans' Home for Girls and pressured other Hollywood doyennes to serve on the board.

As compensation for the efforts of her friends, Maria organized the Swans Ball, which quickly became the most prestigious, star-studded event on the Hollywood calendar. Maria didn't hesitate to use both her father's influence and her husband's connections to promote her pet project, and since no star or studio dared refuse an invitation, the Swans Ball consistently featured a brilliant array of talent. Astaire danced, Garland sang, and famous beauties—the Swans—dressed entirely in white gowns by Adrian or Travis Banton modeled exquisite jewels, which were later auctioned off to benefit the Swans' Home.

Katherine and Leo were happy. By now she was content and felt oddly settled despite his erratic financial status. Leo was a free-lancer, not a contract player like many stars and character actors of the day. His quicksilver nature wasn't suited to life at the beck and call of the Warner brothers or under the crushing paternal thumb of Louis B. Mayer. But although he wasn't a star like Richard Sears, he was a known quantity, a character actor whose face and talents were an asset to any motion picture, and he went from one part to another without a break.

Offscreen he gambled, but he always won more than he lost. He had Katherine, after all; he had his luck and his dreams and his family, and they were the foundation of his life. He had no bank accounts; the hard lessons of the bank failures of the early thirties were burned into his brain, so he kept cash strewn around the house—behind books, in teapots and wineglasses in the kitchen cupboard, in Katherine's coffee can. One day Mrs. Gebhardt was running the Hoover in the spare bedroom and came to Katherine with three thousand dollars in her hand and a mystified expression on her pudgy face. She'd found the cash under the rug.

And he spent money too. He bought jewelry, furs, and beautiful gowns for Katherine, a Russian icon of Saint Nicholas for Mrs. Gebhardt, toys for Rosalind, whom he adored. And people loved him as well. His generous nature and open hand made him many friends, and he was continually lending out money that was never repaid. "It's gambler's insurance," he told his young wife. "Maybe someday I'll be paid back."

At first Katherine tried to curb his excessive spending, his impulsive buying of expensive gifts for anyone he liked, but she quickly gave up. Leo's charm was part of his nature, and gradually she accepted him as he was. She didn't know where his money came from; she didn't know where it went. He simply handed her wads of cash for the housekeeping and told her to charge what she wanted at Bullock's Wilshire. She was content to be taken care of, to tend her child, her house, and her garden, and to be beautifully dressed when they went out to the Coconut Grove or the Trocadero or downtown to the Biltmore Hotel for dinner.

And gradually, subtly, without Katherine's noticing it, her life took on a fairy-tale air. They weren't rich—certainly not by Hollywood standards—but their house was large and comfortable, their life happy and full. She had a new Buick and all the clothes and jewels she could wear or want, and she laughed and dined with the most famous faces and brightest wits in Hollywood's world. Even Gary Cooper flirted with her outrageously one night at the Troc, but when she reported it to Leo he only laughed and told her Coop was a famous ladies' man and couldn't resist a beautiful woman. "If he bothers you again, I'll kill him," Leo said as he laughed and made a deadly mock thrust with an imaginary sword. But Katherine knew he was almost serious, for she'd never forgotten that night near the Magyar Café when he'd broken the thief's kneecap and burned his face. She alone knew how fierce Leo Cole could be.

Chapter
9

It was a surprisingly cold night in early December of 1938, and in a few minutes Atlanta, Georgia, would be destroyed on the back lots of Culver City, California. Producer David O. Selznick was about to film the most crucial scene for his mammoth production of *Gone With the Wind*—the fiery devastation of the city of Atlanta. In a moment he would give the order to ignite the mass of old standing sets filling part of the lot he called his Forty Acres—the back lot of Selznick International Studios. The crew had built false fronts on the old sets that would serve as the facade for the Atlanta Railroad Station so that, on film, the fire would appear to consume the entire city of Atlanta. Actually huge set pieces from *King Kong, The Garden of Allah,* Cecil B. DeMille's *King of Kings,* and many other legendary productions would be set ablaze, and in a matter of minutes an irreplaceable chunk of movie history would be reduced to a thick layer of ash.

They were shooting on a Saturday night because the visionary Selznick needed all seven of the Technicolor cameras available in Hollywood for his production of *Gone With the Wind*. Wisely, he also had thirty-six pieces of fire equipment from both the Culver City Fire Department and the LAFD standing by just in case the wind kicked up and the burning of Atlanta got out of hand.

Katherine Cole stood next to her husband in the midst of a crowd of people huddled under tin sheds in back of the cameras, anticipating a fascinating evening ahead. She wasn't alone in her curiosity. A mass of bystanders had joined the cast and crew for the big event, and there was a vaguely hysterical festive atmosphere in the unusually nippy air. Leo was playing one of the scavengers who would try to steal the horse as Rhett and Scarlett escaped against the backdrop of the flaming city, and his brief close-up was to be filmed tonight, though his actual scuffle with Gable would be shot later. Leo was already in his tattered costume, but like the rest of those at Selznick International, he was waiting.

Tonight David O. Selznick was waiting too. He was about to film the most difficult scene in the book that had swept America. More than two hundred people were jammed onto the set, and all of them were waiting for one man: Myron Selznick, David Selznick's brother, a powerful agent who represented many of Hollywood's biggest stars. Finally Myron arrived with a young couple in tow, all three of them a little tipsy.

"Laurence Olivier, the English actor," Leo murmured to Katherine. "I met him the other day at the Brown Derby. He's here doing *Wuthering Heights* for Sam Goldwyn. An amazing talent."

"I recognize him from *The Divorce of Lady X*. Is she his wife?" Katherine asked, indicating the dark-haired woman with Olivier.

"No, she's his friend." Leo shrugged. "They want to marry, but they're both married to other people—the usual story. She's an actress too. Her name is Vivien Leigh."

"Oh, yes. She was in that silly Robert Taylor picture, *A Yank at Oxford*. They're the most beautiful couple I've ever seen," Katherine said frankly. "They look like a pair of racehorses."

Katherine watched as Myron Selznick introduced Vivien Leigh to his brother, and though David Selznick was clearly irritated that Myron was late, he stared at Leigh intently as he signaled production manager Ray Klune to start the fire.

Klune gave the order, the grips lit the oil in the pipes feeding the blaze, and a blast of fire shot hundreds of feet into the cold night sky, illuminating the entire area. The flames cast an eerie glow over the movie company, and out of the corner of her eye Katherine saw that Myron Selznick was hard at work noodling his distracted brother, talking a mile a minute, and pointing at Vivien Leigh's ivory face. Bored, Olivier scanned the crowd, saw Leo, and waved. He left the little knot of people clustered around Selznick and wandered over to Leo.

"Darling, this is Laurence Olivier," Leo said as the two men shook hands. "My wife, Katherine."

Olivier took her hand gravely. "You have the most beautiful hair I've ever seen on a lady," he said, admiring Katherine's mass of red hair that matched the flames lighting the sky as he bowed low over Katherine's hand. "You're a lucky man, Leo." Then, blowing on his hands, he said, "It's cold in your sunny California." He cast an anxious glance at Vivien Leigh. "You must excuse me, Mrs. Cole. I have to retrieve Miss Leigh before she sweeps Mr. Selznick off his feet. Don't tell anyone, but she's dying to play Scarlett O'Hara, and after tonight I have no doubt she'll get what she wants. Viv usually does. A pleasure, Mrs. Cole," Olivier said before he returned to Vivien Leigh, who was smiling vivaciously at David Selznick.

"I must go as well, my darling," Leo said. "This will take hours, so don't wait for me. Leave when you're bored, yes? You'll be all right by yourself?"

"Of course," she said, squeezing his arm.

Leo smiled lovingly and disappeared into the knot of men surrounding art director William Cameron Menzies, who was directing the fire sequence.

Fascinated, Katherine turned her attention back to the burning of Atlanta and watched in awe as Yakima Canutt, the stuntman doubling for Clark Gable, fearlessly pulled a horse and wagon carrying Scarlett's stand-in past the gigantic flames. The fire was tremendous, and the reflected glare lit up the sky. Puffs of vapor flowed like smoke from the open mouths of the onlookers in the chilly night air and gave them a ghostly air.

"Hello, Red," a man said quietly.

She didn't bother to turn around. She didn't have to. She knew who it was. She held her breath, hoping he would go away and praying he wouldn't.

"Richard," she whispered.

"Come and talk to me," he said, guiding her to the rear of the crowd and behind a tin shed.

Without a word he took her in his arms and began to kiss her feverishly, as if he were starving for food, parched for water. Time made no difference. It was as if they'd parted yesterday, as if every day since they'd last met was erased. She responded to him, and her body melted to his, framed and backlit by the enormous flames climbing quickly over the false fronts of the lost city of Atlanta and into the heart of the old standing sets.

Sanity shot through her mind like a bullet, and Katherine wrenched free of his hunger before it was too late. "No," she said breathlessly. "Richard, let me go."

"No?" he said angrily, shaking her gently. "First time I've seen you in over a year and you say no?"

He kissed her again, one hand in her hair, one hand holding her close to him, his mouth hot on her throat, her face. . . .

She pulled away, but she didn't want to. "Almost two years." she said gently.

"That long?" he said, surprised. "Come with me. No one'll see us."

"Don't be an ass, Richard," she said sharply. "I'm not the girl I was a couple of years ago."

Behind them the remnants of the tremendous wall from

King Kong were outlined in orange flames and black smoke, and embers hot enough to melt steel glowed at the base of the huge fire.

"How's . . . the baby?" he said quietly.

"Rosalind is her name, and she's fine. We adore her," Katherine said, stressing the "we."

"Jesus, Katherine, don't play Lady Astor with me. I think about you every day, all the time."

As she looked at his handsome face illuminated in the growing fire storm surrounding them, she felt as if she were being swept along on a river of flames. She had thought Richard Sears was locked safely away in a small corner of her mind, yet the moment she saw him, her resolve had disappeared. His face was more defined; he'd settled into himself and outgrown his young man's eagerness. Now that Richard Sears knew exactly who he was, he was more dangerous than ever.

"I think about you, too, Richard." She sighed, both sorry and glad it was true. "All the time, in fact. But it doesn't matter anymore. It's over between us, and it won't start again, because I won't let it." Behind them the last vestiges of Cecil B. DeMille's biblical epic, *The King of Kings,* disappeared in the onrushing flames, and though the night air was cold on her cheeks, Katherine felt something more than the heat of the huge fire warming her face, her heart, and her body.

"Listen to me," Richard said with tremendous intensity. "You were right and I was wrong, all right? Marrying Maria was a terrible mistake, and I'm paying for it. She's rotten, just like you said. Everything she touches goes bad, soft in the middle—soft and spoiled. You were right about my career, too. Edgar Lashman is more powerful than ever, and no one believes I've made it on my own. Selznick married Louis Mayer's daughter, and this town won't let him forget it either. 'The son-in-law also rises,'" he said bitterly. "That's what they say about Selznick, and it isn't true about him any more than it is about me, but it still hurts. I live with Maria in the house that Lashman built, but it's a big, beautiful tomb. Christ, I feel as if I'm rotting to death."

"Too late, Richard," Katherine said. "All too late."

"Come back to me, Katherine. I don't give a damn about Maria. I'll leave her eventually, I swear it."

There was a pleading note in his voice she'd never heard before, and Katherine sighed, wishing she could rewrite the past and give their life a second draft. "It doesn't matter what you want, understand? You wanted to get rid of our baby because it interfered with your plans for your career, and when I refused, you abandoned me without a backward glance. Do you honestly think I'll come trotting back to you simply because *you* made a mistake? Good-bye, Richard." Katherine pulled her coat tightly around her and turned her back on him.

The fire was hot, but she was suddenly cold, and once again there was a frozen spear lodged in her heart like an arrow, and a horrible fear washed over her. She would never, never melt; she would be the impenetrable ice queen, frozen for all time. Frightened, she turned back to him. "There's another reason I won't come back to you. You see, when Leo asked me to marry him, I made him a promise. I made it because it was the only thing he asked of me. I promised him I would never see you alone," she said. "That's his polite euphemism for going to bed with you. I made that promise, and I won't break it, even though I want to more than anything on this earth."

"Jesus, I have to fall for the only woman in Hollywood with ethics," Sears said, his voice harsh. "The thing is, you don't understand that I love you, but I love power and money, too."

"More," she said quietly. Perhaps he didn't hear her; perhaps he was pretending. She couldn't tell which. "Richard, your past was dreadful, but it's past. It's dead and gone, and the world's still spinning merrily along. Isn't it time to let go?"

A snarl flicked over his face, and his blue eyes turned as black as a winter pond. "I am what I am, Katherine."

"Rubbish. You're selfish and mean-spirited, and I don't know why I give a damn about you. Leave my husband for you? For *you?* I'd die first. You're not worth his spit, Richard. Give up my husband and ruin my child's life to be your whore? Do you honestly think you're worth it?" she said, her voice devoid of emotion. She knew she spoke the truth, but as his face shivered and broke, she regretted her harsh words. *Richard, Richard, why aren't you the man I want you to be?*

Behind them the great wall from *King Kong* collapsed and a spray of sparks filled the sky like a mass of escaping fireflies. Harsh light danced over their faces as Richard Sears and Katherine Cole looked at each other for a long wordless moment.

Finally Richard broke the silence encasing their small slice of earth. "You've changed," he said softly.

"I should hope so." She laughed shortly.

"I don't know if I like it," he said.

"I don't give a damn if you like it or not."

"You're harder, Red."

"You made me that way, Richard."

"You were so gentle, so sweet."

"I gave. You took."

He couldn't take his eyes off her. "You're on fire."

And she realized she had power over him at last. When they were lovers he'd been in control; he'd set the pace and course of their relationship. But power grew out of strength, and now *she* had the power; she could see it in the new way he looked at her. If he'd loved her before, he admired her now.

"It's just special effects, Richard. Don't let it throw you," she said.

"You're right about me. I'm everything you say. But I love you and you love me, and we both know it," he said urgently. He reached out a finger and tentatively stroked her cheek.

"We do? How?" she said as she pulled away from his gentle touch. She couldn't let him see that it burned her skin like fire.

"This is how," he said as he took her in his arms and kissed her again.

For a brief final moment she allowed herself to respond fully, then tore away from the hard familiarity of his body. "No, Richard," she said quietly. "It doesn't matter how much you want me or how much I want you. I owe Leo Cole my life, and I'll never betray him. It's too late for us." Quickly Katherine turned, walked away from Richard Sears, got into her car, and drove off, the embers of Hollywood's version of Atlanta lighting the sky behind her.

Leo came home at four in the morning. The destruction of the Selznick back lot took less time than expected, so he'd gone over to the Cinegrill with a few of the boys. When he slipped into bed next to her, Katherine woke up and reached out for him, twining her arms around the known quantity of his body, and his mouth slipped over hers with the comfortable yet passionate fit of long-married lovers. Leo molded himself to her joyously, feeling her desire for him was a gift, a glorious present he would double and redouble.

Later, as Leo slept in the crook of her arm, Katherine eased his head onto the pillow and padded down the hall to Rosalind's room. It was barely daylight, and the soft shafts of light seeping into the room marked both the end of a long day and the beginning of a new one. Mrs. Gebhardt was awake, and Katherine heard the soft sound of hymns drifting upstairs from the beehive radio in the kitchen.

Rosalind was asleep and Katherine didn't wake her. She only wanted to look at the baby's sleeping head ringed with copper curls. The child made her even more aware of Richard Sears's presence in her house, and as she watched Rosalind's rhythmic breathing she thought about the three kinds of love she knew.

Richard, the man she had loved with all the passion of a young girl, the man she would never love again.

Leo, the man she'd grown to love just as he'd predicted on the night he asked her to marry him.

Rosalind, the child of her heart, whom she loved fiercely, protectively. Three lives, three loves, three hearts entwined like green vines embracing a tree.

Katherine bent and kissed Rosalind's head, then went back to her own bed and curled her body to fit Leo's. He reached behind him, pulled her closer, and she clung to him. Then he turned to her, and they made love once more as the sunlight of the new morning flooded through the organdy curtains and filled their room.

Nine months later Olivia was born. This time the birth was uneventful, and once again Leo insisted on choosing the baby's name—from *Twelfth Night*.

Katherine's pregnancy had been easy, and as the child had grown heavier throughout the long summer, she had felt a new sense of comfort and emotional security. As the child grew, her love for Leo grew, and their love was coupled with respect. Despite his profligate way with money, Leo was the ideal husband and father. But ever since the night she'd accidentally met Richard Sears on the set of *Gone With the Wind,* an uneasy angel had hovered overhead, shadowing Katherine Cole with its dark wings.

Maria Lashman Sears's second child, Richard Sears, Jr., was born the same week as Olivia Cole, and the moment she read the announcement in the *L.A. Times,* Katherine knew exactly what the timing meant. That night, the night they'd met on the *Gone With the Wind* set, Richard had gone home and made love to Maria just as she'd made love to Leo. As Katherine had lain wrapped in Leo's arms, so Richard had lain encased in Maria's stifling love, a pair of unknowing surrogates. And with her new knowledge, Katherine Cole wondered whether the invisible rope stretching across the Hollywood Hills and binding her to Richard Sears would ever break.

But her home life was quiet and happy, and Olivia's birth brought her a serenity she'd never known before. Perhaps it came from a stable life. Perhaps it came from the growth of trust and security she felt under Leo's protective wing. It was hard to tell. Yet though she still felt connected to Richard Sears, her ties to Leo were stronger than ever before. Loving two men at once seemed impossible, but she grew more and more comfortable with her dual nature as time passed.

Katherine looked out the kitchen window and saw Leo and Roz lying on the grass together, their legs bent in an identical pose as they stared at the sky. The two heads nearly touching, the dark and the red, Leo's hand tracing patterns in the air as he explained the clouds to the little girl by his side. Rosalind idolized her daddy, and when Leo was at home she invariably escaped Mrs. Gebhardt and tagged along after him.

Katherine laughed as she turned back to the salad she was making. Roz was so tiny, still a baby, and yet she shared a special relationship with Leo. They were always together, always sharing secrets. He took her everywhere—to the studio, to restaurants, to racetracks, and probably to crap games—for Roz, too, was Leo's lucky charm.

On September 1, 1939, a month after Olivia's birth, the Germans invaded Poland. Over the next few days Leo was quiet and reflective in a way Katherine had never seen before. He spent the days listening to the sketchy news on the radio in his den and the evenings alone on the brick patio outside the living room, drinking brandy and smoking cigars in the dark.

The night air was growing cool, and Katherine pulled her quilted robe around her as she went out through the French doors and sat down in one of the green wrought-iron chairs that stood around the circular pebbled-glass table. She'd bought the set at the beginning of the summer, and now it was Leo's favorite place to sit and smoke at the end of the day. Somewhere up the canyon a coyote barked and a neighborhood dog answered back.

The tip of his cigar glowed secretively, tracing a zigzag pattern of light in the dark as a lone cricket chirped from the rosebushes. "War is coming," Leo said.

"You've been saying that for years," she answered. "You said war was coming the first day we met." She felt a sudden stab of fear, and there was a desperate shading in her voice. "Maybe it won't. Maybe nothing will happen. Besides, you're not a Pole, you're a Hungarian."

"Ahh, but I'm an American now."

"Leo . . ."

He didn't look at her. "Someday it would be nice to have a pool there," he said, pointing at the big lawn stretching out behind the house in an unbroken roll. And so they talked about the domestic future, relieved to have a safe, comfortable subject and a safe, comfortable world to escape to.

Despite the growing storm in Europe, life in Los Angeles continued in an easy stream for the next two years. Mrs. Gebhardt took care of the children, and Katherine became a young Hollywood matron. As Leo's career continued to flower, she shopped and lunched with the wives of agents and actors and studio executives. She dressed beautifully, her hair and nails were tended, her clothes were ever more expensive, her appointment book was overfilled, and her life seemed completely settled. Until December 7, 1941, the day that changed everything.

After the Japanese attacked Pearl Harbor, Richard Sears was one of the first Hollywood stars to enlist. He joined the air corps, earned his wings in flight school, went to England as a copilot, and began flying bombing raids over Germany in B-17s.

Leo tried to enlist, but he was turned down because of a bad hip. Immediately he started touring with the Hollywood Victory Committee, entertaining wounded troops in hospitals both overseas and at home. He also joined novelist James M. Cain to serve with director Cecil B. DeMille's Hollywood Hills Air Raid Defense Unit, watching the night skies over Los Angeles as an air raid warden.

Katherine volunteered for Bette Davis's newly organized Hollywood Canteen and worked tirelessly, washing dishes, serving food, and dancing with servicemen on leave. Often she gave parties at the house to raise money for the War Bond Committee.

In 1943 Leo worked in Colonel Jack Warner's controversial *Mission to Moscow* for his old friend Mike Curtiz and made a string of short training and propaganda films at "Fort Roach," as the Culver City base of the army's Motion

Picture Unit was called. In Burbank, Warner Brothers made a specialty of producing patriotic war films, and Leo worked steadily, jumping from one picture to the next without a break. But the films were standard flag-waving fare, and Leo longed for a part he could sink his teeth into.

Finally, in May of 1944, the right script came along. The film was *Objective, Burma!,* the star was the unpredictable Errol Flynn, and the director was the masterful Raoul Walsh, whose black eye patch gave him a raffish air. Walsh had specifically asked for Leo Cole in the part of the cynical war correspondent.

Leo stayed up half the night reading the gritty screenplay. "It's a wonderful story," he told Katherine the next morning. "More than just another wartime potboiler. It's a real story, a timeless story about guts and loyalty. Call it my small contribution to the war effort."

But from the first, the picture didn't go well. The swamps around the Santa Anita racetrack were doubling for the Burmese jungle, and the filth, the flies, and the hard work were almost unendurable. The actors playing the American paratroopers waded waist-deep in foul, mucky water for days, and Leo, who was older than many of the others, found it tough going.

Nevertheless, he was proud of his work in the picture, and when he shyly asked Katherine if she cared to drive out to the location one morning and watch the day's shooting, she agreed even though she'd just learned she was pregnant.

In a way, this new baby was the first of her children to belong exclusively to Leo, and the unborn child symbolized the tranquillity surrounding her marriage. Rosalind belonged to Richard Sears. Olivia was conceived in ambivalence on that strange night when she met Richard again on the set of *Gone With the Wind* and then went home to Leo's arms. But the child she carried now would inaugurate a fresh life for Leo and Katherine Cole, and both of them were aware of the new dimensions of their relationship. Leo was unusually tender toward her, and she felt that they'd scaled a huge mountain together.

It was years since she'd been on a location, and when she and Leo arrived at the *Burma* set, the atmosphere brought back waves of nostalgia—the chaotic scene in the early morning half-light, the paper cups of steaming coffee, the rush to get into makeup and costume. But Katherine was no longer an actress. She was simply a bystander, and that made her a little sad.

Leo's character was a hard-bitten journalist whose cynicism would be overcome by the enormity of the pain and sacrifice around him, a man forced to face up to his own convictions. Walsh's initial instinct was correct, the part was made for the mobile face of Leo Cole. His close-ups were superb, not simply automatic reactions; a wealth of experience and emotion was reflected in his world-weary eyes.

After lunch, Leo and the young actor playing his driver were to shoot a pivotal scene marking the turning point for Leo's character. The two men would drive their Jeep up a small incline, and the young driver would be killed by sniper fire. Leo, the cynical journalist, would then take the dead boy in his arms, grab his carbine, and fire blindly on the unseen enemy. As the camera focused on his face and his eyes filled with tears, the audience would know the reporter was no longer capable of sitting on the fence.

Katherine watched as Raoul Walsh set up the long crane shot that would follow the Jeep as it ascended the small hill. Leo and Ted Watkins, the young actor playing the doomed driver, climbed into the Jeep. It was Watkins's first big moment on-screen and he was understandably nervous, but Leo eased the tension by laughing and joking with the boy.

Watkins gunned the engine and the Jeep took off up the hill, kicking up a gigantic dust cloud. The huge crane carrying Walsh and the cameraman was elevated to follow the Jeep, and Katherine heard mumbled cursing at the size of the dust cloud.

"Cut!" Walsh yelled. "No good! Can't see you."

The assistant director waved Watkins back. "I want to see

you, not the dirt," Walsh cried impatiently. "Take it slower."

Watkins nodded and tried again. Once again he accidentally gave it too much gas as they approached the small hill, and the Jeep rocked dangerously on the rutted road.

"Damn it," Walsh said irritably. "Again."

The third take began smoothly. The dust cloud was perfect, but when they reached the crest of the hill the actors playing the enemy snipers leapt up and fired directly at the Jeep, spooking Watkins. The Jeep swerved unexpectedly, then slammed to a sudden halt.

Leo was lighting a cigarette, and when Watkins slammed on the brakes he was caught unaware. He catapulted out of the open car, flew over the hood, and slammed heavily onto the stony road. Then he twitched uncontrollably and lay still.

For a long moment Katherine watched in silence, waiting for Leo to jump to his feet with his characteristic shrug and laugh to cover his embarrassment at the accident. Unexpectedly she heard Richard Sears's words ringing in her head, the slight joke he'd made that day long ago on the set of *The Arizona Kid* when he told her Leo had pushed him out the window at Clara's house. "Fell on my head," Sears's voice echoed out of the past. "No damage."

But Leo didn't get up. He lay on the road, sprawled on his back like Rosalind's favorite Raggedy Andy at the bottom of the stairs, the blue California sky covering him like a glass dome. Katherine tried to call out, but her voice wouldn't work, so she ran up the hill to Leo, heedless of the rolling camera, of Ted Watkins's anguished cry, of Raoul Walsh yelling at the crane operator to get him down. She was part of a knot of people rushing up the hill toward Leo, who wouldn't get up, wouldn't get up, wouldn't get up. . . .

"Leo! Leo!" Katherine screamed, her voice as harsh as a crow's, a raw rasp of metal on metal. *"Leo!"*

Chapter
10

As she stood in the hospital room and watched Leo's pale face grow slack and cold, Katherine knew she was unalterably changed. There was a block of granite on her heart, thick, hard, and unbending. A piece of her soul had been cut out and thrown away, and she would never find it again, no matter how hard she looked. Tonight she was as dead as Leo Cole. The sky outside the smudged window was growing lighter, and though she knew she should call for a nurse, she didn't do it.

Katherine wanted one more minute alone with Leo, one more minute to pretend he was still alive, still vital and strong, still Leo, the man she had learned to love. She took his hand in hers, but the long, delicate fingers that had so often traced their course across her body were limp and cold. Briefly she fancied they vibrated with life, but it was just a fancy. Were the fingers growing colder as they lay in her palm? Another fancy. It was too soon. Death was only minutes old, but the inexorable change had begun. Still, she clung to his lifeless hand, wanting to be his wife for one last moment, his wife instead of his widow.

She looked at his quiet face, put a hand on his chest, motionless, without any trace of life or breath. No more quick smiles or lightning flashes of temper. No more dear jokes and laughter. No more Leo.

"You saved me," she whispered. Funny, how we talk to the dead who can't hear, whose eyes are a dark slab of slate, she thought. We murmur secret thoughts to the dead who will never hear us or betray our whispered confidences. Finally she was free to tell him everything, to confess the depth of her love, but it was too late, all too late.

Do I cut a lock of your hair and wear it in a locket, like a Victorian ghoul? she asked him silently. Do I shriek and cry out "No, no, no"? Do I dry up and blow away like a pressed flower? I don't know how to behave in front of death. What manners do I use? What dress do I wear for death?

Katherine sat down next to his unmoving body and put one hand on her stomach. "You'll never know your father," she said. She placed the other hand on Leo's forehead. "You'll never know your child. You will know each other only through me." And so Leo and Katherine Cole sat alone, together.

Ten minutes later she got up and went to the door to call the nurse. As her hand hit the brass doorknob and the pale light of dawn flooded the room with thin, sharp intensity, she felt the weight of death descend on her, a thick layer of resignation that would cover her like a cloud for the rest of her life.

"Good-bye, Leo," she called softly without turning back. "I'll always love you. . . ."

That night Katherine sat beside Rozzie's bed and watched the child toss fitfully in the hot, rumpled sheets in reaction to the stark trauma around her. She'd had a fever, and now her long red hair was damp with sweat and her voice was hoarse from coughing. Roz kicked the covers off and breathed heavily; a racking noise scraped her throat, and the painful sound sent a flash of anger and fear surging through Katherine's body.

A memory sparked and died as Katherine covered Roz

with a light blanket and tried vainly to plump the pillows. That sound, that sound—she'd heard that sound before, that dry scrape of anger and pain. The night Leo asked her to marry him, the night Richard left her—on that night the dry palm fronds had scraped the window as the winds blew. She put her hand on the child's hot forehead and felt a film of sweat that made her skin slick and oily. Work. The work of children. A hot, sick child took precedence over grief on the night your husband died. Your life continued, because what else was life to do?

But I have no grief, no heart at all, she thought. My feelings have been pounded into dust, dirt, and ruin. I'll never feel anything again, not with this dead space inside me that feels like the surface of the moon. Gray and jagged and covered with anger. Katherine put her hands to her face and realized she was crying. She wiped the tears away, remembering the night long ago at the Magyar Café when she'd christened Leo.

"Leo Cole," she whispered, pressing one of her tears on Rosalind's forehead. "You're his daughter, Rozzie, not Richard's at all. Olivia is so little, she won't remember Leo. The baby inside me will never know him. Leo Cole will slip away. He'll be a memory, or maybe a dream.

"But you—you loved him more than all of us. Your Leo. Damn you for dying, Leo," she said harshly.

Roz stirred and shivered fitfully in her bed at the angry sound of her mother's voice.

"I have nothing left but my children. No future but my children. They are my future."

Roughly Katherine wiped away her tears. Her mind was wandering, and she didn't like that, so she went down the hall to check on Olivia. The little girl was sleeping peacefully, undisturbed by the sorrow around her.

Someone knocked tentatively at the front door, and Katherine wondered why Mrs. Gebhardt didn't answer until she remembered she'd sent the housekeeper home to her Santa Monica bungalow. Tonight she wanted to be alone. The doorbell rang. Katherine sighed and went downstairs.

It was one of Leo's poker pals, Bill Shank, an old character actor who'd been forced out of talkies in the early thirties when an odd collection of verbal tics marked the end of his brief career. He was heavily wrinkled, as if he'd spent years in the sun, but his bright blue eyes were as sharp as those of a magpie hunting for treasure.

Katherine had met him before, but she'd never said more than a few words to him. She wondered what he wanted; then she remembered Leo was dead. Bill Shank had come to offer his condolences.

Bill Shank ducked his head nervously. "Sorry about— about Leo, Mrs. Cole," he stammered. "He was a good man, good pal, see. Look, I'll get right to it. Reason I'm here, see, I owe Leo a little money, see. Well, more'n a little. Fifteen hunnert dollahs." Bill Shank ducked his head again, sadly. "Felt bad when I heard he was gone, see. Sorta been keeping outta his way these last few months. Didden have the dough to pay him back, see. Not that old Leo woulda said a word about it, see." He pulled a creased envelope out of his frayed suit jacket and thrust it into Katherine's hand. "Here's what I owe him, and damn sorry I didden pay before. Fifteen hunnert dollahs. Night, Mrs. Cole." Bill Shank turned quickly and walked away, a small, nervous shadow under the moon.

"Thank you, Bill," Katherine called after him. "Leo often spoke of you." It wasn't true. Leo had never mentioned him.

Katherine sighed and put the envelope down on the mahogany hall table and went back to check on Roz. The child's breath came easier now, and when Katherine put her hand on Rozzie's forehead she thought the little girl wasn't quite so hot. Paying a debt to a dead man. How very . . . gentlemanly.

Tears came again as she sat beside Roz, and this time she didn't bother to wipe them away. She woke a little while later; she didn't know how long she'd slept. Someone was knocking on the door.

This time a thin blond woman with tense eyes and nervous fingers was standing on the doorstep, shifting from foot to foot. A black Chevrolet stood in the driveway with another woman at the wheel. The blond was heavily made up, and a white fox fur was draped over the shoulders of her flowered evening dress.

"Mrs. Cole?" the blond said. "Look, hope it's okay to come here so soon after Leo—Mr. Cole, I mean—so soon after he's passed on and all. I work at Clara's? House with the blue door? You know the place I mean?"

"Yes, I know," Katherine said, confused.

"Leo—Mr. Cole—he used to come and play cards, y'know. But he was a soft touch, and me and some of the other girls used to borrow money from him, time to time. Not much, a five spot here, twenty there if we were short on our rent. But when we heard he got . . . he died and all, we started feeling kinda bad 'cause we never paid him back and all. He talked so much about you and the kids, we figured we oughta pay him back. So, anyway . . . here." The blond shoved a manila envelope at Katherine. "It ain't much, just what we owe. Sorry about Leo, Mrs. Cole. He was a nice guy, and there's precious few of 'em in this town."

"Thank you," Katherine said softly.

The blond went down the steps, then turned back to Katherine, shielding her eyes against the light flooding out of the house and across the driveway. "Mrs. Cole?" she said as she got in the car.

"Yes?"

"He just came to play cards."

"I know," Katherine said to the empty air as the Chevrolet pulled out of the driveway. She put the envelope on the hall table next to Bill Shank's, shaking her head. Leo's dead. He'll never know his friends paid him back. The hall clock struck eleven, and Katherine made herself a cup of tea.

Twenty minutes later the doorbell rang again, and as one of the waiters from the Magyar Café thrust another envelope full of cash into her hands, Katherine began to understand.

After the waiter left, a pair of beat cops from downtown

L.A. showed up. Then a man barely larger than a midget appeared and handed her a thick wad of wrinkled bills. He was a jockey, he said, and he claimed people all around the track owed Leo—jockeys and concessionaires, touts and handlers and a tip sheet owner. A waiter from Musso and Frank's, a grip from Universal—one after another they came with small stacks of cash. All of them claimed they owed Leo money. All of them politely asked about the children and said wistfully that Leo often spoke about her, about his children, about his home.

Slowly Katherine realized that these wads of creased bills shoved into hotel envelopes were the gambler's insurance she'd heard Leo talk about. This was her widow's mite. There was more than twenty thousand dollars in envelopes on the hall table. She hefted the stack of bills in her hand; a debt from the past became a gift for the present. She put the money in the top drawer of Leo's desk and went upstairs.

Roz was quiet. The fever had broken. Katherine checked on Olivia. Her hair was tangled, and one bare leg was uncovered and hanging over the edge of the bed. One hand was clenched in a tight fist. Little fighter. She stroked Olivia's dark hair. As dark as Leo's. Please come home. It's late and we miss you, Leo.

The house was as dark as her heart, as dark as Leo's hair. I am alone. I loved one man and he left me. I loved another and he died. I am alone.

She went into their bedroom, stripped off her clothes, and threw them in a heap. Tomorrow she would burn them. She never wanted to see those things again, the clothes she had worn on the day Leo died.

She got into bed naked. She moved over to Leo's side and smelled his pillow. She wanted the last traces of him imprinted on her bare skin, the creases from their tangled sheets on her body one last time.

Leo. The man I didn't love until it was almost too late. Leo, I should have loved you better. I should have loved you sooner.

The room was full of silence and loss. An empty room.

Tonight I will cry for you. Tomorrow I will change the sheets. But tonight I will cry for you. Good-bye, Leo. . . .

The day after the funeral Katherine went to the lawyer's office and left empty-handed, as she'd known she would. There was no money. Leo Cole had left nothing but debts, although the house was in Katherine's name and it was free and clear. There was only his gambler's insurance, Katherine thought grimly as she took the thick stack of bills from Leo's desk drawer. How long would it last? Leo, once you told me you would take care of me, and you've always kept your promise in your own way. . . . She was too exhausted to make any decisions.

Katherine stumbled forward and her body became heavier and more unwieldy as the baby inside her grew larger. Finally, toward the end of her pregnancy, she was unable to do the easiest things and the days rolled in and out like a slack tide slapping up against a long, wide beach. Leo was gone, and as the baby shifted inside her she knew it was the last child she would carry.

Yet as she sat and stared out the living room window at the fading garden, caught in a haze of Leo's death and the child's life, a part of her mind saw a day of reckoning lying on the landscape ahead. But for now Katherine was content to drift in and out with the tide, sinking further into a static paralysis as night blinked into day and back again. For now she could do nothing.

She had no money, no income, nothing. They were living on Leo's gambler's insurance. She sold her jewelry to pay Leo's debts and kept only her favorite trinkets and the big diamond necklace. Everything else went to pay the bills—Mrs. Gebhardt, the car repairs, the gardener—and it was a terrible, crushing burden. Leo had lived like a prince, dispensing money out of pocket, saving nothing, putting nothing away, depending on his own boundless wit and skill and energy to provide for his castle.

She sat at Leo's rolltop desk sorting through the bills, the markers, the scraps of paper with tips on the horses at Santa

Anita. Overwhelmed, she pushed her chair back, went to the window, and watched the twilight seep over the Hollywood Hills. Crevices that only a moment ago were tinged with gold now were turning deep blue with violet centers. The scrub oak and the manzanita were a dark, indistinguishable mass, and the owl that made its home in the heart of a nearby palm tree hooted anxiously, warning the last of the daylight to fly away, fly away, fly away . . .

Katherine was alone. She had two children to support, and soon there would be three. There was very little money left. Mrs. Gebhardt would stay, of course. Katherine had asked her, and she'd replied that she would stay as long as the Lord left her there. And besides, if Katherine went to work after the baby was born she'd need Mrs. G. to take care of the children.

Katherine saw her face reflected in the windowpane, the bright lights of the study glowing cheerfully behind her. Who'll give me a job? I'm not an ingenue anymore, and I haven't worked in years. But, she reasoned slowly, maybe I don't have to act. Maybe I could be a dress extra, and all I'd have to do is stand still. After all, I have the clothes for it, and a dress extra who can provide her own wardrobe makes more money. Maybe I could make a living that way. . . .

Charles was born late in December, and as soon as she could manage, Katherine went to the business rep for the Screen Actors Guild and asked for help. Luckily, the rep was a longtime pal of Leo's, and he was sympathetic.

"Don't worry about it, Mrs. Cole," he told her. "I got a pal works at Central Casting. I'll call, I'll schmooze, it's as good as done. Believe me, it's not a problem." The rep waved a pudgy hand, and his diamond pinky ring flashed in the light through the dirty venetian blinds. "Too bad about Leo."

Katherine nodded and blinked back the hot tears that still came when she heard his name. "Yes," she said quietly. "Too bad about Leo."

So Katherine went back to work in the studios as a dress extra. At first she filled out crowd scenes, but her elegant bearing and air of quiet sophistication soon got her featured bits. Often she'd be at a front row table at an elegant restaurant while Betty Grable and Don Ameche danced the night away center stage, or she would be selling elegant hats to Hedy Lamarr in a glamorous shop. And all the while she knew her life was twisting in the wind, a lonely flag whipping helplessly in a sharp breeze. There were long hours in too-tight heels on cold, drafty sound stages and endless talking on the phone in order to line up more jobs, for extras had no agents. Extras fended for themselves and worked through the grace of Central Casting, the clearinghouse for the lowly.

But as hard as she worked, she could not earn enough. "I've got to have more money," Katherine told Madeline one night as they sorted through the remains of her jewelry on the bedroom floor. "The kids'll need private schools, and everything is so expensive." she said as she pulled out the marcasite pin Leo had given her when they first met. "I can't sell this," she said, sighing.

"Listen, honey, you've got to have more of a life," Madeline said with her usual practicality. She'd been overseas flaunting her famous derriere on a USO tour when Leo died, and this was the first time the two old friends had seen each other in over a year. "You were in love with Richard, you were in love with Leo, and they're both gone. I hate to put it so coldly, sugar, but that's the way it goes. Sure, you've got the kids, but you can't work your life away."

"What's my alternative? A job at Lockheed? Selling dresses at Bullock's Wilshire? I feel as if I'm falling into a bottomless well," Katherine said as she pinned the little marcasite bow on her blouse.

One day as Katherine hustled up a job at Fox, she managed to include a friend of hers on the shoot. Mrs. Eyles was a tall, graceful British expatriate who'd settled in California in the early twenties after her spiritual master, Swami Yogananda, began the Self-Realization Fellowship in Los Angeles, and she was now the quintessential Angeleno, a vegetarian and a crystal gazer who spent much of her money on tarot readings and communications with the spirit world. Years ago she'd been queen of the dress extras, but lately she'd fallen on hard times.

For some reason Katherine took pity on her, despite her stargazing foolishness, and Mrs. Eyles was tremendously grateful. After the few days' work was over, Katherine realized Madeline was right: she had to carve a life out of the emptiness. If she could get work for herself, if she could get a part for Mrs. Eyles, maybe she could get jobs for the hundreds of Hollywood hopefuls who pounded the sunny pavements of Los Angeles. If she wanted to get out of the hole created by Leo's death, she'd have to stop suffering and grab life by the scruff of its neck. And so, at nine o'clock on a Monday morning, the Cole Agency was born on Leo's rolltop desk in the corner of the living room.

Katherine called every person she knew, every person in Leo's address book, every person she'd ever met who was connected with the movie industry, every person she knew who *wasn't* connected to the movie industry. She begged, she pleaded, she threatened, she was tearful. She was shameless. She talked about Leo, she talked about the children, she talked about money, and she talked about the lack of it. She talked and talked and talked . . .

Mrs. Eyles and some of the other dress extras were her first clients, and Katherine agreed to represent them without charge just to get her foot into the studio door. But oddly enough, Leo's old acting coach, the irascible Madame Lermontov, was the first "big" client handled by the newly formed Cole Agency.

Madame's acting school in New York had gone bust at the beginning of the war, and Madame had passed her time knitting sweaters for Russian War Relief until Leo got her a part in *Mission to Moscow,* and then she had returned to California, where, she huffed, "at least it is varm." Now Madame made ends meet by giving private lessons, and when she heard of the formation of the Cole Agency, she showed up one morning, pounding on Katherine's front door with her pearl-handled cane.

"I sign with you for two reasons. First, nobody else wants me. Second, I loved Leo Cole like a son," Madame announced. "You get me jobs, I send you kids from my classes, boys and girls with talent, yes? Me you don't charge a commission, them you charge plenty, and so one hand washes the other, yes?"

Katherine stared into her shrewd old face, the pale blue eyes buried in the mass of wrinkles. "Deal," she said as they shook hands.

As a client, Madame Lermontov was a tough sell. She was old, she was cranky, she was fat and had gout, and she couldn't walk without her cane, but Katherine took her on. She called every casting director she knew, she called studios and producers. No one would give Madame a job. Desperate, she called Eddie Gibbon.

The little director was working at Metro on a musical, and the moment Katherine told him she was representing Madame Lermontov, Eddie slammed the phone down in her ear with a rude snort. Ten minutes later he called her back.

"I hate her," he announced without preamble, "but I called Mike Curtiz, who is doing some action picture at Warners. I ask him if doesn't he have a part for a fat, mean old Russian woman who can't walk and nobody in town will touch with a crane. It takes a few minutes, but Mike, he doesn't forget he's a Hungarian."

Katherine smiled gratefully. Her first victory was small but beautiful. "Thanks for the help, Eddie."

"Why not help? You'll be a good agent. You got Leo his first job. That's good agenting."

"I won't forget this," she said.

"Ha! In Hollywood everybody forgets to remember," Gibbon snapped as he slammed down the phone for the second time.

Katherine sat at the desk and cried as memories flooded over her. Eddie was right, she *had* gotten Leo his first job, that long-ago day on the hot location in the San Fernando Valley. Maybe the key to a new life had been there all along. Maybe she'd be a good agent. Maybe she had a chance. . . .

Katherine hocked the big diamond necklace Leo had left draped over her toothbrush and went office hunting. A week later she found a two-room suite of offices on the fourth floor of a white stucco Art Deco building on the north side of the Sunset Strip, about a block from the Garden of Allah.

She had the name of the agency painted on the door in gold lettering and went to work. Very quickly, in a few months, there was nothing left but work. She barely had enough time to see the children in the evenings, and she had no time for a private life, but the work suited her. Work became her life, and soon Katherine had accumulated a solid client list. Unlike the bigger, richer agents, Katherine took on anybody with talent, young or old, even those who were having a bad spell. She was a mother to her clients, who called her at all hours, at home or in the office; it made no difference to the Cole Agency. Actors and writers and directors . . . anybody with talent, she thought grimly. And a year after the agency opened, she signed Eddie Gibbon.

And Katherine worked harder.

The war was over, men were flooding back into Hollywood, eager to pick up their lives, but there was a new mood of confusion in the air. The unbelievable had happened. The old studio system was creaking and cracking. No longer were the Mayers and the Goldwyns, the Cohns and the Lashmans all-powerful. The new postwar stars were flexing their muscles.

And Katherine worked harder.

She left early, she came home late, she kissed the children, and she went out again to parties and nightclubs and screenings.

She was single-minded in her pursuit of business, for business was the only way she could protect her family. There was no one to protect Katherine Cole—no husband, no father, no brother. There was only Katherine Cole.

The memory of her old life in the Hollywood Hills, the sleepy, sheltered life she'd shared with Leo when times were good, shimmered in her mind like a mirage in the desert, a dream. I'll have it all back and better, she thought fiercely. I won't let anything stand in my way. She had a vision of the Cole Agency cutting through the ocean like the prow of a ship.

A year after Katherine opened the office on the Strip, Madeline dropped in, sleek and shimmering in beige silk, alligator pumps, and pale furs.

"Listen," Madeline said breathlessly as they kissed hello. "I waited around until I was sure you could make a go of the agency. Well, now I'm sure. You want to be my agent? Fine. Get me something decent. Here I am with the most famous rear end in America, and these guys in the studios don't know how to handle it. Don't say it." She grinned, holding up a hand. *"That* they know, but the screwing I get isn't worth the screwing I get, if you catch my drift. This guy I got, this dumb agent, all he wants to do is play patty-cake. He thinks I oughta be grateful for two scenes in a bathtub. Katherine, you're the only person I trust. Do something with my career. Make it happen for me. Otherwise"—Madeline sliced her neck with a red-nailed hand—"it's curtains, Lefty."

Katherine leaned back in her chair and looked carefully at Madeline. She looked good, stylish but sexy, and there was the glow of a smoldering fire in her eyes that came across on film. With the right management, Madeline could be bigger than Betty Grable. . . .

"Well?" Madeline pressed.

Katherine didn't hesitate. "There's one thing you've got to think about. If I'm your agent, it could ruin our friendship," she said evenly. "I'm a different person now, Mad. I don't tell people what they want to hear. I don't try to make anyone happy. I'm not nice. I'm in this business to win, understand? To take care of my children. There's no man in my family, no one to run things but me. This isn't the way I thought my life was going to turn out when we lived together on Hayworth, but this is what I've got. If you can handle that, tell your old agent good-bye."

"Hell, you think *I* thought I'd be nose art for a bomber?" Madeline shrugged, her pale fur slipping down over her shoulders. "Be my agent. Help me. It won't ruin anything. I love you like a sister, Katherine. More, 'cause I hate my dumb sisters, who only want money all the time. We've got to look out for each other. Men haven't done me much good, either. You ever see Richard?" she asked quietly.

Katherine shook her head.

"Does Rozzie know he's her father?"

Katherine's heart seized up like an unoiled motor. "Of course she doesn't know!" she snapped. "She's just a little girl! And she's never going to know, either."

Madeline arched her eyebrows and shook her blond head. "Don't be too sure, kiddo. She's a Hollywood brat in a Hollywood world. Kids are always listening, and they know more than we give 'em credit for. Hell, I knew Mr. Edmonds, the postman, was boffing the butcher's wife when I was a ten-year-old in Fresno. I used to climb up on a crate, peek in a window, and watch 'em go at it. They did it doggy-style." she said with relish. "Kids know everything."

"God, I hope not," Katherine said as she obsessively reached for the phone. "Back to work."

And gradually the memories began to fade. Work helped, and time helped, and the past didn't hurt so much when she didn't think about it, and for a long time Katherine Cole believed the part of her life that encompassed love was finished. Behind her. In front of her lay years of work supporting her children and building the Cole Agency. The agency and the children—Roz, Olivia, and baby Charles— were her future. They were Katherine's world, and they were her life. Leo, Richard, love . . . all in the past. Everything stood still as Katherine worked for the agency. It was all she had, all that stood between the Cole family and a world of emptiness and defeat.

By 1947 she was earning enough to put in a pool behind the house, just as Leo had suggested the night the Germans invaded Poland, as he smoked a cigar and talked about the coming of the war. In 1948 Katherine bought the building on the Sunset Strip and expanded her office. She took the downstairs floor, opened up the black marble reception area, and put in a waiting room. Not that she needed a waiting room, since the telephone was her weapon of choice, but it looked impressive as hell.

Roz was indifferent to the agency—she preferred flirting with the Ladd boys at birthday parties—but Olivia adored the office. Often she came in with Katherine on Saturday afternoon and went away with handfuls of paper clips and newly sharpened pencils and rubber bands stuffed in her toy-size purse. One afternoon she made a picture of an outsize flower by sticking gummed reinforcements onto a piece of yellow legal paper as she sat at the receptionist's desk.

"Mommy?" Olivia said as they walked to the car. "Can I come to live here? I love the Cole Agency."

Katherine laughed. "Good, darling. Good." And for months afterward, every Saturday afternoon Olivia asked Katherine if they could go to the Cole Agency, as she formally referred to it. Not "the office," not "the agency," but always "the Cole Agency."

By 1949 Katherine was a success. Her hard work had paid off, and her shrewd moves with her clients had made her more than a novelty, more than Leo Cole's widow who had opened some little office somewhere and whatever happened to her, poor thing? She was Katherine Cole, and she was the Cole Agency. Her Tiffany approach endeared her to her clients, and oddly enough, Madame Lermontov was her most conspicuous success. The prickly, irascible old Russian had become a beloved character actress, rather like Ethel Barrymore with a heavy accent, and she'd been twice nominated for an Oscar.

Madeline, too, was thriving. Her marriage to onetime child star Rick "Picky" Thomas had ended in a disastrous Vegas divorce. But by captalizing on her blond hair and lush figure, Katherine had turned Madeline into a comedy star at RKO. Madeline shrewdly bought the film rights to the Rosie Parker stories cranked out by an embittered Hollywood writer for a mildly racy men's magazine. The four Rosie Parker pictures, featuring Madeline as the not-so-dumb blond sexpot who always got her man, racked up impressive numbers at a declining box office, especially since the pictures were programmers and took little more than two weeks to shoot. Madeline Gerard looked great in Technicolor on a fifty-foot screen.

Katherine hadn't exactly lied to Madeline about Richard that day in the office, but she hadn't exactly told the truth, either. After the war ended, she had begun to see him again—up on screen, like the rest of America. The war had propelled his career in a new direction, and he'd transformed his screen image from cowboy star to fighting wartime hero. No longer the saddle pal, Richard Sears was now the brave pilot sacrificing himself for his men, the brave Seabee, the brave escapee from a German POW camp. Katherine saw them all.

And as Hollywood's nightlife resumed some of its prewar ebb and flow, Katherine and Richard began to run into each other at nightclubs and screenings and dinner parties. That was only natural, for Katherine was no longer the wife of a character actor but a powerful presence in her own right, and she maintained a high visibility on the A-list party circuit. But their relations remained formal, always correct, nothing more. Heads nodding, a brief "Hello, how are you?" exchanged at a bar or across a table at a dinner party. Nothing more. Even Maria Lashman Sears was correct to Katherine. After all, as the wife of a Hollywood legend and the daughter of a mogul, Maria had standards to uphold. A scuffle with her husband's long-ago mistress wouldn't be in good taste.

Then, at a party Edie Goetz gave to celebrate the purchase of a new Impressionist painting, Katherine literally bumped into Maria Lashman Sears coming out of the powder room. Maria was wearing a silver sequined gown and a necklace of pavé diamonds resembling a slim spray of leaves. Maria said hello with a gracious smile, then excused herself and sailed over to her husband's side, her jeweled fingers coiling possessively over his arm. Richard's tanned face was an implacable mask.

At home later, as Katherine undressed after the party, her thoughts turned to Richard. Perhaps I'm just not ready, she mused. I'm still young. Can I live alone forever? Do I want to live alone? She looked at her naked body in the mirror, shivered, and hurriedly pulled her pink silk nightgown over her head.

As she climbed into bed, Katherine knew that if there was going to be a man in her life, it would have to be Richard Sears. There had been Richard; there had been Leo. Now there was no one, for Katherine was incapable of loving again. She wasn't like Madeline, who hopped from one bed to another, allowing a train of lovers and husbands to parade across her body like a line of tanks across North Africa. Madeline didn't care; her face and body were currency, and she threw them down on the table without a thought. But Katherine had known only two men, and there would never be a third.

That brief encounter with Richard and Maria Sears at the Goetz party had pushed Richard into the forefront of Katherine's thoughts, and she began to fantasize about him at night. It was more than ten years since he'd confronted her on the set of *Gone With the Wind,* five years since Leo's death. And in those years, Katherine had lived alone, without a man, without even the thought of one. But now she thought about Richard. . . .

Once she saw him across the room at the Polo Lounge. He was having lunch with Darryl Zanuck. She was with Jack Warner. Both men waved, and Zanuck sent champagne to her table.

Then she saw Richard at a screening at Paramount. She was with Madeline. He was with Bob Taylor.

Finally, on December 31, 1949, they met at Sam Spiegel's New Year's Eve brawl.

At Christmas time Hollywood business always shut down, nightlife began, and there were many glittering parties during the holiday season. Dinners, parties, and galas abounded, but no event was quite so fevered, quite so loud, quite so mad as Sam Spiegel's annual New Year's Eve bash at his house on Crescent Drive.

Producer Sam Spiegel was known for his extravagant brilliance and the excesses of his personal life, and every year he produced his most miraculous event—a grand New Year's party featuring French champagne and American hot dogs—all on borrowed money. "To spiegel" was the Hollywood verb for "to con," "to cajole," "to persuade."

That evening, as Katherine dressed for the party, she felt particularly alive. The frightened girl Richard Sears had seduced—and he *had* seduced her despite his impressive claim of honesty—that girl was gone, and a new and powerful woman had taken her place. Idly Katherine wondered if she could seduce Richard Sears.

Why not? She was free, young, and vital, and her promise to Leo had been canceled by his death. She'd grieved, but now her grief was gone. She'd cried, but now her tears were dry. And there was a new element in the equation that hadn't existed before: Katherine Cole didn't want to marry again, and she didn't want to give herself away like a gaily wrapped Christmas present, either. She liked her life exactly as it was. She'd built her own business, she made her own decisions, she relied on her own instincts, and she liked it. No, she *loved* it, and she didn't want her energy to dissipate.

Katherine went to the party alone. She often went to big parties alone because she liked the feeling of independence. Besides, her solitude made her feel powerful. As she pushed her way through the crowd to Spiegel's side to say hello, she saw Richard sitting on the staircase, watching her.

Katherine smiled at him very deliberately, then turned away as Spiegel filled her glass with expensive French champagne. Then, all business, he took her arm and began to cajole her about his latest project. It was an impossible story about a missionary spinster, a lowlife, and a boat in Africa, and Katherine found it hard to pay attention. She could feel Richard watching her from his perch on the staircase, and a new and unknown erotic thrill rippled across her exposed skin.

She was wearing a slim black velvet cocktail dress with no back and a plunging neckline and her dazzling diamond necklace. She'd retrieved it from the jeweler as a Christmas present to herself, and it fanned out across her bosom like a gift.

Richard was still watching her. He was sitting with a group of people, but Maria was nowhere to be seen. It was New Year's Eve, and Katherine felt free, starry-eyed, and filled with anticipation. Teasingly, she lifted her wineglass in his direction, and just like that other night in his house at the top of the hill so many years ago, she knew she was ready for anything.

She turned away, deliberately ignoring Richard Sears, and drank more champagne. She watched one beautiful girl after another parade hopefully around the room in search of love and contacts, chatted with the many people she knew, listened to the drunken piano player tinkle out Cole Porter and Rodgers and Hart, sipped more champagne.

This time it would be different. The world had flipped over a thousand times in the past ten years, and Katherine Ransome was long gone, a pressed flower from an ancient prom pasted in an old scrapbook. Katherine Cole was a different woman.

He was still watching her—she knew it, she could feel it—and she was both amused and excited. She drank more champagne and as she moved through the crowded room chatting and laughing, she knew Richard Sears was sitting on the staircase, watching and waiting.

The party got louder as midnight approached. Nineteen forty-nine was over, and a new decade loomed ahead, a decade in which change would catapult half the people at Spiegel's party into the limelight and the other half into obscurity. Katherine drank another glass of champagne, and as she felt the ridged crystal with the tip of her tongue she saw Richard walking through the crowd to her side.

"Shall we celebrate the birth of the new decade together?" he shouted over the din. They were in the center of a mob, and yet they were completely alone, just like the night on the

170

set of *Gone With the Wind*. He was wearing a dinner jacket, but his tie was loose and his dress shirt unbuttoned. He was thinner now, and the lines around his dark blue eyes were sharper and more clearly defined. Movie stardom agreed with him.

Katherine looked up, laughing. "I was wondering what you'd say. 'Celebrate' sounds so formal."

"It's only part of what I have in mind."

"Oh? Tell me the rest, Richard. Go on, surprise me." She was drunk and sober at the same time, clear and cloudy, high and low. She was in control and eager to see how far she could push him. She leaned back against the bar and looked up at him as shrieks of laughter filled the room, punctuated by the gigantic splash of a human body cannonballing dead center into the swimming pool outside. The guests were taking to the water, and it would be only a matter of time before they took off their clothes.

"Sure," he said easily. "I'll tell you the rest. I've been planning this ever since I saw you at Edie Goetz's house. And tonight, when you came in alone, so beautiful, so . . . exposed," he said, running the tip of his finger across her naked shoulder, "well, I'll tell you, the rest is we'll drive over to the Beverly Wilshire . . ."

"Not the Beverly Hills?" She wanted to taunt him a little, goad him.

"The Beverly Wilshire's closer, and I don't want to waste time. We'll get a suite, go upstairs . . ."

"Without luggage?" she mocked. "What will Hernando Courtwright think?"

"I'll borrow a suitcase from Spiegel. Anyway, Hernando's discreet." Richard smiled, enjoying the game. "Then you and I will go upstairs in the elevator and I'll put my hands under that black velvet dress you're wearing and stroke your thighs."

"Sounds interesting. Go on. . . ."

"We'll walk down the hall and into the room, and while we're waiting for the boy to bring up the suitcase, I'll take your dress off. What are you wearing underneath?"

"Black lace teddy, stockings, garter belt . . ."

"You'll go into the bedroom and lie down on the bed until the boy leaves. Then I'll call downstairs for champagne, and while we're waiting, I'll take off the rest of your clothes. Except the necklace," he said, stroking the stones carefully with his finger. "I want you naked, but leave the necklace on. I'll kiss every part of your body. . . ."

"You sure you want to wait for the champagne?"

"I think so," he told her. "Yeah, I want to wait. I've waited all these years, and I want to wait another few hours, and I want you to wait, too. I want to peel your stockings off very slowly. I want to kiss the backs of your knees. I want you to drive me crazy. I want to lick champagne off your breasts. . . . Want to hear more?"

"Yes . . . Tell me more. . . ."

The party surged around them like a tide, people laughing and eating and drinking and shouting and screaming, and Richard and Katherine were pushed closer together in the isolation of the crowd. The New Year came amid more shrieks and yells and laughter. They were completely isolated, as alone together in the packed room as if they were on top of a mountain.

"You want to dance?"

"I can't hear the music."

"Who cares?" he said as he took her in his arms.

Later, in the darkened hotel room with the curtains throwing a slash of light across the bed, as Richard's mouth traveled languorously over the length of her body, as he thrust himself into her and her body arced in return in the thick silence of the room, as she waited for him on the edge of an uncharted continent, the diamonds around her neck no longer cold but hot and slick with the sheen of sweat, a faraway piece of her mind looked down at the two figures sprawled on the white sheets of the faceless hotel room, and that absolutely private place in her heart said yes, no matter what the consequences. Yes, yes, yes . . .

Chapter

11

A few months later Katherine and Madeline were in the office going over the contracts for the latest Rosie Parker picture.

"How's it going with Richard?" Madeline asked.

"It's fine," Katherine said, averting her eyes. She didn't talk about Richard to anyone but Madeline, because he was a secret she didn't want to share, nor did she talk about their passionate meetings at the cabin—he'd stubbornly refused to part with his old house in the hills. Privately Katherine suspected that he kept it as a reminder of the freedom he'd lost when he married Maria. Richard had been on location in France for the past month making a picture about the effects of postwar devastation on a wartime romance. They'd spoken on the phone once or twice, but the connections were bad and a long-distance call couldn't take the place of a long afternoon in bed.

"You like having an affair with him?" Madeline asked.

"Yes, it's perfect. It's funny, Mad," Katherine said slowly. "If you'd told me ten years ago I wouldn't want to marry

Richard, I would've spit in your eye. But I really don't. I don't want to be tied down. I don't want to be married."

"Ever?"

"Ever's a long time. Maybe. I don't know. I like being my own woman. I know the magazines say I should stay home and bake pies, but I like being an agent. I like being in control of my life. It's a new experience for me." She laughed, aware of the slightly defensive tone in her voice. "I like having a lover instead of a husband. I'm not worried about Richard; I'm worried about Roz," Katherine said. "She's so quiet. She's thinking all the time."

"I told you ages ago, she knows Richard is her father," Madeline said wisely. She squinted at the fine print in the contract. "This deal stinks."

"You're making more than ever before, so quit complaining. The hell she knows and keep your big mouth shut," Katherine said fiercely.

"Okay, okay, she may not know Richard is her father, but she's *got* to know you're having an affair with him. Look, she may not know *what* she knows, but she knows something, I'll stake my life on it."

Katherine didn't take this information well. The phone rang, and she picked it up, cradling it on her shoulder. "Tell him I'll call him back," she snapped. "I don't believe she knows," she said to Madeline.

"If that's your story, you stick to it. By the way, I saw this great gal today over at MGM." Madeline settled herself on the corner of Katherine's desk and straightened her seams. "Blond, big pouty lips, and a figure that, honey, I *swear* is gonna drive men wild."

"Hmmm?" Katherine sorted through the papers on her desk. Another damn letter from the school about Olivia. What the hell am I working for if she cuts class all the time? Her glasses slipped down on her nose, and she reflexively pushed them up. "What?"

"Blond. Divine. You ought to sign her up, except Johnny Hyde's got his love hooks sunk deep in her flesh."

"This year's blond, huh? What's her name?" She'd have to have a talk with Olivia. *Another* talk.

"Marilyn something-a-bunkus. Just finished a John Huston picture called *The Asphalt Jungle.*"

"Good title," Katherine said absently.

Madeline left, and Katherine made twenty or thirty calls before the end of the day, as the anxiety of the high-pressure negotiations for *Rosie Parker in Acapulco* crept across her skin like a spider. Though she'd talked proudly about controlling her own life, she wondered if she could manage to continue at this pace. Deep down, she felt as if she were on a treadmill running faster and faster. Was her life slipping by as she watched? Only yesterday she was eighteen years old and fresh out of the Northwest. Today she was a powerful agent. My God, how did it happen so fast?

The telephone never stopped ringing, and sometimes she imagined the damn thing was a rattlesnake on her desk, its sharp warning rattle startling her day and night, its coiled black cord poised and ready to strike. Faster, faster, faster! her mind cried as she raced to stay on the treadmill. Work harder, make up for lost time, lost life, make up for your sex, work harder than a man, and look good while you're doing it.

Her driving ambition fueled her ability to shift and change with the temper of the times while her instinct and will to win kept her ahead of the wolf pack. Instead of submitting to defeat, Katherine worked longer, harder hours than ever before. The Cole Agency and the success of her clients remained her primary concern. The agency was her fortress, an edifice of steel she'd created to protect her family.

Still, although everything she did was for her family, somehow she never had enough time for the children. Often, as she dressed to go to yet another party, Katherine felt guilty. The most important part of their lives was slipping away while she watched, helplessly chained to the telephone, to the Cole Agency, and to her desire to stave off an uncertain future.

As the aggressively pastel decade of the fifties began, times in Hollywood changed rapidly, and by 1952 the days of glittering premieres and sambas at the Troc were timeworn memories. The war was over, the salad days of the picture business were long gone, and some people thought the fun was gone too, especially when the House Un-American Activities Committee began to cast its jaundiced eye over the sunny landscape of Los Angeles. The making of motion pictures was becoming just another big business, just another industry. But to Hollywood folks it was still *the* Industry, even though many of those who'd been power brokers in Hollywood since the days of silents didn't understand the changes abounding in their now thriving empire. Mayer and Goldwyn and Zanuck and Cohn were simply running out of gas, and the old moguls were dying off, giving up, or giving in.

But not all the old-timers had disappeared. Though the movie business was in a state of flux, Edgar Lashman was thriving. He'd enlarged his small studio into one of the most powerful and one of the last under the control of its founder, primarily because he didn't fight the future. The little box with the grainy black-and-white images creeping into the living rooms of America was changing the face of Hollywood, and Edgar Lashman knew it. To combat this new threat, Lashman became the first producer to film stories that couldn't be seen on TV, garish Technicolor Roman epics and low-budget special-effects monster movies.

Meanwhile, Maria Lashman Sears retained her position as a prominent social power broker and a member of Hollywood royalty. She collected the works of contemporary painters and espoused fashionable causes, although her politics, like her father's, remained impeccably Republican. The Swans Ball and the girls in their white costumes floated on unaware, in suspended animation like Sleeping Beauty. Maria's photograph was often seen in the society pages of the *L.A. Times,* flanked by her son and daughter or by newly important designers and decorators as she pursued her many charity interests. By now she was a stalwart society lieutenant to President Emeritus Mary Pickford and added the Lashman Wing to the Motion Picture Country Hospital.

Ever since the formation of the Cole Agency, Madame Lermontov had continued to send Katherine talented hopefuls from her acting classes, though Katherine usually accepted them purely as a favor to Madame. But for some time, Madame had pestered her about a young man she claimed was going to be a star despite his obvious eccentricities. "He is impossible. So full of himself. He thinks he is the greatest actor since Olivier," Madame announced. "Unfortunately he is right."

Finally Katherine met with Simon Wyler, and at first she thought he was an egotistical monster. He certainly wasn't a sleek product destined for the studio star factory. He was scruffy, he mumbled, he slouched, and she thought he was altogether too tough to handle until she saw him at Madame's workshop.

Simon Wyler was reading *Hamlet* from an open script. "To be or not to be," he spat out, peering over his horn-rimmed glasses at his audience, one bare foot up on a three-legged stool. "That is the question."

It was the most famous question in literature, and in Simon Wyler's mouth it became a sneering joke. The effect was powerful, electric, and Katherine instinctively knew Madame was right: Simon Wyler was a rare find. He had run away from his home in Ohio, unable to live with his alcoholic mother after his father died on the beach at Normandy during the war. He was still a child, unformed and raw, but Katherine agreed to represent him because he was too talented to ignore.

Simon was a problem from the beginning. He irritated casting directors and mumbled his way through auditions. He got a few small parts and invariably caused tension on the set. He was late, he was autocratic, he was grandiose. And he had an odd habit that bothered everyone he met.

"What's with the notebooks?" a casting director asked Katherine nervously. "My secretary says he sits in the waiting room looking around my office and scribbling things down. I get the feeling he's making notes on me. What is this guy, a writer or an actor? Does he work for that scum rag *Confidential?*"

A year later Katherine was still having trouble with Simon Wyler. Despite his enormous talent, his grating personality caused problems on every job he got, and he spent his time scribbling wildly in his big blue notebooks when he should have been going to parties and getting his face seen around town. Half the time he couldn't pay his rent, so he'd moved into the pool house that Katherine recently installed at the end of the garden.

But the girls adored him, and Roz, now sixteen, had a crush on him. . . .

"Stuff it, Cole."

"You stuff it, Sears. Snitchy Sears. Snitchy Bitchy Sears. No one's talking to you, and no one ever will." Roz Cole rolled the words lovingly in her mouth, enjoying her moment of triumph. She stuck out her tongue childishly at Linda Sears, then gave her the finger and poked her in the stomach. Not too hard, but hard enough to hurt.

Linda, who had her mother's thick black cap of curls and her father's startling cobalt blue eyes, began to cry.

"Oh, shut up, snitchy bitch. I didn't hurt you," Rosalind said as she grabbed her lunch and walked across the green grass toward the back entrance of the Miss Lilys' School. "Stinkface!" she called over her shoulder as she went inside the big clapboard house. Even in the California heat the building was cool and dark, and Roz loved the feel of the damp, dark air on her skin after the blaze of sun outside.

The Miss Lilys' School was a huge Victorian pile on Hollywood Boulevard, and by 1953 it looked exceptionally out of place on the street, which was unraveling around the edges. But Miss Susan Lily and Miss Jane Lily didn't care. They'd hung on to the big house for over forty years, and they had no intention of giving in now. Not when the Miss

Lilys' School was the top-ranked private high school in Los Angeles, consistently attended by wave after wave of wealthy Hollywood kids whose generous parents made it all possible. So the old house remained, a testament to the golden past of the Golden State.

The Miss Lilys were a pair of California oddities, unlikely originals in the nouveau glitz and glamour beginning to seep in around them. They'd been born in Los Angeles in 1888 in the big bedroom they now shared upstairs, and by the fifties they'd increased the Lily family's forgotten splendor by their own hard work. The huge moss green mansion their father built was a gingerbread masterpiece of the past, replete with leaded stained-glass windows, turrets and cupolas, ornamental moldings, and an unaccountable widow's walk borrowed from New England.

When their father died in 1923 and left the girls with nothing but the house, they shrewdly managed to hang on to the old pile by turning it into a fancy day school for the children of Hollywood's new elite, the movie people. The DeMilles sent their children to Susan and Jane Lily, and so did the Mayers and the Schulbergs. Maria Lashman Sears had gone there as a girl, along with the rest of Hollywood's royal offspring.

Rosalind and Olivia Cole went to the Miss Lilys', and they were the acknowledged leaders of the school's troublemakers. Roz was smart, and at sixteen she was growing wild, bored with the daily life of books and studies and Mrs. Gebhardt's tender care. She was interested in boys, in sneaking a smoke in the garden shed and tasting the scotch her mother kept in the crystal decanter on the sideboard. Adult life loomed ahead of her like a busy highway, and Roz Cole was fascinated by the prospect of her own future.

Usually she led and Olivia followed, but this time the crime they committed was masterminded by Olivia. One afternoon during study hall, they slipped upstairs to the Miss Lilys' private apartment where they smeared great gloppy hearts on the bathroom mirrors with lurid red lipstick and short-sheeted the prim twin beds. Worst of all, they left a dead lizard with a tiny red bow around its desiccated neck on each pillow.

Miss Susan, who was prone to hysteria, demanded that they burn the bedding, but Miss Jane, who was tougher, took a watch-and-wait attitude. Though she had her suspicions, the crime went unpunished for several weeks because nothing could be proved.

It looked as if the Cole girls would escape until Linda Sears, prompted by gnawing jealousy and helpless anger, did the unforgivable: Linda Sears snitched.

Linda was as charming and petite as her mother, and she didn't understand why she wasn't the leader of the Miss Lilys' girls. She was pretty, she was smart, her mother was the daughter of a powerful studio head, and most important, her father was the biggest box office draw in the United States, neck and neck with Clark Gable one year and with Gary Cooper the next. Gable was the King, John Wayne was the Duke, but Richard Sears was the Prince. Prince Richard. Salesgirls swooned as his dark eyes burned a hole through the pages of their movie magazines and into their lonely hearts. The combination of his dark blue eyes and his broken nose gave Richard Sears a cocky, know-it-all panache on-screen, and throughout her childhood his adoring daughter had basked in her father's luminous success. Prince Richard, the Star.

So why wasn't Linda Sears popular? Why did she always wonder if the other kids would show up for her birthday party? Why was she always anxious about her place in the hierarchy of Hollywood brats? Stinky Sears, Roz Cole called her to her face. Stinky Sears and now, worse, Snitchy Bitchy Sears.

Linda Sears couldn't help herself. Like her father, she was ambitious, and like her mother, she had a cunning streak of cruelty concealed beneath her polished exterior, and her helpless resentment of Roz Cole persuaded her to report the episode of the dead lizards, the short-sheeted beds, and the smeared hearts to Miss Jane.

Miss Jane instantly called Katherine Cole and reported the heinous crime and the damage caused by her errant daughter. Katherine apologized abjectly, promised a large donation to the building fund, and swore that Roz would be confined to room at home for a month. Roz was lectured and threatened with expulsion and then made to scrub the Miss Lilys' bathroom with Lysol until it shone, even though the gloppy hearts had been washed away weeks ago. At home, Roz was lectured again about setting a good example for her little sister. She took it with courage and didn't squeal on Olivia.

But at the school, Linda Sears paid the highest price of all. She was blackballed by the other girls for having committed the worst possible schoolyard crime, snitching. And so her position was worse than ever. Linda was more isolated and more confused, and she still didn't quite understand why she wasn't loved.

That night, as Katherine was dressing for the evening, she lectured Roz one more time. "What's the matter with you, Rozzie?" she asked impatiently as she clipped on her diamond earrings and blotted her lipstick. "You're supposed to set a good example for Olivia. You're older. You're the big sister."

"Yes, Mother." Roz scuffed the blue Chinese rug by Katherine's dressing table with her foot. "Where're you going?"

"I'm taking a client to dinner, and then there's a screening at Metro."

"What picture?"

"No Can Do. It's Richard Sears's latest," Katherine said without missing a beat. Was it her imagination or did Roz ask her more questions about Richard Sears's movies than about, say, Bogart's? She kept her eyes on her reflection in the mirror.

"Richard Sears, huh? What's it about?"

Sometimes Katherine thought Roz knew she was sleeping with Richard Sears, but how could she? They were *so* careful. They never exchanged furtive glances at parties, never touched hands accidentally over the buffet at the Beverly Hills. Madeline knew, and Mrs. Gebhardt knew, although she didn't admit it, but no one else knew. Katherine was sure of it.

For three years, ever since the New Year's Eve party at Sam Spiegel's, she and Richard had stolen time together. In between meetings and screenings and months on foreign locations, Katherine Cole and Richard Sears spent every minute they could manage wrapped in damp sheets, the late sun casting a diffused glow across the room, as if the cameraman had coated the lens with a thin film of Vaseline to create a softened effect. Von Sternberg had shot Dietrich through lace, and that was what the long, tangled afternoons felt like to Katherine. Lace and hot sheets.

But no one knew. She was sure of it. So why did she wonder about Roz?

"What's the picture about?" Roz said again.

"It's a romantic comedy, and don't change the subject. You disappoint me, Rozzie."

Big deal, orange peel, Roz thought bitterly as she worked a long blue thread out of the rug with her toe. So what, chicken butt? You don't care about me. You're always out. She nodded and tried to look ashamed of herself, but she wasn't ashamed at all. At sixteen Roz was smart, observant, and curious. Everybody from Beverly Hills to Bel-Air to Brentwood knew her mother had been sleeping with Richard Sears for centuries. That was why Snitchy Bitchy Sears had ratted on her. All the kids at school knew who their parents were sleeping with, how their careers were going, who was on the up-o-later, and who was taking the long cold haul on the down. People in the movie colony were constantly marrying and divorcing and dating or screwing, and the kids knew more than Hedda or Louella, and they knew it first. Olivia, in particular, was always aware of the latest gossip around town, and she reveled in surprising her enemies at school with the latest news of their parents' failures or successes.

"I'm sorry," Roz said contritely as she left the room. She stuck out her tongue at her mother's back.

"And remember," Katherine called. "You're grounded for a month."

Slowly Roz went down the hall to her room. Most of the time she hated her mother. All of the time she wondered why Daddy had to die. Why Daddy? Her mother spent her life at the precious Cole Agency, and Roz knew Katherine loved the agency and the glittering whirl of parties and movies and dinners far more than she loved her or Olivia or stupid Charles, who was only a shrimp and didn't count anyway.

She took Leo's picture in its silver frame off the shelf and put her little finger on Leo's mouth in the secret kiss she shared with the photograph when no one else was around.

"Daddy, why are you dead?" she asked him softly. When she talked to Leo she felt like a little girl again. She didn't want him to be dead even though the Leo Cole who lived in her memory was far more perfect than the real Leo had been.

Leo Cole watched the progress of her life, comforting her from his home in the silver frame. It was a studio portrait taken one Saturday afternoon by his friend George Hurrell, and as a handsome, quizzical Leo in evening clothes looked out on Rosalind, the smoke from his cigar cast a dim screen behind his head. The faint curtain of smoke put him in soft focus, and sometimes she imagined he was looking at her with a dreamy, faraway look in his dark eyes.

At night she talked to Leo in a secret language, asking his advice and telling him secrets. She knew it was childish. She knew she was too old to talk to a photograph, but these shadowy conversations were an old habit she didn't want to break, because Leo—the Leo who lived in the silver frame —was her link to a secure past, a fantasy childhood when her life was safe and warm, as whole and complete as an egg. A life filled with parties and ponies and ice-cream sundaes and bound on every side by the unbroken security of a daddy who worked and a mommy who didn't. Now her life without him was unsure. Her mother spent all of her time chasing stars, building up the precious Cole Agency, and Katherine loved the Cole Agency more than she loved Rosalind. Olivia said that was a crock, but Olly was only a kid. What did she know about real life?

All Roz knew was that Katherine was never at home. She was always going out to some stupid party or other. Her nails were always wet, and her face was always primed with a coat of perfect makeup, so she couldn't be touched. In the hallway the perfume from her fur coat lingered long after her car had roared out of the driveway. Roz heard the stinging crunch of tires on gravel that meant Katherine was gone for the evening. The sound was indelibly impressed on her mind.

Roz put Leo's picture back on the shelf and turned out the lights. The best thing about her room was the view from the window seat where she could lie down and look out as the stars above took flight across the dark, pathless California sky.

She woke up an hour later, pulled on a shirt and loose shorts, and went downstairs for a glass of milk. The big house was quiet. Olivia was in her room, Charles was in his, and though the kitchen was dark there was a slice of light shining under Mrs. G.'s door. The faint sound of gospel music on the radio echoed into the dark kitchen, and Roz felt the familiar sweep of childhood comfort flooding over her.

She got her milk, and as she stood at the sink dipping a fudge brownie into cold milk she suddenly saw the light from the pool house webbing across the backyard. Simon Wyler. Roz finished her milk and quietly put the glass in the sink.

Simon Wyler had been living in the pool house for a year, off and on, and Rosalind had watched him with interest. Once she'd waylaid him in the garden, thrown her arms around him, and kissed him on the mouth. Then she ran away, embarrassed and afraid he'd tell her mother, but he didn't. When she thought about it afterward, she realized Simon had kissed her back and pressed his body into hers. He had kissed her back. *She* was the one who ran away.

Simon was difficult and moody, tall and thin with sandy hair and a malleable face. No matter how closely she studied him, she didn't know exactly what he looked like. He was changeable, his thoughts were reflected on his face, he was disconcerting, often brutally frank, and people shied away from him. Could he be trusted? Was he what he said he was? Who he said he was? He was opaque. Roz had overheard Katherine saying his untrustworthiness was a big part of the reason he hadn't been successful as an actor. There was something secretive about Simon Wyler, but it was just that compelling secret that inevitably pulled Roz Cole in his direction.

Thoughtfully, Roz washed her mouth out with water and went quickly out the back door and through the dark yard to the pool house. The night air was soft on her skin, and her bare feet were cold on the flagstones, watered that afternoon by the gardeners.

She went around the side of the pool house and looked in the window, shrouded partially by a ragged banana plant. Simon had his shirt off and was sitting cross-legged on the bed, writing in one of the big blue cloth-bound record books he was never without.

She wondered what he wrote about. She'd asked him once, and he'd said he was just making notes. Very offhand, very casual. She watched him for a few minutes more, single-minded, completely absorbed, his back curved over his work like a tailor. He was very pale, with his sandy hair and untanned skin.

Roz ran her hands over her bare arms, and as she stood at the window spying on the half-naked man, she realized a new emotion was rising inside her. She hesitated, wondering if she was going to make a fool of herself. But, she thought with a smile, she could always pretend to be a child.

Rosalind had learned about sex three years ago when she found a sex manual her mother had hidden on the top shelf in the library. Roz had read it with interest, avidly, over and over, though a lot of it was confusing and icky. It was clinical but explicit, with line drawings of people's insides and a boring discussion of penetration and ejaculation. She wondered if it hurt to be penetrated, but the book didn't say. Apparently there was blood the first time, which didn't sound like any fun at all. The part about the blood put her off. Blood usually hurt, her period hurt, but she was sixteen and penetration seemed inevitable. Linda Sears claimed she'd let one of the Royce boys put his finger in her, but Linda lied all the time. Roz Cole wasn't about to let some schoolboy do any penetrating, let alone draw blood. No, it would happen with someone older, someone who knew what he was doing. With Simon Wyler.

Roz was tired of waiting for her life to begin, tired of being a child. Her childhood had ended when Leo died, and she was ready to cross the next bridge. Now, as she stood at the door, hand upraised, fingers about to fall on wood, the moment solidified in her mind.

She knocked and went in without waiting for Simon to answer. The pool house was a tiny room meant for changing clothes, but over the past year Simon Wyler had turned it into his own private camp. His clothes hung on the wooden pegs lining one side of the room, and piles of books were everywhere. The room was flooded with yellow light from the brass gooseneck lamp on the floor next to the single bed shoved up against one corner.

He didn't look up. "What's the matter, brat? Can't sleep?"

"Bored."

"You're too young to be bored," he said. He kept on writing.

Roz wandered over and sat down on the end of the bed. "No such thing as too young," she said deliberately.

Simon stopped writing and whistled soundlessly between his teeth as he closed the blue book and carefully capped his pen. He always wrote with a thick-nibbed fountain pen and black ink. "What does that mean, brat?"

"Means I'm bored, is what it means." She pulled back a little. She wanted to say, "It means I want you to take me to bed with you, get rid of this wall I have inside me that I don't want, this childish thing holding me back from the beginning of my real life." But she couldn't say it until she was sure he'd do it. "What are you writing all the time, anyway?" Now she sounded like a petulant child, not the woman she wanted to be.

"Just keeping notes."

"I thought you were an actor, not a writer."

"I'm a double threat. You're the first one to find out." Simon smiled and lay back on the bed, hands clasped behind his head. "Why are you here, brat?"

"Roz, or Rosalind, okay?" She avoided his question.

"Okay. Roz, then. You want to go to bed with me, is that it?" His voice was gentle. He wasn't taunting or mocking her.

"No." She knew she was turning red; she could feel the heat flooding across her neck. "Mom turns red, too, she thought irrelevantly. "Yes," she blurted out. "With somebody. Simon, I'm tired of being me. I want to be somebody else."

He laughed. "You think screwing does that?"

"I don't know. Something must."

He trailed his bare foot along her outstretched legs, skin dragging on skin. "Is that why you kissed me?"

"Maybe." Help me, she thought. Help me.

"Come up here," he said. He didn't move, simply lay still with his hands behind his head.

She crawled up next to him on the bed. Suddenly the smell of his bare skin frightened her, and a flood of panic washed over her as quick and hot as the blush that had spread through her a minute ago.

"Touch me," he said. "Run your hands over me. See if you want to do more."

She giggled nervously. "Is this a science experiment?"

"Yeah, kind of. Go ahead. See if you like it. I won't move."

She giggled again. "Promise you'll be my prisoner?"

"Always. I promise. Always."

Very tentatively she ran her hand over his chest, covered with a light mat of blond hair. He lay quietly, watching her as she explored his chest, his arms, feeling the length of his neck. As she trailed her hand over him, Roz felt a new sense of power and put both hands on him, beginning to move in a slow, teasing circle. His nipples hardened under her touch, and he smiled.

"Like it?" he asked.

"I think I do," she said slowly. "You won't move?"

"Promise." His skin was warm, soft, yet he was hard underneath. "Want to kiss me?"

She bent toward him, but he shook his head slightly. "Not my mouth. Not yet. Kiss my body first. Take it slow, okay?"

"Okay. Show me. Tell me . . ." She sank down and ran her mouth over him. She felt her heart beating between her legs as she took his hardened nipple in her mouth and licked it. "Do boys . . . Do you like that?" she asked as she lifted her head.

"Yes, I like it. Go on. Do it again. No. Take your shirt off first so I can see you a little. If you want to. Roz, are you sure you want to?"

"I want to." She crouched over him on the narrow bed and pulled off her shirt. She wasn't wearing a bra. Her breasts were small and firm, and bras were ugly and itchy, so most of the time she didn't wear one.

His eyes widened briefly as he looked at her bare breasts. "Christ, Roz, how old are you?"

"Sixteen."

Simon moaned softly. "I thought you were older. I could go to jail for this."

"Why?" She got on top of him, straddling him. "I want you to do it, Simon. Really." She bent down and rubbed her breasts over his bare chest, then buried her mouth in his neck. "I want it, Simon. I want *you*, not some jerk in the backseat of his daddy's Jag. I know all about it, Simon, really I do, and I want it to be nice. I want it to be something special." She stretched out on top of him, fitting her body to his. She felt how hard he was, and for the first time in her life, Roz Cole felt the triumphant thrill of the power that women had over men. He *was* her prisoner. This grown man was hers and hers alone. She controlled him now, completely.

He groaned, pushed her up, and cupped her breasts in his hands. "Sixteen. Jesus H. Christ."

"How old are you?" she asked, arching her back a little so he could see how beautiful she was.

"Twenty-three."

"Seven years." She laughed. "Big deal, orange peel." She sank down again, kissing him, and he wrapped his arms around her and rolled her over, one hand slipping inside her loose camp shorts, briefly caressing her between her legs.

His probing fingers startled her, but she reached down and unfastened her shorts and arched so he could slide them off. He got on top of her, one hand lifting her up and spreading her legs open.

"Put your hand on me," he said, his voice hoarse and insistent, his skin damp with sweat. "Look."

Tentatively, she reached down and took him in her hand. She was astonished that his . . . thing—*penis* was a dopey word—was so big. It didn't look like the line drawings in the sex book, and it didn't look like the little curlicue worms she'd eyed at the County Art Museum. It was too big to go inside her.

"Don't worry," he told her, his voice muffled in her neck. "It'll be all right." He began to spread her open, working his way inside.

Roz felt him going deeper and deeper and heard her own breath coming faster and faster. Something was happening, something new and unknown, an explosion of emotion she hadn't anticipated, and as she wrapped her arms and legs around Simon Wyler, as he bore down into her and she arched up to meet him, sensation and joyous feeling overwhelmed her. Somewhere far away Rosalind Cole heard an airplane flying over the hills, and then she heard herself laughing and she realized she'd made a good choice. She was something, all right. Something, something, something . . .

At midnight Richard Sears stalked into Musso and Frank's and grabbed a stool at the bar. It was years since he'd been in the joint, and he went there now because he felt like hell and Musso's was the perfect place to relive old disasters.

He sat at the bar, nursed a J&B and thought moodily about the night he'd sat in this same bar and told Leo that Katherine was pregnant and he wasn't going to marry her; he was going to marry Maria Lashman. Disaster all around.

As he stared into the mirrored backbar he realized he'd been married to Maria for years and he still thought of her, of his wife, as Maria Lashman. They had two children, houses and cars and bank accounts in common, and in the back of his mind she was still Maria Lashman, not Maria Sears. "Crap," he said aloud as he signaled the bartender for another drink.

His latest picture, *No Can Do,* was a disaster. He could see the reviews already: "Richard Sears proves he *No Can Do.*" The audience was painfully silent, burping out little heh-heh-hehs when there should have been uproarious laughter. His costar, Trish Wilman, looked so young; he looked so old. The whole thing was a goddamn disaster.

Years of marriage and the Lashmans, father and daughter, were choking his life away. Edgar the Magnificent made a fortune on Richard, loaning him out to other studios, collecting fat fees and skimming the cream right off the top, dangling the promise of more money in front of his eyes. Maria spent as if she'd turned on the tap for a long, hot shower and money flowed out and swirled down the drain. He should have married Katherine and been his own man. The second J&B was gone, so he had another. Maria and her charity broads having tea, the kids, his mother and sisters whining for money . . . His whole life was a goddamn disaster.

On that long-ago night with Leo, he'd thought it would be

simple. He could handle marriage to Maria. He thought his sisters, Lila and Claire, would marry, settle down with some East Coast blue bloods and breed chinless children and he'd never see them again. Instead, the silly bitches kept getting divorced and inevitably turned up at his house, giggling with Maria and Linda. Disaster. His fans, more silly bitches, wrote sad little notes saying how much they liked his old pictures and the old days, complaining ever so gently that his movies weren't as good as they used to be. Jesus, since the war, nothing was!

Nothing would ever be the same again. Couldn't they see that? Of *course* he wasn't the same, and the world wasn't the same. Did they expect the Arizona Kid to ride into the sunset forever? Katherine . . . Christ, why hadn't he married her when he had the chance? And why had Leo died? But this latest picture was no good—that was clear.

"Hey, fella." A light hand tapped him on the shoulder. Richard spun around, half expecting to see Leo, and upset the tag end of his drink. The watery ice cubes clipped over the bar like wet hooves, and the bartender hurriedly wiped up the little pool of scotch.

It was Dick Powell.

Richard was relieved. At least it was a friend, not an autograph hound. "Jesus, Dick, good to see you. Take a pew."

"Evening, Mr. Powell, what's yours?" the bartender said as he slid a fresh drink in front of Richard.

"Scotch. Just a short one, Richard. June's due in any minute. How's the new picture?" Powell said as he sat down.

"Stinks, Dick. But thanks for asking."

"Another one'll come along." Powell laughed as he reached into his pocket and pulled out his pipe. "Just like waves at Malibu."

"I wonder."

Powell eyed Sears and tapped his pipe softly against the ashtray. "Feeling your age, are you, fella?" he asked.

Richard started to say "No, I'm great, the picture's great, Maria's great, the whole damn world's great," but he didn't feel like playing the scene that way. He felt like playing it straight. "Something like that," he said, his voice tight.

"I'm getting into TV. I'm tired of being a studio dog who barks every time somebody jerks my leash," Powell said easily. "And I want to direct. That's where the future is. Look, Richard, this business is about change. You think I'd still be a star if I'd kept going as a hoofer?" Softly, he hummed a few bars of "42nd Street," then ran his hand through his hair. "This widow's peak ain't gonna last forever. Try TV. There's room for all of us."

"Christ, Dick. That little box?" Richard was surprised. TV? It had never occurred to him. Nobody took TV seriously. It was for kids. Puppet shows and clowns.

"Know so, pal. Since the war, people have been staying home. Everybody's got kids and cars and lawns to mow. Ain't got time for three, four movies a week to get 'em away from the tenement. Don't need to go up into the balcony to neck with the girlfriend. Nowadays the girlfriend's the wife, and they've all got homes of their own."

Instinctively, Richard knew Powell was right, but he didn't want him to be right. "But TV's so . . ." Richard paused, thinking of his face filling the screen, his horse riding into the camera in a cloud of dust, his plane spitting bullets straight at the audience. He thought about Technicolor and thunderous music. Could the tiny TV screen recreate his gigantic moments of glory or would he be reduced to a midget version of himself? "TV's so goddamn small!" he said angrily.

Powell laughed as he drained his drink. "World's shrinking, fella. Get used to it. There's June. I gotta go."

"I've got to do something," Richard said as they lay in their tangled bed at the cabin the next afternoon. "I've got to get in on TV before the big guns swallow up the whole damn pie and there's nothing left but burnt crust."

Katherine rolled toward him. "Being a movie star isn't enough for you? Do you have to have everything?" she teased, tracing her finger down his side.

"Tickles," he said absently. "Sure, I like being a movie star, but nothing lasts forever. This picture stinks."

"It's not that bad—" she began.

"It stinks and we both know it," he said impatiently. "I'm not a kid anymore, Red. Times have changed, audiences have changed, everything's changed. I want to start my own production company and make product for TV."

A little chill of fear ran across her back like a spider. The past few years had been wonderful—meeting in hotels, quickly embracing in parking lots, holding hands like kids at out-of-the-way mom-and-pop cafés stuck out at the ends of the earth where no one would ever see them. Wonderful, fun, exciting, but nothing could last forever, right? Especially with Richard Sears . . . "But you're a movie star," she hedged. "If people see you every week in their living rooms will they pay to see you in a theater?"

"Why buy the cow if the milk is free?" Richard laughed, then turned serious. "I think they will, and so does Dick Powell. I ran into him last night at Musso's, and he's got the first dime he ever made. He gave me the idea."

"He's a very smart businessman," Katherine said slowly. "How much would you need?"

Richard rolled out of bed and went into the bathroom, his hips still slim, his body the same soft tan all over. "That's always the problem, isn't it? A lot."

"Where would you get it?" she called. Money again. Always money. Yet he was so beautiful! Odd, to think of a man as beautiful . . .

"Bank. Maybe." His voice was muffled by the sound of running water.

"I could invest something," she called.

Richard stuck his head around the corner. "A: not a chance. B: you ain't got enough. And C: pull that sheet down so I can have a good look at you."

She pulled it down very slowly, laughing as she exposed herself to him. It was strange, the way their relationship had changed. Now that she had nothing to lose, she felt comfortable and free with Richard, free to make no demands and expect no rules. An affair was perfect if you didn't dream of marriage. Love and fun and sex all rolled into one big beautiful ball, without a long-term commitment.

Richard dropped his towel, came over to the bed, and began to caress her. Just the thing . . . Her mind wandered as he stroked and kissed her. Just what I want. It suits me, Katherine thought, these secret meetings, casual love in dark corners. And maybe it *will* go on forever. . . .

The only problem was, Richard Sears couldn't raise a dime. All of a sudden an iron hand clamped down over Hollywood and began hammering Richard into the ground. He went to the bank. He went to the lawyers. He went back to the bank. He would do a western, tried and true, starring himself, tried and true. Surely . . . But no.

All of the bankers listened politely, smiled, shifted uncomfortably in their leather chairs, and said they were sorry. He was a great star, much loved by the American public, and the fact that his last few pictures hadn't done well meant absolutely nothing. Nothing at all. He'd be back on top in no time. There was nothing to worry about. The problem, they explained—oh, so gently—was that he didn't have a track record in business. All these years he'd paid no attention to his investments, hadn't bought real estate like Joel McCrea or art like Eddie Robinson. He had nothing to show for his years of stardom but strips of celluloid. And without the foundation of business experience his sudden venture into TV was just too risky for a major investment.

Katherine kept her mouth shut and found him a blacklisted writer who worked cheap and fast and who cranked out a couple of terrific sales synopses, but the rebuffs keep coming, and Richard was getting angry and desperate. The onetime rich kid turned movie star couldn't understand the word *no*. Richard Sears believed that if he planned and schemed and worked like a dog he could reach out and grab what he wanted. This was America, after all. The world is yours. Take what you've earned.

"I can lend you a piece if I take a second mortgage on the

office building," she said finally. They were lying in bed, and the warm scent of summer blanketed the room with hot, thick air. "And maybe we can pry some dough out of Madeline."

"Katherine, I told you before, that's not the way I want it. It's my way or nothing at all," Richard said sharply.

"Just like always."

"Dammit, the Cole Agency is yours, Red. For you and your children. You think I'd take a piece of that?"

"Rosalind is yours too, Richard."

"No, she isn't," he said quietly. "I have no right to Roz. She belongs to Leo and she always will. He loved her and cared for her and nurtured her as best he could. I ran out on her and on you, too."

"Let it go, darling. It's all in the past."

Restless, Richard got out of bed and groped on the dresser for his cigarettes. "Damn Maria, she's eaten up my life," he said bitterly. "No, that's crap. I've done it to myself." The match scraped as he looked back at Katherine, his naked body outlined in the sunlight streaming through the window. "I had a chance with you and didn't take it. Leo Cole was always the better man, Katherine," he said lightly. "I've never given you a damn thing, and I won't take any more from you. Let me put it this way: I'll take your love but not your money."

"Beggars can't buy biscuits, my love. Look, I hesitated to say this before, but there's a reason you can't get financing and I want to know what it is. I know a guy, I'll call him."

Richard looked at her in astonishment. "What the hell do you mean, you know a guy? How the hell do *you* know a guy, Katherine?"

"I have clients, they have problems. They want divorces, they want their wives or husbands followed. Simple. I know a guy who follows people for a living. It's okay, darling, believe me. I've used him before."

Richard shook his head and laughed as he climbed back into bed beside her. "Boy, have *you* changed!"

As soon as she got into the office the next morning she

phoned Frank Perrow, who ran a modest detective agency, and explained the problem. Four hours later Perrow called her back with an answer. "Why didn't you call me right off?" he said in his thick Brooklyn accent. "Coulda saved you a lotta grief."

"What's going on, Frank?"

"Katherine, these days life is complicated. You want the scoop on how come Richard Sears can't raise the dough? You won't like it," Frank Perrow said slowly.

The fear she'd felt the other day had grown like a tumor. "Tell me," she said.

"Two words: Edgar Lashman. He doesn't want Sears to get away from him, and he's let it be known, very politely, that any banker who loans Sears money will no longer be welcome at Lashman Films. That's it, straight and simple."

"Straight and simple, huh? Thanks, Frank. I'll send you a check," Katherine said as she hung up. Of course. I should have known. Edgar Lashman . . .

Chapter

12

Like many movie moguls, Edgar Lashman was a self-made man. He left high school at fourteen to work in an iron foundry, later became a junk dealer, and now he was the head of his own motion picture studio. He'd sandblasted his rough edges, amassed an art collection second only to Norton Simon's, and filled his home with French and English antiques.

Richard Sears had known Edgar Lashman for over fifteen years, and though they'd never liked each other, Richard respected Lashman for his tough, combative nature and his unyielding, rock-hard will to win. Lashman had a ferocious ability to bend life to his own advantage, yet Richard was always on edge in his presence because he knew Lashman didn't trust him. The house was a wedding gift from Lashman, and it was in Maria's name. Their expensive furniture and the contemporary paintings Maria collected had been doled out as birthday gifts. Lashman provided the income Maria spent on her lavish wardrobe, and even the children's large trust funds were fueled by Edgar Lashman's choice of stocks and bonds. Lashman's hold over his daughter and her family grew tighter every year, and Richard could do nothing but finance the staggering expenses of his family's lavish life-style. He'd always suspected the old mogul would never loosen his iron grip, and Lashman's refusal to allow him to raise money for his company proved it.

As Richard walked up the broad steps toward Lashman's front door he considered his peculiar position of husband-as-gigolo, wondering what Byzantine maze of reasoning Edgar Lashman was about to reveal. The old mogul's motives inevitably ran deeper than they appeared. Was there a sadistic crimp in Lashman's nature that enjoyed the spectacle of Richard Sears, the faded aristocrat, bending his knee in the presence of the patriarch?

The butler showed him into the library immediately. Lashman was seated at his walnut desk, reading a script in a pool of golden light cast by a pair of black marble lamps. On the wall behind him was a jewellike collection of drawings: a Picasso, a Bonnard nude, a van Dongen sketch, a Forain pastel of a woman in black. The assortment of breasts and eyes stared out from the wall like Lashman's guardians.

Lashman looked up as Richard came in and motioned to the armchair across from his desk. "That'll be all, Turner. I'll give Mr. Sears a drink if he wants one."

The butler nodded, closing the library door softly as he disappeared.

"Nothing to drink, Edgar."

"Good. Better to keep a clear head." Lashman looked at Richard expectantly, his taut face ready for battle. "Well?"

"Tell me about the money, Edgar. Why don't you want me to go into TV?"

"Took you longer than I thought to figure it out," Lashman said, smiling. "I don't dislike you, Richard. I hope you know that."

"Not the point, Edgar."

Lashman held up his hand. "Listen to me, Richard. Listen and learn." He leaned forward, and the pool of light from the marble lamps cast lacy shadows over his face as he steepled his fingers in front of him. "You know how I started out, so I won't be tedious about my early life, tell you any lies about my Abe Lincoln childhood and walking through the snow in cardboard shoes, though most of it is true. I worked hard, made money, built a movie studio, destroyed lives in the process. What price power, yes? I am rich. Some people say I'm dangerous. I would be the first to admit I have no claims on sainthood." He laughed harshly, and it sounded like he was choking. "You'd agree?"

"I agree, Edgar," Richard said impatiently. "But . . ."

Lashman held up his hand. "Listen and learn," he said again. His tone was imperious. "I have everything the world offers, but like so many men who have everything, I also have nothing. My wife—the love of my boyhood, for whom I built this empire—is a hysterical bitch who weeps constantly and will not agree to a divorce because of her equally hysterical devotion to her church. She sleeps with the saints, never with me, and no longer concerns herself with things of this world. So I content myself with a parade of empty-headed beauties who appear in my office and then disappear like phantoms, hoping their lush favors will persuade me to give them the career they are incapable of earning themselves. But here's the point." Lashman smiled bitterly. "When my wife deserted me for her spiritual sanctuary, I turned my familial attentions to my daughter—my only child, for my wife was incapable in that area as well as every other. Richard, I spoiled Maria. I made her the monster she is. I gave her every toy, every dress, everything her greedy fancy desired. And when she wanted you, I bought you."

Anger exploded like a rocket in Richard's head, but he knew Lashman spoke the truth. Lashman recognized my weakness and made use of it, he thought. Who am I to resent him after all these years?

Lashman sighed. "I see you are angry. Control it. You amused Maria for a short while. As I told you, she's a greedy girl. Like her father, after the children were born she turned her attentions elsewhere. This doesn't shock you, I hope?"

A funny thought hit Richard Sears as he sat in his father-in-law's library and admired his Bonnard, his van Dongen, his Forain, and his Picasso. In all the years of their marriage he'd never cared enough to wonder who Maria was sleeping with. At least she'd been discreet about her affairs.

"So. My daughter is vain and spoiled, thoughtless and self-involved. I made her that way, so I should know, yes?"

"Go on, Edgar."

"Ah," Lashman said grimly. "I have your attention at last. When Maria's little . . . foibles became too apparent to ignore, I reluctantly turned my attention to my grandchildren. Linda and little Dickie." Lashman sighed, and his eyes filled with tears. "Richard, I will give you the money you need, but there's a price: you must give up Katherine Cole."

A dark pit opened up at Richard's feet, begging him to jump in. Control, he thought. I must be in control. "Edgar, forgive me, but I don't follow your logic. What dirty thread binds your story together?"

"Where's the through line? How is the plot resolved? I'll tell you. Richard, I don't deny you pleasure, but I must deny you love. You see, my daughter is a dead loss as far as I'm concerned, but my grandchildren can't survive without you as an anchor in their lives. If you prosper on your own and marry the lovely Mrs. Cole, Linda and Dickie won't stand a chance," Lashman said slowly. "It may be too late now. If you leave Maria she will destroy her own children—merely a sin of omission, nothing deliberate. Spoiled, eh? Ruined by Hollywood like so many other unsuspecting children. Richard, if you didn't love Mrs. Cole, your affair wouldn't matter to me in the slightest. It is *because* you love her that she is a threat to me. Richard, Richard, I know all about your affair with her years ago. I know her oldest child is yours. But you can't have her, now or ever. When you married my daughter you mortgaged your soul to the devil; I am that devil and I'm here to collect. Nobody held a gun to your head, Richard. Nobody forced you to give up Katherine Cole and marry my daughter. You made a choice, and now you must live with it. That's the sad truth. I have my business, my studio, and my art collection, but my wife and daughter are the casualties of my success. Now I fight to protect my grandchildren." Edgar Lashman got out of his chair, came over to Richard's side, and put a paternal hand on his shoulder. "You have fame, and I will give you money and power, but you will be forever strapped in harness with Maria. I've told her the same thing, by the way. Find another woman," he ordered, his voice as rough as gravel. "One you don't love. You can never have Katherine Cole."

Richard Sears lay sprawled on the couch at his cabin staring out the big windows, waiting for Katherine, and thinking about the night lying shattered behind him like a broken headlight on a wet highway. He was Lashman's hostage, nothing more, imprisoned by his love for his own children just as Lashman himself was imprisoned by his love for Maria, his dissolute daughter. Defeat and disaster and loss were everywhere, and Richard felt a horrible combination of immense fury and complete helplessness. For a long moment he was a boy again, and he saw his father lying on the floor of his bedroom, the metallic stink of blood mingling with the tang of gunpowder in the air. But as anger surged through his veins Richard realized he felt stronger and younger than he had in years. His anger was infusing his spirit with new life.

He heard Katherine's car in the driveway and got heavily to his feet. Lashman owned him, had owned him for years, but his new knowledge brought him a sense of freedom. He would take this twisted opportunity, take his father-in-law's money, and use it to break free of the Lashman stranglehold. He was caught in a net, but it couldn't hold forever. One day, with skill and cunning and patience, he would have his own wealth, his own power. One day he'd have Katherine again, for she was his too. One day he would win.

"But, Richard, I always knew our affair was temporary. Did you think I would scream and cry and throw myself at your feet when it was over?" Katherine shook her head sadly. "I've learned a thing or two in Hollywood. I'm not the same naive girl you abandoned years ago, my love," she said lightly. "I wanted an affair, Richard, and I knew nothing would come of it. I wanted you for a lover, not a husband. Once I thought the sun and the moon revolved around you; now I know we are the ones who revolve. I love you, but I have my children to protect. Nothing comes before my children, do you understand? Not you, not me . . . Nothing in this world."

"We both have families to protect," Richard protested. "Maria will destroy the children unless I can temper her insane sense of entitlement. The Hollywood princess." He laughed bitterly. "My God, what a joke. Lashman holds all the cards. I've been living in an idiot's paradise," he said softly.

"That makes us even," Katherine said. "When I came to Hollywood I was a fool. I believed the rules were the same in this town as they are in the rest of the world. Wrong. It's a tough game here, as tough as it gets in America, and it gets tougher every single time the big ball drops another year in Times Square. When you left me pregnant and alone, I didn't quit. When Leo died, I didn't quit, and I won't quit now. I'll never quit, because now I know the rules of the game. Everything I've done, I've done to protect my children. I'm not a fool anymore, Richard. People think I take talent and push it through a grinder until star sausage pops out the other side, but I can't create stars. They create themselves, but their egos are as fragile as glass Christmas ornaments. I merely coddle talent, wrap it up in tissue paper so it doesn't get broken. I give advice and a little mothering. And I never, never quit, because I am all my children have. There's no cushion of money behind them, Richard, no Edgar Lashman. There's only me. I'm powerful because I've taken the body blows. I've had my heart crushed, and I'll never let anyone crush me again. Not in this lifetime."

"My God, you're like a wall."

"Yes," she said simply. "A wall that's still standing."

Richard Sears shook his head in disbelief, his illusions shredding around him like torn bits of ragged paper. "I've never seen you like this, Red. You're magnificent. And to think I let you go." He sighed, saddened. "We're even, darling: I broke your heart, and now you've broken mine."

As she got into her Cadillac and drove away from the cabin for the last time, Katherine was oddly surprised it didn't hurt more. Perhaps she had told Richard the truth. Perhaps expected blows caused less pain. Or were her senses simply dulled by another in a long line of losses?

Big things don't hurt, and small things don't count. The thought ricocheted inside her head like an echo across a deep canyon. The pain wouldn't last. This time around with Richard was just another spin of the carousel. But as she wound her way out of the Hollywood Hills she realized she'd known only two men in her life and now she'd lost them both. No more men for me, she thought as the lights of the Sunset Strip filled her eyes like multicolored tears. No more love.

Richard's always been willing to trade me in on his career, the empire he needs to soothe his fears. But I don't need his empire; I'm building my own. Work saved me when Leo died; it'll save me now. I have my family, my children, and they are all that counts. I have my work. My family and my success belong to me alone. I've begun to build, but now I'm going to create. Double, double, redouble.

Unlike many others in Hollywood, including Edgar Lashman and Richard Sears, Katherine Cole didn't see the encroaching face of television as the enemy; she saw it as an ally. So with Lucille Ball's "I Love Lucy" proving to be the hit of the decade, Katherine Cole and Madeline Gerard formed Double Productions, and quickly were hot on Lucy's heels with the TV version of Rosie Parker. Like Dagwood and Blondie, Rosie's scatterbrained but lovable character made an easy transition from small-scale features to big-scale TV. Her trademark sweetheart neckline and red and white candy-striped bow became a nationwide fad, and her astonished catchphrase, "You mean *me?*" permeated the small talk of a generation. Madeline Gerard was the darling of Saturday night. But success didn't make Katherine's life any easier.

Roz and Simon managed to hide their affair for over a year before Katherine, purely by chance, found out about it. She'd been at a meeting at Warner Brothers and afterward she drove over to Toluca Lake to get gas. There, at the Hot Dog Show, she saw her daughter and Simon Wyler sitting at the counter with their heads together like Archie and Veronica sharing a malted. The hot Valley sun was beating down on Rosalind's red hair as Simon smiled at her adoringly, his big blue notebook casually propped up on the counter beside him. As the tiny details of the scene etched themselves forever into her mind Katherine thought reflexively that it was all too perfect, too loving, too soon.

She pulled around the corner and stopped the car on Moorpark, her hands trembling on the steering wheel of the Caddy. But she's only a baby, only seventeen. She's too young to start sex and love and the whole procession of events emanating from love. It's happened too fast! I thought I'd have more time. I didn't think I'd have to work so hard. I thought I'd have more time, more time. . . . She was pounding the dashboard when she realized how futile and foolish her reaction was. Katherine opened her hands and started to laugh. "Just what the hell I need," she said to the air. "My daughter's screwing a goddamn no-good actor."

That night she joined Madeline at her new house in Holmby Hills. She badly needed to talk, but first she had to admire the decor, of which Madeline was inordinately proud. The living room was done in movie-star white with gold-veined mirrors accenting the walls. Overstuffed white couches and chairs and huge gold brocade pillows littered the sunken area by the mirrored bar. Crystal lamps scattered rainbow chips of light across the white carpets, and an assortment of white and gold plaques of musical instruments adorned the walls. A life-size portrait of Madeline as Rosie Parker wearing her "you mean *me?*" expression hung over the white marble fireplace.

"Roz is having an affair with Simon Wyler," Katherine said as she sipped her martini. The thick, oily drink made her feel nauseated, and she put the glass down on the coffee table.

"What?" Madeline arched her eyebrows in amazement. "You're kidding. Roz? Little Rozzie? She's not old enough!"

"She's seventeen."

"She's old enough!" Madeline said shortly. "My God, *I* must be getting old. How the hell did she get to be seventeen so damn fast? Are you sure they're having an affair? How do you know?"

"I saw them together, and of course I'm sure. There's no mistaking it. Oh, Mad, I thought I'd have more time! Everything happens too soon! I met Richard too soon, Leo died too soon, Roz grew up too soon . . ."

"Right, right, right. And my tits are falling too soon, believe me. So what are you going to do?"

Katherine smiled thinly. "I've been thinking about getting Simon a job in New York."

"Can you? Everybody knows what a pain in the ass he is."

"I can do it," Katherine nodded grimly. "To get Roz away from him I can walk on water. Maybe if they're separated for six months she'll get bored."

Madeline frowned. "Maybe I could use him on 'Rosie Parker' if New York doesn't work out. We could write 'Rosie Goes to Paris.' "

Katherine shook her head. "They'd smell it. God, what if she gets pregnant?"

"She won't. She's a lot smarter than you were," Madeline said wisely.

A week later Katherine called Simon Wyler, who was now living down the Strip at the Chateau Marmont in one small room with a hot plate.

"Good news, darling," she told him. "I've got you a part

in *Blindfold,* the new Tim Harold play in New York; Timmy's an old friend of mine. Simon, attend to my words. This is your last chance for gas. It's a *tiny* little part in a Tim Harold play. Are you hearing me? You're a crazed murderer, and you have one good scene, Simon. *One* scene. Now, let me put it to you straight, Simon. It's make or break time."

"What are you? The mother of the universe?" Simon grumbled. It was noon and the phone had woken him up.

"I'm your surrogate mother, and listen to me well, my son, since I'm paying for your trip. If you ruin this, Simon, I won't be able to help you anymore. Neither will anyone else."

Simon started to protest, but Katherine steamrollered right over him.

"You're a big talent, Simon, and everybody knows it. But you're also a big pain in the ass, and you've been knocking around town far too long. If you were a star, people would put up with you, but you're not and they won't. You're a day player who's having trouble getting work because you've alienated too many folks. So act nice for Timmy or else, okay? Got it? Is it clear enough for you?" She held her breath. Would her fevered sales pitch work?

For once, Simon was quiet. "Why do you put up with me, Katherine? I don't make a nickel for you. Hell, I cost you a fortune."

"You've got talent, Simon, that's why. You think I'm just another bloodsucker? Shame on you, you should know better." She was conning him now. "If you make it big, the Cole Agency will be known far and wide for its foresight, its perseverance, and my genius."

Simon laughed. "Right, right. You're brave, clean, and reverent. I get it. And I'll try to behave."

Two weeks later Tim Harold called Katherine in hysterics. "Wyler is a lunatic!" he shouted. "He walks through rehearsal like he's at Coney Island looking in the fun house mirror! I can't get anything out of him. He's a living lox! *Shtick fleish mit oigen!* Meat with eyes!" Harold moaned. "He don't act. He sits around scribbling, writing all the time like he's keeping score on all the broads he's diddling! What is he, Boswell? Katherine, I took this lunatic on your say-so, and if my play, which I wrote personally in my own blood, flops because of this schmuck-prince Wyler, I expect you to get me a movie deal for eighty bezillion dollars, at least!"

"Tim, how many years have we known each other? Don't answer that. It's his style, I swear it."

"He scratches so much I think he's got lice!"

"The moment he gets in front of an audience, he's bright, he's incandescent, he's electric!"

"Enough Edison analogies! I don't need Edison, I need an actor! Swear to God, if my play goes in the tank because of Wyler, little Timmikins checks into the Old Show Biz Home!"

"I'll make it work. Believe me," Katherine said firmly. Two minutes later she picked the phone and began to scream at Simon Wyler.

It was twilight. Roz lay in her bed, turning her predicament over and over in her mind, waiting for the sound of her mother's car pulling out of the driveway, waiting until she could dial New York, let the phone ring twice, hang up, and wait for Simon to call her back. It was their private code, a secret way to keep Simon's New York number off Katherine's phone bill. He'd been gone for almost six months, and Roz was amazed their affair was still a secret, because no one knew except Olivia. But how much longer could they be separated? Roz knew he wasn't faithful to her. Winchell's column had mentioned Simon's appearance at a theatrical benefit with one of his pretty costars, and Roz Cole had a practical mind.

But the truth was, Simon's autocratic nature combined perfectly with her own desire to be dominated and controlled. He liked to manipulate women, and she alone had managed to tap into the depths of that murky well. Thus, Roz owned a piece of Simon Wyler no other woman had touched, and their long-distance relationship had only reinforced that highly charged quirk in Simon's sexual nature. Now, while he was ostensibly the hunter, he had also become the game.

Finally she heard Katherine's Caddy spitting gravel and grabbed the phone, though she knew Simon would be at the theater until eleven-thirty, at least. *Blindfold*'s success was a thrill. His one scene was a smash, but Simon had a run-of-the-play contract, and he was stuck in New York for the duration. She liked hearing the phone ring in his empty Greenwich Village sublet, a delicious, sexy vibration shooting across the country through the telephone line. She tried three times over the evening, and finally he was there.

"I've been lying here, waiting for you," he said.

"Liar. You were in bed with a blond. I bet she's there now."

"Yeah, yeah. Two blonds. Want a description? One of 'em is fat; one of 'em is skinny, and she's got a mole on her—"

"You rat," she said, laughing. "I wish I were in bed with you."

"Honey, so do I. But honest to God, you've got to finish high school first. Jesus," he moaned, "I can't believe I'm in love with a girl who's in the twelfth grade."

"I graduate next month."

"What am I supposed to do in the meantime?" he teased.

"Get a blond," she said lightly. "An ugly one."

"I like redheads."

"Are you writing?"

He laughed, the spell of bed broken. "Yeah. Almost through. You gotta read this, Roz. Tell me if I'm a double threat or just a threat."

"Talent is talent. You're a terrific actor, but you're a better writer, I know it."

"Acting's for whores," Simon said shortly. "Writers are in charge of their own lives."

"Only rich ones," she said.

"I bought you a present today. You wanta know what it is?"

"Twenty questions?"

"Five."

"Is it sexy?"

"Yeah."

"Lacy?"

"Nope."

"Tight?"

"Could be."

"Hard?"

"Better believe it."

"Hey, hey!"

"That *was* the answer!" He laughed. "One more."

"A belt."

"Close. A thick gold choker so you'll always be my prisoner."

"I love you. I want to be your prisoner."

"Me too you. I love you. Tomorrow?"

"Ummmm. 'Night." She hung up the phone, took off her clothes, and lay in bed, the moonlight flooding in through the open window. Later she dreamed she was tied to Simon Wyler by a long golden rope. And from high on his shelf, Leo Cole looked down protectively from his silver frame at the girl who was now a woman, the girl who was never his daughter but would forever be his child.

The hot June sun shone down on the quadrangle behind the Miss Lilys' School as Rosalind's graduating class, their black gowns over their long dresses and dark suits, walked across the freshly mowed Bermuda grass to collect their diplomas in a simple ceremony.

Afterward, as parents, teachers, and students flooded the quad, congratulating and kissing one another under the warm California sun, Rosalind Cole thought she'd never been happier. She even liked her deep blue dress and the string of pearls Katherine had given her as a graduation present. Everything in her entire life was precisely on course, and as she smiled at her friends and their parents she realized she was finally free of Susan and Jane Lily and the tedious pretense of being a child. Soon her new life with Simon would begin in earnest.

Linda Sears was vibrant in yellow chiffon, her dark hair shining as she stood between her handsome parents, her little brother Dickie behind her. "Oh, Roz," she called out. "I don't think you've met my mother and father."

Roz shook hands with Mr. and Mrs. Sears and nodded politely.

Linda smiled up at her father. "Daddy darling, you don't mind if I slip away with Roz for just a sec, do you? There's something I want to tell her."

"Of course, baby," Richard said, deliberately keeping his eyes off Rosalind. "Come on, Maria. Let's circulate."

Linda Sears grabbed Roz by the hand and pulled her toward the end of the lawn.

"Let go of me, idiot," Roz said impatiently.

"You really think you're something wonderful, don't you Roz?" Linda's beautiful face was spoiled by her mouth, twisted into a torn slash. "You think you're better than me, but you're not. We're just the same."

"That's a revolting idea, Bitchy. Being like you."

"Oh, but you are like me, Roz pie. You're just like me." Linda said the words slowly, clearly enjoying her game.

The unpleasant gleam in Linda's eyes sent an ugly quiver through Roz, frightening her like the sudden flick of a garter snake across the brick path in the heat of summer. What was Linda talking about?

Linda Sears pursed her lips and made a nasty wet, kissing noise at Roz. "C'mon," she teased. "Don't you want to ask me *how* we're the same? Don't you, don't you, don't you?"

"Shut up, Linda."

Linda leaned forward and put her face close to Roz's. She smelled of lilacs, and when she spoke, her voice was low and hoarse. "We're sisters, you and I. A long time ago your mother was my father's whore, and Leo Cole wasn't your father, so you can stop worshiping his memory. You're my bastard sister—half sister, really, but what's the diff? My father fucked your mother, Roz pie. Your name isn't Cole at all. Or maybe it is," Linda said slowly. "You're certainly not a Sears, that's for sure. Now, isn't that a nice graduation present?"

Rosalind stood quietly as the full impact of Linda's words hit her. She felt as if she'd been socked in the stomach. All her ideas, thoughts, and memories of her happy childhood began to disintegrate like an old photograph tossed into a roaring fire, edges curling and contracting, turning brown, black, gray, and disappearing into the flames. It was all turning to ash because, as the horrible words came out of Linda's twisted mouth, all the odd suspicions she'd had over the years fell into place. Rosalind knew her hated enemy was telling the truth.

"You always were a lying bitch, Linda," Roz said lightly. The sun was a poker stabbing her eyes. "Why should I believe you?"

"Because it's true, that's why," Linda laughed, enjoying her victory. "Last night when my parents came in, they were having a real big fight. Throwing stuff downstairs, that sort of junk," she said disdainfully. "They do it all the time. Then, when they go into their bedroom they usually make it up, and I like to listen. They shut the door, of course, but I can hear them through the heating vent in my bathroom. My mother was laughing at him. She's known all about *your* mother for years. Dad said he and Katherine stopped seeing each other, and Mother said that was a crock. She knew you were his daughter years ago, but she doesn't give a damn as long as he leaves her alone." Linda smiled grimly, maliciously.

"You're a goddamn fucking liar, Linda," Roz said.

"No, I'm not." Linda laughed. "You and me are half sisters, but in this case I think a half is as good as a whole, don't you agree, Roz pie?"

Leo's face shot through Rosalind's mind, and she clung to his sharp black-and-white image as if it were a saint's relic. Leo Cole *was* her father. He would help her if she could only get home to him and take him down from the shelf. "You're a goddamn fucking liar, Linda," she said again, trying to make her voice strong and sure, defiant and unafraid. "And if you ever come near me again I'll kill you." Rosalind turned and walked briskly away from Linda Sears.

Behind her, Linda Sears was laughing. "I'm not lying, Roz pie. And you know it."

Roz pushed her way through the crowd at the school, desperately trying to escape her impossibly childish girlfriends in their long graduation dresses and the impossibly awkward boys in their brand-new suits. All around her their expensively dressed, impossibly self-confident parents laughed and chatted about the latest deal at the studio, whose latest picture had bombed in Sheboygan, and the latest bath on Wall Street. What had been a happy scene took on a jagged, surreal air and Roz Cole was no longer a part of it. All the kids were happy that high school was finally over and they'd been set free to live life as rich kids in Hollywood where the sun shone every day, the streets were paved with fool's gold, and everyone was a star. But for Roz it was just a rich blur of money.

Olivia grabbed her arm, jerking her out of her daze. "What's going on?" Olivia asked, suspiciously, her thin, intelligent face dark and intense. "What did Snitchy Bitchy Sears want?"

"Later," was all Roz managed as she ran into the big building, through the cool, dark halls, and out the other side to where the chauffeurs and Cadillacs and Continentals and Rolls-Royces were waiting in the circle in front of the school. "Take me home," she told Katherine's driver, but as she got into the stifling car, she realized she'd lost her home along with everything else.

She fled back to the big house in the Hollywood Hills, the house that had been her home, and sent the driver back to the school. Mrs. Gebhardt was at the graduation ceremony with the rest of the family, so the house was empty. Roz took a cool shower and let the water beat down on her head, then, naked and wet, she went into Katherine's room and tossed her graduation pearls on the dressing table. She put on jeans and a white shirt, but as she wandered through the silent, familiar rooms she knew she no longer belonged. She was a stranger.

Finally she went into the living room, poured herself a glass of scotch from the bar, and sat down to wait for Katherine. She didn't want to go back to her own room. She could hold back the tears as long as she didn't see Leo's picture looking down at her. She didn't want to think ever again. She didn't want to know any more secrets about her parents. She didn't want to grow up, and she didn't want to make any decisions. But it was too late.

Leo's face surrounded by a silver nimbus danced just behind her eyelids, and Rosalind fell asleep in the chair.

She woke up an hour later when she heard the car pull up and the sounds of Olivia and Charles running across the driveway and up the steps. Nervously Roz took a Parliament from the white marble box on the table, lit it, blew a stream of smoke into the room, and idly watched it break up into an intertwined pattern that reminded her of an Oriental rug. She heard her mother's key click into the front door lock, the characteristic squeal of the hinge that forever needed oil, Katherine's bag and keys hitting the marble table in the hall, and Charlie's feet clattering up the stairs, his stout little voice calling out, "Rozzie, Rozzie, where are you, Rozzie?"—a symphony of sounds she knew by heart but which now seemed completely foreign.

"There you are! I've been worried half to death. What's the *matter* with you!" Katherine snapped as she stormed into the room. "Are you smoking? I've told you a thousand times—"

"Close the door and sit down, would you?" Rosalind said, her voice low and automatic. "I want to talk to you."

Olivia stuck her head in. "Where have you been, Rozzie? We were worried!"

"Honey, give Charles a sandwich, please? And close the door." Katherine's anger had evaporated instantly, and her face was watchful, guarded.

Olivia's eyes flicked between Roz and Katherine. "Okay." She frowned and left the room.

"What is it, Roz?

Roz threw her head back, the weight of her long hair trailing down the back of the chair. A poodle cut, she thought irrelevantly, short hair. Time for a change. "I'm leaving for New York tomorrow. I have a nine o'clock reservation."

Katherine frowned, anger spurting up unbidden. Simon, that bastard! He'd won. "Absolutely not!" she said.

"I'm leaving, and I'm never coming back. That little bitch Linda told me about you and Richard Sears."

There was a brief second when Katherine prayed Roz didn't know Richard was her father, a moment of faith as the headsman's ax began its long, inexorable descent, a moment that was utterly destroyed when she saw the loathing on her daughter's face. "Roz darling . . ."

"Don't waste my time. I knew it was true the minute she told me." Roz laughed harshly. "And how she enjoyed telling me! I hope I'm able to do her a good turn someday, my sister Linda."

Then Katherine knew there was no hope, none. A few cruel words and her daughter was lost to her forever. A few seconds was all it took. The hard nights and days in the studios, at the Cole Agency, all the sweat and anguish and work so the kids could go to a good school and have clothes and cars and friends and all the things she never had, the conning and the courage and the labor were all swept away by a few ugly words, and only emptiness was left. But the emptiness was so familiar! She'd felt the same pain when Richard said he wouldn't marry her, when Leo died, and now it was back. Katherine sighed heavily and sat down.

"Darling, please," she said, though she knew it was useless. "It's easy to be hard when you're young—"

"Oh, stop, will you?" Roz was bored. "Why don't you tell me how the early bird catches the worm or a stitch in time saves nine?" She smiled bitterly as she got up and walked to the door. "That's all I have to say. I'm leaving in the morning, and I won't be back. Please don't come to my room later thinking you can talk me out of leaving or explain all this or reason it out. I don't care about you anymore, and I never will again. Good-bye."

As the door closed softly behind her daughter, Katherine Ransome Cole sat in her chair and mechanically smoothed her raw silk suit over her knees. She'd been going to Bullock's Wilshire for such a long time, but new shops were springing up in Beverly Hills every day. Perhaps it was time for a change. . . . A thousand trivial details flashed in and out of her mind. Nylons, she needed nylons. The dining room chairs ought to be cleaned. Were there enough raisins in case Mrs. Gebhardt made muffins for Sunday breakfast?

All at once the inconsequential thoughts fell away like dead skin, and as she began to cry, Katherine was overwhelmed with a grief she hadn't felt since the morning she had sat in the hospital and watched Leo's face grow slack and cold, watched the rich fervor of his life drain away to nothing. "No!" she cried dully. "Not my Rozzie! No, no, no. . . ."

Roz left the house in the hills early the next morning with one small suitcase and took a Yellow cab out to the airport. She had very little with her—no clothes, nothing to remind her of the past. When she got to New York and started her new life with Simon she wanted everything to be fresh and clean. No memories attached. She carried only a few photographs of Olly and Charles, some books, some cosmetics so she'd look good when she got there, a pretty nightgown, and Leo's photograph in its big silver frame, carefully wrapped in tissue paper. After all, Leo Cole was the only father she'd ever known, the only father she needed, the only father she wanted. Ever.

Chapter
13

Roz woke with a start as the engine's tempo shifted. Then the drone of the prop jets became more pronounced, and the big plane swooped and began its lazy descent into La Guardia Airport.

Far below, Manhattan shimmered in the twilight, like an intricate maze. The sharp buildings jabbed their fingers at the sky, their windows reflecting the glow of the setting sun as the Statue of Liberty searched the horizon for lost immigrants and the green patch of Central Park nodded serenely in the heart of the great city. Like all newcomers to New York, Roz Cole was looking for a fresh start to smooth out the ragged edges of her old life. Here in New York she would find her future.

She walked down the steps and onto the tarmac. Simon was waiting for her at the gate, a bunch of daisies in his hand. With his hat pushed back on his head he looked like an imitation cub reporter.

"I've missed you. I need you," he said as he buried his face in her hair. "What the hell happened? Katherine called. She's frantic."

"I'll tell you later," Roz said as she smelled his cologne and remembered the comforting fact of his craving for her. To everyone else she was still young, helpless, and bland. But to Simon Wyler she was a desirable woman.

"I've hired a car," he said as they pushed their way through the busy terminal toward the front doors. "The chauffeur can get your luggage."

"Very extravagant." Roz laughed. "Can you afford it on an actor's pay? And by the way, can you afford me?"

"No," Simon said promptly as he opened the door to the limo and settled her inside. "But I can afford it on the advance I got from Simon and Schuster. They're going to publish *Crowded Avenue* this fall."

"Darling! You submitted it without telling me! But that's wonderful," she said quickly, covering her vague disappointment. "How did it happen?"

"Fate. Timing. New York." He laughed, turning his head slightly so Roz couldn't see his eyes. "Yeah, New York's lucky for me, Roz. I met an editor at a party. She'd seen the play and was telling me how great I am. Of course I agreed with her, but I was half drunk, so I told her I was really a writer moonlighting as a ham actor. One, two, three, she read it, threw pots of money at me, and here we are. I didn't want to tell you in case the deal fell apart. Forgive me?"

"There's nothing to forgive. It's wonderful news, and you deserve it." He's sleeping with her, Roz realized with a sudden, stabbing glimpse into the future as she leaned forward to kiss him. He'll always sleep with the women around him. He can't help it; he's weak, and he has a streak of amorality running through his heart as wide as the Mississippi. The word *fidelity* simply isn't in his lexicon. Simon thinks he's a genius and genius deserves its prize but I know the women who throw themselves at him only want him for a trophy, another notch on their sexual gun belts. But Simon wants to imprison a woman, mold her into an image he can worship, and I can be that woman. I *am* that woman, and I'm the only one who knows his secret.

Possessively, Roz curled her fingers over his arm. "Take me home," she whispered. "By the way, do we have a home?"

Simon laughed happily. The petulant shadow had passed and he was all sunshine again. "Wait till you see it! I was saving it to surprise you. As soon as I got the money I junked the sublet in the Village and moved uptown. This is another sublet but much grander. Belongs to an actress who's gone to Paris for God knows how long, and the only word for her taste is *fabulous.*"

"Good," Roz said as she nestled into him. "I want to be fabulous. I'm tired of hearing my mother's nagging voice in my ear, telling me to work harder, faster, achieve her impossible standard of perfection. I'll never match her if I live to be a thousand. Maybe she wants to spend her life working for the glory of the damn Cole Agency, but not me. I want to sleep all day and go to parties at night. Listen to jazz, go to the theater, have my hair done, and go shopping. I want to be a wastrel. Simon, now that you're a writer, can you afford a female wastrel?"

"New York was made for you, darling," he said, laughing. "It's a twenty-four-hour town. There's something doing every minute, and we'll do it all. Baby, I've always wanted to be a writer; it's the only thing I really give a damn about. Now I want to enjoy myself. And yes, I can afford it. Here's where we start!" he said as the car pulled up in front of a white town house just off Park Avenue.

Simon was right, the apartment was fabulous. With six rooms on two floors and twenty-foot ceilings, it was gigantic, and by New York standards it was a palace. And though the architectural detail was beautiful it was the decoration that pushed the place over the edge into a land of fantasy and desire. A deep patina of green, gold, and silver gleamed everywhere; a white marble angel with huge, outstretched wings watched over the hallway; and stained-glass windows running the length of the front wall threw brilliant chips of soft light across the Oriental carpets. There were cut-glass bibelots scattered across black marble tables, deep cut velvet couches, the results of a lifetime of collecting. The musky scent of Rigaud candles wafted through the air, and the whole effect was of a courtesan's salon in the glittering golden age of the last century, or perhaps of a time that never really existed at all. . . .

Roz was amazed. "It's a stage set," she said slowly as she took in the complex variety of objets d'art in every corner.

Simon nodded. "And we're the star players. Come upstairs, my darling, and see the biggest bed in the world. You climb in on a little set of brass steps."

"First give me a drink, Simon," she said seriously. "I have something to tell you. But it's just for us, all right? It's important, so you have to swear you won't tell anyone." Swear, she thought dully. I want him to swear like kids at camp. Swear he won't tell the other kids my mother's a whore and I'm her bastard.

"What is it?" he asked, curious. He saw the intensity in her eyes and held up his hand, palm out. "Okay, I swear," he said. "Now tell me, who's it about?"

Always the writer, she thought. Tell him a secret and he begins digging for material. "It's about me," she said slowly. She turned away as she heard him clinking glasses at the bar. She didn't want him to see her face.

"Brandy's good for secrets," he said. "Warm and thick."

The colored light from the windows danced around Roz, throwing a kaleidoscope of color across her face, her hands, her hair. "Richard Sears is my father," she said. It was the first time she'd ever said the words flat out, and she was surprised how little they hurt and how little they meant. "Richard Sears is my father, not . . . not Leo Cole." Another loss. In the space of a few words her beloved daddy had been transformed into plain Leo Cole. An ordinary man with a first and last name.

"Son of a bitch!" Simon whistled.

Roz turned and saw Simon staring at her. The bottle of brandy was in his hand, and some of it had splashed on the green marble bar. "Well, I'll be goddamned," he said finally.

"Jesus, I heard a rumor last year that Katherine and Sears were carrying on."

"Carrying on *again,*" Roz said lightly.

"What a great story," Simon said thoughtfully. "Lovers before, lovers again. . . ."

"Simon, will you forget your passion for plots just this once? It's not such a great story to me. It's my life. Besides, you swore you'd keep it a secret." Roz sighed, fighting back the tears stinging her eyes. "I never want to talk about it again. This is one tale that's not for publication. Richard Sears may be my father, but he doesn't exist for me and I don't exist for him. You know how I feel about . . . Daddy. About Leo. He's my real father. He'll *always* be my father, and I never want to see my mother again. Do what you want about your business relationship with the agency, but I won't see her. Simon, don't you understand? I want a new life; I want to change everything I am, live every day. The hell with the past and the hell with the future. Can't we drink champagne and be thoughtless?"

"Darling one, of course we can! I have the play to do, but it won't last forever. Let's be thoughtless children until the mood wears off or the money runs out," he said with a crooked smile. "Hell, everything wears off sooner or later. But for now let's spend money and have fun. Oh," he said as an afterthought, "let's get married next weekend."

Six months later *Crowded Avenue* came out, got good reviews, and sold briskly—even more briskly after it was sold to the movies. Simon's gritty tale of a writer seduced by a young girl was widely taken to be autobiographical. Wisely, Simon and Roz did nothing to dispel the illusion, especially as they were now famous as a couple linked in literature as well as in love.

In the aftermath of *Crowded Avenue* Mrs. Simon Wyler became New York's newest, most chic face. Her youth, her cropped red hair, her daring gowns, and her flair for the high life promptly brought her to the attention of the city's older and wiser hostesses, who recognized the wild and beautiful young wife of a lionized actor-turned-author as a valuable asset to any dinner party. Especially since Simon was at the theater between 7:30 and 11:30 and Roz could be counted on to flirt outrageously with wealthy brokers and businessmen who might back a play or fund a boutique or endow a museum. The rich and thin Babe Paley took Roz under her elegant wing and taught her the ins and outs of the fashion world, Diana Vreeland spotted her at a fund-raiser and put her on the pages of *Vogue* along with Gloria Vanderbilt, Jacqueline de Ribes, and the Bouvier sisters. Roz was everywhere. She drank at "21," dined at Chambord, and shopped at Saks.

Simon was amazed at her chameleonlike adaptation from California schoolgirl in jeans and scuffed penny loafers to New York sophisticate dressed by Chanel, but Roz only laughed as she unwrapped her latest boxes from Bonwit's. Charvet ties for Simon, Dior for her, Hermès bags and Liberty scarves by the dozen from London. Anything she wanted was hers, and Roz wanted it all.

"Spend everything, I don't give a damn," Simon said one day when they were at the Plaza having drinks in the Oak Room. "By the way, I've got a contract for a series of stories for *Esquire.*"

"Pat Hobby in New York?" Roz laughed. "Hollywood's child in the Big Apple?"

"Well, I'm no Fitzgerald," Simon said thoughtfully. "And you're no Zelda, thank God. But it's a good idea. I think I'll steal it."

"Everything I have is yours," Roz said lightly, sipping her martini.

"Yeah." Simon nodded slowly. "I'll write a series of stories about a desperate young actor on the make in Gotham City."

"After all the press on *Crowded Avenue,* you should keep the stories autobiographical. Let people think they're about us. Make them sexy."

"Yup," Simon said thoughtfully. "How a low-born lad screws his way through the upper classes."

"But the girl is always true blue," Roz said, her voice deliberately light. "The source of his strength."

Simon kissed her hand. "Let's go home, get drunk on champagne, and make love."

They drifted along on the tide of Simon's success. After the play folded, he acted off-Broadway—he was now a draw as Simon Wyler, actor with a wild life turned writer with a beautiful wife—and he was halfway into another novel. For Roz and Simon Wyler, life was a perfect blue-white diamond, and New York City was their Cartier setting.

Like Leo Cole before her, Roz flowered into her own creation, and a completely new woman took the place of the child she'd been in California. But she didn't forget her anger at her mother and she never mentioned Katherine's name. Occasionally, when some visiting Hollywood luminary asked about her connection to the Cole Agency, Roz would smile brightly and acknowledge that, yes, the powerful Mrs. Cole was indeed her mother.

But over the course of the next several years, she spoke to Olivia often, and the transcontinental reach of the telephone over three thousand miles brought the two sisters closer together than they'd been as children living in the same house. Roz told Olivia all about Katherine's relationship with Richard, though she wasn't surprised to learn that Olivia had already heard the whole story from Linda Sears. Olivia was Rosalind's only confidante, the only person who knew the depth of her anguish over Simon's constant, meaningless infidelities.

"It's a cliché, but he's like a child. He can't control himself where women are concerned. He sees, he wants, he takes. He never thinks of controlling his sexual desires; he never worries I'll be hurt. I honestly think *he* doesn't think I know. Especially since sex is so easily available to a famous writer. Goddamn debutantes at the Stork fall out of their panties every time he walks into the room."

"Leave him or shut up," Olivia offered succinctly.

"Olly, you don't know what marriage is like."

"Never will, either."

"Oh, you'll get married. You'll fall for some guy and marry him. Everybody does."

"Not a chance. Olly Olly oxen free, that's me," Olivia said. "I'm going to be rich and famous and have men falling all over me, but I'll never let some guy run me around like you and—" She stopped abruptly, unwilling to mention Katherine.

"I'm not like her. Not at all. How's Charles?" Roz sidestepped the question mark that was Katherine.

"Goofy," Olivia answered. "Moons around all the time and doesn't say much. He's just a kid."

"Kiss him for me," Roz said absently.

"Hey, hey, don't hang up. I've got big news. I'm going to quit school. I think I've got a job with Violet Rawley. I've been peddling her bits for her column, and she likes me. So maybe it's good-bye unemployment and hello to Hollywood's newest legwoman."

"Are you serious? You're too young."

"The hell I am," Olivia said belligerently. "I'm twenty. You think I can't do it?"

"Darling Olly, that's not the point. I know you can do it. You know all the gossip in town before it happens."

"You bet I do, and I know it first 'cause nothing gets by me. You don't get it, Roz. Rawley needs me, and she's smart enough to know it. Nobody knows this town better'n me. I'm in touch with the younger Hollywood crowd. Hell, I went to school with most of 'em. Hedda and Louella are on their last legs, the old bats. All they do is go to lunch at Romanoff's every day, wear silly hats, and run press releases as items. They're part of the old world. I want to be part of the new! Rawley's younger, so she's a little more in touch. You know what's gonna be big in the next few years? Teenagers," Olivia said promptly. "Teenagers and Los Angeles. L.A.'s the wave of the future—not just the movie crowd but the whole damn town. In a few years everybody in America's gonna wake up just like their alarm clocks all went off at once, and they're gonna say, 'Hey, I want to be in L.A.' We've got it all—sunshine, movie stars, studios, the beach, the beauty, and the business. Honey, this is my hometown, and I intend to squeeze the Big Orange till the juice runs dry!" Olivia laughed happily. "Teenagers don't want to know about Joan Crawford and Bette Davis; teenagers want to know about Robert Wagner, Elvis, Rock, Tab. That's why Simon's book did so well."

"I don't understand."

Olivia was irritated. "Think about it. *Crowded Avenue* was packed with steamy sex in an expensive setting."

"A thinly disguised portrait of famous people," Roz said slowly.

"Famous *young* people. Simon's readers think they're getting a peek at the inside poop. That old studio-arranged stuff is over. I'm going to have my own column someday, and working for Violet Rawley is just the beginning."

"Olivia, if anyone can do it, you can. So I'll give you your first scoop, direct from the Big Apple to the Big Orange. It's hot and I guarantee you're the first to know."

"Fantastic. What's the story?"

Roz smiled happily and snuggled down into the beige satin comforter in her magical apartment. "I'm pregnant," she said dreamily.

Rosalind's departure drastically altered the carefully ordered balance of Katherine's life. Though she bore down at work as she always did, emotionally Katherine drifted. Olivia had always been sturdy and self-sufficient, and she no longer needed or wanted a mother. Now, Olivia was quickly acquiring a tough, brittle hardness from the influence of the fast-paced newspaper business and the pressure of daily deadlines coupled with Violet Rawley's moody antics. For the first time since Leo's death so many years ago, the cohesive family Katherine Cole had fought to protect and maintain was slipping away, disintegrating into a set of disconnected pieces. And behind it all was the dreadful, gnawing fear that Rosalind and the baby Katherine had never seen were lost to her forever.

From time to time she was swept away by a deep nostalgia that forced her to drive by places from her past, to look at old photographs and dream of her history. Curiously, Olivia's West Hollywood apartment was only a few blocks from the cubbyhole Katherine and Madeline had shared so many years ago, and one evening after a quick visit with Olivia, Katherine drove by the old place just to see if it was still standing. It was. The same palms and bananas waved. There was the little courtyard where she'd seen Maria Lashman coiled on the hood of her car. The door was open to the apartment where Richard Sears had refused to marry her, where Leo Cole saved her. . . .

And deep down, beneath her love and concern for her children, Katherine felt cheated. Richard was lost to her, Leo was dead, her children were slipping away. Yes, she had the work she had taken on in order to save her family, but her work was destroying her life, eating her up. Rosalind hated her for past mistakes. Olivia's new toughness was incomprehensible and foreign to Katherine. Only Charles was left.

But it was Charles who worried her most. By the time he was fourteen, he was still bewildered and unsure of himself. He remained an unformed baby at an age when the girls had been precocious and outgoing. He was shy and withdrawn and innocent. So Katherine coddled the last child left to her and desperately tried to save the boy from the cruelties of the world, cruelties he took to heart. Like his sisters, he went to the Miss Lilys' with the rest of Hollywood's brats, but as he got older, he often disappeared after school. Even Mrs. Gebhardt didn't know where he went. . . .

Charles Cole didn't care about Hollywood; he hated it and everything it represented. Unlike his mother and his sister Olivia, he was sick to death of the place, of the constant dinner table talk of who was making what picture where, of the endless bickering and backbiting and infighting permeating every facet of life around him. The thin, intense boy, his dark eyes burning as bright as Leo Cole's, secretly dreamed of a land where no one had ever heard of the Cole Agency, where no one gave a damn about grosses, where Hollywood was just another town, and where he could escape the crushing burden of his movie-dominated past.

At night, when he heard his mother deal-making on the phone or when he sat on the stairs watching the cocktail party below, Charles Cole put his hands over his ears and hummed loudly so he wouldn't have to hear any more crap about the star, the picture, the billing, the points—all the endless trivialities he hated. Charles knew he wasn't one of them, and secretly he thought of himself as a freak.

He was nine years old when Katherine told him the story about how Leo Kartay became Leo Cole, and at that moment his own freakishness became clear to him and his estrangement from the fast-paced world around him began. Secretly Charles Cole thought of himself as Charlie Kartay.

A few years later he began to read. Baudelaire and Villon at home, Henry Miller purchased secretly at Campbell's Book Store in Westwood Village. Delmore Schwartz, Dos Passos, Algren, Nathanael West. . . . Books were his life. Books were real, and his life was not, especially after Roz left and Olivia moved out. Mother was always on the phone yakking or at the office yakking, and there was too much noise.

At home or at school, Charles was always alone, and there were a lot of rumors about Mother at school. Dickie Sears—who wasn't a bad kid for a jerk, even if he was fat and nervous—had said his sister Linda said something about Mom and Richard Sears, but Roz had said Linda was a lying bitch and you couldn't trust her. Anyway, Charles didn't care. But now Roz was gone to New York with Simon Wyler, and Olivia was gone too. He didn't blame them. But that left him alone with Mrs. Gebhardt and though he loved her he needed something else, an open door leading to his own life.

So he read and learned about grown-up life from books, which were far more interesting than real people. Real people were scary—too loud, too grabby—but books were manageable. Charles like to take a few books and go out to the unused patio behind the pool house and read the summer days away. It was always sunny and quiet back there, even when the gardeners were running the lawn mowers or washing down the pool area. The patio was drenched with sun, and as the bees buzzed around the golden copa de oro vines twining across the trellis, the sound of chain saws clearing away brush across the Hollywood Hills buzzed in the distance like even larger bees. There Charles spent long days drenched with sun like maple syrup on Mrs. Gebhardt's Sunday pancakes.

Lately he'd figured out he could cop a glass of wine or two from the half-empty bottles stuffed in the back of the refrigerator and Mrs. G. wouldn't know the difference. He'd take his book and his glass outside when the afternoon turned sticky and golden. Peaceful. He'd take off his shirt and feel the sun and the wine spreading across his stomach and down his legs, and the heat would change the character of his hidden hours. Alone in his sanctuary, Charles was no longer lost and the wine made him feel strong and invincible.

Even though the life of literature filled his hungry mind and the stolen wine he was coming to depend on more and more soothed his frightened dreams, Charles Cole was ready for a new turn in the road. He wanted an escape, a departure, something wild, anything to get away from the weight of Hollywood that constantly crushed him into the ground like a slab of granite. And one day as he left his mother's office on his way home after school, he found it.

The Griffin was a small stucco building set back from the Sunset Strip with a black and gold heraldic flag waving lazily in the shimmering afternoon heat. He'd seen it often and been intrigued by the weird kids in black clothes who hung around smoking cigarettes outside, their paperback books scattered on the cement like dice. They reminded him of the crows that inhabited the Valley, shrieking and cawing their sharp warnings whenever anyone came too close.

Charles turned tentatively into the flagstone pathway leading to the Griffin. A young girl with lank blond hair and pale, thin arms sat slumped against the side of the building, smoking a cigarette. She had a guitar across her lap and was aimlessly plucking on a single string. A copy of *Howl* was lying at her feet.

"What's up, man?" she asked, blinking at Charles as he stood nervously in front of her.

"Nothing," Charles said, a little frightened. "Just looking around. It's okay, isn't it?"

"Everything's okay." She shrugged, twanging on the guitar. She was wearing black pants and a sleeveless black top with a high neck, but her arms were white in the California sun, and she looked as defenseless as a rabbit. "You're just a kid, aren't you?" she said, tucking a strand of thin hair behind one ear.

"Fourteen," Charles said.

"Lucky number," the girl said. "You want to smoke some weed, lucky boy?"

"Sure," Charles said, feeling very bold. "I'm a viper." He'd read *Really the Blues* a year ago, and he knew all about marijuana. Musicians smoked it all the time, and it made you feel very good. "Let's get stoned."

The pale girl looked at him and laughed. "Viper, huh? What a crazy town," she said. "I love it here." She reached into her bra, pulled out a loosely rolled cigarette, and handed it to him.

Charles took it, uncomfortably aware it had been between her breasts, small as they were. He put the crushed cigarette in his mouth.

She snapped a stainless steel Zippo, and as he bent toward her he smelled lighter fluid and heard the rush of the flame and the tiny crackle as the white paper caught fire. It sounded like dry brush burning. He inhaled deeply and held the musky smoke in his lungs; that was how musicians did it. As the smoke sank in, Charles felt a universe of happiness open up to him, and for the first time in his life he felt excitement and danger cover him like a net.

Smoking marijuana in broad daylight at the Griffin, where beatniks played. Smoking marijuana at the Griffin in broad daylight. The words rang through his head like a love song. Wonderful! Dangerous!

"So what's your name, man?" she asked.

"Charlie," he said as he took another drag and held the smoke in, just like Mezz Mezzrow in *Really the Blues.* "Name's Charlie Kartay."

"Charlie parlie darlie," the girl said.

"Oh, yeah," Charlie said as happiness enfolded him. The Griffin's white stucco walls turned prickly and speckled with dancing stars of light. "This is great."

But after the brief episode at the Griffin, Charlie retreated even further into solitude. He went home after school, stole wine from the fridge whenever he could get away with it, and took it out to his patio hideaway behind the pool house.

The strange golden expansion he'd experienced as he shared a joint with the nameless girl frightened him, so he locked it in his memory and resigned himself to the idea of waiting out his childhood. Charlie was determined to break free of the quicksand of Hollywood someday and have a different life, but until then he had to wait for age and time to set him free. So he learned to live a double life. At home he was quiet, reserved, polite but always remote. He answered questions, but his responses were superficial and his thoughts were hidden. His reading intensified. Ginsberg, Corso, Kerouac . . . Someday—Charlie knew the day would come soon—he would be on the road, free of the pervasive influence of Hollywood. One day he took the bus to Santa Monica and saw a weird black-and-white movie called *Little Shop of Horrors,* about a man-eating plant. That was how Charlie thought about Hollywood—as a beautiful Venus's-flytrap with a great red mouth chewing up all of the people in the movie business and turning them into a pulpy, homogenized mass of jelly. Charlie's real life lay behind the pool house on the brick patio in the late afternoon haze. Books and sun and solitude enhanced by wine.

Olivia Cole rapidly became indispensable to Violet Rawley. She often wrote Violet's column, "Seen on the Screen," by herself. She also wrote articles and interviews for *Tiger Beat* and *Sixteen* magazine and was a contributing editor to *Teenzine,* a new venture featuring interviews with budding rock and roll stars as well as actors. Olivia, who illustrated her articles with her own carefully posed "candid" snapshots, was a dynamo, working sixteen hours a day. Like her mother, she never stopped. She moved quickly through a whirlwind of parties, interviews, editorial sessions, and screenings, and she devoted every moment of her life to the heady business of gossip.

Secrets held no charm for Olivia Cole. In fact, she'd made a conscious decision that nothing would ever be hidden from her again. If there was a deal, an affair, or a marriage in her town, Olivia Cole was the first to know and, more importantly, the one to spread the news. And her determination played directly into the hands of Violet Rawley, a somewhat younger beehive-blond version of those famed purveyors of rumor, chatter, and idle speculation, Hedda Hopper and Louella Parsons.

Times had changed. Television was here to stay, the studio star system and the old moguls who'd made it run were long gone, and new stars were passing across the panoramic sky, stars like Rock and Tab, Marilyn and Jayne, Frankie and Annette and Sal. Glamour gave way to glitz, but Violet Rawley knew the show must go on.

Violet Rawley was a southerner, and when she first came to L.A. she wore a flirty-southern-belle trademark—a bunch of silk violets on her lapel, in her hair, or in the depths of her generous cleavage. After she reached one of her goals, the triumphal watershed of syndication in over a hundred newspapers, she had a delicate spray of diamond and enamel violets made at Tiffany and featured them as her personal logo. Jewelry was Violet Rawley's only passion other than her column, and she wasn't shy about letting Hollywood's elite know it. Come Christmastime, her Colonial house on Heather Drive was swamped with velvet boxes from every chichi jeweler in town.

"How boo-ful!" Violet would chirp in her famous baby-talk voice. "For wittle me?"

Her husband Al Tinker, an alcoholic stockbroker whose firm had benefited enormously from his wife's connections, groaned inwardly and poured himself another stiff scotch. For despite her baby talk and predilection for flowery prints, Violet Rawley didn't become a syndicated Hollywood columnist by being a silly absentminded dame.

She'd started out as an actress. For many years she was the mistress of a big studio producer, and when he dribbled his career away on a series of third-rate horror movies, some wag remarked that Violet Rawley had slept her way to the bottom. They'd mistaken her dogged southern loyalty for stupidity, but though Violet had many bad qualities, stupidity wasn't among them.

Finally, when the producer had a stroke and moved to the Motion Picture Country House in Woodland Hills, Violet did the only thing a decent woman on the skids could do. She got a job on the local Encino paper covering what passed for social life in the San Fernando Valley. Low rent, but not for long.

Violet dished the dirt as if she'd been born for it. She spent her evenings stalking the piano bars, lounges, and little restaurants up and down Ventura Boulevard, then mentioned every soul she saw in her first column, "Valley Chatterbox." Violet quickly realized that whenever she mentioned famous names and faces alongside those of the wealthy non-pros in the neighborhood, her column was avidly read and discussed in the local business community. The wealthy executives in the Valley loved to see their names in a column about movie stars.

Her byline spread, and very soon Violet Rawley was a force in the gossip industry. And, having been an also-ran, she was determined to remain a queen. Violet Rawley had experienced the depths, but she found the heights far more attractive.

She worked every morning in an office at her house on Heather Drive, making and taking an endless stream of phone calls. Then she went off to lunch, usually for an interview, then to her larger office in Beverly Hills, where she hammered her tidbits into a column.

"Olivia darling, isn't your sister having another baby?" Violet called one afternoon as she stormed into her Beverly Hills suite.

"'Bout a month, Vi," Olivia called. She was working on a heartbreaking story she hoped to sell to the Sunday supplements about the desolate small-town girl Elvis had left behind. "You'll be the first to know."

"That's the way I like it, dear," Vi called. "Don't ever forget it."

In New York, Simon Wyler bounced higher and higher, a rubber ball in a room with no ceiling. *Crowded Avenue* was followed by *Angels Cheer,* a wry, comedic tale of a show biz marriage. Then *Angels* went to Broadway and Simon went with it. Now that he didn't have to act, he was able to enjoy it and he won a Tony for his supporting role as the bemused neighbor. The short stories Roz had once laughingly characterized as "Pat Hobby in New York" were turned into a prestigious production for the "Hallmark Hall of Fame," and Simon was hard at work on a new novel.

After the birth of their first child, Danny, Roz and Simon had it all. They left the sublet and lived like royalty in the Carlyle. They had a house in the Hamptons, a live-in housekeeper, a nurse for Danny, and a bank account that gushed like a river, since every dollar Simon made flowed out the door like floodwater.

They ate and drank and gave parties, and Roz spent and spent and spent. She bought whatever she wanted, because in her secret heart she was desperately afraid, although she never admitted it. Except for Danny and rare moments with Simon, spending money was her only pleasure. Oddly, she liked to buy little things, things she characterized as trinkets. A cloisonné vase, not a couch. A Mogul miniature, not a Bechstein grand. A jade Buddha with onyx eyes, a jewelry box inlaid with mother-of-pearl. . . .

Objects were stable, constant, and reliable; Simon Wyler was not. Now that he was an overwhelming success, Simon's temperamental behavior was even more erratic than it had been when he was a struggling actor in Hollywood. He seemed to enjoy making trouble and felt his talent made it all right. He ate and drank too much in public places, got into a fistfight over another guy's girl in the momentarily chic restaurant La Vie, and he was prone to shouting fits when frustrated. Roz knew he slept around—the young actress who played opposite him in *Angels* told Earl Wilson that Simon was "divine." Then there was the chorus girl, the dancer, another chorus girl . . .

But though she bought and bought to fill the black hole expanding inside her, Roz believed no other woman understood Simon's need to control, and she clung tightly to this little raft as she spun faster and faster in the torrent of New York's nightlife. Their lovemaking was less frequent but more intense, and lately she noticed he was more interested in game-playing than he'd ever been before. Once he made swift, hard love to her in a dressing room at Saks. Once he sent her a note asking her to meet him at two-thirty in the afternoon at a sleepy Village bar. They drank too much, and Simon's hands slid up under her dress far too publicly. Afterward he took her to a room at the Sherry, and they made love with all the lights on and the windows open. Later, in the dark, she blindfolded him with his tie and felt, briefly, the same sensation of power over him that she'd felt the first time they'd made love in the pool house. Power bound them together—his power over her, her power over him. She didn't care. Simon fulfilled her deepest need, the need to belong. She was his.

So first she ignored his brief affairs, then finally accepted them as just another manifestation of his famous talent, feeling that no matter what, he always came home to her, to their life, to Danny. But try as she might not to notice, not to care, each new girl he took and tossed away was a loss, a wedge between them that was widening, widening, widening.

And as the crevice became a chasm, Roz shopped and bought and spent, because only things filled her up, because each new success of Simon's made her feel desperate and lost as he slipped away from her into another world. But objects weren't demanding, and they were incapable of causing pain. Besides, her second child was due any minute and another child would bind them together even more tightly. Wouldn't it?

Chapter

14

~~~

Katherine stared vacantly at her reflection in the mirror over the dressing table. The tired, wrung-out dregs of the day had seeped into her bones, and the bright light cast by the cut-crystal lamps on either side of the beveled mirror threw the shadows lying across her face into sharp relief. It had been a horrible day at the office, filled with angry phone calls, problem clients, and nervous studio bosses.

And Madeline was the worst. "The Rosie Parker Show" was long gone, but Madeline's prima donna truculence continued to grow by leaps and bounds. She was anxious about her age, and recently she'd insisted on taking every two-bit part she was offered, over Katherine's strenuous objections. Why couldn't the silly woman understand that she wasn't an ingenue anymore and that her overblown comedy style was highly individual? Without the right vehicle she was a grotesque, laughable caricature of herself. If Madeline's career was going to survive the sixties, she *had* to try something new, take a risk, and make a change.

The relationship between the two old friends was

stretched to the breaking point, and deep down, Katherine knew it wouldn't survive, primarily because Madeline went through cash like a shark through water, using most of it to finance a string of ever-younger muscular boyfriends. Her latest, a stuntman, wasn't helping matters any, and Madeline was dying to play Sheba in a ridiculous costume epic produced by a flamboyant Italian businessman. The idea of some quickie cash from a quickie flick in Rome sounded too good to resist, especially since the boyfriend was eager to travel. Angrily, Katherine uncoiled her hair and brushed it out.

Tonight was the Academy Awards ceremony, the capper on a long, unpleasant day. Oscar night, the grand culmination of the hopes and fears of stars, hairdressers, writers, executives, costume designers, directors, composers—every single moth inhabiting the incestuous, cloistered society circulating around the flame of the Hollywood studios.

It was the biggest night of the year, and shortly Katherine Cole would sit in the midst of a bejeweled audience and watch the elderly Edgar Lashman receive a special Oscar for lifetime achievement in Hollywood. Edgar Lashman, the man who'd denied her even those few stolen moments with Richard Sears. Edgar Lashman, whose power had forced Richard to abandon her for the second time. Edgar the intolerable would bask in his moment of glory as he climbed the steps to receive a special Oscar, and she'd have to sit there and watch it with a smile—an appalling prospect. Never give in, she told her reflection. Never show fear. Never.

Katherine groaned as the gold clock on her bedside table peacefully ticked the minutes away. Late already and she hadn't even started dressing.

Richard would be at the Academy Awards ceremony, and they'd smile and say hello in a very friendly way. Not too friendly, of course, because Maria would be watching and so would Edgar Lashman. Names rang through Katherine's head as she pulled the sapphire satin evening gown from her crowded closet and held it up, examining her image in the big mirrors lining the closet doors. Leo ... Olivia ... Charles ...

Roz ... A picture of Roz at fifteen smiled down from the shelf with the rest of the family pictures in their silver Tiffany frames, and Katherine automatically wondered how she was. But this was no time to leaf through the past. A tough night lay ahead, and Katherine was determined to play her part flawlessly.

"Lady Bountiful, *c'est moi,*" she said to her reflection.

You have nothing left but memories, a voice told her.

The hell you say, she answered, fierce as fire. She shook the dusty thoughts out of her head and began to brush her long red hair.

But to watch Edgar Lashman get an Oscar! To see Maria Lashman Sears gloating, a captive Richard by her side like a trophy. It was horrible, galling, infuriating, and there was no escape. Sitting for hours in an uncomfortable chair, smiling blindly as Edgar Lashman accepted his Oscar and mouthed inanities while Maria Lashman Sears basked in her father's reflected glory. A long, boring evening at the Governor's Ball after the ceremonies, the same old beautiful faces anxiously circling this year's studio chieftains, then another round of parties. But she had to go. She'd promised Olivia, and besides, she wouldn't give Maria the pleasure. She would go to the Oscars, she'd look beautiful, and she'd make people think she was enjoying herself. No one would hear her grinding her teeth. Nothing ever changes, she thought. Illusion is everything, and Hollywood's the same small town it was when I first came here.

"Too spoiled, too fast," she said aloud. "Ten years ago— no, twenty—you would have killed to go to the Oscars." Still, if she could have a hot bath and a cold martini and slip in between freshly ironed sheets, her mood would change, and in a few minutes she'd be ready to do battle with the human elements again. Or would she?

Methodically she creamed off her old face and reapplied a fresher, prettier one. Lately she needed more makeup to hide the tired circles beneath her eyes and the little lines digging in deeper every day. Nothing an Aida Grey facial won't cure, she lied to herself.

Nevertheless, when she had finished her face, piled her still-bright copper hair on top of her head, and slipped into the beautiful sapphire gown that accented her full breasts and small waist, she knew she looked spectacular. The years hadn't passed her by, but the hand of time had been gentle and she was still a handsome woman, sure of herself and confident of her footing in the Hollywood quicksand. Katherine Cole and the Cole Agency were a combined natural force, twin powers to be reckoned with. If she had to face Edgar Lashman, she'd push herself to the limit and there would be no cracks in her composure.

She put on her diamond necklace and as she stood in front of the full-length mirror, misting herself with Le De Givenchy, her favorite perfume, a funny thought hit her. I have no husband, one daughter hates me so much I've never seen my grandchildren, my other daughter's indifferent, my son worries me with his strange moodiness, I'll never have the man I love, but at least I've still got my figure. Not much consolation.

On her way downstairs Katherine looked into Charles's room, but it was empty. The bed was unmade, and the room was a mess. Books and records littered the floor, the desk, the bedside table. What's the matter with him? she wondered desperately. I don't know what to do. I'm afraid he's slipping away from me too. God, I'm afraid he's already lost.

"Charles?" she called into the kitchen.

Mrs. Gebhardt was polishing the silver. She had laid down a thick mat of newspaper to protect the table, and the radio was whispering gospel music into the night air. "In the living room, Mrs. Cole," she said without looking up from her work.

Katherine walked down the hall and opened the door to the living room. Charles was playing solitaire on the coffee table. The TV was on, but the sound was turned off. Atonal rock and roll music played on the radio, but at least he had the volume down. "Didn't you hear me calling?" she said. She knew she sounded sharp and impatient.

He looked up at her lazily and smiled. "Was that you? Where you going?"

"Oscars."

"Win one for me, will you? I hear Dickie Sears's granddad uses 'em to crack nuts with." He giggled.

"Good night, Charles," she said lamely as she walked outside and got into the limo she'd hired for the evening.

She didn't know what to say to Charles. He was so strange lately. Did he know about Richard? Was that why he'd made that crack about Dickie Sears? Did everybody know? Did *everybody* in this damn town know *everything?* Olivia said if two people know something, it isn't a secret. Olivia ought to know. She knew where everybody in this town was buried and how long the body been there.

Two hours later Katherine sat impassively, a wide fixed smile pasted on her face as Edgar Lashman slowly mounted the steps to the stage, waving to friends in the huge audience like a king as a thunderous ovation surrounded him. He blew a kiss to Maria, who was sitting in the front row with Richard, and accepted the applause reverberating through the room as his right. He was awash with the adulation of his own town, full of his own glory.

Katherine's face betrayed nothing of the fire storm brewing in the pit of her stomach. You son of a bitch, she thought grimly as Lashman accepted the golden Oscar from an ageless Cary Grant. Her smile was set in cement, but she applauded wildly, like the rest of the crowd. You bastard. It was just an affair. Did you have to deny me that one little flyspeck of happiness? We didn't want a lifetime, only a few hours a week. Nothing more. Couldn't we have that? A shiver ran across her naked shoulders as she remembered her hectic affair with Richard, that night after Spiegel's party when they went to the Beverly Wilshire and made love, the long passion-filled afternoons as they lay in the half-light high in the Hollywood Hills.

Onstage, Edgar Lashman motioned the crowd to silence, the king quieting his subjects. Despite his years, Lashman was trim and taut, and his dapper figure in his beautifully cut Savile Row dinner jacket was a tribute to years of tennis, polo, and the cutthroat croquet parties he hosted at his weekend home in Palm Springs. His military mustache matched his suave bearing as his manicured fingers lovingly caressed his own perfect golden Oscar.

Katherine looked at Richard, who was in front of her and to her left. He was smiling, but it was a polished actor's smile. Maria was posed elegantly beside him in a beautiful white peau de soie gown, her face glowing and triumphant as her father began to speak about his career.

"My friends," Lashman began. "This is a great honor, not only for me but for the rough-and-tumble studio that bears my name. At first many people thought our studio wouldn't survive. Many people didn't want us to survive. Many people thought Hollywood would be better off without our particular brand of low-budget moviemaking and the serials for the kids in the balconies." Lashman's tone was wry, and the crowd dutifully responded with a murmured laugh. "But we *did* survive, and by the time Lashman Films won its first Oscar"—Lashman leaned forward over the lectern and smiled intimately at the crowd—"for *Dangerous Skies,* just in case you've forgotten . . ."

More appreciative laughter from the crowd.

An ugly thought darted into Katherine's mind like a spider as she watched Richard's profile: I'd like to kill Edgar Lashman. I'd like to see him dead at my feet. I didn't want to take Richard away from his children, or even from that bitch Maria. All I wanted was those few hours a week— Richard's hands on me in the darkness, the touch and smell of love around me, his smile above me, his body on mine. A thrill ran over her, and she shivered violently as the memory of Richard's violently plunging body filled her thoughts. God, I hate Lashman. He has the world, but he wants more, like everybody in this goddamn town, she thought savagely.

He wants all he has and all I have, too. He sucks happiness dry as he'd suck the pulp from an orange.

"And many other Oscars followed, for many Lashman pictures. . . ."

"Dickie Sears's granddad uses 'em to crack nuts with." Charles's voice echoed in her head. . . .

"But a special Oscar is different. It's not just for one film, great as that film may be. It's for many films, for a lifetime's work spent in the entertainment business. It's for the privilege of giving something back to the American people. My friends, all I can say is that it's been a lifetime of happiness, and I thank you all from the bottom of my heart." Edgar Lashman dropped his head in a parody of modesty. Wave after wave of applause surrounded him, and when it was at its apex, Lashman slyly raised the gold statuette and kissed it on the mouth.

The crowd roared with laughter, and even Katherine was forced to recognize that his wry, cunning gesture bore the touch of a master. I'd still like to kill him, she thought as she smiled gracefully, applauded, and finally rose to her feet with the rest of Hollywood to pay tribute to Edgar Lashman. I'd still like to see him dead.

Finally the ceremony was over. Smiling, waving, Katherine and Olivia pushed their way through the crowd. Katherine watched Olivia proudly as she talked to disappointed stars, questioned studio executives, busily gathering bits and pieces of gossip for Violet Rawley's column. Violet had reserved one of the big post-Oscar parties as her beat for the evening, and Olivia was covering the ceremony and the Governor's Ball afterward.

Katherine smiled as she watched her daughter work the crowd. I had to learn that skill, she recalled. I had to overcome my insecurity and my fear that the famous people around me knew a secret I'd never know. Besides, I was forced into the industry when Leo died. Olivia's been swimming in this sea since infancy, and this town holds no mysteries for her. To her it's an industry town, like a steel or a coal town, and she knows it right down to the grit. Leo, you'd be proud of our daughter. For a moment maternal pride washed away the bitter taste of Edgar Lashman's triumph.

In the lobby, hyperactive people pressed together and debated the awards while the winners flooded toward the press room where they would give ingenuous, unaffected, thoroughly rehearsed interviews expressing their shock at receiving an Oscar. Smoke and noise and hysterical laughter filled the air like a flock of sparrows. Outside, reporters descended on the losing stars as they waited impatiently for their limos, ready to get on to the relief of a drink and a party where they could console themselves by making big plans for next year.

Katherine wasn't claustrophobic, but the crush of the crowd and the intense noise level was giving her a fierce headache. "Olivia, meet me outside when you're through," she called.

"Got to get some quotes," Olivia said, yanking the skirt of her silver lamé gown out from under a photographer's foot. "Five minutes."

On her own, Katherine moved a little more easily through the crowd, though it was only a blur of black dinner jackets, bare shoulders, and the sleek shine of the stars at play. Suddenly, without any warning, the throng broke open and she unexpectedly found herself face-to-face with Edgar Lashman, his Oscar dangling loosely in his hand like a golden club.

"Congratulation, Mr. Lashman," she said without missing a beat. "I'm Katherine Cole." She'd be damned if she'd show fear. She'd be damned if she'd give Edgar Lashman another victory. One was enough.

He gave her a slow, obvious once-over, and his interest was evident. "Of course. I know who you are, Katherine Cole," he said, his voice as rough as rock. "You worked on one of my pictures a long time ago. My first with Richard Sears."

"It was *The Arizona Kid,* Mr. Lashman." She laughed, refusing to be intimidated by his blatant reference to Richard. Lashman looked a good deal older close up. His face was tense and drawn, and deep blue shadows mottled the hollows of his eyes. My God, I thought he was invincible, but he's sick, she realized slowly. He's old, he's tired . . .

"Funny we've never met before, Mrs. Cole. You're very beautiful," Lashman said frankly. "Is it hard to be a beautiful woman? I've always wondered."

"It's hard to be a beautiful agent," she said swiftly. "So many men in Hollywood don't take you seriously."

He snorted bitterly, an imitation laugh. "Very funny. Very clever. You handle Madeline Gerard?" he asked.

"For years," she said. He knew that. Why was he asking?

"I'm thinking about using her in a picture," he said, still swinging the Oscar back and forth in his hand. His eyes traveled over her in a leisurely manner. "Perhaps you'd care to accompany me to a small party I'm giving? Very few people. Very intimate."

"I'm waiting for my daughter," Katherine said. "My second daughter. My older daughter is in New York." As she spoke the words she realized there was no doubt Lashman knew where Rosalind was. He'd probably kept tabs on her for years. Funny, I never thought about that before. I wonder if he would have offered me hush money after Leo's death? Probably, but I would have repaid the debt in his bed. . . . She remembered Maria Lashman talking caustically about her father's little book and his descriptions of the women he'd bedded. At least I'm not among them, she thought as she smiled up at Edgar Lashman. "I'm a grandmother," she added, driving the stake in a little deeper.

"Yes?" he said slowly. "How . . . nice."

As she watched, a curious change was spreading over Edgar Lashman's face, erasing the seams and the tired blue hollows. All of a sudden he looked younger, not as tired and drawn as he had a moment ago. For a brief flash Katherine imagined that he was melting like the Wicked Witch. Then his free hand clutched feebly at his tie and pulled the bow apart, leaving the ends dangling around his neck like a black satin rope.

"Hot," Lashman gasped. "Hot . . ." The Oscar slipped from his fingers, and Katherine automatically reached out and caught it before it hit the floor.

Lashman groaned and pitched forward, slumping heavily into Katherine's arms, pushing her backwards. As the weight of the old mogul pressed down on her, she realized with astonishment and horror that he was having a heart attack.

The crowd around them shrieked and split apart, recoiling from the scene in their midst. For a long moment Katherine Cole and Edgar Lashman were locked in a twisted embrace reminiscent of a frozen waxwork tableau. Lashman's breath rattled in deep gasps on her bare shoulder, and she felt the heat of his body seeping into her like a dreadful fog.

Horrified, she tried to wrench herself away from Lashman's fatal grip, but he wouldn't release her. Instead, he clung to her greedily, his grip unrelenting, as if he could drain the life from her body and into his own. Katherine searched the crowd, and across the room Maria Lashman's contorted face stood out in sharp relief, her neck corded with anger. Her white face was shining like a ghost's, her mouth a red circle of horror against the background of her white skin and her white gown.

Maria moved forward in slow motion, swimming through the air as if it were hot, sticky maple syrup, Richard behind her, his hands outstretched as if he would save Katherine if he could. She heard him yell for a doctor, but it was all so far away. A doctor? Louella's husband was a doctor, but he was long gone, she thought inadvertently. She heard Olivia call her name, but her voice was tinny and far away.

Katherine couldn't support Lashman's weight any longer, and the two of them slipped to the floor as she tried to loosen the collar of his white silk evening shirt. Air, she thought desperately. He can't breathe.

"Get away, bitch," Maria Lashman snarled as she reached her father's side. Her hands clawed at the Oscar lying on the floor at Lashman's feet, half covered by the hem of Katherine's sapphire dress. "Give me that!"

Katherine pulled her hem back as Maria kept clawing at her, and there was a sharp, tearing sound as her dress ripped under the weight of Lashman's body. His breath was harsh and painful, his eyes wide and puzzled as he stared blindly at the gawking crowd.

Richard pulled Maria backwards, and Katherine saw that his face was as cold as ash. Still, the event proceeded slowly, lazily, a fantasy ballet. There's no hurry, no rush, she thought dreamily. We have plenty of time. But as Lashman's cold fingers dug into her flesh, she realized he was dying. I've seen death before. I watched one man slip away through that gray door, and now I'm watching another. Lashman is dying and I wished him dead only a few minutes ago. Strange that a man who was my enemy for so many years should die in my arms.

Lashman shuddered and exhaled a long, thin stream of damp breath that went on forever. Then his unseeing eyes glazed over, and he jerked sharply and lay motionless in her arms.

Flashbulbs popped all around her, and as Katherine looked up and saw Richard Sears staring at her, she read an unexpected message in his strangely naked face: Edgar Lashman was dead, and there was nothing left to bind him to Maria Lashman. Nothing at all.

Edgar Lashman's funeral was the biggest social event of the season, and Olivia's firsthand account of the occasion—"the last of Lashman," as she jokingly referred to it—made the front page of the *L.A. Times* and was picked up by papers throughout the country. Violet Rawley behaved graciously in public, but privately she was livid she'd been scooped by her young protégée. For months afterward, Olivia languished in the Rawley doghouse, interviewing fallen stars, plugging bad movies, and living on a very short leash. Olivia fumed, but she confided to Katherine that the best course of action with La Rawley was to bide her time.

"I can wait," Olivia said confidently. "I'm young, and she's an old bat. I'll outlive her, I'll outsmart her, and I sure will outwrite her. Lashman's death was my first big scoop, but it won't be my last."

In New York, Roz read Olivia's article and saw the photograph of Edgar Lashman lying dead in her mother's arms, Richard Sears's shocked face in the background. It was literally too close to home for her battered nerves, and the photo threw her into a new frenzy of buying and redecorating. Lashman's death frightened her. It meant change, and change would upset the carefully ordered hothouse routine she'd erected around her life. She busied herself with the children, Danny and Zelda, the baby. Simon, who'd bought an old barn in Connecticut and liked to spend weekends there, was working on a new novel that promised pots of money—the story of a womanizing detective. Luckily, the decoration of the country house gave Roz an excuse for her increasingly frenetic shopping. She loved the binge-and-bust feeling that shopping gave her, the excitement of preparation, circling the stores—for there were different stores for different moods—looking, touching, deciding, and finally carrying off her purchases and enjoying the glowing afterplay of drinks when it was finally over. Antiques at the auctions at Sotheby's, jewels from Bulgari, clothes from Bergdorf Goodman. Bags and bags filled with treasure, bits and pieces of other people's lives, scarves and rings and crystal perfume bottles, and any other glittering trinket that caught her eye. She bought far more than she could use and often thrust the unopened packages in the back of a closet or under the bed so Simon wouldn't see them. Sometimes the bags were forgotten and accidentally ripped by the maid when she vacuumed.

Not that Simon gave a damn. He never noticed what she bought or how much she spent, although he admired her clothes and liked her to be well dressed. In fact, Simon liked her to be admired by his friends and enemies alike, especially by other men. Though his affairs with empty-headed girls were painfully public, he pressured Roz to be the most startlingly beautiful woman in the room. Any room. This was a central fact of Simon's character—the need to be seen and admired by other people. But Roz still believed she alone saw him accurately. She knew about his many girls, but she also knew he'd drop them at once if she needled him about it. The scenario was always the same: she'd confront, he'd deny, she'd demand, he'd apologize, she'd forgive, they'd make love, she'd shop. . . .

Katherine's life continued on like a wide, placid river as a new calm engulfed her. She heard nothing from Richard Sears, nor did she expect to—immediately. It was a question of time. Now that Edgar Lashman was dead and the last remaining bars to their relationship were torn down, it was time to wait and take things as they came. Sooner or later she would turn a corner and Richard would be standing in front of her. Sooner or later they would have one more chance.

By October Edgar Lashman had been dead for over six months, and Katherine had all but erased the memory of his cold grasp on her skin. It was late morning and the autumn day was warm and sultry, as fall often is in southern California. As Katherine parked her new Mercedes behind the Cole Building and walked up the stairs to her office, she felt the dampness on the back of her blouse from the leather seat of the car. She'd driven Cadillacs for so long that the foreign-built Mercedes was a new experience, but the European cars were growing in popularity and awfully pretty.

She opened the door to her suite of offices and saw Richard Sears sitting on the pale pink couch in the receptionist's office, reading *Variety.*

They looked at each other with years of knowledge in their eyes. He wore a light brown suit that set off his tan. His temples were going gray, she noticed. He looked terrific, and she was glad she'd had her hair done.

"Richard, how nice," Katherine said smoothly.

The receptionist, a pretty girl fresh out of an East Coast drama school and unused to movie stars, gawked openly at Richard.

"I assume you're here to see me?" Katherine said. "Come into my office. We'll have coffee." Her tone was light, neutral, and her smile was pleasant. Two old friends greeting each other. Two old friends who hadn't seen each other in ages. Two old friends intent on business.

Richard carefully put *Variety* back on the pile of papers and magazines on the coffee table, got up, and straightened his brown silk tie. "I need some advice," he said, his tone smooth and even.

Katherine led him through the corridors behind the receptionist, past the offices of her two junior agents and their secretaries, past her own secretary, Dolores.

Katherine poured coffee from the electric percolator Dolores kept on the breakfront. Carefully she set the delicate Belleek cup and saucer beside him on the end table.

Richard said nothing as he picked up the cup and held it gently, the pale porcelain trembling slightly in his hand.

"I've missed you," he said quietly.

Katherine sat down behind her desk. She felt light, deflated. Now that they were finally face-to-face, a strange awkwardness swept over her and she hadn't expected it. "Yes," she said. "I've missed you too. What are we going to do about it?"

"Get married, of course," he said without hesitation.

"Will Maria give you a divorce?" They might have been talking about buying a book or making a movie.

Richard sipped his coffee. "Oh, she'll give me a divorce all right. She'll be glad to get rid of me. There is, however, one small hitch." He laughed bitterly.

Another barrier to climb? Momentarily Katherine was furious. She felt a hot spurt of anger, and then her sudden fury disintegrated like a fallen soufflé. She looked at him; his tan movie-star face was so familiar to her. Like the rest of America, she'd watched him age on the screen, but after all they'd been through together, she knew him intimately, knew every nook of his heart. "Richard darling," she said with a laugh, "with you there's always a hitch."

"I never repaid the loan Lashman made me when I started Beachwood Productions. So . . ." He put the cup down on the table, and the spoon jangled slightly on the saucer, startling her.

"Maria owns Beachwood? Is that it?"

He nodded. "If I don't repay the loan in ten days, she'll take over. She's informed me she plans to dismantle the company and sell it off piece by piece just to twist the knife in a little deeper. She knows I want to marry you, so she'll try to destroy everything I've built." He laughed bitterly. "The viper in my bed. She'll give me a divorce, but she'll ruin my company. Strangle me."

Katherine got up and began to pace back and forth angrily in front of the long window looking out over the Sunset Strip. "Richard, it's always money, isn't it? Always money. Nothing comes before a buck with you. You threw me away to marry money; you threw away our daughter. Rosalind hates you. Did you know that?"

Richard shook his head. "I didn't," he said quietly. "When did you tell Roz I'm her father?"

"*I* didn't tell her; Linda did."

"Linda? *My* Linda? How did she—"

"Oh, grow up, Richard. Everybody in this town counts every breath you take. Olivia tells me the kids know everything first. Star kids, she calls them. Roz hates me, too, if that's any consolation to you. I haven't even seen my grandchildren."

"*Our* grandchildren."

"Richard, after Leo died we could have had a life together, but money and power were more important to you. Until today everything that's happened to us has been your choice, do you know that?"

Richard came over, grabbed Katherine by the arms and began kissing her neck. "I know I've made all the mistakes, Katherine," he said as she pulled away. "I was young and stupid, and I didn't know what love was worth. But, darling, I've changed," he said roughly. "I swear it. Look, I want you above everything. If I can beat Maria and keep Beachwood, so much the better. But I've learned from my mistakes. When Lashman forced us apart—"

"You forced us apart, Richard. Don't forget it." Funny, now that he was hers, she was free to be angry with him. After all these years of holding things in, she was finally able to let her feelings out and be herself with Richard Sears. "We both made the decision, but you were the lever. Not Lashman. You."

"Listen to me, damn it. God, you're an impossible woman! Are you listening to me, Katherine? I love you. I don't care about Maria. I'll fight to keep Beachwood because that's how I am. I don't lie down anymore. I fight. I've given in before—caved in, more like it. But if she strips me to my shorts, at least I'll have you."

Katherine was silent. Was he telling the truth? Could she depend on this mercurial man after twenty-odd years of dangling on the end of a hook?

"Well?" he demanded. "Do you love me? For Christ's sake, Katherine, that's why I'm here. Tell me you still love me. Tell me you forgive me for all the crap and agony I've put you through." Richard sank down on the couch and ran his hands through his hair angrily. "Red, we can have a future together that's much longer than our past. I was a monster; I know it and I'm sorry. But I didn't set out to be a monster. I acted out of ignorance, the ignorance of youth. Look, after we stopped seeing each other I went into therapy. You don't know what my father's death did to me, Red. It took me years to fight my way out from under his shadow, and when I finally did it, I was trapped under the Lashman legend, father and daughter. I've paid the price too, you know. Living like an indentured servant in my own house. Prince Richard, they call me. Slave Richard is more like it. Katherine, I swear I'm going to spend the rest of my life making it up to you. Look," he said, an ironic smile on his face, "if I lose Beachwood, I'll keep house for you. I'll make you coffee, I'll pick up the dry cleaning. If I win, if I can keep my company, we'll be rich as hell, and we'll buy the damn moon."

"You idiot! This is not about money. Can't you get that through your skull?" she yelled. "Don't you get it? Look around. I built this all by myself! The girl you threw away built the Cole Agency. I had nothing, less than you. No education, none of the advantages of schooling and family and position and name, and I built this alone! I didn't sell myself to do it."

He looked at her. "God, I was a fool to let you go. You are absolutely the most gorgeous, the most desirable . . ." He took her in his arms and started kissing her again. "Tell me you love me," he prodded. He lifted her up on the desk and hiked up her skirt, his hands caressing her thighs. "Say it, Red. I want to hear you say it." His hands cradled her on the desk as she pushed forward to meet him.

"Of course I love you," she said softly as the familiar warmth of his body spread through her. "In spite of it all, I love you." A wave of desire washed over her, but Katherine pulled back from his embrace, looked at him, and laughed, their bodies still locked together. "I'll say one thing for you, Richard Sears," she said breathlessly. "Life around you has never been dull. But, Richard, one thing . . . This is the last chance you will ever have with me. Ever. If you fail me now, if you run out on me, I swear I will find a way to ruin your life. Understand? Next to me, Maria Lashman will look like Shirley Temple."

Chapter

15

Katherine drove up the sloping driveway of the Beverly Hills Hotel with trepidation, her hands trembling on the leather wheel of the Mercedes. In a few minutes she would face Olivia and tell her about Richard Sears, even though she suspected Linda Sears had spread her own version of the story years ago. Still, now that she and Richard had a future together, Katherine believed Olivia deserved to hear the truth from her mother. As she slowly walked up the path and into the cool, familiar environs of the Polo Lounge, she wondered if she was about to lose another child. . . .

Olivia, wearing a neat blue silk suit, was already at the table, talking on the phone. She waved at her mother across the room and hung up as Katherine made her way through the crowded dining room. I'm not going to draw this out, Katherine thought fiercely as they touched cheeks. If I'm going to lose her, I won't wait for dessert to do it. Quickly, without embellishment, she told Olivia the story of her affair with Richard Sears. Painful as it was, Katherine wanted Olivia to know the unvarnished truth, but she glossed over one point in order to spare her daughter's feelings: she didn't admit that she didn't love Leo when they were married; she simply ignored the issue.

Olivia listened quietly, nodding as Katherine spoke. When her mother was through, she smiled and squeezed her hand. "I've known it since Roz left, Mom, but thanks for telling me yourself. Linda Sears—we call her Bitchy, by the way—has a mouth bigger than the Grand Canyon. She made sure I knew."

"Charles too?"

Olivia shrugged, eyes roving the room. "I guess. He's tight pals with Dickie Sears, who's a dumb kid but basically okay. Charles keeps to himself; it's hard to tell what he knows or what he thinks. But us star kids know everything in this town." She laughed scornfully. "Hollywood's forgotten victims, the offspring of the stars, studio magnates, directors, big-time agents like you. Some of us hate each other, like Roz and Linda, but Hollywood brats are a tight little group all the same. Hell, who else lives the way we do? Who else understands? Not civilians, that's for sure. Chauffeurs and screenings and shopping in Beverly Hills after school. Why should we go to college? To learn about English history? We saw *Elizabeth and Essex*. What else do we need to know?" She giggled. "Thing about us is, by the time we grow up, we're not fit for anything but Hollywood. That's why so many of us go into the business like our folks. What's Dickie Sears gonna do with his life—become a dental surgeon? Think Linda Sears'll fit in down at the Garden Club? We're Hollywood brats, and once the non-pro kids find out your father is Richard Sears or your mother runs the Cole Agency, they look at you funny. You just don't fit in anywhere else," she said again. "Star kids are freaks in the Hollywood sideshow; they're show biz aberrations. End of tirade."

Katherine was taken aback by Olivia's cynical thumbnail sketch of her childhood. "I'm so sorry, darling," she said quietly. "I never knew you felt this way."

"Don't feel guilty. God knows, it's not the worst fate in the world. If you can't adjust to being rich, gorgeous, and privileged, you're a big dope!" Olivia laughed at herself harshly. "Hell, I'm making the most of it," she said, waving her hand at the packed Polo Lounge. "I sure can't beat 'em, so I've decided to join 'em."

"I wish I'd known all this before," Katherine said slowly. "Maybe I could have made life easier for you."

"Comes with the territory." Olivia leaned forward conspiratorially, like a sorority sister. "Forget about it, Mom. It's not important. But this is: either Violet Rawley doesn't know about your past with Richard or she knows and can't back it up with hard facts. Either way, she's dangerous, and you'd better watch out for her. Rawley's part of the new breed of columnists, and she's got no ethics. Hedda and Louella were old bats, but they had a code of honor where the movies were concerned. Richard's a Beloved Star, and they never trashed a Beloved Star, especially one with big studio connections. But Rawley's the illegitimate offspring of yellow journalism and *Confidential* magazine, and she'll do *anything* to advance her career. And there's something else: I've heard rumors about Maria Lashman. Is she giving you trouble? More to the point, is she giving Richard trouble?"

"She'll divorce Richard, but she'll keep everything." Katherine's eyes filled with tears. "The house is hers anyway, the pictures, the furniture, everything, but we don't give a damn about that. The problem is, Edgar Lashman loaned Richard the money to start Beachwood Productions, and Richard never repaid it."

"Not very bright on his part," Olivia said thoughtfully. "And now Maria wants to screw him? So to speak?"

"Olivia, your language is impossible! Yes, she does. Unless he can repay the loan in ten days, and he can't do it. I could lend him the money, but he won't take it. So, Richard and I get each other, but his company goes down the drain, and everything he's built financially goes with it. It's an emotional issue. His father was a suicide, and Richard's terribly, terribly afraid of poverty."

"Aren't we all?" Olivia laughed cynically.

"Yes, we are," Katherine said slowly. "But for Richard it goes far deeper than fear, and Maria knows it. Taking Beachwood is her way of gouging out a chunk of his flesh."

Olivia leaned back in the booth, an enigmatic Mona Lisa smile on her face. "So that's the deal, huh? Well, she's got more than she bargained for this time, Mom. Don't worry about it. I told you, star kids know where *all* the bodies are buried. Leave Maria Lashman Sears to me."

At nine o'clock that evening Olivia got out of her Thunderbird and knocked on Maria Lashman Sears's front door.

"Olivia Cole for Mrs. Sears. I'm expected," she told the butler.

He led her into a sunken living room and left her there alone. The room was startling—stark white walls splashed with a pair of huge, disturbing Jackson Pollock paintings on either side of a black marble fireplace. The paintings were the focus of the room, and they drew the eye down into a bottomless swirling vortex. The other walls were lined with black-and-white George Grosz etchings, a stark counterpoint to the huge Pollocks. The furniture was bland, colorless, white shot with gray-black threads, serving as a background for the magnificent madness of the canvas and paper lining the walls. There was no doubt about it: the room was designed to disturb, and the violent emotions on display made Olivia distinctly uncomfortable.

A smooth voice came out of the shadows. "My father was a great collector, but you probably know that. I collect, too, but in a different style. Do you like pictures, Miss Cole?" Maria Lashman Sears was curled in an armchair, hidden in the shadows at the far corner of the big room.

Olivia turned quickly, caught off-balance.

Maria got up and went to the bar. She was tiny, her black hair was a mass of curls, and touches of gold gleamed in her ears and around her wrists. She was wearing a black jumpsuit with a thick gold belt around her tiny waist. A gold choker circled her neck, and her red toenails shone through gold sandals.

"Generally," Olivia said, recovering skillfully. "I was just wondering if I like these."

"Pollock can be overwhelming to the uninitiated," Maria said smoothly as she poured scotch into an old-fashioned glass. "You work for Violet Rawley? Drink?"

"No, thank you. I work for Violet, but I'm here on my own. Did I give you the wrong impression on the phone?" Olivia said, her voice cloying.

Maria frowned, swirling the scotch in her glass impatiently. "Yes, you did. I thought Violet wanted an interview."

Olivia shook her head. "No. This visit is not about an interview. It's personal. I want you to leave my mother alone." She said it flat out, hoping her bombshell would startle Maria Sears.

Maria burst out laughing. "You're awfully young to be issuing ultimatums, Miss Cole. Mind your manners."

Olivia shrugged. "I'm old enough to play hardball, Mrs. Sears. Leave her alone, give your husband a divorce, and give him time to repay your father's loan. You see, I know quite a bit about you . . . about your affairs. *Quite* a bit," she stressed. "So leave them alone. Hell, you have everything you want." She gestured at the room, the huge pictures, the insulated world of Maria Lashman Sears.

Maria slammed her glass down on the marble bar, and Olivia heard the crystal chip on the hard surface. "You little bitch! Get the hell out of here!" she snapped, flushing brick red to her hairline. "Who do you think you are, talking this crap to me?"

Olivia didn't back down. She walked over to the bar and looked Maria full in the face, the cut glass and crystal behind her casting a splintered light across the smooth marble surface. "I'm the little bitch who knows where the bodies are buried, honey. That's who the hell I am. So shut up and listen. You don't scare me. I know all about the Swans' Home for Girls, Mrs. Sears."

Maria's anger faltered like a stumbling racehorse. "Know what?"

Olivia laughed harshly, and for the first time she felt the

unbridled thrill of power that knowledge brings. "God, do we have to dance? Cut your husband loose or I'll spread the news of your extracurricular activities at the Swans' Home around this town. You and your rich, bored friends take those girls into your homes, and then you take 'em into your beds."

"How the hell do you know?" Maria asked sharply.

"I'm a star kid. What you Hollywood people don't understand is that your servants don't talk, but your kids do. Star kids know everything, Mrs. Sears," she said softly. "We *all* know *everything*. We know who you sleep with and where your money goes. We know who's on booze or pills and how your careers are going. We know what you're going to do before you do it. See," Olivia said ruefully, "half of you didn't want us, and once you got us, you thought we existed only to enhance your image, but now we're grown up, and you're stuck with us as bitter equals. Well, I'm grown up now, and I'm in the business I know best. Gossip. Dirt, rumor, and innuendo." Olivia smiled, a trace of the gleeful schoolgirl showing through. "Do what I tell you, Mrs. Sears. It's the best offer you're going to get. Give your husband his company and his divorce or I'll make sure the press finds out about your predilection for girls. You'll look like a damn fool, not because of what you do—God knows, nobody in this crazy town gives a damn who you fuck—but because you got caught. I've got a lovely set of eight-by-ten glossies, enough hard proof to satisfy the *New York Times*. You don't believe me? You should. I bought them a few years after your little Linda told my sister that they were related. Want to see them? They're nice and sharp."

Maria Lashman Sears turned abruptly and walked away from Olivia. She sat down on the couch and delicately scratched her long red fingernails on the fabric like a cat. "You're an evil little monster, Miss Cole. Are you sure *you're* not my daughter? You remind me of myself."

Olivia shrugged. "Heaven forbid. But since I think you mean that as a compliment, I'll take it as one."

"I guess I have no right to complain," Maria said, her

voice as cold as ice. "I've lived in this town a long time, and I know the rules. After all, I'm Hollywood's child too. Some wise man once said, 'It is not enough to succeed; others must fail.'" Maria Lashman smiled maliciously. "You may have won this round, but there'll be another. Hollywood's a small town, and we'll meet again."

"Don't threaten me, Maria," Olivia said. "I'm as tough as you are. First thing in the morning I expect to hear that Richard will have no more problems where you're concerned. I'm reliable. You be the same."

Olivia opened the living room door and went into the hall without waiting for the butler to show her out. As she walked through the big dark foyer she heard the sound of feet running lightly up the stairs.

Linda, she thought as she got into her car and drove away. Snitchy Bitchy Sears was eavesdropping. I wonder how much she heard. Didn't I just say star kids know everything?

Unexpectedly, Simon's detective novel, *Stone Cold,* was a failure. It was his first flop as a writer, and he didn't take it well. He'd failed before—but early in his career, and as an actor. He'd never really cared about acting, merely used it as a stepping stone to the career he really wanted—writing— so the scathing reviews of his latest book were agony. Simon was crushed and enraged. To fail so publicly, to be panned so viciously by the same critics who'd recently fawned over him . . . his humiliation was excruciating.

And there was a secret kicker intensifying his anger that only Roz understood: *Stone Cold* was his first work of pure fiction. His other books, his successes, were thinly disguised portraits of his own life—his life with Roz, with the Cole family. Always before, his own affairs, his marriage, and his tangled emotions were the basis of his books. Did the apparent stability of their marriage make him fear his well of talent was running dry? Simon began to drink heavily. He gained weight. He was combative. Without constant reassurance from Roz, Simon's usual unpredictability grew to king-size proportions.

"I'll never write straight fiction again," he said moodily one morning over the breakfast table. He was drinking red wine with his steak and eggs; he hoped it would chase away his hangover. "Trash they want, trash I'll give 'em." He knocked over his glass of orange juice. Danny laughed happily and did the same.

"Monkey see, huh, sport?" Simon rumpled the little boy's hair as the lake of juice spread over the tablecloth.

As she watched the man who was her husband, the man she no longer knew, a vast chasm opened at Rosalind's feet, like a dark, grinning mouth, a pit with no bottom. Here in New York she was completely alone, an infinitesimal ant isolated in the huge city. Oh, she had friends—acquaintances, really—actors from Simon's plays, his editor, his agent's secretary, women she lunched with—but she had no life of her own, no one to pull her out of the morass. Olivia was the only link to her past, and she was three thousand miles away.

"Olly, I'm afraid," she said when she phoned her sister later in the morning. "Simon's erratic. His behavior's undependable. He's drinking too much."

"What's too much?"

"He was drunk at breakfast this morning."

Olivia was silent for a long, painful minute, sighing heavily. "That's too much. Roz, he's got to stop drinking or you don't have a chance. Make him go into therapy. *You* go into therapy."

"Maybe he'll change," Roz said, pleading.

"Maybe he will," Olivia said. Her voice wasn't hopeful.

Roz knew her sister was trying to humor her. "The worst thing is, the new book's a dud, and it's sending him over the edge," she said.

"Yeah, I know. A pal of mine at Fox sent me the Story Department synopsis, and I could barely get through *that*. Sounds like a stinker."

"He wanted to break out of the mold, try something new."

"Big mistake," Olivia said wisely. "He's got a great

formula; he ought to stick to it. He's the biggest thing since Harold Robbins. This sprawling sex epic stuff is terrific! Push him back to it for his own damn good."

"Simon wants it all, Olly. There's a greedy streak in him he can't control. Gimme, gimme, gimme, that's Simon Wyler. Critical acclaim, money, love, sex, power . . ."

"Dreamer," Olivia said.

"Are they really getting married?" Roz asked, switching subjects without warning.

"Are they ever!" Olivia laughed. "Come out for the dream wedding, will you? Mend fences, let bygones be bygones. They've bought a huge house in the Hollywood Hills, up above our old house."

"What's she going to do with *our* house?" Roz asked angrily. A stab of pain cut through her as another piece of her childhood slipped away.

"Rent it."

"Rent our house? *Our* house? Who's going to live in it?"

"Me! And Charles is going to stay with me for a month while Mom and Richard get adjusted."

"You? Olly, you're insane! What do you need that big house for?"

"I'll give parties. Be a Hollywood hostess. Have wild orgies with handsome men. Besides, it's *our* house, and I don't want anybody else living in it. And if I've got a great house I can be oh-so-social, and I can do twice the work in half the time. I'm gonna improve my visibility quotient. Come out, Rozzie. Richard's a good guy, and he's nuts about Mom. It would mean so much to her."

"I can't do it," Roz said shortly. "I don't care if my life *is* falling apart, I'm not crawling back to L.A. like a failure. I can pull Simon back together. I've manipulated him in the past, I can do it again."

"Manipulate?" Olivia said slowly.

"Grow up, Olivia. That's what marriage is all about. Simon gets what he wants, I get what I want. Everybody's happy."

"But *is* everybody happy?"

"No," Roz sighed. "That's the damn trouble."

Katherine Ransome Cole stood at the window of her house and looked out at the garden. *Her* garden. *Her* house. The house she'd worked for, the house she'd wanted so her children would have a home. In a few minutes she would take the limo waiting for her in the driveway and ride a short way up the hill to the house she would share with Richard Sears.

They would marry in the garden of the new house, a house untouched by memories of the past, of Leo, of Maria, of their children, of the problems and difficulties they'd faced together—but never really together, always apart. Will my life change the minute I say "I do"? Yes. My life will change forever.

She wondered how it would have been if she and Richard had married when they'd first met. What kind of life would they have had together? Would they have lasted this long? In Hollywood that was a real question. The separation from Roz was her only regret. Katherine looked at the ring on her finger—Leo's plain gold wedding band covered with the nicks and scratches of years of daily life.

"He gave me a chance," she'd told Richard. "I don't want to forget him. Richard, Leo's between us but not as an enemy. He's an old and trusted friend, and it would be disloyal to discard his ring. I've worn it so long."

Richard had laughed, his eyes warm and happy. "Darling, Leo kept me on my toes for years. No reason for him to stop now. I'll get you another ring, a second wedding ring. Wear them both."

A week later a red leather box arrived from Cartier in New York. Inside was a huge square-cut diamond and a card reading "from Richard with my heart."

Katherine was ready to begin her new life. We have years ahead of us, she thought. I've had years of work and years of solitude. I never expected that Richard and I would be allowed to have a life together. We had a past; now we are being given a future.

She took one final look at her bedroom, the bedroom she'd shared with Leo Cole. This was the last time she would see it as Katherine Cole, as Leo's widow. The next time she returned she would be Olivia's mother, helping her pick out new drapes or carpets or rearrange the furniture. She would be a new woman. She would be Katherine Sears.

Six hours later Katherine and Richard went up the stairs to their bedroom in the new house, and for the first time in their long life together, they were hand in hand at the end of the day. The room was dark; everything was new. Flowers cascaded from vases on every table. There was nothing from the past—no beds slept in by other people, no tables holding the ghosts of other family dinners, no paintings picked out to fit other walls, no traces or mementos of the past except for the framed photographs of the children in their separate offices downstairs. A clean face to the world.

The day that took so many years to arrive was over. The guests had eaten the caviar, drunk the champagne, and danced the evening away. They'd deposited their wedding gifts in the library—silver from Tiffany and David Orgell, Porthault linens, and antiques from all over the world. It was over. The big new house was empty, and Katherine and Richard were alone. The evening was quiet; a few sounds echoed over the hills: laughter from a party farther down, crickets humming busily in the damp grass in the garden.

They'd decided against a honeymoon. A few weeks of hectic travel abroad would only increase their tension and prolong the arrival of the moment they wanted most, the moment of evening solitude in the quiet Hollywood Hills with a few peaceful hours stretching out ahead of them like an unbroken ribbon of highway. Time. They wanted time. . . .

How do you feel?
Stunned. Amazed.

I'm relaxed. I haven't been relaxed since . . . maybe never.
Have we done the right thing? The children . . .
We can't live for our children. We have to live for ourselves.
I've only lived for my children. Now I want to live for you.
I've never lived for my children, only for myself.
Men and women are utterly different.
Utterly . . .

Charlie Kartay—for that was how he thought of himself
—was lying on the warm bricks behind the pool house
smoking a joint and thinking about his secret life. The sky
was flat and dull, the color of a dirty ocean, and the roof of
the pool house overhead reminded him of a tall building. A
skyscraper. Did they still call tall buildings skyscrapers? Roz
would know; she lived in New York, and that was the kind of
thing New Yorkers knew.

He liked living with Olivia because she was never home,
just like Mom, but he missed Roz. Everything had fallen
apart after she left. Or maybe not. Maybe things were always
fallen apart. Maybe *he* was the fallen-apart one. In a little
while he'd get up and go down to the Strip and see if Star
was there. Star was her freak name. She'd chosen it herself
because she didn't like her old name, which was Susan or
Mary. He'd go in a little while. Till then the ground was
warm and there was no reason to hurry. No reason at all.

It was warm here, and there was always the beach. He was
taking a few classes at UCLA, but that was a drag. Easy,
though. Just like home. He did what they wanted and they
thought he was a good kid and left him alone. He'd learned
long ago that all you had to do was give older people the
right answers and they went away and didn't bother you.
How's school? Fine. Having fun? Yeah, just great. Simple. All
you had to do was be a parrot. That's what they wanted.
Parrots.

Most of the time he hung out on the Strip, had a
hamburger at the counter at Schwab's. Ate Danish at Pupi's
and listened to the half-baked writers and out-of-work

publicity guys at Barney's Beanery lie to each other about how great they were doing and how they had a job at Metro all lined up. Charlie thought it was pathetic.

If you're born into a Hollywood family you can't escape, no matter how far you go. Funny, his mother's office was on the Strip and her new house was so close to her old house, yet the two were worlds apart. L.A. was a small town masquerading as a metropolis. Now she was married to Richard Sears, which meant he and Dickie Sears were brothers, which was also pretty weird. Dickie was okay, though. It was Linda Sears who was a pain in the ass.

Mom and Richard had moved to the new house, and that kept her off Charlie's back. Richard Sears was okay. At least he didn't try to be fatherly or bug Charlie with stupid questions. Dickie Sears said his father wasn't a bad guy, but kind of dense and a real prude about sex. Besides, it didn't matter who Mom married. Just act like a parrot. *How's school? Fine. Having fun? Yeah, just great.*

Wheels within wheels, thought Charlie Kartay. Wheels within wheels within wheels.

Simon's detective novel sold to the movies for an absurdly low price, but he took the deal because it gave him the opportunity to write the screenplay. It was purchased by Columbia, and in typical Hollywood fashion the background of the book would be transposed from New York to London because the British producer had interested Kim Corbin in the project and she was a rising star in the international firmament. Besides, a British film with American backing was financially advantageous.

"If I write a hit movie—and this'll be a hit if I have to kill myself in the process—I can write my own ticket in L.A.," Simon told Roz repeatedly. "Big money. I can produce. Anything. *I'll* be in control."

Simon's depression had lifted. He was riding the crest again, feeling the wind of success in his thinning hair. He'd tempered his drinking, and he was no longer spiraling downward but skyrocketing higher and higher emotionally with each transatlantic phone call. Roz was terrified the deal would collapse and his mental balance would slide away with it, but after weeks of intense negotiations, the deal jelled.

He would jet to London alone and stay at the Dorchester until he found a flat. Then she would follow with the children. Their separation was to last a few weeks at most, but as Simon's departure date approached, Roz grew increasingly nervous. They'd known each other so long—grown up together, really—that it was hard to imagine life without him, even for a few weeks. But Roz knew the separation was worth the anxiety. With the London trip on the horizon, Simon's mood improved, as if a rain cloud had blown across a mountain range, and he was his old self again. Difficult and unpredictable as ever, but that was Simon's nature, after all. Work was the center of his life and as long as he had work—a book, a project—he was Simon Wyler the novelist. Without it he was a one-dimensional cardboard man with a brittle paper soul.

But two weeks after he left, Roz was at the breakfast table in their Fifth Avenue apartment, the sun streaming in on the yellow pottery dishes scattered across the bright yellow tablecloth like sunflowers, feeding Zelda Wheatena from a silver spoon while Lena, the rail-thin Polish maid, did the dishes. Routinely, Roz opened the *Daily News* to the columns and gasped. Simon was snarling out at her, one hand up in a vain attempt to shield his face from the camera's prying eye and one hand on the pale, beautiful, bare shoulder of Kim Corbin.

Roz looked at the photo for a long, unbelieving moment as the impact settled around her heart like a shroud. Simon in evening clothes. Kim Corbin poised on the brink of fame, her lush figure outlined in a tight white satin sheath, teetering on spike sling-backs, her blond hair tousled as if she'd just wakened from a long nap, her blue eyes childlike, shocked at the presence of the camera.

Roz let her eyes flick over the squib in the column: ". . . Kim Corbin and writer Simon Wyler. She's starring in the steamy film version of his novel, *Stone Cold*. Funny, Kim and Simon look plenty hot to me. . . ."

Plenty hot, Roz thought dully as she put down the paper. Simon's blank eyes stared out at her, and she carefully placed her cheery yellow cup over his face. Plenty hot.

Kim Corbin was trouble, no doubt about it. A famous blond film star. Young and pliant. And Simon appreciated youth in a woman. Young women were easy to impress, easy to control, especially for the polished, sophisticated man Simon Wyler had become. He'd had women all along, but chorus girls and hopeful actresses were never a threat to Roz; they were flirtations. But Kim Corbin was a sex goddess poised on the brink of megastardom. Ladylike yet shameless, voluptuous yet restrained, Kim Corbin was everything Simon Wyler craved. Yeah, plenty hot.

Roz booked a flight to London for the next day. She'd held on to Simon before; she'd given him everything. Simon was hers. She took a cab from Heathrow directly to the Dorchester. The streets were damp and bleary through the smudged window of the big black cab, and the world outside looked confused, backwards, until she remembered the English drove on the left side of the street. She realized the sense of unreality clouding her mind was merely a product of her exhaustion. She was wound up, dizzy, disconnected, and the long flight had drained the last of her inner resources. She wondered if she had the strength to face Simon.

She stopped at the desk and told the clerk she was Mrs. Wyler, joining her husband. Did she see a gleam in his proper eye or was that a product of her exhaustion as well? The bellboy led her upstairs to Simon's suite. She tipped him mechanically, and she was alone. The room was empty and dark; only a pale slice of morning light shone through the half-drawn curtains. Traces of Simon were scattered over the room like fine dust—the inevitable blue notebooks, his talisman from the past, his typewriter, his books, clothes thrown carelessly on every chair. A bottle of Glenlivet stood next to a box from Turnbull and Asser on the writing table, and at least twenty shirts of every color cascaded out of the half-open box like pale jelly beans.

The table lamps were on in the bedroom, the bedclothes tossed back to reveal creased sheets and a rumpled bedspread. A white satin brassiere hung from the knob on the bathroom door. Gingerly Roz picked it up and checked the label. Saks Fifth Avenue, size 36 C. She replaced it on the knob, went back to the living room, and lay down on the couch. Years of marriage evaporating in a few days. The children, their life together, the ideas, the books, the fights, the days and nights spent catering to Simon, indulging his whims and foibles, disappeared with the crack of a closing door.

The cloth of the couch felt electric on her skin, the room swam, and she realized she was crying. Her life? She had no life. She had only the dregs of Simon's life. Mrs. Simon Wyler—laughed at by the columnists and by his battalion of girlfriends, used by her husband like a convenient hotel, a dry cleaner, a watering hole sandwiched in between binges. But losing Simon was a terrifying idea, and she didn't know if she could bear life on her own. He was a lifeline whipping out of her hands in the midst of a hurricane. The silence of the unfamiliar room was suffocating, but eventually Roz fell into a heavy, uncomfortable sleep. She woke an hour later, to the tick-tack of a key clicking in the brass lock on the door.

"What the hell are you doing here?" Simon was startled, but he covered it by blustering. He was wearing a dinner jacket, his white shirt was open, and his tie was dangling out of his pocket. He'd been drinking, and his voice was rough with hours of smoke and talk.

"I missed you," she said, rubbing her eyes. I'm placating him already, she thought through the haze of sleep, her voice stiff and false. Did he believe her? If she didn't confront him with the truth, would he pretend it was business as usual? She'd *never* confronted him, she'd *always* placated him, and now she was going to break the pattern. "I saw the picture of you and Kim Corbin in the paper."

Simon shrugged. "That sort of thing never bothered you before, Roz. Why start now?"

She would be courageous. No more placating, no more. . . . "I'm through with your arrangements, Simon," she said sharply. "I want a real life with you or . . ."

"Or?"

"Or without you."

"Roz, leave it alone. Be smart. Don't shred our life over nothing."

"Tell me, Simon," she said slowly. "If we get divorced, who will you write about? Kim Corbin?"

He looked at her curiously, his eyes like pale stones. "Have to write about something, don't I?" He shook his head and poured a glass of Glenlivet from the half-empty bottle sitting next to his box of shirts. Absently he rubbed the material of one shirt between his thumb and forefinger. "Warm scotch?" he asked, meticulously straightening the shirts. "No ice. Very British." He didn't look at her.

The lifeline slipped out of her hands, a raveled end of rope slapping into a cold, dark sea. Roz felt very small, smaller and younger and more helpless than she'd felt on that long-ago evening when they'd made love in the pool house.

"No scotch." She hated him for letting her slip away without a second thought. All these years she'd believed their relationship was unique, but *he'd* known she was merely a cog, a gear, in the magnificent machine that was Simon Wyler. Then the lifeline disappeared into the darkness ahead, and Roz was alone. "Simon, tell me a story. Tell me about Kim. What she is to you? Who you are with her?"

"That's not a story."

"Make it one. That's what you do, isn't it? Tell stories? Create people?"

He snorted a harsh, ugly laugh. "Kim's a creation, all right, but not mine. She's a manifestation of the coming media hegemony, the days ahead when TV will dominate the world. Her managers and publicity people and agents run her life. Kim doesn't exist; she's just a pretty little Frankenstein monster. She's wonderful, Roz—so artificial, so modern. Nothing is natural; every move she makes is studied and planned. But I know her secret, and her handlers don't. *She* thinks she has talent, and she's shrewd enough to realize I can write parts she can play. Is that story enough for you, Roz?"

Loneliness engulfed her as Roz Wyler looked at her husband and didn't recognize him. The man she'd known and loved, the man she'd hoped would protect her, was a complete stranger to her. Somewhere in the long-suffering past, Simon Wyler had disappeared, and now there was only an inflamed egotist standing in front of her, clutching a glass of warm scotch in a foreign hotel room. How had she missed his transformation? But deep down, she hadn't missed it at all. She'd simply ignored it, buried it underneath a stack of shopping bags and packages piled to the sky.

"Jesus, Simon, I knew you were a bastard! I knew you'd sacrifice everything to your ambition, but I didn't think that included your family! I thought Danny and Zelda and I had a unique place in your heart, that no matter what went wrong, we were your family and we were paramount. God!" she said half to herself, hating the note of pleading she heard in her voice. "Did I think you were Leo? I've made a terrible mistake, and I don't know what to do."

"Don't worry, Roz," Simon said impassively, staring out the window. "Somebody'll come along and make the decision for you, like always. Go buy something. Soothe yourself with shopping," he said sardonically. "Spend my money on some useless piece of junk. How about a Sevres cachepot or a silver-framed Georgian mirror? Remember, those who can, do. Those who can't, decorate."

"Fuck you, Simon!"

"Ohhh, nasty, nasty. You used to be so wonderful, so pliable, malleable. God, you were like a lump of clay. I could make anything I wanted out of you."

"And now I'm not clay anymore? Is that it?"

As he poured more scotch, his hand trembled and the bottle hit the rim of the glass. "Nah, not anymore. Not pliable, not supple. Kim, now, she's a woman made to be made, if you know what I mean. You're all dried up," he said critically. "Not your fault, though. It's the kids. Kids take it out of a woman. No more fun and games."

Anger filled her, and Roz leapt forward and slammed her fist into his stomach as hard as she could. He was unprepared for the blow, and her fist sank into the soft pit of his gut. It felt good, and she lashed out again, catching him on the arm.

"Bitch!" Simon shouted, clutching his stomach. He grabbed her arm, twisting it backwards. "Fuck's the matter with you?"

He slapped her face, and she stumbled and fell to the floor, her face pressed into the forest green carpet of the Dorchester. Years of dust assailed her, the smell of spilled liquor, of other couples and other fights, of the past and the present, mingled into an acrid stew. She kicked up at him, grazing his leg.

"Little bitch," he said. He threw himself on top of her, tearing her blouse and exposing her breasts. "Bitch," he muttered, wrestling her arms over her head and burying his mouth in her neck. "Bitch," he mumbled as he unbuckled his belt and pushed her legs open with his knee. "Bitch, bitch, bitch, bitch!"

Simon's weight bore down, and as he entered her, Roz realized it wasn't happening to her. It was happening to somebody else, somebody who wasn't Rosalind Wyler. Over Simon's shoulder she saw a crack running diagonally across the ceiling from the corner of the room to the brass chandelier in the center. Just a hairline crack, but if she could focus on it, rivet her attention on its spidery trail, nothing bad could happen to her. Follow the lines, her mind said. That's all you have to do. This isn't happening to you; it's happening to somebody else. Follow the lines. . . .

After Simon left, Roz lay on the floor and cried for a long time, clothes torn, legs wet, bleeding from a scraped shoulder where he'd ground her skin raw. Pain, rage, frustration, humiliation—one emotion after another shuddered over her body until she was empty and there was nothing left but an uninhabited void. She staggered into the bathroom and stood in the shower until the scalding water turned her skin red.

She slept on the couch for an hour, and when she woke up, she was starving. The body made its demands even in the midst of disintegration. She called room service and ordered a steak and a bottle of Piper Heidsack as a bitter afterthought to celebrate the death of her old life. When the food arrived, she tore into it ravenously, and when she finished she was clutching the steak knife so hard there were welts on her fingers.

An idea struck her. A wonderful idea! An inspired idea! She took the knife and went over to the box of multicolored Turnbull and Asser shirts and methodically cut them apart, ribboning each one into ragged streamers. Even the tiniest revenge brought relief, and she ran into the bedroom, threw open the closet, and attacked Simon's suits one by one. A conservative blue with chalk stripes, a gray houndstooth sport coat, a Burberry trench coat—she slashed them all to rags. She saw four or five pairs of made-to-order Lobb shoes, complete with wooden shoe trees, lying on the floor. Roz got down on her hands and knees and carved a deep X into each burnished toe. The knife handle broke before she could finish, and for a long, agonized moment she clawed furiously at the last pair of shoes with her nails. Finally, her rage spent, she collapsed on the floor, panting.

An hour later Mrs. Simon Wyler left the Dorchester as beautifully dressed and coiffed as she'd been when she arrived. The doorman hailed her a cab, and she rode over to Bond Street and bought an expensive antique diamond bracelet for herself and a little diamond and sapphire pin for Zelda. Mrs. Wyler billed everything to her husband at the Dorchester and went back to Heathrow to wait for the next plane out. There was nothing left to do but go home and start all over again.

Chapter
16

Roz flew home to New York, went to bed, and stayed there for days. Danny and Zelda played outside the bedroom door, but they made only faint faraway scratching noises like puppies whimpering in a distant basket. Roz lolled in bed and studied the heavy diamond bracelet glittering on her wrist.

Lena brought food on a tray, but eggs and toast grew cold and went uneaten while Roz slept the week away, caught in a troubled swamp of twisted dreams. When she was awake she couldn't shake the disconcerting feeling that she was somebody else and none of this was happening to her.

She was a balloon tied to the earth by a long silver thread, a tiny sphere bobbing up and down in the sky, tethered only by a piece of thin silk. But even as she was floating high in the air, she also saw herself lying on a carpet of leaves on the floor of a forest far below. Whatever was happening down on the ground, it didn't concern her.

After a week she dragged herself out of bed to write Lena a check for the housekeeping, but Lena came back from the bank empty-handed. "The money not there," she said helplessly in her thick accent. "Gone. Empty."

Roz pulled on her bathrobe, dragged herself back down the hall to Simon's study, and called the bank. Lena was right: Simon had closed the account and there was nothing left. Roz started to cry. She felt helpless and exposed, the same way she'd felt as she lay on the floor of the Dorchester, the dust in her nostrils and her husband's weight bearing down on her, stripping away her self-respect and making her powerless. Simon handled the money. She didn't know where it came from, how much there was, or where it went. She merely spent it.

She phoned her sister. Olivia listened intently, said she'd make a few calls, and called Roz back a little while later.

"Sister mine, here's the scoop. You're broke, the lease on your snazzy apartment is up in two months, and I'll bet my life Simon's stopped all your charge accounts. Is Gristede's still delivering the groceries?"

"I don't know."

"You don't *know*? What the hell are you eating?"

"Lena's cooking for the kids. . . . I don't know what. I've been sick for a few days."

"Sick or sad? Roz, listen to me." Olivia was firm, almost parental. "Get up, get dressed, and get moving. Sell what you can. Send the good stuff to Sotheby's and flog the rest to the same antique stores you got it from. You won't get half what you paid, but the cash will keep you going until we figure something out. Then get on a plane and come home. Bring the kids and Lena."

"Go back to L.A.?" Roz asked dully, looking across the room at the big mirror with the gilt frame of intertwined angels she'd bought Simon for his birthday. It had cost a fortune, but it was so pretty she couldn't resist. Always the easy way, she thought as she stared at her frightening reflection framed by angels. She was gaunt and drawn, her hair was stringy, and there were dark smudges under her eyes that hadn't been there a week ago. "God," she said to

Olivia. "I just saw myself in the mirror, and I look like a witch! I can't come to L.A."

"Yes, you can, and you'll do it in one week, you hear me? Listen, Roz, you don't have a choice. Do the words 'no money' register with you? Huh? You're broke. You haven't got anything except what's in the apartment."

Slowly it began to sink in. "Nothing?"

"Nothing."

Roz looked at the diamond bracelet she'd charged to Simon after he . . . did what he did to her. But she wasn't going to think about that. Ever. "I have a very expensive diamond bracelet," she said slowly, hefting its cool, perfect weight on her slender wrist, the stones catching the faded light in Simon's study.

Olivia snorted audibly. "Just like Mother."

"What?"

"Rozzie, c'mon, this is Olivia! Don't you remember Mother's story about how after Daddy died she didn't have anything left but the diamond necklace? She hocked it, and that's how she kept body and soul together, bought us oatmeal, and financed the agency? C'mon, c'mon, it's her version of walking ten miles through the snow to the little country school."

"I remember," Roz said. "Call you tomorrow, Olly."

"Reverse the charges," Olivia said as she hung up.

Roz leaned back in Simon's chair, the leather sticking to her bare legs. My God, she thought, I'm just like my mother. . . .

Ten days later Roz was back in the old house, in her old room, in the same single bed she'd slept in as a child. The sense of familiarity and comfort was overwhelming, and Roz lay in bed and looked at Leo's picture up on the shelf. The children were napping in Olivia's old bedroom, Lena was in the guest room, and Olivia was at work. Somewhere downstairs Mrs. Gebhardt was vacuuming, a soothing throb in the background as peaceful as a calm ocean.

Roz was thrust back into her childhood, into the secure

world she'd hated as a child and craved as an adult. She closed her eyes and pretended Leo was downstairs. She was a good little girl and her daddy was still alive, smoking a cigar and reading the Sunday funnies aloud as bees hummed in the purple azaleas beneath the front window. She was safe and warm and dreamy, and nothing bad could happen here in the warm embrace of a past long gone. Later there'd be plenty of time to get out of bed, go downstairs, go outside. No rush. No hurry. There was plenty of time for a good little girl. . . .

"I'm worried about her, Mom," Olivia said several days later, pacing up and down impatiently on the rich Oriental carpet in Katherine's office. "She won't tell me what happened with Simon, but I know it was pretty bad. She cleaned out the apartment and got out of New York, but she didn't have a choice. The rat bastard left her without a dime. Then, as soon as she got here, she went to bed and I can't get her up. Mom, you have to do something."

Katherine toyed with her crystal paperweight. Half a heart, a jagged edge cut down the middle. Richard had the other half on his desk. "Darling, what can I do? Roz won't see me," she sighed, squinting into the depths of the crystal heart. "She hates me. She thinks Richard and I betrayed Leo."

Olivia shook her head. "Mom, this is serious business. She *has* to get out of bed, and you're the only one who can make her."

Katherine frowned and pushed the heart onto the far corner of her desk. "Olivia, are you happy in the gossip business?"

"I love it, Mom. I was born to stir shit and raise hell," she said happily.

"Olivia Cole, your language is atrocious!"

Olivia laughed, delighted she'd teased a reaction out of her mother. "Why do you ask?"

"Roz has to do something with her life—get a job, make money, and support her family if Simon won't."

"She can sue the bastard for all he's got and all he's gonna get," Olivia said grimly.

"Yes, but that's next year or five years down the road or who knows when? Besides, money isn't the only issue. Rosalind can't go on depending on Simon to shape her life. She has to make a world of her own. Olivia, would you be offended if I took her into the agency? Would you feel I was giving her something you had to work for?"

"You mean train Roz to take over? No, Mom, I wouldn't be offended. I love the Cole Agency, but I don't want it. Remember when you used to take me to the office and I'd make paper-clip necklaces?" Olivia said, her voice pensive as she looked out the window. "Remember when I told you us star kids weren't fit for anything but Hollywood? It's true. And that's exactly the reason I want to be my own boss. No acting, no agenting, nothing that runs in the family. Besides, I've always felt . . . different, and in this town a gossip columnist is the ultimate outsider, the only person free to point out that the emperor ain't wearing any skivvies. Give the agency job to Roz, Mom," Olivia said briskly, business as usual. "Just don't let some big company gobble you up. Keep the Cole Agency in the family."

That evening Katherine stopped at the old house on her way up the hill to meet Richard for dinner. It was the same, white-walled and sturdy, but it was smaller than she used to think, a piece of her past that had slipped away like so many others. How hard she'd worked to keep this house and give her children a good education and nice clothes and a happy life. And now Roz was in bed and wouldn't get up, and Roz's husband was splashed all over the papers with that damn blond cupcake. . . . Katherine shook her head angrily. Time to read the riot act.

"Rosalind?" she called out as she went inside.

Mrs. Gebhardt saw her come in, and her broad face split into a happy grin. "Oh, Mrs. Cole, thank heavens. I told Olivia you had to come. Roz won't get up, Mrs. Cole."

"Make us some tea, will you, Mrs. G.? I'll get her up," Katherine said grimly. "Rosalind!" She marched upstairs, acting a lot braver than she felt. She stopped at the bedroom door, took a deep breath, and went inside.

Roz was curled up in bed in the fetal position, her face turned to the wall. "Go away," she mumbled. "I don't want to see you."

"Tough. Turn around and look at me, Rosalind. Now." Katherine's voice was commanding, the tone of a mother who would brook no disobedience from a recalcitrant child. It worked. Roz turned her head and stared bleary-eyed at her mother.

"Rosalind Cole, get up this minute and comb your hair! You look like a fright! What's the matter with you? You have children, and they need you. Either you get out of bed or I'll take Danny and Zelda home with me. No housekeeper is going to raise my grandchildren."

Roz burrowed down under the covers so only her pale, drawn face was visible. "Mrs. Gebhardt raised us," she said, her voice muffled.

"That's a lie and you know it," Katherine said sharply. "I love Mrs. Gebhardt, but I was your mother then, and I'm your mother now. So do as I tell you! Get up!"

"Oh, Mom, I can't. . . . What am I going to do?" Roz moaned.

Katherine smiled to herself as she felt a double wave of relief and victory. She's talking to me. She has to talk to me; I'm her mother and she needs me. "Put on your robe and come downstairs," she told Roz. "Mrs. G. is making tea. I've been at the office since eight, and I need a lift."

Roz obeyed without complaining. She pulled on her satin bathrobe and slid her feet into flowered slippers, then quietly followed Katherine downstairs to the living room, moving as stiffly as an invalid. Mrs. Gebhardt brought in a tray loaded with hot tea and cookies and hefty slices of her own date nut bread, then scurried out of the room, leaving mother and daughter alone.

Katherine poured tea and slid the tray of bread toward Roz. "You think your problems with Simon are original, Rosalind? Is that why you won't get out of bed? God, for a woman whose face is all over *Vogue* you're awfully naive! It's post time, darling. Time to get moving."

Roz sat silently, pulling at the belt of her robe and staring out the window at the purple twilight. Across the canyon lights were popping on over the hillside like flashbulbs. I'll never tell anybody what Simon did to me, never, she decided. Not Mother, not Olivia. I'll keep it inside me until I'm as hard as a rock. Just like Mom. "Post time," Roz murmured inadvertently. "Daddy used to say that, didn't he? His phrase for getting started."

"Leo's dead and buried! And don't look so damn shocked, Rosalind. I loved him more than you know."

"You loved Richard more."

Katherine turned away so Roz couldn't see the fury and pain twitching across her face. "No. Not more," she said in a restrained voice. "Differently. Roz, love has more than one aspect and wears more than one face, like Janus. You've never understood that, and it's made you afraid. You're married, you have children, but you've stayed inside yourself in a private cocoon. Nothing touches you in there, does it? No wonder Simon left you for that idiot woman—maybe she feels something for others. You've got no damned empathy."

"I hate you. I've always hated you."

Katherine felt as if she'd been stabbed, as if a knife blade had sliced through every layer of her flesh straight into her heart, splitting her open. Then she heard her own word, *empathy,* ringing in her ears, and suddenly she knew that Rosalind's hostility was a fragile facade shielding her vulnerability. "No, you don't, darling," she said softly. "But Simon's gone. Time to rejoin the world."

"He'll come back. He's just having a fling." Rosalind's voice was plaintive, desperate.

"Maybe he will, maybe he won't. Right now it makes no difference what he does."

"No difference? Are you kidding? He's my husband!"

"No difference," Katherine said firmly. "He's gone, you're alone, and you can't freeze-frame your life and your children's lives on the chance that he'll come trotting back when he's tired of Kim." A thought crossed her mind. "Is he writing a book about her, I wonder? She's a great character."

"Always the agent, aren't you?" Rosalind said ironically.

"What if I am? How do you think you've lived all these years?" Katherine looked out the window. "You had a terrible fever the night Leo died. Did you know that?"

"No." Roz wrinkled her brow. "Does it matter?"

"It mattered to me," Katherine said. "I sat up with you. You were hot and fretful, and you kept kicking off the covers. God! Leo was dead, and all I wanted to do was shriek, get drunk, kill somebody! But you were sick. You needed me. We were alone in the house, you and I and Olivia, and the wind was blowing and Leo was dead, but I sat next to your bed until your fever broke, and strangers brought me money in rumpled envelopes because he hadn't left us a dime."

"I don't understand."

"I know you don't. Maybe someday you will. Darling, pull up your socks before it's too late. Come to work at the agency."

"The agency? The hell I will!"

"You have other offers?" Katherine said wryly. "People are busting down the door offering an inexperienced social butterfly well-paying jobs? Funny, I haven't heard the phone ringing. Rosalind, you can't spend the rest of your life moaning in your bed because Simon left you for another woman."

"I hate that neurotic bitch. I hate her! I hate her!"

"Good for you, but hating her won't pay the bills. Roz, dear, we all have to work in this life, a fact both Simon and I kept hidden from you for far too long. Come to work at the agency. You'll learn the business, support yourself and the kids, have a career. Who knows? Maybe you'll like it. And maybe if you do something with your life Simon will find you attractive again."

"I hate him too! Jesus, I never knew I had such a bitch for a mother."

"Didn't you?" Katherine laughed easily. "Just think of bitchiness as a job skill. Come to work at the agency, Roz. Make a new life for yourself—*your* life, not Simon's. Don't depend on him. You've been nothing but a little gold charm dangling from his watch chain."

"He's a great writer."

"He is indeed. I agree with you. Simon has a terrific talent, but he's pissing it away."

"Mother! Your language," Roz mocked.

"It's the perfect description. Simon Wyler's been pissing away his talent, and you've been helping him do it— spending money like a fool on parties and clothes and cars and all sorts of silly things you don't need. Oh, I know all about it," she said when she saw Rosalind's look of surprise. "Olivia talks to me, even if you don't, and she's as worried about you as I am. How the hell can Simon concentrate on his work when you want him to be Mr. Famous Writer and go to parties all the time? Don't you know what writers do? They sit alone in a goddamn room and smoke cigarettes and look at the typewriter, and if they don't do that ten hours a day they don't get anything written. Grow up, Rosalind. Simon's talent isn't the question, whether he comes back to you isn't the question, and whether Kim Corbin's a bitch isn't the question. The question is, what are *you* going to do with your life? It's *your* life, not Simon's." Katherine got up and began to go around the living room turning off the lamps until Roz sat alone under a single lamp shedding a pool of pale gold light around her. "Come to work at the agency."

Roz looked up, her face trembling and uncertain. "But I've never worked anywhere," she said slowly. "I don't know how to work."

"Time to learn," Katherine told her daughter. "Monday morning. Ten o'clock."

As she went out the door, Katherine grinned happily, amazed at herself, at Rosalind, at life's unexpected turns. I'm giving her the damn Cole Agency, and she isn't sure she wants it. The toughest deal I've ever struck, and I'm not going to make a dime out of it!

Nothing went right for Charles. When Roz and her kids settled in with Olivia, he moved up the hill to the new house with Richard and Katherine, but they were too busy with their own life to notice him. Richard was a nice guy but he was producing a TV series and Katherine was teaching Roz the agency business. In the evenings they went out or stayed home, sat on the redwood deck, and watched the twilight seep across the scrub oak lining the canyon below the house, and besides, they were old.

Charlie knew they were happy, but their very happiness shut him out and he was lonelier than ever before. He had no interest in college, and the days stretched ahead. There was nothing to fill them, so he lay on the patio and got drunk, went down to the Griffin and hung out.

The trouble was, he didn't belong. Kids his own age bored him. The trouble was, he was lonely. Katherine loved him—he was her son—but she was receding into the distance and the happiness she shared with Richard Sears didn't include him. The trouble was, he didn't know where to turn. The trouble was . . . The trouble was him.

"Do you want me to talk to him?" Richard asked. They'd been to a dinner party and now they were lying in bed, drinking brandy and watching "The Tonight Show" in their bedroom.

"Would you? I'm at a loss. I don't know what to say to him. Do you think he'll resent it if you talk to him?"

"Maybe. But I think I know how to talk to kids. Boys, anyway," Richard said, a trifle defensively. "Even Linda's come around now that she works for me."

Katherine was silent. She had nothing to say about Linda.

"She works hard, and she's serious about learning the business. I'm going to let her coproduce an episode of 'Beachwood Theater.'"

"I'm glad you're happy," Katherine said lightly. Linda Sears remained a sore spot. She'd been barely civil the few times Katherine had run into her at Richard's office, so Katherine skirted the issue of Linda's rudeness and avoided her.

"She wants to use Madeline," Richard said, eyes on the TV screen.

"Oh? Don't ask me. I'm out of it," Katherine said. "Madeline doesn't listen to my opinion anymore. You know that. . . . How's her latest husband?"

"Don't ask. He looks like a little bird. I figure he must be a killer in the sack. Look, Linda wants her."

"Offer Madeline money, she'll do it," Katherine said.

"Don't be bitter, darling. It doesn't suit you."

"I'm not bitter; I'm sad. Madeline and I were friends; now we're not. She's so afraid of getting old it's made her afraid to live. She's an emotional zombie."

"*And* Linda wants her boyfriend to direct."

"Oh, boy, am I glad I'm out of it! Is that wise? How old is he?"

"Young. They're all young. Christ, I know just how Madeline feels. These kids make me feel like Father Time. Linda's boyfriend is English, he's done plenty of series TV, and if Linda's carrying the ball I have to back her up, right?"

"Right, right," Katherine said. "I just don't want you to fall into a hole of your own digging."

"What syntax. I admit I've got my problems with Linda, but Dickie's turned out okay. He wants to go to film school. Who the hell goes to film school? You want to learn the business, you get a job in a studio," Richard mumbled. "Film school, for Christ's sake."

Katherine flicked off the TV set and rolled toward her husband. "Back to Charles for a minute. I'm worried about him, and I can't shake it. He's different. He's always been so quiet, standoffish. He's grown up in a house full of vociferous women, but he never talks," she said. "Even though I've fought with Roz, we used to talk and now we're talking again."

"How's she doing at the office?" Richard asked.

"Tentative, but she'll shake out," Katherine said confidently. "She's frightened, though. Simon knocked the stuffing out of her. I wish I knew what really happened."

"It's Danny and Zelda I miss," Richard said. "I miss that I can't be their grandfather. I want to dote on them. I want to act like a fool, and I can't do it."

"They love you, darling."

"Maybe they do, but as your husband, not as their grandfather. Funny," he said. "Linda is her mother's daughter, and she was lost to me years ago. Dickie always belonged to Edgar Lashman. Roz belongs to Leo. I'm left with nothing."

Katherine laughed. "You know who's most like you? Of all of them? Olivia," she said. "Maybe you're not her father, but she idolizes you; she always has. Where do you think she gets her drive? Her ambition? She learned it from you."

Richard sighed, and Katherine heard the loss in his voice. "My family has always been my mainstay," she said, reaching out for his hand. "They can be yours too. Let it build slowly. Roz'll come around. She loved Leo so much, she's afraid if she accepts you as her father Leo will disintegrate and blow away like dust."

"Leo . . ." Richard laughed and shook his head.

"Do you resent him?"

"Maybe. Sometimes I'm amazed the guy still has so much power."

"Roz will come around," Katherine said confidently. "I know it. But Charles worries me. When I ask him how he is, he responds like a robot!"

"It's the times, darling," Richard said, leaning over to pour another brandy from the decanter by the bed. "I used to think I knew what was going on. Hey, I'm a movie star, I must be a pretty hip guy, right? But all of a sudden I feel like a fossil! Have you seen those kids on the Strip—their hair, those beads? What the hell's the matter with them? Even Dickie looks like a weirdo. Tell me honestly, do you think women find long hair attractive on men?"

"Why, you thinking of doing an aging Prince Valiant? Don't ask me, darling." Katherine laughed.

"Whole goddamn world's upside down," Richard muttered.

Katherine ran her hands down Richard's stomach, admiring how firm and taut his body was. "Listen, we're not that old. Let's forget our children for a little while. Rub my back."

"I can do better than that. . . ."

Charlie was in front of the Ashgrove on Melrose one Saturday afternoon, high from smoking dope in the car on the way down the hill, when Tinker Bell Pope came up to him.

"Here," Tinker Bell said, opening his hand. "Take these." There were two pink tablets lying in his palm.

"Sure," Charlie said, popping them down dry without a second thought. "What are they?"

"Acid," Tinker Bell said vaguely. "Dreaded LSD, the scourge of Switzerland. This guy Owsley over in Hollywood makes 'em. Righteous dose, man. You're gonna love it. Very pure."

"Oh, wow," Charlie said. He'd heard about acid, but he'd never done any. Time to try it, he figured. He started to come on about forty-five minutes later, so he went over to Barney's Beanery and ordered a burger, but when it came, he didn't want it because it was undulating on his plate and looked like brown worms. He went back outside and sat on the fender of his VW for a while. People smiled as they came out of Barney's, and Charlie felt good. The world around him got bright and sparkly, as if everything were made out of mica, and there was an aurora borealis hanging in the sky over the Hollywood Hills he'd never noticed before. He left the car and walked slowly up Holloway to the Strip, admiring the beauty of the sidewalk. The kids on the street looked different, vibrant and alive, filled with possibilities. The very molecules of the buildings were visible to the naked eye. Charlie was a brilliant sun exploding with warmth, shedding his golden light on everyone around him. "Oh, wow," he said as he drifted into the sky. "Oh, wow."

The next day he found Tinker Bell Pope and they went over to Owsley's place in an alley below Santa Monica to buy some more acid. Owsley was a small bearded man who used to be a commercial chemist but was now in business for himself.

"Now we're dope fiends," Tinker Bell said, laughing as they left, loaded down with pink tabs.

Charlie went back to the new house and dropped acid every day for a month and thought about doing it every day for the rest of his life. It was that good.

Katherine found him by accident. A minute later and he would have been dead. She'd picked up Danny and Zelda at the dentist's in Westwood, dropped them off at the old house, and continued on up the hill to the new house to meet Richard for dinner.

As she pulled the Mercedes into the garage she noticed that the interior door leading to the pool in the back garden was open. When she went over to shut it, she saw Charles floating face down in the shallow end of the pool, arms and legs spread as wide as a crab's.

Her long, hollow scream reverberated through the garage, and as she ran for the pool she felt herself swimming through the air, hands and feet parting the leaden atmosphere, her body stretched forward as she raced down the broad steps and into the water. The full skirt of her green silk dress filled with water and billowed out behind her, slowing her down as she clawed her way forward, desperately reaching out for her son.

She pulled his head up out of the water by the hair, yanking ferociously at him, dragging him into the safety of her arms. She heard herself shrieking Richard's name over and over.

She got Charles up on the lip of the pool, his legs still half sprawled on the steps, and rolled him over on his stomach. Violently she pressed down on his rib cage, hoping to force the water out of his lungs, damning herself because she didn't know how to save her son's life.

Charles moaned and coughed, spitting up water and gasping for air. When his eyes opened, he looked Katherine full in the face and howled dreadfully, lashing out at her, flailing his arms and legs, furiously trying to get back into the water.

"Richard!" Katherine screamed as she struggled to hold on to the boy, who was slipping away. "Richard!" Her voice was hoarse, some other voice, not her voice at all. "Richard!"

A door banged, bare feet slapped the concrete, and the sound rang in her mind. Funny, how every sensation was heightened. . . . Charles slipped out of her grasp and twisted back into the pool like a fish escaping the net. Desperately she pushed into the water, but Richard bulldozed past her, grabbed Charles by both arms, and lifted him bodily out of the pool.

Charles was screaming incomprehensible sentences, kicking, biting, scratching, but Richard was stronger than he was and wrestled him up onto the lawn. Charles curled up into a tight ball, and Katherine heard him weeping and croaking out unidentifiable noises as she ran back into the house to call an ambulance.

Two hours later Richard and Katherine sat in the waiting room at UCLA's Neuropsychiatric Institute listening to Dr. Sughrue, an earnest, bearded young psychiatrist with a mild demeanor.

"I've pumped him full of Thorazine. That'll cool him off. How long has he been taking LSD, Mrs. Sears?"

Katherine shivered. She felt like an idiot. "I didn't know he was," she said lamely, pulling Richard's windbreaker around her. Her clothes were still wet, her hair was damp and stringy, and she wore no makeup, no Katherine Cole Sears armor. "He's always been moody. It's hard to get through to him, he's so quiet."

"Not inside he isn't," Sughrue said very gently. "Inside, he's in turmoil. The acid just stirs the kettle."

"Why do they take drugs?" Richard asked, one hand on Katherine's arm to steady her.

Sughrue sighed. "Hallucinogens, you mean? Mostly, they do it for fun."

"Fun? What the hell does that mean?" Richard was belligerent. "I don't understand."

"Parents never do, Mr. Sears. Listen, these kids are rich, they're bored, they're alienated, they're lonely. Smoking dope and doing acid makes 'em feel connected to a larger family of freaks. That's what they call themselves—freaks." Sughrue grinned and tugged his beard. "*Hippie* is a square word."

"What was he doing in the pool? He didn't want to come out. Was he trying to kill himself?" Katherine asked. Suicide was unthinkable, but she had to ask.

"Maybe he thought it was a pool of happiness and as long as he was in the water, he'd be happy," Sughrue said. "From his reaction I figure he took a busload of acid. God knows how many mikes he swallowed. Charlie's seen stuff nobody on earth ever dreamed about. He thought he'd be safe."

"Safe from what?" Richard said.

Sughrue sighed. "Go home, folks. There's nothing to decipher here. There's no Rosetta stone. This is brand-new territory," he said gently. "See, the dope's just a symptom. Charlie's all whacked out inside. That's what he's got to fix."

Katherine and Richard looked at each other and started to protest, but Sughrue cut them off with a wave of his hand. "Charlie's gonna sleep twenty-four hours, easy, and you two have taken a helluva beating," he said as he maneuvered them toward the elevator. "Go home, get some sleep. I'll take care of Charlie."

Charles stayed in Neuropsych, pale, not talking much, just sitting and staring out at Westwood Village through the wire-mesh windows. He apologized over and over again, crying fitfully when Katherine came to visit him. It was apparent that he was both frightened and mortally embarrassed by the episode in the pool.

Sughrue left him alone for the first week, correctly gauging that Charles needed time to recover from the enormity of his experience, but finally, as they sat in his small hospital office in a private session, Sughrue confronted him. "So when you gonna do it?"

"What? Do what?"

"Kill yourself. You gonna wait awhile or take a shot as soon as our backs are turned?"

Charlie shook his head, and his voice rose apologetically. "What makes you think I'm gonna kill myself?"

Sughrue laughed. "Because I'm a shrink and I work in a psycho ward and you tried it once and I'm betting you'll try it again. You think you're the first?"

Charlie felt the tears coming; ever since that day in the pool, he'd been crying all the time. He couldn't stop, couldn't control himself. He felt as if the water were up to his lips and if he let go, he'd sink in and disappear.

"What?" Sughrue said softly. "What's going on in there?"

"I'm just tired is all," Charlie said. Okay. He had the tears choked back. He was okay now.

"Tell me about it."

"I feel like they're on top of me. I feel like they're crushing me. I'm afraid I won't measure up."

"To what?"

"My mother. Richard. My sisters . . . Everybody."

"Say more."

Helplessly, Charlie whacked his fist into his palm. "Everybody in my family is talented, driven. All they care about is winning. It's like they all know how to swim in this weird river and I don't."

"What river?"

"Hollywood."

Sughrue frowned. "How is Hollywood like a river?"

"More like quicksand." Charlie laughed.

"Look, I'm a shrink, okay? All I know about Hollywood is what I see on the screen. I don't know what kind of place it is, what it's like to be a kid and to grow up there. C'mon, Charlie, tell me how it feels."

"Feels like drowning," Charlie blurted out, surprised by

the anger in his own voice. "Look, every single day of my life I hear about Hollywood. Hollywood is all that matters. How you have to fight to survive, win, make it to the top. Okay, they've done it, but I'm not tough enough."

"There's all kinds of toughness."

"Don't you get it?" Charlie said desperately. "I'll never measure up! They win at everything! I'll never be like them."

Sughrue leaned forward, and Charlie felt his level of intensity change, as if he'd shifted into shrink overdrive. "Do you have to be like them? Why not be like yourself?"

"Because I don't know who I am, and I'm afraid I'll never find out!" Charlie cried. "I'm trapped under their shadow. They're all talented and important, and I'm a weirdball with no talent. I'll never win," he said desperately. He could feel the damn tears again, drowning him.

Sughrue pulled his beard and looked out his office window at Westwood Village. "Two things. Why do you have to win at a game you don't like? And if you can't win, why do you have to kill yourself? Charlie, listen to me. The secret of life is that there's no secret."

"You're a very weird shrink."

"Thank you." Sughrue smiled. "But look, as long as you're living out other people's lives, or what you think their lives are, or how you think they want you to live, you won't be happy. Sooner or later, Charlie, you have to stop *trying* to measure up to their standards. You have to be tough enough to have your own standards. This is *your* life, Charlie, and *you* have to decide how to live it. Not your mother or your stepfather or anybody else. Just you, man. You have to decide what you want and how you're gonna get it."

"I don't want to die. I don't want to be another Hollywood casualty," Charlie said, twisting the cord to his bathrobe. "I *do* want my own life. Can I have my own life in L.A.?"

Sughrue looked out the window. "What do you think?"

"My own life," Charlie said slowly. "I don't know. I know I want to be happy."

"Be forewarned, man. These days, happiness is a tough thing to find." Sughrue sighed. "Money and fame and power are easier to find than happiness."

"My own life," Charlie repeated.

Sughrue cocked his head to one side and pulled at his beard for a minute. "Okay. With the power vested in me as a shrink, I've made a decision. I'll spring you from Neuropsych in a week or so, but you gotta promise me you won't try to kill yourself, okay? You have to make a contract with me. I have to believe you won't try it again. If you feel like killing yourself, you'll call me."

Charlie nodded. "Okay. I swear."

"This is serious business," Sughrue warned. "You break the contract and God zaps you with a lightning bolt."

"Man, you're a *very* weird shrink."

Charlie disappeared three days after Sughrue let him out of Neuropsych.

At first, Roz hated the agency. She hated getting up early in the morning, she hated the menial work, made worse because she didn't know how to do it. Answering the phone, filing. She hated the simple fact that Coral, the receptionist, knew twice as much as she did. But after a few months Roz didn't feel so stupid. She adjusted to the routine of work, getting up early, going to bed early, or staying out late and pumping herself up with coffee in the morning like the rest of the world. These were simple facts of grown-up life that Roz had never faced before.

Katherine started taking her along to lunch and occasionally to a screening or a dinner party on the strict condition that Roz keep her mouth shut and listen. Slowly Roz began to see the webs her mother wove, the way she knit people and money into a seamless fabric, marrying a writer to a producer to an actor to a director to a studio. Lunch by lunch, meeting by meeting, Katherine built a deal out of her relationships, and Roz realized the creative process of a movie deal was fascinating and the film itself was the end result.

At first, Roz and Katherine were tentative together, almost formal, but slowly a new, more equal relationship began to develop. As the days passed and Rosalind saw the intricacies at work behind the walls of the Cole Agency, she became more interested in learning the business. And Katherine was a good teacher. She'd trained young agents before and instinctively knew when to press Roz and when to hold back, when to goad, when to counsel patience, and when to call it a day.

Finally, one late afternoon at the office, Katherine began to talk to Rosalind about Richard and Leo, and for the first time, Rosalind listened.

"I grew up with a lot of foolish ideas floating through my head," Katherine said. "I don't know where I got them, probably a combination of Gloria Swanson's movies and Elinor Glyn's books, throw in some Shakespeare and add a little Dickens. I thought a woman fell in love with a man, he loved her back, and they lived happily ever after. That was that, finished, end of story." She paused and looked out the windows across the Sunset Strip below her office. "I wanted Richard to sweep up my life the way he swept me up onto his horse that day on location and carried me off into the Valley."

"I can't believe he really *did* that!" Roz said incredulously. "God, you guys must have been something! It's so damn romantic."

Katherine smiled ruefully as the faraway black-and-white day in the heat of the San Fernando Valley spooled through her mind. "I wanted him to order my life the same way you wanted Simon to order yours. I thought Richard would cut a road for me through the jungle."

"Richard must have loved it. He still thinks he's Allan Quatermain."

"Did he tell you that?" Katherine asked curiously, remembering the day Richard had told her that when he was a boy he wanted to be Allan Quatermain, the gentleman adventurer.

"No, it's just how I see him. As if he ought to be wearing a pith helmet and puttees and discovering buried treasure. White scarf whipping in the wind . . ."

Katherine laughed. Are we that transparent to our children? she wondered. Can't we hide anything? "But when Richard . . . failed to live up to my expectations, I thought I was used up. I couldn't understand how he could love me and walk away. Then I married Leo. At first I didn't think I would ever love him, but I did. I loved Leo Cole, and I loved Richard Sears. Even now, Rozzie, Leo's been dead more than twenty years, and I still love him. Do you understand? Maybe you'll understand in twenty years. You'll say to yourself, my God, *that's* what Mother was talking about. . . ." Her voice trailed off. "I love them both, dear, both of them at once. I always will."

And slowly Katherine and Rosalind became mother and daughter again, their sympathy for each other expanded by the similarity of their experiences as they worked together, a pair of professionals pulling in the same harness.

After Charles disappeared, Katherine hired Frank Perrow to find him. Perrow, the same detective who'd helped her years before, did a lot of work with wealthy runaways, and he tracked Charles from San Francisco to New Mexico to an Oregon commune in a small logging town the Cascades, where he'd settled, at least for a while. Charlie had a girlfriend. He did carpentry, and he worked in the communal hardware store. Since the commune was macrobiotic, Perrow figured his drug use had tapered off or stopped.

Katherine was relieved, yet the sheer fact of her privileged son living in a hippie commune and throwing away everything she'd given him appalled her. Her sacrifices had been for nothing, tossed overboard into the whirlpool of the sixties. She went to see Dr. Sughrue.

Sughrue smiled and combed his beard with his fingers. "Let him go, Mrs. Sears. Let him try to grow up. By the way, that's advice, not therapy. Maybe he isn't living the life you chose for him, but Charlie has to live his own life, not yours.

So what if he doesn't want to be an agent or a director? Is that the end of the world? Isn't he better off as a happy carpenter than he would be as a miserable studio executive? Believe me, I've had lots of Hollywood kids in here pressured by their hard-driving parents, and I should know."

"Have I driven him?" Katherine wondered. "I didn't think so."

"Maybe not directly, but certainly by example. Let him go, Mrs. Sears. You can't live his life."

Richard's point of view was similar. "It's his life, his world. How the hell can he grow up if we make all his decisions? Look how many mistakes we made, Red, and we've survived. So will Charles."

Roz didn't divorce Simon, but for over a year they simply ceased to exist for each other. Then, about the time Katherine started taking Roz along to meetings and lunch, a curious thing began to happen. Roz realized she'd become a minor celebrity in her own right. Simon was much in evidence in the papers; as Kim Corbin's latest constant escort, publicity was inevitable. Roz, cast as the discarded wife bravely carrying on for the sake of the children, was definitely the sympathetic heroine of the melodrama, and folks around town began to take notice of her. She was asked to parties, not as Simon Wyler's reflection, not as Katherine's daughter, but as Roz Wyler, a bright girl who was having a tough time with her no-good husband. Slowly, with all the speed of a glacier creeping across the face of a frozen continent, Roz began to feel whole.

She didn't have time to go shopping for sport, only for necessities—summer clothes for the kids, tires for her secondhand BMW, a garden hose. Gone were the bibelots of the past—the lacquered nesting boxes, the Chinese screens, the Georgian silver. Like her life, objects took on a practical reality, and Roz discovered she liked that too. One day she was having lunch in Beverly Hills when a moonstone ring in the window of Frances Klein caught her eye. She bought it on a whim, and it wasn't until two days later that she realized it was the first piece of jewelry she'd ever bought with her own money.

So when Simon called late one night, she took it in stride.

"Kim's pregnant," he said quietly. "I wanted to tell you myself."

"How thoughtful." Roz was so angry the phone shook in her hand as the static in the line from London crackled in her ear like fire.

Simon didn't respond.

"Now you've told me," Roz said. "Now drop dead." As she cradled the phone she heard his tinny voice squawking in the distance, trying to defend the indefensible.

Chapter

17

Roz and the children stayed on with Olivia in the old house. It was convenient, there was plenty of room, and Mrs. Gebhardt and Lena could take care of the children while Roz and Olivia were at work. Roz kept the kids out of the Miss Lilys' where they'd only have met star kids and sent them to public school instead. Though her anger at Simon was unabated, she knew it wasn't over between them. Not by a long shot.

Life went smoothly for Olivia. Her transitions were flawless, from errand girl to legwoman to full-fledged reporter with her own byline, and she moved up the ladder swiftly, as if every step were part of a chess match and she alone could see three moves ahead. Although she was never embroiled in a serious relationship as her mother and Roz had been, there were usually a few handsome men tagging after Olivia like lost puppies, validating Roz's claim that success came to those who didn't give a damn. Work was the only arena that mattered to Olivia, and when she won her own column for a rival news syndicate she was thrilled to be

Violet Rawley's chief competition. "Hollywoodland" fulfilled another goal for Olivia.

It was Saturday afternoon, and Olivia and Roz were sprawled by the pool under a green striped umbrella while Danny and Zelda splashed and played in the water. "I don't want kids, I don't want to be married, and I don't want to be somebody's wife or somebody's mother. I want my own life on my own terms," Olivia drawled lazily, her voice muffled by the straw hat over her face.

"Olly, you'll be sorry later on," Roz said as she watched the children. Danny was so sturdy now. His skin was brown, and his light brown hair had a blond streak running through it from the California sun. He was pretending to be a sea horse pulling Zelda around on a rubber raft.

"So what?" Olivia said, pulling the hat off her face. "Everybody's sorry about the way life goes. You got married, and you're sorry about it."

"Yes," Roz said as she shielded her eyes and watched the kids shrieking and splashing each other. "Quiet down! Danny, come out, you're turning blue. But I'm not sorry about the kids."

"Okay. Not now," Olivia said with her sharp practicality. "But don't you think Richard's sorry Linda's such a twerp?"

Roz said nothing. She'd never acknowledged Richard as her father openly, although she was faultlessly correct with him, kissing his cheek smoothly when they met and chatting pleasantly at family dinners. Their relationship was friendly but distinctly cool and formal.

"You think Mom's sorry about Charlie?" Olivia went on. "She never hears from him and it's killing her."

"Sorry? No, she's sad about Charlie. She's sad she's lost him, same way she was sad about losing me, but she's not sorry."

"See? Everybody's sad about something. You can't have a perfect life, so I'm going to play it for laughs instead of trying to measure up to other people's expectations and bizarre rules I can't decipher."

Roz sipped her orange juice and lay down again on the

chaise. They were friends, they were sisters, they were two utterly different people.

"All I want is power," Olivia went on, half to herself, half to Roz. "Then they can't get us."

"Who can't get us?"

"Them! The Lashmans of the world, the powermongers in this town. That little bitch Linda is gunning for us, and she won't stop until she's got us in the cross hairs."

"What happened between you and Maria that night, Olly?" Roz said, curious.

Olivia laughed, gleeful and triumphant. "I had *her* in the cross hairs. She knew it, and she backed down. But it's not over yet. Maria Lashman will spend the rest of her life trying to destroy me. Destroy us. That's the name of the game in Hollywood, and that's why I want power. Power keeps 'em off your ass," Olivia said as she looked across the garden. "Hey, you know what's funny? You and I have lived in this house all our lives, but Mother grew up and moved out."

Rosalind looked at Olivia and laughed, the bond between them stronger than ever before. "You're right. We're the parents. We're working like dogs, and she's having a high time with her hot new husband."

"Nothing like the old switcheroo." Olivia hooted.

Danny and Zelda heard them laughing and Danny craned his head up out of the water to see what was going on. "Grown-ups are so weird," he told Zelda.

Finally Roz broke down and filed for divorce. The decision had nothing to do with Simon; it was simply the easiest way to realign her life. Over the course of the next year Roz heard rumors about Simon and Kim but nothing concrete. They married in a very public ceremony on a barge on the Thames. They bought a country house in Surrey and a town house in Chelsea. The baby, a girl named Eliza, seemed to catapult Kim and Simon into an excessive life-style that even Olivia's network of sources couldn't penetrate; it was impossible to divide truth from the thick tissue of public fiction surrounding Kim Corbin and Simon Wyler. Their wild life in London, the time Simon drunkenly put his fist through a plate-glass window at Harrods, the wrecked cameras of the paparazzi, the torn gown on the way to Albert Hall, the fight in the streets of Highgate Village—it was all in the papers. Kim's fragile nerves and obvious insecurity combined with her startling beauty to make her the most photographed woman of the day. In the early seventies she made several films in Europe, and Simon was constantly at her side. He hadn't published a book or written a movie in years, though the papers referred to him as Kim's screenwriter husband. Then he and Kim began battling constantly, and their public fights and private reconciliations made even richer fodder for the papers as they were relentlessly pursued by London's feral tabloid press. But the news was amorphous, and the events surrounding them were clearly tricked up for shock value.

But popular fascination with Kim Corbin never waned. She was in a permanent state of flux, always changing before the world grew tired of her. Nobody could nail her down, and that was the secret of her celebrity. She was never the same woman twice, never the same hairstyle, never the same personality, and her wide blue eyes reflected the uncertainty of the times. With Simon at her side, Kim moved from one film to another, one hotel to another, one city to another. She'd raised instability to an art form, and both press and public adored her.

Roz and Katherine ate chili at Chasen's once a week after work, ostensibly to discuss agency business, but as their relationship solidified, Roz began to talk about her emotional life as well. "She's the most beautiful, most talked-about woman in the world, and I feel as if I'm constantly being compared to her, and it drives me wild because I can't win. Everyone looks at me and says, 'Well, Roz is all right, but she's no Kim Corbin.' I'm always going to be second best."

"Don't believe it," Katherine said. "And don't let anything stop you. You'll survive. Kim Corbin's a disaster waiting to happen. You mark my words."

Roz pushed her food around on her plate. "It's too late for

anything to stop me now. When Simon first left me I thought I was dead. I felt dead. Annihilated." The memory of Simon's weight crushing her into the floor sent a violent shudder through her body. Her fork trembled faintly against her plate, and the sharp *ping* cut through the polite murmurs of the dining room. She shook the feeling away. "But not anymore. Maybe this'll sound self-serving, but after Charlie . . . after you found him in the pool I decided I wanted to be happy. I had this thought," Roz said reflectively. She leaned forward, eager to explain herself to her mother. "I had this thought that all I had to do was *decide* to be happy and give up the past. Happiness is a choice, and I've made it."

Death does that to you, Katherine thought. Leo's pale face cut into her brain, etched into her thoughts forever. She remembered Edgar Lashman's frantic grasp, the wild look in his eyes as he realized he was dying and all the power in Hollywood couldn't drive death away. "Death makes us crazy to live," she whispered.

"But the problem is, Simon's still a part of me. We've been through too much together, good and bad, to be completely separated. We aren't through with each other. I feel it. I'm afraid of it," Roz said as another shiver ran across her bare arms.

Three nights later Roz was in bed dozing over a boring screenplay when the phone rang.

It was Simon.

"Listen to me," he said, pleading. "Listen to me."

His voice was flat but filled with a shivering urgency Roz had never heard before. Shadows bounced against the bedroom walls as Roz pulled herself out of her foggy half sleep and into the present. "What do you want?"

"Kim's dead."

She couldn't help it. Roz was filled with a flush of triumph. Then jubilation evaporated into pity. "Dead?" she said. "Why are you calling me, Simon?"

"I need you," he said. "Come to London."

"Go to hell."

"Roz, I need your help."

"Go to hell, Simon."

"Roz, I'm begging you."

She was silent, then sighed. "Tell me what happened."

"Christ, I don't know! I was asleep in the guest room. I heard Eliza crying, and when I went into Kim's room I found her swinging from the chandelier. That's what happened!" He was desperate, ragged.

"Did you fight?"

Simon laughed bitterly. "We always fight. Eliza's crawling around under her feet like a puppy! Kim loved a grand gesture," he said sardonically.

Eliza wailed in the background as if on cue, and Roz had a bizarre sense of unreality. "Wait a minute, you son of a bitch! Is Kim still . . . hanging there? Simon, cut her down, for God's sake! Call the police!"

"I will, I will. Rozzie, come to London. I'm so tired."

"Simon, you bastard. Just because you need me you think I'll—"

"Goddammit, come! You still love me; you know you do. Besides, there's more. I've written something new, and nobody's seen it. It's the greatest fucking book I've ever done."

Roz laughed. Still the old imperious Simon, the egoist par excellence.

"Simon *über alles,*" she said. "Call the police."

"You're an agent, aren't you? You want to see the book? Come to London, Roz."

The transatlantic wire stretched between them across seas and continents, and Roz felt the familiar lifeline being spliced together again. It was thin, it was frayed and raveled, but it was still there. This was what Mother was talking about, she thought. Didn't she say Richard failed to live up to her romantic expectations and someday I would know what she meant? The Santa Anas were blowing across the desert, and the white curtain billowed into the room like a ghostly ocean spray. "I'll come," she said tiredly. "Call the police, you bastard."

The next day Roz flew to London in a haze. *Setting my demons to rest, putting my demons to sleep . . .* The words ran through her head like a tinkling nightmare tune as she watched the clouds scud past beneath the plane over the stone-gray North Atlantic.

Did she want to put an end to it or begin all over again? She had to find the answer. *Simon and I are linked by our history, and history is stronger than love. Love ends, but history endures. Love disintegrates, but history binds you tighter and tighter and tighter. Was that what Mother felt when she and Richard finally married? Funny, he's just Richard to me, but he's everything to her. When she told me how he carried her away on horseback, I found it hard to believe they were ever so young and loved each other so much.*

She took a cab from Heathrow to Simon's house in Chelsea, feeling a painful sense of déjà vu as she rode through the busy London streets, so drab and gray after Los Angeles. The city was timeless—the same damp, foggy streets, the same glowing lamps reflected on shining concrete, the same dun-colored shops. The memory of the musty smell of the Dorchester carpet burned her nostrils like a smoky fire.

A small group of reporters in shabby raincoats were clustered on the front steps of the town house, and they accosted her as she rang the bell. Someone shouted inside the house.

"Who're you, then, luv?" one of the reporters sang out.

"I'm nobody. I'm the new nanny," Roz said, her face averted.

"Be my nanny, then. Put me to bed, luv." He and the others laughed. The door opened, and Roz hurried inside before they shrieked any more questions at her.

Simon slammed the door behind her, and they looked at each other in the glare of the overhead light in the paneled foyer.

She was shocked. He'd aged terribly since she'd seen him

last. Puffy pouches drooped under his eyes, and his thin, once-boyish face was fleshy and worn. His skin was blotchy, and he looked as if he'd slept in his clothes.

"Time catches up with Dorian Gray," she said.

"Don't push me, Roz," he said flatly. "I need you, but I won't eat shit for you." He turned, and she followed him into the living room.

The room was cold, half empty, devoid of character. No one had attempted to make it cozy or homelike. Pictures leaned casually against the walls, cigarette butts overflowed from the ashtrays, papers littered every surface, and the sharp smell of dirty diapers hung in the air. A tray of crusty breakfast dishes sat on the floor beside a huge coffee-colored couch. The drapes were drawn, but the glare of the wet, gray day pierced through tears in the heavy, once-elegant brocade.

Eliza cried upstairs, a mournful wail that trailed off and stopped a second later.

"Eliza's getting her lunch," Simon said, running his hands through his unkempt hair. "Thank God for the nanny." He sank onto the couch and fumbled a Rothman to his lips.

"When's the funeral?"

"Tomorrow. Want to go?"

"Christ, Simon. Look, I flew all night to get here, even though I swore I'd smash your face in the next time I saw it. I'm here because we used to be married. So don't push me, either."

"We were way more than married, Roz. We still are married, and you know it." He looked her in the eye briefly, then let his glance wander off.

Roz turned away from him, looking at the paintings stacked against the wall. Was the blue clown a Picasso? Simon always had taste in pictures. "All right, Simon, tell me why I'm here."

He lifted his face, and she saw the burned-out eyes again and the weary wisdom that hadn't been there before. "To help me," he said simply. "Help me, Roz."

"You're amazing! Help you? After what you did to me?

Simon, you raped me, do you know that? Do you realize that I didn't say yes to you? All the times before, no matter what we did, we did it together, and I always said yes to you. Yes to what *you* wanted. The hotels, the games, I always said yes. But that time I said no, Simon. You raped me on the floor and now you want my help? I ought to kill you."

Simon leaned back on the brown couch and dragged on his cigarette. "Listen to me," he said as the smoke made dragon patterns in the air. "Listen to me."

She had the same eerie feeling she'd had when his disembodied voice floated out of the phone. Simon the hypnotic genius . . .

"Let me tell you something, Roz. I'm not like other people and I never will be. I'm rough and rotten, but I make things happen. That's who I am, and that's what you like." Simon leaned forward, his hands knotted together under his chin. "We've known each other too long to live with bullshit, my darling. You love me because I'm interesting. You love me because I change and I'm unpredictable. You always have. That first night in the pool house, you were how old? Fifteen?"

"Sixteen."

"Oh, yes, that one year makes all the difference, doesn't it?" Simon said ironically. *"You* took *me,* my darling. I wanted it, believe me. I'd dreamed about you for a long time. But you love me because I'm not boring. All right, at the Dorchester I was drunk and I forced myself on you. I admit it. I left you for Kim. She was a bitch and a whore, and it was a ghastly mistake. I admit that too. I'm sorry, I am truly, honestly sorry, and I'm not asking you to take me back as your husband. Not now. Not yet. But make no mistake, Roz, I want you and I intend to have you. You probably won't believe me, but I'd been looking for a way to break things off with Kim and patch it up with you. But this isn't what I had in mind," he sighed.

"Go fuck yourself."

Simon smiled. "Business before pleasure. I've finished a new book, and it's the best thing I've ever written. Also, I'm broke, and I need money fast before my creditors move in on me."

"Spoken like a true writer." She laughed bitterly. "All right, Simon, I'm here. Tell me about the book. What's it called? What's it about?"

"It's called *Fools in Love,* and it's about us. You, me, and Kim. There's even a great part in it for Madeline as Kim's mother," he said, his eyes glittering like dark marbles.

"Madeline? Fat chance she'll play a mother; she still thinks she can do Juliet." He was baiting the hook and she was the fish he hoped to catch, but beneath her anger, Roz was intrigued. After all, she was an agent, and Simon Wyler was a major talent. "Okay, you've got my attention. Let me read it."

Simon reached under the pile of papers on the couch and pulled out a box bound with thick rubber bands. "I thought you'd never ask," he said ironically. "Read it tonight. Tomorrow we'll decide how much the swine will have to pay. I'm going to buy a house in California for Eliza so I need lots of money."

"Dreamer," she said, hefting the box. "This must be a thousand pages long! I'll never get through it in one night."

"Darling, you won't be able to put it down," he said with certainty.

And Simon was right, as always. That night, alone in her room at the Connaught, Roz read *Fools in Love* in one sitting, the pages floating down around her bed like snow. It was all there. The complete story of their relationship from the day they met. Marriage. The children. Katherine's initial animosity. Incidents she'd forgotten, like that strange day at the midtown hotel. Kim Corbin. The beautiful, ethereal, doomed Kim Corbin, was as compelling in death as she had been in life. Kim's mother, a hard-driving monster filled with overweening ambition for her talented, unstable daughter. What a part for Madeline if only she had the brains to see it! The book had been written with a baseball bat. Simon, that bastard, had done it again.

Roz was unable to stop, and as she read on deep into the

night, the agent in her took over. Yes, it was her life, but Simon could write a script that would never be forgotten. The only trouble was, the book was so damn big, sprawling across so many intertwined lives and relationships, that it would be impossible to cut it down to screen length without gutting it. But that was Simon, that was the story, she thought. Did it have to be shortened? She turned out the lights and lay in the dark hotel room, listening to the rain tap against her window and the restless roar of the city, car horns, planes, an occasional murmured voice in the hallway outside. Slowly, an idea began to form in her mind. What if they didn't compress it? What if they did it as a TV series and ran it every night for a week?

Simon's a bastard, but he's immensely talented, she thought as the thin light of dawn seeped through the window of the Connaught. Is that reason enough to endure his monstrous behavior? Does he really think I'll come back to him? Will I? Is that why he's shown me this book, to bind me to him? *Am* I bound to him? Finally she fell asleep, the manuscript pages mounded on the floor beside her.

She called Simon a few hours later, a patina of business laid over her voice.

"Okay, you bastard, the book's great, but it's too long."

"Tough."

"Shut up and listen to me. I'm going to pitch it to Richard Sears as a series. But we do it over a week's time. A series in a week. A miniseries. You like it?"

"Not a bad idea, Roz," Simon said after a long moment. "Very creative, I gotta say. I knew I came to the right agent."

"But even if we sell it to Richard, production is still a year away. What'll you do in the meantime?"

"Why a year? Go to Richard now. I told you, I need money."

"Simon," Roz said patiently, "you have to write a script."

He laughed, and she heard all of his school yard victories in his voice. "I'm way ahead of you, sugar. I've already written an outline and most of the first half of the screenplay."

Rosalind flew back to L.A. with Simon's script in her briefcase and dropped it off at Katherine's on the way home from the airport. "No one else has seen it, Mom. We can set this up in-house, an all-Cole, all-Sears production."

"What do you have in mind?" Katherine asked as she pushed her glasses up on her nose.

"Richard produces it on TV. Big stars, an important television event. Simon does the screenplay."

Katherine hefted the manuscript in her hand. "Richard, huh? Who's going to talk him into it?"

"You are," Roz said.

Katherine shook her head. "Not me. It's your project, you do the pitch."

Roz was silent for a long moment. "You want me to have it out with him, don't you?"

"There's no solution, no 'having it out,'" Katherine said. "Just talk to him. Richard's a human being like the rest of us. He knows he can't take Leo's place, and he doesn't *want* to take Leo's place, but he *does* want a relationship with you. He's not perfect, but who is? By now you've probably figured out people are faulty. There are seams and cracks running through all of us. Besides," she said guilelessly, "he probably won't go for it. I've got ten hours of TV in my hand. It's too long."

Roz rose to the bait. "Not if we do it in short episodes. Five nights, prime time! Ten hours in all. It'll be a miniseries, a TV event, a first from America's biggest literary talent."

Katherine said nothing, but the look on her face told Roz she was intrigued. "A miniseries?"

"Casting is easy," Roz went on. "A beautiful blond. Hell, it's a great part—she kills herself, right? How much drama can you take? A handsome guy. And Madeline as Kim's mother."

"She'll never do it. Besides, we're not speaking."

"Sure she'll do it," Roz said wisely. "I'll warm her up and you move in for the kill, like the last reel of *Old Acquaintance*. You and Madeline in the flickering light of a fading fire. Listen, Mom, she'll talk to you. She needs the work. Madeline's a has-been. She always said she was more than just a pretty fanny. Well, this is her chance to prove it."

"Ten hours?" Katherine said slowly.

"It'll work." Roz was firm, determined.

"It might," Katherine admitted. "TV's the right medium for a story like this. Richly textured, sprawling, multi-paneled, great star parts . . ." Katherine stopped in mid-sentence. "Roz, are you going back to Simon?"

"Oh, God," Roz said, throwing herself into a chair. "I don't know. Certainly not now. Maybe not ever."

"You've changed, Rozzie. You're not the child you were when he left you, the beaten little girl who wouldn't get out of bed. You've grown up, and I'm proud of you. Don't let Simon drag you down again. If you still love him, then make him come up to your level. Don't go down to his again."

"Simon has to prove himself to me. If he wants me back, I've got to see a real change in him. Don't worry, Mom. I know what I'm doing."

"Darling, I believe you do."

That night Rosalind drove up to the big house and explained her concept for *Fools in Love* to Richard. At first she was stiff and awkward, but as he listened, shrewdly pointing out both problems and solutions, she realized she'd become comfortable with him without knowing it. Strange, she thought as she looked at him, strange to think that Richard Sears was her father. He'd made mistakes when he was young, but he'd carved a second chance out of the rock. Maybe someday they'd have a second chance to be father and daughter.

"The miniseries is a brilliant idea, Roz. Very creative solution to a tough problem." Richard watched her brighten visibly at his compliment. My daughter, he thought. Mine and Katherine's. God, she looks like her mother at that age! He wanted to take Roz in his arms, tell her he was sorry he'd been no good as a father, but he held himself back. If he pushed her too hard, she'd spook like a thoroughbred, he thought as he fought back the tears in his throat. "Sign up

Madeline, for starters. That'll give me enough ammunition to wrestle an okay out of the network." Maybe someday he and Rosalind would have a second chance.

"You've got a deal," Roz said.

Madeline hadn't aged well. Despite numerous lifts and tucks, there was a quality of despair in her eyes the camera picked up and magnified, and her once-pretty face had a bitter, mournful cast. Too many younger men, too many drinks, too many late nights, and too many parties had turned her desperate. Only a few weeks ago she'd made the papers by getting into a public shouting match outside La Scala in Beverly Hills. She had slapped her latest young man. He'd slapped back and sent her sprawling into the gutter in front of the restaurant. Later, while she was at Cedars having her cracked rib bandaged, the boyfriend broke into her house and stole a fur coat and several pieces of jewelry. It didn't look good.

But the incident gave Katherine the perfect excuse to phone her old friend, and though Madeline was cool at first, her bubbly nature quickly reappeared. Katherine sent her a copy of Simon's manuscript and a week later, when Madeline's black eye had disappeared, they met for drinks at Scandia.

Madeline shook her head, frowning. "You're wrong, Katherine. I can't do it. I won't do it."

"You *have* to do it, Mad. It's a great part."

"It's an old lady's part! It's not for me! I'm young, I'm beautiful, I do glamorous parts, *star* parts. Costumes, cleavage, fabulous locations . . . Look, nothing against Simon, he's a great writer. Is Roz still in love with him?"

"I don't know," Katherine said. "He's such a bastard."

"What man isn't?" Madeline shrugged, slipping her champagne-colored mink off her shoulders. It fell over the arm of the chair and trailed on the floor of the restaurant, but she paid no attention. "So he's no great shakes as a husband. So he cheats. All husbands cheat. The point is, this is a character part. It's not for me. I'm a star."

Katherine heard the edge of uncertainty in Madeline's voice and pounced on it. "Madeline, listen to me closely. Hear every word I say. I'm your friend, and every word I say is in friendship. You're *not* a star. You're an ex-star who's on the verge of becoming a has-been. Wait, wait, wait! Don't storm out of here. I'm on your side! You're not a star for two reasons. First of all, stars are passé, the studio system is over, and we're entering the age of the celebrity, the personality. Second of all, you're a woman. Face facts, if you were a man you'd be playing the lead for the rest of your life. Nobody cares if a man is fifty or sixty. He's still a hot ticket, still does love scenes, right?"

Madeline lifted her delicate eyebrows in a tired parody of her former self. "Go on," she said quietly.

"So, if you want to keep working for the next thirty years, you're going to have to play your age."

Madeline laughed harshly, the old anger flaring again. "When hell's an ice rink, toots." She stood up angrily, grabbing for her fallen fur.

"Damn it all to hell, sit down! Take a chance, take a risk, take the damn part! Yes, you'll look like a fright, but you've got a drunk scene that'll win you an Emmy." A brilliant idea began to form in Katherine's mind, and she laughed out loud. "God, sometimes I'm so smart I can't believe it. Mad, let's get Simon to age the character. Get the point? Make the character *older* than you are. Don't try to look younger than you are; try to look older! You'll look fabulous by comparison, young and gorgeous," she added shrewdly.

Madeline frowned, a cautious light in her eyes. "You mean," she said slowly, "you mean the worse the character looks, the better *I* look?"

"Exactly! Mad, listen. *Fools in Love* is going to change the face of TV forever, give it more depth. TV's the hub of all the media in the world. TV's the future of entertainment, not just in America but in the world. Look, I'm not supposed to tell you this, but Roz has had an absolute brainstorm, and both Richard and I think the network will go for it. You've read *Fools,* right?"

"I read my part," Madeline said. "Skimmed the rest."

"You know how big the damn book is."

"Too big, you ask me. That's another thing. How the hell is he going to boil it down to a two-hour TV movie?"

"He's not. That's the brilliant idea. *Fools in Love* is going to run for ten hours."

Madeline stared at Katherine. "You're insane."

Katherine shook her head. "No, we're not."

"Ten *hours?* Ten *hours* on television? You've lost your mind. Tell Roz I said so."

"Will you please shut up and listen to me? It's a brilliant idea. The book is great, but you can't cut the story without destroying it. So we're going to do it all. The whole, sprawling story. All the characters, all the relationships, the whole shebang. It'll be like a serial, a miniserial. A miniseries. The network's going to run a two-hour episode every night for a week. They figure if it bombs, at least it'll be over fast. But it won't bomb because it's going to be great. This is no schlock production. It's going to have 'great stars in great stories' as Sam Goldwyn used to say."

"Let me understand this," Madeline said carefully. *"Fools* is going to be on every night for a week?"

"Two hours a night for five days. Exposure, Madeline, exposure. Ten hours in all. I believe and Richard believes it will be the most watched television program ever made," Katherine said quietly. Madeline was going to do it, she could tell. "Mad, you're better than the sexpot roles you've done. You're . . ." Katherine pretended to be groping for words. "You're an *actress.* So *act!"*

Madeline sank back in her chair and buried her face in her hands. "Oh, Katherine, I'm not! I can't act! All I can do is pose and show my tits! Knockers and blond hair, that's me! I need a touch-up, too. My roots are showing and so are my wrinkles."

"Do it, Mad, do it. Stop whining and *do this part."* Katherine wondered why it was so hard to persuade creative people to act in their own best interest. Why did they fight so furiously to protect their mistaken ideas about themselves?

Did their insecurity force them into bad decisions? "Do it," she whispered. "I'll be with you every step of the way. My God, woman, look what *Virginia Woolf* did for Liz Taylor. Madeline Gerard is *back!*" Katherine wrote in the air.

"I could try . . ." Madeline said. "Pull out all the stops. Those bastards, for years they've said I was a joke, a cutout. . . . I wonder . . . Do you have a copy of the script lying around?"

Bingo! Katherine thought. *Bingo!* "Simon's not through with it, but I'll send a copy over if you promise to read every word this time. Not just your part, the whole bloody thing. I'm telling you, it's a great, great part. Call me when you've finished it, okay? I want us to go to Simon together and talk him into aging the character. God, the contrast'll be great. Mad, you're doing the right thing."

Katherine went back to the office, put her feet up on her desk, exhausted and drenched in sweat. Bingo!

It took close to two years to get *Fools in Love* into production, and the day they filmed Madeline's big scene, Katherine went down to the studio to watch her old friend. As she did, she knew she'd been right all along. *Fools in Love* would be the biggest thing in the history of TV. Simon's sprawling story and the passionate emotions of the complex characters were bound to capture the country's fancy, and the young actors who played Simon, Roz, and Kim would be catapulted to stardom. And as Katherine watched Madeline Gerard, the sly fox herself, she knew Madeline's boozy, blowzy star turn as the late Kim Corbin's greedy, ambitious mother would kick-start her stalled career. As the long day wound to a close, she met Madeline in her tiny trailer dressing room behind the sound stage. "Darling, you're wonderful," Katherine said as they embraced. "If you don't get an Emmy there's no justice."

"Hah! No justice in this town, that's for sure. But thanks," Madeline said as she stripped off the gray-streaked wig and put it on the eyeless Styrofoam head on her cluttered dressing table. "The worst thing about doing this part is that I now know just how bad I'm gonna look in ten years. Jesus! That damn makeup man's got no mercy. He's outlined every wrinkle. I look like a thousand-year-old raccoon lying dead on the side of the Ventura Freeway."

"Nine hundred, tops. You've got guts, Mad."

Madeline began to cream off her makeup. "It's a funny thing. Remember back in the bad old days when you and me were living on Hayworth and Leo was sleeping on the couch? He took me to Madame Lermontov's class?"

Leo . . . so many years, and my heart still lurches when I hear his name. . . . "Of course."

"Funny thing." Madeline frowned. "I got a taste for acting. Real acting, like this. Not the glamour girl va-va-voom dog and pony show I do for the studios. . . . Used to do," she added. "Guess those days are lost and gone forever, huh, kiddo?" Madeline leaned forward and peeled off one strip of eyelashes, then the other. "No more," she whispered to the mirror. "If I'm gonna spend my golden years in front of a camera, I'm gonna make good and goddamn sure the old black eye gets it *all*. Every crepey droop of my neck, every little crow's foot. Let 'em like it or lump it," she said cheerfully. "Love me, love my gracious, ruined beauty. Thank you, thank you," she said, turning away from the long mirror and bowing to an imaginary audience. "I'd like to thank my mother, my agent, and, of course, the Academy. But most of all, I'd like to thank you, my fans, the *little* people out there in the darkened theaters who made this night possible." Madeline clutched an imaginary Oscar to her bosom and dropped her head humbly.

Katherine laughed as she felt a second or two of the old days flick by. The year it had all started, the year she and Madeline lived together and were bachelor girls on the loose. Well, Mad was on the loose. I was so young, so frightened. And look how we've turned out.

"Yup," Madeline continued happily. "You're looking at the new Madeline Gerard."

"Another new Madeline Gerard? I was just getting used to the old new Madeline Gerard."

Madeline waved her down. "All these years I've been chasing after one man or another, and once I caught 'em I'd spend all my energy trying to hang on. I squeezed 'em so hard they couldn't stand me six weeks later. Just little ol' try-to-please Madeline, love-me Madeline. So fuck 'em if they can't take a joke," she said emphatically, slicing her hand through the still air. "From now on, they can take me as I am."

Chapter
18

After the triumph of *Fools in Love,* Katherine's life had a new, calmer center. Over the next few years she handed over to Roz day-to-day control of the agency, although she remained active in major decisions and went into the office several afternoons a week. But now she wanted time to herself, time with Richard, time to go with him when he went on location, and they both wanted to enjoy their new house in Rancho Mirage while they were still young. Roz handled the Cole Agency brilliantly, and Katherine was proud that she'd recovered so well from her disastrous marriage to Simon. Roz had flirted briefly with the idea of remarrying Simon, but had finally discarded it when she fell in love with an orthopedic surgeon from Pacific Palisades who knew nothing about movies. Olivia, too, had maneuvered her life in exactly the direction she'd dreamed of when she first began her column. Olivia Cole's "Hollywoodland" was a fixture in the newspaper firmament, and though at first the column was filled with snappy tidbits of show business gossip, as the eighties wore on Olivia began to accent the business side of show business and featured a regular update on media-related stocks.

But Charles was still an ache, an empty spot in Katherine's heart that had never completely healed. Over the years, she'd asked Frank Perrow to keep track of him now and then—not on a day-to-day basis, but occasionally, just so she'd know where Charles was. The last she'd heard, he'd left the commune and moved to Eugene, Oregon, a college town. Often, Katherine would lie awake at night and wonder how he was. Was he healthy? Was he happy? Would he ever come home? Or was her son lost forever?

Olivia was alone on the patio, watching the aquamarine lights shift as the wind kicked up tiny swells of water across the pool. An hour ago she'd left the network with the chocolate taste of victory in her mouth. She'd done it! All these years she'd pushed and prodded, the years as Violet Rawley's slavey, the years of covering mediocre stories, promoting her column, but she'd done it!

She'd won! The network was giving her the show! Her own show—"Hollywoodland," named after her column. How many people remembered that the famous Hollywood sign began life as an advertisement for Hollywoodland, a housing development that went bankrupt? No one knew, no one cared. Now only Olivia Cole's "Hollywoodland" existed, her tribute to her personal vision of her hometown. Nothing mattered to Olivia but the column; nothing mattered but her work. Men, she thought derisively. Men. My mother and my sister traded away their lives to men but not me. Everything I have is mine and mine alone. *I* am the prize. . . .

Olivia took a sip from the bottle of champagne she'd carried out on the patio to celebrate. She didn't like champagne much, but what else can you drink to celebrate the victory of a lifetime? At last she had everything. . . .

Two weeks later Violet Rawley asked Olivia to have a drink with her at Le Train Bleu, a newly chic bistro in

Beverly Hills that had been tricked up to look like a French railroad car. Olivia accepted, partly because the idea of La Rawley and La Cole cozily celebrating "Hollywoodland" together would make great copy and partly because she wanted to rub Violet's pug nose in her success, ever so gently. Olivia dressed beautifully for the occasion, knowing she'd be seen and noticed. Lately she'd been experimenting with a new image that she planned to use on the show—hair very smooth, huge diamond earrings, faintly tanned skin. She wore only pale, elegant colors, and the look was soft, smooth, professional, but decidedly upper crust. Golden. She felt golden.

Olivia arrived early, carefully selected a banquette, and seated herself with her back to the light. Let Violet face the glare, she thought cattily as she ordered champagne.

Violet arrived promptly at five, followed by a young muscle man who settled her in the banquette, then trotted off with her fur.

"Violet," Olivia began as the waiter poured the champagne, "how lovely you look. Mauve does *so* much for your skin."

Violet Rawley sighed happily. "I'm *so* glad you're here, Olivia," she said, aping Olivia's treacly tone. "I've been looking forward to our little meeting."

There was a nasty shade in Violet's voice, the shrill edge of an imagined victory. Olivia didn't like the sound of it.

Violet Rawley smiled maliciously at Olivia as she drank her champagne, printing a crescent of lipstick on the rim of the glass. "No show, dear. No 'Hollywoodland' for our wittle Olivia. . . . Surprised? Wondering what this is all about? I'll tell you. Did you think I'd lie down and play dead, let you roll over me on your way to the top? It took a while, but I've been stocking up dirt on you and your family for ages. Your mother's affair with Richard Sears so many years ago and her marriage to Leo Cole right before Rosalind was born is *such* a romantic story. And your brother tried to kill himself, didn't he? Drugs, was it? Then he disappeared. That must be so painful for your mother. And there's Roz and Simon Wyler and poor Kim Corbin hanging herself! Of course, Simon's been mining that particular field for years and he *is* a genius, but can he be worth the trouble? I hear he's banged every ingenue from here to New York and back again. It's a sad commentary on our times, but these days, no one's blameless, I suppose." Violet snorted delicately.

"You can't blackmail me." Olivia tried to sound calm, but she was enraged. Violet Rawley was threatening to expose every mistake her family had ever made. Katherine and Richard, Roz and Simon, everything. The image of Charlie floating face down in the pool hit her like a strobe light. Eliza whimpering in the basket like a lost pup while Kim Corbin dangled overhead . . . "I've worked for 'Hollywood-land,' and I'm going to get it."

"Read the news, sweetie. Your TV career is over before it's begun," Violet said, toying with the jeweled spray of violets on her mauve print dress. "Olivia, it's only natural that you want to kill me off, and it's only natural that I cut you off at the knees. It's my job, it's who I am. No one is bigger than Violet Rawley," she drawled, all southern lace and molasses. "Go ahead, have your little TV show and enjoy your moment in the sun. But you'll pay, because no one tops me, understand? Either you give up 'Hollywoodland' or I spill every dirty secret I know about your family. There's no other way." Violet laughed prettily, light notes running up a harsh scale, and her big gold charm bracelet clanked like a jailhouse door closing.

"What do you have on that bracelet, Violet? Shrunken heads? Go ahead, amuse me. Tell me how you found out."

"Oh, darling, don't be naive. Don't you know the Lashman family can't be trifled with? Maria is quite the power broker in this town, and Linda takes after her."

Linda, Olivia thought angrily as she remembered the light sound of running feet the night she confronted Maria Lashman. Snitchy Bitchy Sears. "I'm as tough as you are, Violet. I have some lovely candid shots of Maria, and I told her a long time ago that if she fucked with me or my mother,

I'd publish them," Olivia said, but she knew she was treading water.

"Don't be naive," Violet said again. "You won't publish those pictures, if you have them at all. The world turns, and timing is everything. You lost your chance with Maria years ago. Besides, if you do publish, you'll be through for good. Networks don't want little bitches with mud on their hands," she said shrewdly. She leaned forward, her pudgy hands toying with her champagne glass. "Trade secret, Olivia. Blackmail's a secret vice. It only works when the lights are off and the shades are drawn and we're all cozily undercover. Your family has secrets to keep, and I'll keep them. *That's* why blackmail works. It's good for private threats. I'll keep your secrets, Olivia, but cross me and I'll nail every one of you to the wall. Believe me, I have the ammunition." Violet Rawley stood up and smoothed her silk dress over her hips. Magically her young man appeared and draped the fur over her shoulders. "Thanks for the champers, Olivia. Let me know when you cancel 'Hollywoodland.' You know how I love an exclusive."

Olivia watched Violet sweep out of the big room, laughing and talking with people on her way out. When she was gone, Olivia sat quietly for a long time as Le Train Bleu filled with the evening's crop of celebrities and thought about Violet's threats. I'm not giving up, she thought fiercely, sipping the champagne. Mother never gave up, and neither will I. Slowly, as she watched the brilliant crowd filling the room, an idea formed in her head, and as she sat alone in the midst of Beverly Hills, Olivia Cole started to laugh.

Katherine was in the living room reading a script when Olivia showed up at the big house later that night. "Where's Richard?" she asked as she flopped down in a chair and hooked one leg over the arm.

"Outside. He's turned the pool house into a little studio. He's taken up watercolors, if you can believe it." Katherine laughed. "What is it, dear?"

"Trouble in Glitter City," Olivia announced. Her voice was expressionless, flat.

Katherine could tell it was bad. She took off her glasses and pushed the script away. "What is it?"

"It's my old friend and mentor, Violet Rawley. She wants me to cancel my show. She's dug up quite a bit of information about us, all of us, and she's threatening to go public with it, make me look like a jerk, and trash us all. You know, Simon used Roz like a slate in *Fools in Love,* but that was only an appetizer. Now Violet's ready to spoon-feed her readers the main course. She's pieced it all together, Mom. Everything. You, Richard, Roz, Simon, Charlie—the whole shebang. She and Maria Lashman are just like this." Olivia waved crossed fingers in the air. "And I smell Linda Sears's stinky hand in here somewhere. Violet's so pissed about 'Hollywoodland' she'll do anything to cause us grief. If I back out of the show, she'll keep quiet." Olivia rubbed her eyes. "God, sometimes I hate this town."

Katherine stood up, went to the window, and looked across the garden. The light was on in the pool house, which meant Richard was having a good time with his paints. She felt oddly buoyant, relieved at the prospect of a future without any lies. At last the past was going to come out, and she'd be rid of it! The secrecy, the guilt, gone! Years of pretending things didn't happen. Years of pretending other things did. She touched her wedding rings, rubbing Leo's gold band for luck. Funny, but the prospect didn't frighten her at all—quite the opposite. She felt a tremendous exhilaration coursing through her blood.

Olivia mistook her silence for anxiety. "Mom, I'll give up the show. Let the old hag have it, I don't care."

"The hell you'll give it up, Olivia Cole!" Katherine snapped. Her voice was light but her fist was clenched. "Darling, I've done some silly things in my life," Katherine said, softening as she turned away from the window. "I came to Hollywood when I was young, naive. I've made every mistake a woman can make in this town, and I've still survived!" She held up her hand and began to tick her life off on her fingers. "I fell in love with a man who wouldn't marry me. I got pregnant and still he wouldn't marry me, and that was back when those things counted, when a woman with a child and without a husband was a slut. So I married a man I didn't love. I fell in love with him, and then he died. I loved him, and he died on me! That was a mistake, wasn't it? I wanted to die too, wanted to give up and float away like a tumbleweed down the Los Angeles River in one of those floods we have every few years. Do you think that's the life I wanted? Do you think I wanted to be alone while other women . . ." Katherine stopped, fighting back her tears. "Who cares about other women? They have their lives, I have mine. I finally found Richard again, and that bitch Maria is still trying to destroy me. Another mistake! I lost him once, and I lost Leo, so loss is no stranger to me, my dear. Loss . . ." Her voice dropped, and she looked deflated. "Loss is my constant companion. Loss is always dependable. I sleep with loss every night of my life, and I'm used to it. You know that? You know I used to go to bed every night and lie there like a board, a rock, stiff and immobile and hard. Do you think I chose that as a way of life? That's what I do at night. Think about my losses. I count mistakes like sheep. But I'm still here. I keep getting kicked, and I keep coming back. Maria won't win—this time or ever. She may have me now, but I'll wait and watch, and someday I'll cut the ground out from under her and she'll fall like a load of bricks. She'll never win."

"Cut and print." Olivia laughed. "God, why did I worry about you? You're tougher than all of us. Look, Mom," she said slowly. "I sat in Le Train Bleu for an hour after Violet rode off on her broom, and I think there's a way I can beat Maria and Violet into the ground. But it's up to you. . . ."

Olivia stopped her car by the wrought-iron gate to the Hollywood Hills, rummaged in her briefcase, and pulled out the duplicate set of photos of Maria Lashman Sears and her lady friend. Amazing, she thought clinically, that two human beings can get into that position. I would've thought only a contortionist . . . She took a large manila envelope, addressed it to Linda Sears, and slapped on plenty of stamps, just in case. She slipped the pictures inside, but as she was about to seal it, she had a nasty little thought. Smiling, she took out a sheet of the new "Hollywoodland" stationery she'd ordered from Cartier. "Dare I say tit for tat?" she scrawled across the thick gray paper. "Lots of love, Olivia."

She leaned out the window and dropped the envelope into the mailbox, and as she drove away she remembered a song she and Roz had made up when they were at school. Olivia laughed out loud. "Whistle while you work," she sang happily. "Linda is a jerk. . . ."

Richard Sears got off the plane in Eugene, Oregon, and walked down the steel boarding steps to the wet tarmac, the brilliant blue sky looming overhead like a tremendous eye. Gigantic white clouds were sailing steadily eastward like soldiers in battle formation. Mahlon Sweet Airport was sleepy. There were no tubes to shuttle you inside without a breath of air, and he was reminded of the old days shooting some war picture out at Burbank Airport. The poor ingenue —he couldn't remember her name—was so nervous she kept stepping on his feet when they shot the good-bye kiss in front of the plywood planes. He shook away the memories and went inside to get his bag. No one recognized him, and in a way, that was a shock. He was wearing sloppy clothes— jeans, a polo shirt, and thick horn-rimmed glasses—and for the first time in years no one knew who he was. No one looked up as he got his rental car, no eyes widened as they realized who he was—"Omigod, it's Richard Sears!" There was no limo waiting for him. No gofers to run interference, get his bags, open the door. You're spoiled, Sears, he told himself as he headed east into town on a two-lane highway. Spoiled, like a kid.

He drove the short distance from the airport into Eugene. It was a college town and he felt lost in a time warp. The kids

were still embedded in the amber of the long-ago sixties—
long hair, madras skirts dragging on the pavement, ethnic
jewelry. It amused him that Hollywood was only a few hours
away from this sleepy, easy place. No wonder Charlie liked
it here. He felt the tension slipping out of his body as he
searched for the address Katherine's detective friend had
given him. He found it easily, a small, neatly painted saltbox
house on a side street. A split rail fence enclosed a tiny front
yard. Richard knocked on the door.

Charlie answered. Crosby, Stills and Nash were playing in
the background, something about carrying on. "Richard,"
he said slowly, eyeing his famous stepfather. "What are you
doing here?"

"Can I come in?"

Charlie shrugged. "Of course you can."

Charlie was older, but why was that surprising? He'd filled
out in the chest and was no longer the skinny rail Richard
remembered, but he didn't look that different. He wore
patched Levi's and a flannel shirt, like everyone else in
Eugene. Dark hair hung down across his forehead, and he
pushed it back with Leo's characteristic impatience. The
house was sparsely furnished but neat and clean, a square
living room with a wood stove in one corner, secondhand
furniture, brick and board bookcases crammed with paper-
backs, and a bright God's eye on the wall.

Richard moved a pile of books and sat down on the couch
while Charlie made coffee. An Irish setter trotted over and
smelled him gravely, then lay down in front of the wood
stove and showed her stomach. "I have to talk to you,
Charlie," Richard began, his mug of coffee steaming in his
hand. "It's important."

"It must be," Charlie said. "For you to come all the way to
Oregon."

"Your mother needs you to come home. Violet Rawley's
threatened to publish every detail she knows about our
family. Our families, I should say. You see, Olivia's gotten a
TV show. It's called 'Hollywoodland,' after her column. It's

something she's wanted for a long time, but Violet Rawley wants it too and she's a tough enemy. So your mother's going on Olivia's show to do an interview about her life. Our lives. She's going to talk about everything, Charlie, you understand? You, me, Roz, Simon—all of it. We're hoping to beat Violet Rawley to the punch with the truth. Charlie, your mother needs you to come home."

Charlie shook his head slowly, very firm, very sure of himself. "I can't go back to L.A., Richard. I have a life here. I work. I can't up and leave, I have responsibilities to other people."

"You *have* changed, Charlie. I never heard you talk about responsibilities before."

"That's right. I've changed, and I don't intend to change back. I can't go to L.A.," Charlie said again. His tone was friendly. "Too much bad past, I guess. Richard, I'm a grown man. It took years, but I finally managed to grow up. It was hard, it was damn near impossible, but I think I've made it."

Richard heard the decision in Charlie's voice, but he pressed on for Katherine's sake. "Afraid if you come back, you'll be the old Charlie?"

"Maybe," he said easily. "Look, I work in a drug rehab center. I'm going to school nights so I can be a therapist. Make any sense to you?"

"That's not my decision to make, Charlie. All I know is that your mother needs you."

"Richard, you saved my life once so I owe you an explanation. You lived in Hollywood when it was a boom-town. I saw it disintegrate from the last get-rich-quick scheme in America into a slum with sequins. Olivia calls us star kids. Well, Olly and Roz like living their parents' life. I don't. I always felt like an outsider. Always the stranger, always watching other people having fun and telling jokes."

"You're still part of the family, Charlie."

Charles shook his head, his hands splayed open on his knees. He bent forward, determined to explain himself. "See, I'm not funny. I'm serious. I'm *good* at being serious.

People are lonely, and no one listens to them but me. Mothers afraid their children will burn down the house, fathers afraid their teenage son is molesting his little sister, kids afraid Dad is going to get drunk and beat them up again—all these people talk to me," Charles said slowly. "And I listen. That's what they need. That's what I have to give. Not very glamorous, is it? No movie stars in limos, no premieres, no audience rising to their feet to applaud when my face fills the screen. But it's who I am. It's my life. That's why I can't go back to L.A. with you."

Richard looked at the boy he'd pulled screaming from the pool, the boy who'd pushed so hard to become a human being, the boy who'd finally become a man. "I wish you were my son, Charlie. You make me feel I've wasted my life," Richard said slowly. "I'm not asking you to come back to L.A. permanently. Your life is here, and I respect the choices you've made. Just come back for a little while, a few weeks. Come back because your mother needs you."

"She has you and Roz and Olivia. She has the agency."

"She needs *you,* Charlie. *You.* Oh, she needs Roz and Olly, too, but one person isn't a substitute for another. You're her son. And mine, in a way." Richard looked past Charlie's dark head framed by the blue Oregon sky beyond the window. "Your father was my friend. Maybe this is hard for you to understand, but the fact that Leo and I both loved your mother brought us closer together. He's not here for you, Charlie. Let *me* be here for you. Violet Rawley's cut your mother deeper than she knows. Your mother and I made mistakes. We were young, we were in love, I was stupid. God, when I was your age I was such a selfish little prick! I let Katherine drift away, and I spent years paying for it. But she's not embarrassed about her past. Our past. You're not embarrassed about *your* past, are you?"

"You mean the drugs and nearly killing myself? No, I'm not embarrassed." Charlie paused, rubbing his hand over the patched knee of his jeans. "I feel sad that I wasted so much time, I suppose. Rueful."

"Well, so does your mother. Violet Rawley is going to try to split us open, and that includes you, Charlie. I want us to present a united front. Hell, I want us to have dinner at the Polo Lounge. Front row, center table, all of us together. I'm damned if we'll sneak around with our tails down."

There was a knock on the front door. Charlie frowned. "Just a minute," he said to Richard as he went to the door.

A young woman with long blond hair stood there holding a small boy. "Here he is," she said. "See you tomorrow." She put the boy down, waved, and left without another word.

The little boy ran in, clutching a Tonka truck in both hands. He had black hair slicked straight back from his face and high cheekbones and dark eyes. He was wearing Frisco Can't Bust 'Em overalls and a little plaid shirt that made him look like a diminutive lumberjack.

"Richard," Charles said gravely, "this is Leo Kartay, my son. Leo, this is Mr. Sears."

The little boy looked at Richard shyly, dropped his truck on the floor, and marched over to him. "Hi. I'm Leo," he said, sticking out his hand.

Richard started to laugh as he swept the boy up in his arms and hugged him close. "You sure are, sport," he said, pressing the child to his heart. "You sure are Leo in spades." He looked up at Charlie, smiling. "But don't you see? This is why you have to come back, this guy right here. Call it continuity, call it family, call it anything you want, Charlie. Just don't deny your mother this moment."

Charlie said nothing, but as he watched Richard embrace little Leo, the unlikely combination of the world-famous movie star and the tiny boy in his lumberjack outfit suddenly gave him a sense of a long bridge spanning the generations. Slowly he shook his head. "I always tell people they have to face the past before they can find the future," he shrugged. "Maybe it's time for me to take some of my own advice."

* * *

"Mother, we're here," Roz murmured as the limo pulled up to the Warner Brothers Barham gate. Her voice was shaking slightly, and she had wrapped the long gold and leather chain of her quilted Chanel bag around her fingers so tightly it cut into her flesh.

The driver leaned out the window and gave Katherine's name to the guard. "On the list for 'Hollywoodland.' "

The guard, a balding man with sleepy eyes, flipped slowly through his list of drive-on passes and ticked off Katherine's name. As the arm on the gate went up, he gave the driver a world-weary nod and went back to reading *Variety*.

"I hate this," Roz moaned as the limo wound through the dark Warner's lot. "I feel sick."

Katherine roused herself from her light sleep. "Don't be nervous, darling," she said softly as she watched the familiar studio roll by, the hulking sound stages, the trailer dressing rooms, the narrow streets. It was all so familiar.

"I'm not nervous, I'm terrified. There's a qualitative difference," Roz muttered.

The car pulled up in front of Stage 28, and Katherine saw Richard, Charles, and little Leo standing by the open door. A brand-new Leo Kartay is ready to face the world, she thought as she got out of the limo.

"Darling," Richard said, kissing her on the cheek. "You look beautiful. You too, Rozette."

Rozette, Katherine thought. He calls her Rozette.

Inside, they were assaulted by a blaze of lights. The stage was jammed with a large crew complaining nervously about the number of setups and the lousy quality of the catering. The stale, fetid air rang with noise, and the cavernous room vibrated with coffee nerves, clashing tempers, and the tense, electric smell of a countdown.

The set was simple—a pair of deep, comfortable gray chairs, a Plexiglas coffee table, and a few plants to soften the scene. It gave the impression of an intimate living room, but only an impression, since "Hollywoodland," the show's instantly recognizable logo, floated behind the chairs on invisible wires.

Katherine had a nostalgic sense of recognition as she threaded her way over the mass of thick cables zigzagging across the floor like rubbery seaweed tossed up on the shore. This was the same stage they'd used for *Pilot Down,* Richard's last war movie. She looked up and saw a lighting man she knew from the old days perched on a scaffold and stopped to call out to him. "Billy . . ." She waved.

"Yes, ma'am?" Billy said in surprise as he recognized Katherine.

"Why so formal? You used to call me 'doll' in the old days."

Billy flipped her an appreciative salute, and his wrinkled face split into a huge smile. "I'll light you myself, doll," he called. "Knock 'em dead."

"Big crew for an interview show," she said to Roz.

"C'mon, Mother, the whole damn town knows you'll be on tonight."

Roz was right. An unusual number of rubberneckers were scattered around the sound stage, and the instant audience meant the word had spread throughout the studio hierarchy via the secretarial drums that the premiere episode of "Hollywoodland" would be hot. After all, tonight Olivia Cole would interview her famous mother in front of a television audience of millions.

Katherine's heart rocketed into hyperspace. Her face was hot, and her hands were cold and sticky damp as she stared blankly at the set and the oh-so-casual onlookers. In a few minutes she would sit down in a gray chair and talk to Olivia about her own long, complex life, and she knew without a doubt that the meaning of that life hung in the balance. Katherine Ransome Cole Sears was about to toss her past, her present, and her future into the hungry, gleaming mouths of the media. She was taking a terrible risk—in a flash, the foundation of her life could crumble like a sand castle under a tidal wave. As she made her way across the crowded stage to the small dressing room, she was assailed by momentary doubts. Was she doing the right thing? Or was she about to make a fatal error?

"Roz, darling," she said. "I'd like to be alone for a little while."

Roz frowned as she reflexively smoothed an escaping tendril of red hair into place. "I . . ." she began.

Katherine cut her off, shaking her head as she opened the dressing room door. "Nonsense. I won't wander into the traffic," she said tartly, indicating the crowded stage.

"If you're sure . . ."

"I'm sure. I need a few minutes to compose myself. Now, scoot on out of here and leave me alone."

Katherine closed the dressing room door and looked around. Bland. Faceless. A mid-range motel room for weary television travelers, the wild-eyed promotion tour vets shell-shocked by endless interviews and the ceaseless plugging of their one and only product—their shopworn souls.

She took a critical look at herself in the mirrored walls, and a hundred Katherines looked back at her, outwardly calm and composed. Still chic, she thought with pride as she draped her sable coat over a chair and surveyed her timeless black wool Dior suit.

She saw her hand toying with her rope of pearls and felt a little shock tickle across her mind as the difference between her past and her present flooded over her. That old woman's hand again! She couldn't get used to that hand! Her wedding rings gleamed in the mirror. Both of them.

Katherine sat down in the tan chair in front of the long makeup mirror, and the combination of overhead fixtures and the glowing white globes surrounding the mirror washed the shadows from her face and made her look suddenly young again, as fresh and careless as an ingenue of twenty.

She leaned forward and gently placed her hand on her own reflection in the big mirror and covered her face. Her diamond ring caught the lights overhead and a rainbow of color scattered fragments of chipped light around the room.

"But I'm still the same woman inside," she told the watching mirror defiantly.

There was a knock on the dressing room door.

It was Roz. "Mother? It's time. Are you ready?" she called.

Katherine got up and opened the door. "Darling, I've been ready for years," she said as she faced the blaze of lights from the sound stage.

Olivia was already seated in one of the gray chairs, and as she walked toward the set, Katherine distantly heard Olivia's clear voice beginning her introduction.

"Tonight, on the premiere episode of 'Hollywoodland,' we're proud to bring you an in-depth interview with a woman who knows this town inside out. A woman who knows every secret in Hollywood, a woman with a lifetime of love and work behind her, a woman who knows exactly what the movie business can give . . . and what it can take away."

Olivia's voice faded away as the faces of the people she'd loved flooded across Katherine's mind. I'm the same woman I was all those years ago when I first came to Hollywood, the same girl, loving the same people. . . .

. . . Leo in his ragged suit and broken shoelaces the first day they met, a Monte Cristo trembling in his long fingers and cigar smoke floating around his head like a cloud of bees . . .

. . . Richard as the Arizona Kid, leading a posse across the hard, flat face of the long-ago San Fernando Valley . . .

. . . Rosalind, Olivia, Charles . . .

Olivia's voice broke into her thoughts: "The founder of the Cole Agency and my mother, Katherine Cole Sears."

"Mother," Roz whispered. "That's your cue."

. . . Pieces of a lifetime of love and loss, happiness and pain, appeared and disappeared in quick succession as snippets of the past melded with the present, assaulting her from all sides. Conversations, words, faces, and gestures cut quickly from one to the other as Katherine's life flipped by in an unending montage.

Applause echoed behind her as Katherine stepped into the bright circle of light on the "Hollywoodland" set. Olivia was smiling up at her, and suddenly Katherine was utterly calm, completely unafraid. I've had it all, she thought, the moon above and the stars below. I've won and I've lost, but I've faced it all. And nothing will ever frighten me again. . . .